PRAISE FOR S.D. ROBERTSON

'Parts of this story will have touched most of our lives, and the sensitivity the author gives to it is wonderful. This is a real tear-jerker.'
The Sun

'You don't realise how quickly this story draws you in and then takes you on an emotional roller coaster ride.' **Welsh Country Magazine**

'Unputdownable. A real page-turner.'
Maria Felix Vas, BBC Radio Lancashire

'Nobody writes about the tenderness and brutality of life like S.D. Robertson.' **Miranda Dickinson**

'A tender and beautifully told heart-tugging story.' **Caroline England**

'With great skill and humour S.D. Robertson guides us through a minefield of family misunderstandings and discontent. I'm not sure I've seen such dynamics tackled better.' **Stewart Foster**

'A wonderfully told tale of devastation, grief and ultimately hope, with a narrative that grips from the start and doesn't let go until the final page.' **Kathryn Hughes**

'What's really, really clever about this book is that you don't realise you've been drawn in until it's too late to stop. The story leaves you sliding down an emotional knife edge until you freefall. It's soft, subtle, and engaging, then devastating.' **Helen Fields**

'Real. Emotional. Powerful. A must-read for anyone who loves to lose themselves completely in a book.' **Claudia Carroll**

'Mind-blowing . . . I cannot express just how much this book has gripped me!' **Cara's Book Boudoir**

'S.D. Robertson writes excellent books about messy lives and true emotions.' **Books of All Kinds**

D1102230

C334512984

'Such a powerful and emotional read . . . Had me hooked till the very end.'
Echoes in an Empty Room

'A really fascinating study into the vagaries of family life.'
Jaffareadstoo

'A perfectly executed story and a great read.'
Reading, Willing & Able

'Sensitively and superbly written . . . I was under the book's spell until the last word.'
Gingerbookgeek

'Pick up the book today and prepare yourself for an uplifting and glorious journey!'
Kristin's Novel Café

'S. D. Robertson's writing is so vivid and real that it takes you right there, into each moment with the characters and once you're there, there's no escape. You feel everything they feel.'   *A Novel Thought*

'One of those unique books that once read will truly stay with you for a lifetime.'
Compelling Reads

'A strong contender for my favourite book of the year . . . Emotional, heart-warming, tragic, bittersweet, charming and very, very satisfying.'
Silver Thistle

'Gave me hope, renewed my faith and made me feel like there is more to look forward to on the other side of life than just an empty space.'
Comfy Reading

'A sad, sweet, thought-provoking tale about the love and bond between parents and children.'
Lovereading

ABOUT THE AUTHOR

Former journalist S.D. Robertson quit his role as a local newspaper editor to pursue a lifelong ambition of becoming a novelist. *How to Save a Life* is his fifth novel, and he is a *USA Today* and Kindle Top 20 bestseller.

Stuart is a reluctant DIYer and unofficial tech support provider for his family. He lives in a village near Manchester with his wife and daughter. There's also his cat, Bernard, who likes to distract him from writing – usually by breaking things.

Also by S.D. Robertson

Time to Say Goodbye
If Ever I Fall
Stand By Me
My Sister's Lies

How
to
Save
a Life

S.D. ROBERTSON

avon.

Published by AVON
A division of HarperCollins*Publishers* Ltd
1 London Bridge Street
London SE1 9GF

www.harpercollins.co.uk

A Paperback Original 2020

First published in Great Britain by HarperCollins*Publishers* 2020

Copyright © S.D. Robertson 2020

S.D. Robertson asserts the moral right to
be identified as the author of this work.

A catalogue copy of this book is available from the British Library.

ISBN: 978-0-00-837476-1

This novel is entirely a work of fiction. The names, characters
and incidents portrayed in it are the work of the author's imagination.
Any resemblance to actual persons, living or dead, events or localities
is entirely coincidental.

Typeset in Sabon Lt Std by
Palimpsest Book Production Ltd, Falkirk, Stirlingshire
Printed and bound in UK by CPI Group (UK) Ltd, Croydon CR0 4YY

All rights reserved. No part of this text may be reproduced,
transmitted, down-loaded, decompiled, reverse engineered, or stored
in or introduced into any information storage and retrieval system,
in any form or by any means, whether electronic or mechanical,
without the express written permission of the publishers.

MIX
Paper from
responsible sources
FSC® C007454

This book is produced from independently certified FSC™ paper
to ensure responsible forest management.

For more information visit: www.harpercollins.co.uk/green

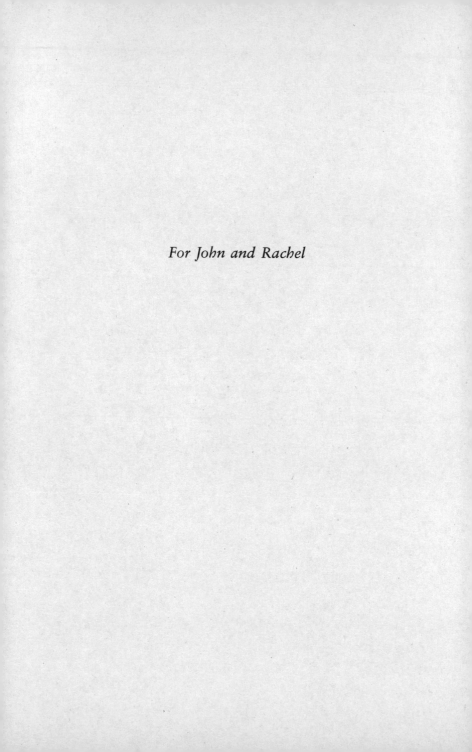

For John and Rachel

CHAPTER 1

I see him in the mirror as a gust of wind sweeps him up to the locked door, his dark curly hair bedraggled and blowing from side to side. After staring at the CLOSED sign for a few seconds, he squints through the rain-flecked glass in my direction. I know exactly what's coming next and my muscles tense up in anticipation.

He tries the handle. Of course he does. And when the door doesn't open, instead of getting the hint, he knocks on it.

'Hello?' he calls. 'Are you still open?'

Snarling internally, I shake my head. Without turning around to look at him or downing tools, I reply in a loud voice: 'What does the sign say?'

His answer is delivered with a satellite delay. 'Um, but I can see you're still working.'

Bloody idiot, I think, refusing to look at him other than through the mirror. 'We're closed!' I bellow. 'Like it says on the sign.'

There's silence for a moment and I hope he's got the message. But my heart sinks as he remains huddled in the doorway, chin tucked into his flimsy coat, which clearly wasn't designed with a British winter in mind.

'Can't you squeeze me in?' he pleads. 'It won't take long. Come on – it's horrible out here. I'm soaked through and freezing cold. Can't you cut me some slack?'

I squeeze my left hand into a tight fist and take a deep breath in a bid to stop myself from really lashing out. 'No. Try somewhere else. We're closed.'

Incredibly, he doesn't give up for another few minutes. He stays there, moaning and groaning, like it'll make a difference, but I tune him out and get on with the job in hand, no longer acknowledging him. Eventually he goes away, with a sullen, half-hearted kick to the door to mark his departure and a few choice insults.

'Does that happen a lot?' the ruddy-faced chap in the chair asks as I continue to hack through the top of his thick grey hair with the thinning scissors.

'Often enough,' I reply.

He chuckles and says no more, which suits me perfectly. Barbers have a reputation for enjoying small talk – chatting for the sake of it – but that's not me. I hate all that. I'm here to cut hair, full stop. I've no interest in what people have got planned at the weekend or when and where they're next going on holiday. Seriously, who cares? It's not like we're friends or anything. And I'm not an advice service or a counsellor either. Got a problem? Get help from a specialist. Need a short back and sides? *That* I can help you with . . . I'll do a damn good job of it too, particularly if I'm left alone to get on with it. It'll be decent even if I'm distracted. Better than most cuts you'll get around here – on the edge of Manchester's Northern Quarter – and almost certainly lower priced.

That's thanks to my no-nonsense business model. I'd call it cheap and cheerful, but for the fact I'm a grumpy sod. There's no faffing around with fancy décor. I definitely don't try to court the hipsters with any of that vintage nonsense, or by providing organic coffee and a fridge full of craft ales. And rather than huge wall-hung TVs and a snazzy sound system, there's a cheap FM tuner locked into Radio 2. But if what you want is a good, quickly executed, well-priced haircut with minimal chat, then I'm your man.

I'm not exactly rolling in cash as a result – hence the reason I work alone, despite the two empty barber chairs alongside me – but I do okay. It keeps the wolf from the door.

A while back, I came up with the bright idea of renaming the place No Frills, Top Skills. I'll hold my hands up: it was something I initially thought of on a rare night out, having had a skinful. I chewed it over for some time afterwards, though. Unlike most of my drunken ideas, I still liked it sober. I even messed around designing some potential logos. And yet in the end I never got around to changing it from what it's always been: Luke's Barbershop, plain and simple, named after me.

If it ain't broke, don't fix it. That was my late father's motto – and I guess it rubbed off on his son. The faded, peeling shopfront sign outside is a good example. I have thought about replacing it, but I seriously doubt the cost would be worth my while. So why bother? Would it really generate enough new customers to pay for itself? Besides, as the hub of Manchester's alternative, bohemian scene, the Northern Quarter is all about shabby chic, right? That's what I tell myself, anyway.

Having finished my final cut of the day, I go through the motions of showing the customer the back of his head with a hand mirror. 'Is that okay for you?' I ask.

'Perfect, thank you,' he replies, nodding vigorously.

A couple of minutes later, payment dealt with and coat retrieved, he heads to the door and I let him out, greeted by a strong gust of wind that rattles the door in its frame. 'There's talk of a really nasty storm this evening,' he says, turning up his collar and shuddering. 'High wind warnings and all that. Looks pretty wild already.'

'It's probably the press blowing things out of proportion, as usual,' I reply, having heard the same on the radio. 'There's always a storm about to batter Britain these days. Desperate for sales, aren't they? I take it all with a pinch of salt. They'll be issuing panicky heat wave warnings again before we know it.'

'Let's hope you're right,' he says, screwing up his face dubiously. 'Thanks, anyway. Bye now.'

'See you,' I add out of habit, although I've no idea whether I actually will or not. I'm fairly sure I haven't cut this bloke's hair before and, since we barely spoke, I don't have the foggiest idea whether he's local or passing through, maybe going to or from one of the nearby train and bus stations. He sounded vaguely northern to me, although accents don't mean much in the city, since people from all over the place live here.

If he hadn't been a customer, I wouldn't have bothered engaging in his tedious weather chat. One of my neighbours at home, a busybody pensioner called Doreen, tried having a similar conversation with me as I left the flat this morning.

'Not wearing any waterproofs?' she asked, collaring me as I headed down the communal stairs to exit the building. 'You might regret that later on. There's talk of a big storm coming.'

'Whatever,' I told her, keeping walking. 'I don't have time to worry my head about that nonsense.'

'But it's—'

'Listen, some of us have jobs to go to, businesses to run. Can't chat. Goodbye.'

Recalling the disgruntled look on Doreen's face after I said this earlier, I lower the shutters on the shop, so as to avoid any more chancers asking for a quick last-minute cut. Then I turn up the radio as I clean and disinfect all my scissors, combs, clippers and so on. I move on to sweeping and mopping the floor before wiping down the mirrors and other surfaces, making sure everything is spick and span for when I open up again tomorrow morning. I might not run a fancy barbershop, but I take pride in keeping the place clean and hygienic. That's really important to me – and not just to avoid getting closed down. Certain things in life need to be done properly, end of story.

By the time I get outside, it's dark and bitterly cold,

pretty much as you'd expect for a Thursday evening in late January. The rain has eased, but the wind really has got up, despite me pooh-poohing the forecast earlier, and I'm glad to be in my long wool overcoat and beanie hat. The headgear is not a good look, especially for a man due to turn forty later this year, but it's something of a necessity for a baldy like me when there's a bite in the air.

I might be a barber, but ironically my own head of hair is pathetic. There's very little left of it on top; it's gradually ebbing away on the back and sides, leaving me with little choice but to shave what remains. I can at least do this myself: small mercies. Not a great advert for my business, though, is it? I'm like a dentist with rotten teeth.

I spot a homeless person crashed out on the ground, apparently asleep or in some kind of stupor. They're lying in the doorway of a neighbouring shop, which is already closed for the night. I stop for a moment and cough, before saying in a loud voice: 'You shouldn't be here. You're on private property. I've just called the police and they're on their way to move you along.'

I hope this lie will be enough to get them to shift, assuming they've registered it. Wrapped up as they are in a sleeping bag and hoodie, facing away from the pavement, I can't even tell if they're male or female. Whatever, they shouldn't be here. This is outside the main 'begging zone' at the heart of the city centre; the last thing I want is for that to start spilling over here, potentially affecting my business. The bargain service I offer is already undervalued. I definitely don't need down-and-outs dossing on the doorstep and putting off customers.

'Go on, shoo,' I add, after my first comment goes ignored. 'There must be better places to crash than this.'

Still I get no reply other than a faint groan. I'm tempted to persevere, but in the end I'm too tired and cold to bother. So with one final hollow threat that the police will be here any minute, I let out a noisy sigh before continuing on my way.

As I walk along the pavement in the direction of my flat, all the buildings around me seem to rattle and shake in sync with one another, like a menacing percussion ensemble. Various pieces of litter – newspaper sheets, snack wrappers, cans and bottles – bob and weave their way alongside me, occasionally making contact. A couple of times I really have to fight to hold my ground as a strong gust threatens to sweep me off course. One minute I'm almost being blown into passing traffic; the next I'm dodging a fellow windswept pedestrian.

Plodding on, regardless, dreaming of a hot shower and a brew when I get home, I curse repeatedly under my breath and wonder how this walk could get any worse.

As if in reply, and without prelude, the heavens open. Driving rain and hail take it in turns to hammer down on me. I'm soaked through in seconds and look around desperately for shelter. My flat is still several minutes' walk away, but having left the busy shop and bar-lined streets near work behind me, there's nowhere immediately obvious to wait out the worst. On one side of the street is a large open-air car park, where I can see various people running to their vehicles. Most of the other side is taken up by the rear of a former warehouse that's been converted into offices. Sadly, all the entrances are round the front, so there's not even a doorway in sight to run towards.

'Come on, think!' I shout at myself, continuing forward. Drenched like I've jumped fully clothed into a swimming pool, I'm racking my brains for somewhere to go as the deluge continues and the wind does its utmost to knock me off my feet.

'Come on,' I cry again, my voice carried away in a fierce gust. It makes a nearby lamppost jiggle around in a way that looks comical and precarious at the same time. Having walked this way on so many previous occasions, I really should be able to think of somewhere to take shelter, but still nothing comes to mind.

I spin around full circle, scanning my surroundings, but it doesn't help.

Screw it. I'm wasting time now and only getting wetter in the process. I decide to press on towards my flat, running for a bit until I'm out of breath and even more infuriated at the bloody weather.

The rain eases off for a minute or two and I pray the worst is over. Then it's hailing again with a vengeance – of course it is – and I feel like I'm being bombarded with mini golf balls.

Turning a corner, I see a ramshackle old building wrapped in scaffolding. Someone else, wearing a canary-yellow raincoat, is already cowering under the lowest platform of the towering temporary structure, so I make a dash to join them. It doesn't exactly look like an ideal shelter, but better some cover than none.

'All right?' I grunt at the brightly dressed figure.

It turns out to be a woman – late twenties, early thirties at a guess, from what I can see of her. She jumps at the sound of my voice, having been looking in the other direction. But once her wide brown eyes land on my face, she soon flashes me a smile from within the circle of her coat's wide hood.

'Gosh, you startled me,' she says in a husky, confident voice. 'You look like you could have done with getting here a few minutes ago . . . and maybe wearing something a bit more waterproof.'

'Hmm,' I reply, wiping the ice-cold moisture out of my eyes with my right hand.

'I don't know about you, but I wish I'd taken the weather forecast more seriously,' she adds. 'I figured they were probably exaggerating, based on past experience.'

I raise my eyebrows and nod. 'You're not kidding.'

The wooden planks above us do offer protection from much of the downpour – although we have to take care to avoid the leaky spots, which are like mini waterfalls. The creaking, rattling sounds all around, particularly when the wind gusts, are disconcerting to say the least.

Relax, I tell myself, as an extra fierce squall makes everything around us shudder and shake. My new companion and I both look upwards and then at each other; I stretch my mouth into a grimace.

She keeps smiling, looking way calmer than I feel. 'I'm sure it'll ease off soon.'

'You reckon?' I reply. 'I'm not convinced.'

We remain where we are for several more minutes as

the rain and hail keep on coming in alternating onslaughts, like a freakish tag team working at the wind's behest.

And then all hell breaks loose as the fiercest gust yet roars, pounces, bites and refuses to let go.

Heart in mouth, I see and hear the scaffolding above and all around teeter and then finally tip.

'We need to move now!' the woman shouts. But I'm frozen to the spot in terror as, with a series of mighty and devastating crashes and crunches, it all starts coming down.

That's it, I think. Game over.

Then I feel myself being shoved to one side and, with a sudden jolt of intense pain to my head, I'm out of it.

Nothingness envelops me.

CHAPTER 2

When I come to, shivering and achy, it takes a moment to get my bearings. My initial thought is that I must have been having a bad dream and I'm at home in my flat. But the uncomfortable, scrunched position I find myself in and my pounding headache soon set me straight.

I try to sit up, only to find I can't. I'm enclosed by what's collapsed around me. And yet miraculously, other than my head hurting, nothing else appears badly injured or crushed, as best as I can tell lying on my side, wedged into such a confined space.

I know this because I make a point of wiggling everything, from my fingers to my toes, and it all still appears to work, despite a few aches and pains. My limbs are free to move, but only as much as this small space I find myself in – this bubble amid the destruction – will allow.

As my mind grinds through the process of fully rebooting, like an ancient PC, I start to recall further details of what happened. I realise it's probably safest not to move, in case I unsettle something.

Next my thoughts turn to the woman who was with me before I lost consciousness. How on earth did I not think of her until now? And what was her name? I don't even know. We never properly introduced ourselves. Is it thanks to her that I'm here and not squashed beneath some other part of the wreckage? She definitely shoved me to the side, presumably out of the way of some danger she spotted while I was incapacitated by fear. So where is she now?

'Hello?' I call out. 'Can you hear me? Are you okay?'

Nothing. Not a huge surprise, as my initial attempt is pathetic – little more than a raspy groan. After clearing my throat, wincing from the extra pain this brings to my pounding head, I take a slow, deep breath before trying again.

'Hello? Are you there?'

I repeat this several times, as loud as I can manage in a bid to be heard over the still raging storm, but no reply comes. Nothing at all. Shit. She can't be far away, so if she's not replying . . . she must be unable to, for whatever reason.

She's probably unconscious, like I was until a few moments ago. How long was I out? It must have been several minutes at least. Maybe longer.

I try to peer at my watch, but it's too dark to read the analogue face. I think of my phone, but once I manage to dig it out of my pocket, my heart sinks as I remember the battery died earlier. Dammit. If only I'd got around to keeping a spare charger at work. I don't usually need it, though. Not unless I forget to plug in the bloody thing before going to bed, like I did last night.

Desperate, I try to turn it on anyway. The sudden brightness of the boot screen hurts my eyes, but before they have time to adjust, the phone gives up the ghost and switches itself off again. Fantastic. I narrowly resist the urge to smash it on the ground in frustration.

Unable to see anything other than vague shapes and shadows from the position I'm stuck in, I cry out for assistance; not only to my silent companion this time, but generally, in the hope of attracting some passer-by's attention.

'Help! Help me!' I bellow with everything I've got. 'I'm stuck here. Is anyone out there? Please help!'

I keep at it for what feels like forever: shouting variations of the same desperate words over and over again until my throat is throbbing in time with my banging headache and I'm out of breath.

Am I going to die here? All it would take would be for some more scaffolding or masonry to come down on top of me and that would be it. I fight to calm my breathing, to steady my mind before it races into a blind panic from which there might be no coming back.

But the negative thoughts won't leave me alone. Who would actually care if I didn't make it out of here? Would anyone really miss me? There were people who might have done once, but now they've all been taken from me, or they left of their own accord, or I pushed them away.

There is Alfred, I suppose, although I'm not sure if he

counts, being a cat. I'd certainly miss him; I hope he'd be okay without me.

'Don't be so defeatist,' I imagine my mother telling me. 'You sound like you've given up already. Where's that fighting spirit?'

I wasn't always so gloomy and bad-tempered. The younger me would never have spoken like I did to that homeless person earlier: putting my own concerns over the welfare of someone down on their luck and struggling to get by. Far from my finest moment, that. Not exactly a Good Samaritan, am I? And yet here I am, lying on the ground myself now, calling out for others to help me. I guess I got my comeuppance.

'Sorry, Mum,' I say, recalling her perched on the edge of my bed, reading that very parable to me as a young child. 'I must be a huge disappointment to you and Dad. I didn't mean to end up this way.'

I picture her shaking her head and giving me that disappointed look I used to get from time to time growing up, like when I was a teenager and she once caught me smoking in the back garden while I thought she was out. That look was always infinitely worse than being shouted at.

As desperation is on the cusp of setting in, I hear something: a woman's voice, faint but just audible. 'Hello?'

Initially I think my mind's playing tricks on me; that it's the echo of another resurfacing memory. But when I hear it again, a little louder this time, I realise with a jolt that I'm not imagining it.

'Hello!' I call back. 'Is that you: the woman who was taking shelter with me? Are you all right? Are you hurt?'

There's a long pause and finally a reply. 'Yes, it's me, Iris. I must have blacked out.'

'That's your name? Iris? Mine's Luke. How are you doing? Are you also trapped?'

'Hi, Luke. I, um, I'm not great.' Her voice sounds strained. 'It hurts . . . I'm losing blood. And yes, I'm stuck here.'

'Blood? How come? Are you sure that's what it is? You're not just wet from all the rain?'

There's a delay before she replies, during which my heart is in my mouth. Then finally – thank goodness – I hear her voice again, although what she says sounds strangely clinical. 'I'm sure. Something, um . . . never mind. It's not good. Are you hurt?'

'No, I'm all right, Iris. I'm trapped and a bit knocked around, but otherwise I'm fine, most likely because of you. You pushed me out of the way of something, I remember. Thank you.'

'Glad to help.' She breaks off before adding: 'Listen, if we don't get out of here soon, I think I could be in real trouble.'

'Don't talk that way. You're not a doctor. You can't know such things. Can you reach the wound? Maybe you should try applying some pressure to it.' This last suggestion is something of a desperate one, based purely on stuff I've seen in movies and TV shows. But I figure it's worth a try.

'I am actually,' Iris says, her voice sounding a little louder now; closer than I initially thought, maybe only a couple of metres away.

'What, applying pressure?'

'A doctor.'

It takes a moment for me to digest this information but, once I do, I feel particularly embarrassed about the two-bit medical advice I offered her.

'Right. So we need to get help ASAP,' I say. 'I've tried plenty of shouting, but I don't think anyone's heard me so far apart from you. The noise of this damn storm is muting everything. I can keep going, but we really need to get word to the emergency services.'

'Have you got a mobile with you?'

'Not a working one,' I reply, mentally kicking myself again. 'My battery is totally flat.'

'I have one, in my bag, but I'm not sure I can reach it. Let me try.'

She falls silent. I'm soon tempted to ask how she's getting on, but rather than distract her from her mission, I start calling for help again, knowing that might still be our best hope of escape. Eventually, I stop and listen, but all I hear is more wind and rain.

'Iris?' I ask. 'Any luck?'

She doesn't reply, even when I shout out to her. I call her name at least a dozen more times, but to no avail. She must have passed out again. I pray it's nothing worse than that; her words about being in trouble and losing blood bounce around my head.

Yet again, I curse myself for not charging my mobile and try not to fly into a full-blown panic.

As my mind whirrs, analysing the situation, looking for options, I become increasingly convinced there's little chance of us being found here while this storm is raging. Anyone with an ounce of sense will be safely indoors or at least in a vehicle.

I feel so cold, despondent, alone.

And then I hear Iris's voice say my name.

'Yes?' I reply. 'Are you all right? You stopped answering me. I thought—'

'I blacked out again. It was . . . hard to reach.'

'Don't worry about that now,' I tell her. 'Stay still. Take it easy. We'll figure something out.'

As these words leave my mouth, what I'm thinking is very different, but I want to try to keep her spirits up, unlike my own.

'I got it,' she says.

'Your phone?'

'Yes, I'm dialling now.'

I can't make out every word of what she says to the emergency operator, but I get the important stuff. She pinpoints exactly where we are, better than I could manage. And she requests both ambulance and fire crew assistance, which makes sense, as we'll need to get all of this wreckage carefully lifted off us before we can be freed. God knows how they'll be able to work safely in these conditions, mind.

'Please hurry.' That's how she ends the call. Then she tells me: 'They're coming, Luke.'

'Fantastic. You did so well, Iris. How long did they say?'

'Not sure. Really tired. Need to rest.'

'Of course,' I say. 'You do that. You've earned it. I'm sure they'll only be a few minutes. We'll be out of here in no time.'

17

'Hope so,' she says. Or at least I think that's it, as it comes out really quiet. I want to ask how she's doing, but I also feel it's best to let her rest, if that's what she needs. Then I start worrying that maybe she ought to be trying to stay awake. Again, the only basis I have for this is what I've seen in films – so who knows if that's right? Iris almost certainly would, being a doctor and all, but she's in no position to offer advice to herself right now.

'Stay with me, Iris,' I say as loudly as I can, trying to ignore the rising sense of claustrophobia in my belly. Why am I feeling this now, knowing help is on the way?

In the absence of a reply, I start gabbling, even though I realise I'm probably talking to myself. 'Do you reckon the storm has died down a bit, Iris? I think it might have. The wind sounds a little lighter to me. It could have stopped raining too, although it's hard to know for sure under here. I can't see much. What about you?'

Eventually, goodness knows why, I start singing. Part of me hopes Iris can hear it, even though she's no longer answering me, and that it gives her something to hold on to. I go with the old time-killing classic 'Ten Green Bottles', but I add some extra bottles, starting with thirty, to make sure it goes on for a while.

I'm down to sixteen bottles when I finally hear sirens.

Breaking off from singing, I shout: 'They're coming, Iris! They're coming. We're going to be all right.'

Her silence is deafening.

CHAPTER 3

'Oh my God. You gave me a heart attack when you called earlier. I can't believe what happened. How are you doing?'

I smile weakly and nod at Meg. 'Tired and sore, but I'll be fine.'

'I heard about the scaffolding coming down on the news last night, but they didn't mention any names, so I had no idea you were involved. Otherwise, I'd have been here right away. Why did you take so long to call?'

'My phone battery was flat. Luckily, I managed to borrow a charger this morning from one of the other patients.'

'Right.' She's holding an unfamiliar sports bag, which she raises to my eye height, as I'm sitting up in the hospital bed, and jiggles it around. 'I got the stuff you asked for, including your phone charger.'

'That's not my bag, is it? I don't recognise it.'

'You're welcome. No, it's mine – and I want it back, please, once you're done. It's my yoga bag.'

'Yoga? Seriously? Since when do you—'

'I do have a life, Luke, and it's not like we've seen each other much recently. Don't pretend to know everything about me.'

'Hmm. Let me guess: you bought all the stuff and have only used it a handful of times. Am I right?' She screws up her face and looks away. 'Ha!' I continue. 'I know you well enough, Meg Craven.'

Not wishing to push my luck with her, I change the subject. 'Was Alfred okay?'

'Yes, fine. I cleaned his litter tray and left him plenty of food.'

'Was he upset about me not coming home last night?'

'Seriously, Luke? How do I know? He's a cat; it's not like he can talk.'

I shake my head. 'You know what I mean. What was he doing when you arrived?'

'Sleeping, curled into a ball on your bed. There was still food left in his bowl, although he got up to have some more after I washed and refilled it.'

'Good.'

'Again, you're welcome. A little thank-you once in a while wouldn't go amiss.'

'Thanks, Meg.'

Alfred's a fat tabby I've had since he was a kitten around ten years ago – and the closest thing I have to a flatmate. I named him after Bruce Wayne's butler in *Batman*, hoping naively – not having owned a pet before – that I'd be able to train him to do things for me, like you can with a dog. As it turns out, I'm the one who waits on him, hand and foot, making his name pretty damn ironic. Honestly, he has me wrapped around his little finger. I realise now, of course, how utterly ridiculous it was of me ever to think I could get a cat, of all creatures, to be helpful. You live and learn.

It's rare for me to stay away from home but, on the odd occasion I have, my cousin Meg has looked after Alfred for me. The daughter of my late dad's brother, she lives nearby, unlike her parents, who emigrated to New Zealand when we were both still in our twenties. My uncle, who has some kind of high-powered role in finance, was offered a job opportunity in Auckland that was apparently too good to miss. They tried to convince Meg to go with them, but she was having none of it, happy with her life here in Manchester.

My cousin is a year older than me so has already had plenty of time to embrace the joys of being forty. We used to be very close, particularly after Mum and Dad died, but we had a big row a few months ago that really set things back between us. We didn't go as far as cutting off all contact with each other, but our relationship cooled significantly. Up until that point, she'd been like a sister and best friend rolled into one. This is the first time since our quarrel that I've had to call upon her for a favour. The simple truth is that there isn't anyone else I can turn to.

A young nurse I don't recognise walks by, on the way to see another patient, and I get her attention by clicking my fingers. 'Hello? Do you know how Iris is doing?'

I reply to the blank look she gives me by adding:

21

'The woman who was brought in with me last night, who'd also been trapped under the fallen scaffolding.'

'I'm sorry, I don't know anything about that. What's her surname? Do you know what ward she's on?'

'No, I don't,' I snap. 'For goodness' sake. You're the one who works here, right? Surely you can get that information yourself. There can't be many other people who went through what we did yesterday.'

In a calm voice, she says she'll speak to her colleagues in a few minutes and see what she can find out.

'Was there any need to be so rude to her?' Meg asks once the nurse is out of earshot. She sits down on the chair at the side of my bed. 'I know you've been through a lot, Luke, but still. It's hardly her fault. And clicking your fingers like that to call her over. Really?'

'What?' I shrug. 'It's not my fault there are different staff working here every time I look up, is it? Honestly, I don't think I've seen the same nurse twice since I've arrived. They should be more organised and know their stuff better.'

'You'll get more out of people if you're nice to them,' my cousin adds.

'Whatever.'

'So the other person involved in your accident is in a bad way, is she? I remember hearing something on the news about an emergency operation. Who is she? Do you know her?'

'I didn't until yesterday. We met as we were both taking shelter from the storm and spoke to each other while we were trapped. She probably saved my life, first by pushing me out of the way of some falling debris and then by calling for help on her mobile when mine was out of action. I knew she was hurt at the time, but I didn't realise how serious her injuries were . . . She was impaled by one of the scaffolding poles.'

Meg winces, running a hand through her short, spiky hair, which is currently dyed a very light blonde colour. 'Oh my God. That's awful. Poor thing.'

'The pain must have been excruciating. And still she managed to make that phone call. I hope she pulls through. It's been touch and go so far.'

I recount to Meg how the accident unfolded and how lucky I was to have escaped pretty much unscathed. 'I've got a few minor cuts and bruises, but that seems to be about it, amazingly. I think it's only because of the blow to my head that they've admitted me, to make sure I don't have a concussion or anything. Fingers crossed, I should be out of here by tomorrow, I reckon.'

'Does your head hurt?' she asks, her eyes scanning me up and down.

'Not as much as it did yesterday. I'm stiff and achy all over, but that's only to be expected. It's a miracle I wasn't crushed. Loads of chunks of masonry came down with the scaffolding. That old building was in a right mess. I couldn't believe the state of it, from what I could see when they pulled me out. I feel incredibly lucky.'

'Well, if one good thing has come from this, it's that you're seeing the positive side of life for once.'

I frown. 'What's that supposed to mean?'

Meg rubs her chin. 'You're not exactly Mr Blue Sky, are you, Luke? If I looked up the word *pessimist* in the dictionary, I wouldn't be surprised to see a photo of you looking back at me. You're the very definition of a glass-half-empty person.'

'Charming,' I reply, although I don't bother arguing with her. Life has served me my fair share of lemons and, well, I've always preferred a pint of bitter to a glass of lemonade.

A little while later, the nurse I asked about Iris reappears at the end of my bed. I know immediately from the fidgety way she stands there that she has news – and not the good kind.

'Hello, Mr Craven,' she says in a timid, sombre voice. 'I, er, made some enquiries about your, um . . . about Iris. Her surname's Lambert, by the way. There's no easy way to say this . . . It's bad news, I'm afraid. Miss Lambert suffered very severe injuries and I'm so sorry to have to inform you that she passed away about an hour ago.'

Her words hit like a baseball bat to my face and gut. 'W-what,' I stutter. 'No, that can't be right. She was stable the last time I asked. I know she was badly hurt, but . . . are you sure?'

The nurse looks at Meg and then back at me. With an audible gulp, she adds: 'Yes, I'm sure. I'm really sorry. I wish I could tell you more, but that's all I know. Is there anything I—'

'It's okay,' Meg says. 'I'll take it from here. Thank you for letting us know.'

Once the nurse has shuffled away, Meg leans over the bed and takes my hand in hers. 'That must have been tough to hear. Do you want me to pour you a glass of water or—'

'No, don't.' I can't stop shaking my head in disbelief. 'Please, give me some space, will you? I feel like throwing up.'

I knew it was possible that Iris wouldn't make it, but I really thought she'd pull through. Burying my face in my palms, I take one deep breath after another. 'She seemed lovely and kind. And so young: she can't have been much over thirty. A doctor too, with her whole life and career ahead of her. Her poor family. They must be beside themselves.'

'She was a doctor?' Meg asks.

'Yes, that was one of the few things she told me about herself. She mentioned that she was losing blood and . . . Oh God, it should have been me, not her.'

Meg stands up and pulls me into a tight hug, which I resist initially before giving in to it. 'Don't you say that, Luke. It's not for us to decide how these things work. And you have nothing to blame yourself for.'

I hear what she says, but I can't accept it. I can't stop thinking it should have been me rather than Iris to have been killed. Why do I deserve to survive and she doesn't? What do I have to offer to the world compared to her: a young doctor with the potential to make a genuine difference to so many other people's lives? If she hadn't had to push me out of the way like she did, while I was being a rabbit in the headlights, maybe things would have turned out differently.

When was the last time I made a difference, other than by tidying up someone's hair? It's true what Meg said about me being a pessimist. And that's only half the story.

Misanthropic, crotchety, self-centred – all words that could, objectively, be used to describe me. If I was stuck in hospital for a month, I'd be shocked if anyone other than my cousin came to visit. And considering our falling-out, I'm lucky she's here. I'm not even sure that Alfred would miss me much, as long as someone else kept him fed and watered.

'Luke?' Meg snaps her fingers in front of my face, dragging me back into the moment. 'Is everything all right? Where did you go just now? You were away with the fairies. I was about to call a nurse. Could this be something to do with your head injury?'

I shake my head to clear it. 'Um, no. I'm fine. I was thinking, that's all.'

'What about?'

'Iris mainly. I can't believe she's gone. I really thought she'd make it, even if the odds were stacked against her. She seemed so capable – so together. It probably sounds ridiculous for me to say that. Like such characteristics would make any difference when—'

'Take it easy,' Meg says, knitting her brow, her piercing blue eyes scrutinising mine, silently reiterating her concern for my wellbeing. I do as she says and stop talking. Try to clear my racing mind. It works to a degree, but there's a knot in my stomach that's not going anywhere and I can't get Iris out of my head. I'm picturing her standing before me in that bright yellow raincoat when I realise there's a blank where her face should be.

Try as I might, I can't picture it. Not too surprising, considering we only met that one time – and yet it was only yesterday. I desperately want to remember. She deserves that at the very least. But it's no good. I can't do it, and it's frustrating the hell out of me. Then a thought pops into my mind and, as soon as I think it, I have to say something to Meg.

'I'm going to go to her funeral,' I tell her. 'There's no way I can miss it.'

'Okay. I get that.'

'Could you do one little thing for me? It's related.'

'What's that, then?' There's a wary tone to her voice.

'Could you see if you can find out some details of Iris and her family now, while everyone's here in one place? Otherwise, how will I know where and when the funeral's going to be held?'

Seeing my cousin's wariness become hesitance, I add: 'I'd do it myself, but I'm effectively chained to the bed. They've told me I need to stay put. And I doubt the medical staff will simply hand out that kind of information if I ask them.'

Meg lets out a little sigh. 'You want me to approach her grieving family now – right after they've lost her?'

'All I know is that I really need to go to that funeral. I have to pay my respects.'

'Fine, leave it with me, but on the proviso that you stop stressing yourself out. Close your eyes and try to have a snooze, yes? You look like you desperately need it. Deal?'

'Deal.'

CHAPTER 4

'Well? How do I scrub up?'

Alfred opens his eyes as I kneel to ruffle the fur on his head. He slides them shut again when he sees there's nothing exciting going on, such as a snack from the magic jar of cat treats – guaranteed to get his attention and temporary subservience, thus kept well out of his way on a high shelf.

'I'll take your silence as a compliment,' I say, stroking him in slow, sweeping waves along the length of his body, which is stretched out on the carpet next to the radiator in the hall. 'You think I look very smart, right? Perhaps I should get suited and booted more often. People might take me more seriously.'

Alfred meows at me, his eyes still shut.

I'll never forget when I first wore this outfit – charcoal suit, black tie, white shirt, black brogues. How could I? I bought it specially for my parents' funeral. I close my eyes for a moment and I'm back there again, sitting on a hard pew at the front of the church on that horrendous day.

There were people – family and friends – on either side of me, and so many more behind them, but I'd never felt more alone.

How could Mum and Dad both be gone, torn mercilessly away from me without even the hint of a warning . . . forever? How could I be expected to manage without them?

I kept asking myself if this was actually happening. It didn't feel real.

The dreaded day's events were unfolding like a terrible dream. But this was far worse: a living, breathing nightmare from which there was no waking up, no escape. It kept inching forward. I couldn't stop it.

The vicar started speaking. Had there been music before that? I couldn't recall. Nor could I tune into the words being spoken in front of me. And the very last thing I wanted to do was look up, because that would have meant seeing the coffins again – both of them – knowing they contained the vacant, broken bodies of my parents. So I stared down at my stiff new shoes and tried to keep breathing, despite the tightness in my chest. I willed my heart to harden to spare me any more of this unbearable pain.

'Luke, are you okay?' More words, whispered into my ear this time, accompanied by a squeeze of my hand. But that felt no more real than anything else. I nodded all the same. But I wasn't okay, of course. What an absurd question.

How could anyone be okay on the worst day of their life?

I drag myself back into the present and to the bathroom mirror. A red swarm now shrouds the light blue hue of my eyes; my cheeks glisten with tears.

'Come on, Luke,' I tell myself, splashing my face with cold water. 'Today's not about you. It's about Iris and the family she left behind.'

A few minutes later, the buzzer goes and I tell Meg through the intercom that I'm coming down.

'I'm going out now,' I say to Alfred. 'You're in charge. There's plenty of food and water to keep you going. Don't do anything I wouldn't do.'

Slipping on my black, double-breasted mac as the final piece of my sombre outfit, I let myself out. Ideally, I'd like to wear a hat too, but since I don't own one smart enough, I'll have to accept having a cold head. Oh, the joys of going bald.

While exiting through the front door of the building, I flinch as I spot my elderly neighbour Doreen approaching from outside.

'Please could you hold the door?' she calls, speeding up her walk to the point where she starts to waddle.

Doreen's in her late seventies, I think. She has white hair, wavy and short, neatly brushed into a side parting. Today she's dressed in brown cords, a thick red woolly jumper and a green raincoat.

I haven't run into her since the scaffolding incident. I wouldn't blame her for saying 'I told you so' after the

30

abrupt way I dismissed her storm warning that day. But if she's aware of what happened, she doesn't let on, to my relief.

'Thank you, Liam,' she says as I let her inside. 'Just been for my daily constitutional.'

She's always called me Liam, for some reason. I used to correct her at first, but it didn't make any difference, so eventually I just accepted it.

I keep myself to myself when it comes to the other folk in my building, not wanting to get too friendly in case they get the wrong idea and start bothering me with annoying stuff like watering plants when they're away or helping them to put up shelves. It's not like I specifically chose to live near any of these people. So why do we need to be friends?

You'd think my general surliness would have made my feelings about this pretty clear. However, Doreen has always persevered, regardless.

'You look very smart today,' she says. 'Going somewhere special?'

'Something like that,' I say, not wanting to discuss the funeral with her. 'Anyway, my, um, cousin is waiting to pick me up. Got to dash.'

Meg's white Mini is parked just along the road. I climb into the passenger seat and greet my cousin with a kiss on the cheek. 'You look nice,' I tell her. She's wearing a demure black midi dress with a pleated front and matching cardigan; her hair is a little less spiky than usual and her makeup more subtle. The result is a fresh-faced, naturally pretty look that she doesn't present to the world too often but suits her well.

'You don't look too bad yourself,' she replies. 'How are things?'

'Fine. Thanks for offering to pick me up and come with me. I appreciate it, especially after . . . you know, the last few months.'

'Wow, someone's on their best behaviour today.' Meg smiles and squeezes my hand. 'I'm happy to help.'

'Is Ellen covering the shop for you?'

'Yep.'

Must be nice to have someone to do that. It's not so easy when you run a business with no employees other than yourself. I've decided to stay closed all day today – and not for the first time since the accident. I may have escaped more or less uninjured, but it hasn't exactly made me feel like grafting. Luckily, I'm in a position where I can afford to miss the odd day's work, knowing it won't break the bank.

'Is that one of yours?' I ask, pointing towards a swirly ring on her left hand that looks like it's made from barbed wire.

Meg runs a small contemporary jewellery store on the other side of the Northern Quarter from my barbershop. It's not the kind of jeweller where you buy fancy watches and diamond rings, but rather one with lots of affordable, quirky original designs, mainly using silver. Most of what she sells, she makes herself in a little studio at the back. It's amazing how creative she is. She's great at what she does and seems to really enjoy it. Ellen's a long-term employee and friend who serves in the shop a couple of days a week so Meg can focus on the production side of things.

There's a twinkle in my cousin's eye as she replies: 'Yes, it's a new design I've been working on. Do you like it?'

'I do. It looks great, as usual.'

She throws me a raised-eyebrow glance. 'Flattery will get you everywhere. How's the head, by the way?'

'It's fine.'

'It doesn't hurt at all any more?'

'Thankfully not.'

'That's good news.'

The conversation inevitably turns to the funeral, which is being held at a church in Prestwich, a suburb to the north of the city centre, followed by a cremation.

In light of our chat, Meg managed to speak to someone from Iris's family at the hospital while I was still an inpatient there. They exchanged phone numbers and so, once the arrangements were finalised, by which time I'd been released back home, she was able to furnish me with details of the ceremony.

Just over two weeks have passed since that fateful night when Iris and I were trapped. If anything, it feels longer. I've been itching for this day to come, hoping the funeral will give me the chance to get some kind of closure. However, now it's finally here, I'm not sure what I'm hoping to achieve by turning up. I feel increasingly nervous as we make the short journey, with Meg using her mobile, mounted on the dashboard, to direct us to the right location, since neither of us has been there before.

'Why do you keep sighing?' she asks me at one point.

'Do I? Sorry, I didn't realise. It must be nerves.'

'You do seem really on edge, Luke. We don't have to go if you don't want to. I can turn around and take you back home if you like, no problem. There's zero pressure from anyone other than yourself. No one expects you to attend.'

'I'm fine,' I reply, taking a deep breath and then, suddenly aware of what I'm doing, letting the air back out as slowly and quietly as possible. 'Honestly, it's cool. I need to do this, Meg.'

The church is at the end of a long, winding street off the main road we've followed most of the way out of Manchester. As we drive down it, the trendy bars and restaurants at the top end give way to a mix of traditional terraced houses and a few modern semis. We pass an electricity substation and a working men's club before reaching a small parking area that's full to the brim. A crowd is already gathered in the churchyard: a mix of old and young, sombre faces, wrapped up in dark coats.

'Did you notice any parking spaces on the side of the road?' Meg asks me as she swings the car around. 'There's no way we're fitting in here.'

'No. I, er, wasn't really looking. Sorry.'

It takes a few minutes of searching, as the street is chock-a-block with traffic, but we eventually find a spot with enough room to wedge in the Mini.

'You've done this before,' I tell Meg after she reverses into the space in one go and turns off the engine.

'Only about a million times.'

It's a bit of a walk back to the church; when we get

34

there, the tail end of the crowd is shuffling into the main entrance, so we do the same.

'Let's find a spot somewhere near the back,' I whisper into Meg's ear, glad to have her with me. She nods in agreement, but once we get inside, it's clear that's not going to happen. All the rear and middle pews are full, with the only room remaining being on the front four rows, which have presumably been left clear for close family and friends.

Until now, I haven't been inside a church since Mum and Dad's funeral. They used to take me regularly as a boy, being churchgoers themselves. However, I drifted in my teenage years, once other interests started taking over my Sunday mornings, and so the habit faded. As an adult, I did initially still believe in the essence of religion, not least because my parents never forced it down my throat or judged me for taking a different path. My faith died when they were both killed, though, at which point nothing made sense any more.

Just being here now is tough, because of how much it reminds me of their funeral. However, I push those thoughts far away into the depths of my mind, for fear of my emotions getting the better of me, like they did before I left the flat.

'What do we do?' I ask Meg as discreetly as possible. 'We can't go there.'

But before she can reply, we're being ushered towards the front, our mutters of resistance falling on deaf ears. Meg's directed to a single remaining spot next to the aisle on the fifth row, while I'm sent alone to the wall side of the fourth.

Once seated, I look over and to my rear, attempting to convey the awkwardness of the situation to my cousin in an open-eyed stare. She gestures with a subtle nod of her head that I should look forward, so I do, focusing on the order of service that was shoved into my hand on entry.

There's a striking headshot of Iris on the front, her beautiful brown eyes complemented by a glorious jumble of shoulder-length, brunette corkscrew curls. I had no idea she had such amazing hair when I met her, as it was hidden inside the hood of that colourful raincoat she wore.

Before I can delve inside the A5-size pamphlet, my attention – along with everyone else's – is drawn towards the arrival of the main funeral party at the back of the church, accompanied by sombre organ music.

It's a big group and the first of them are directed next to me, drawing attention – in my mind at least – to my hugely inappropriate positioning. Part of me expects to be challenged, like a fifteen-year-old who's somehow managed to sneak into a nightclub, but the stooped, besuited pensioner who takes a seat next to me merely nods and purses his lips in my direction. I reciprocate in a way I hope silently conveys my condolences and then avoid his eye for the rest of the ceremony.

It passes in a blurry flash of kind words, hymns, prayers and grief-stricken faces. It's heartbreaking to see those who must have been closest to Iris in bits, holding on to one another for strength, dumbstruck and devastated.

As much as I try not to think of when I was in that situation, paralysed by the unbearable weight of losing my parents, it's a real struggle not to slip back into those dark memories. I focus on Iris's photo and fight to stay strong for her, like she did for me. How unworthy I am to have survived her, considering what an extraordinary, intelligent, kind and selfless woman she was in her short but notable life.

She was truly amazing. I'm already incredibly aware of this fact, based not only on my encounter with her but having seen several TV reports and newspaper articles about her death. Some journalists have approached me to be interviewed about what happened, but I've declined to comment. This is partly down to how unworthy I feel to have survived when she didn't. Also, I have no idea what to say and, from past experience, I worry they might twist my words. I had feared a press presence here today, but thankfully that's not the case, presumably at the family's request.

When I first heard Iris had signed up to be a voluntary doctor for a charity scheme, which would have seen her travelling to poverty and disease-stricken countries in Africa in the near future, I literally felt unable to breathe. I mean, imagine the difference she could have made over there; how many lives she could have transformed, saved, whatever. I'd found it hard enough thinking of all the good she could have achieved at the city centre GP practice where she'd been working on the day of the accident. So learning about this on top was really tough. Talk about feeling unworthy.

Even though I know it's coming, I struggle to cope again when this overseas aid trip is mentioned during the ceremony. I feel hot and panicky as an older male doctor colleague makes a short speech about how passionate she'd been about volunteering her services. As he explains how donations in her memory are being collected for the charity, I find myself growing paranoid that everyone is looking in my direction, wishing it was me, not her, who died.

Being stuck here at the front of the church – a charlatan among the real mourners – only serves to heighten my guilt. It takes all of my effort to stay quiet while I'm screaming inside.

This isn't about me, I tell myself over and over, fighting to steady my breathing and desperately trying to stay focused on the funeral rather than my own issues. Concentrate on Iris. Think of her devastated family. Calculate what donation to give in tribute to her, if that helps. Like any amount of money I could give would be enough.

A redhead with similar style curls to Iris stands up at the end of the front row. She slowly makes her way to the lectern, as it's vacated by the previous speaker. When she turns to face forward, I see she's middle-aged and, without a doubt, related to Iris. Could it be her mother?

As I'm wondering this, she takes a shaky deep breath into the microphone and wipes her puffy, teary brown eyes with a tissue. In a voice quivering with emotion, she announces: 'For anyone who doesn't already know me, I'm Rita, Iris's aunt.'

Having paused to compose herself, she adds: 'I'd like to say a few words on behalf of the family. You'll, um, have to bear with me, I'm afraid . . . This is even harder than I imagined.'

As Rita continues, fighting the swell of her emotions with every word she utters, the whole congregation looks utterly wretched and broken. It's gut-wrenching to witness and my heart feels ready to burst in sympathy for her and the rest of Iris's family.

'She was always special, right back from when she was a little girl,' Rita says. 'Whenever we saw each other, she'd always start by asking: "How are you, Aunty Rita?" I can picture her doing so right now, like it was yesterday, in that . . .' She breaks off; gulps audibly into the mic. 'That . . . sweet little voice of hers.' Her own voice rises to a crescendo of sorrow as she says this, which makes me well up. I try to hide my emotions from those around me; though they're genuine, I still have the sense of being a fraud, like I have no right to feel this way.

'That might not sound much,' Rita continues, 'but as anyone who's had kids will know, most children aren't wired that way. They tend to focus mainly on themselves when they're little. Well, not our Iris. And she was so clever. She was always destined to do something great with that combination of head and heart. We're all so proud of what she achieved, getting into university and becoming a doctor.'

Following another emotional pause, she concludes, with a catch in her voice: 'The tragedy is she was only just getting started. She had so much still to give. We'll never forget you, Iris: our shining star.'

CHAPTER 5

'How are you doing?' Meg asks me in a quiet voice as we find each other in the crowded churchyard once the service is over.

'I'm okay, near enough,' I tell her. 'Tough, wasn't it? Really hard. I tried not to think about Mum and Dad, but . . .'

'I know,' she says.

I take a deep breath and stare into the distance, trying to swallow down the lump in my throat.

For a moment I'm in the past again, staring out of the empty barbershop window, the smell of coffee rising from the mug in my hand; answering the phone call that's about to crush me – turn my life upside down.

'Mr Luke Craven?' I'll never forget the solemn sound of that heavily accented voice. I immediately knew something was very wrong, even before he identified himself and asked if I was sitting down. Before the mug tumbled from my hand and shattered on the floor, shedding its dark contents all over.

I imagined the worst, so I thought, but I didn't come close.

Meg nudges me back into the here and now with the gentle touch of her hand on my back.

When I turn to look at her, her eyes are glistening. 'It was hard not to get drawn into the emotion,' she says. 'I couldn't stop myself crying a few times, even though I never met Iris. It was so intense, like the air in there was charged with grief. I've never been to a funeral for someone so young before. The sense of loss felt even more raw than usual – I suppose because it's against the natural course of things.'

'Yep,' I reply, blowing cool air up on to my face. 'It feels totally unjust, doesn't it? Wrong.'

'Exactly. There aren't even any "at least she had a good innings" type platitudes to fall back on. People aren't meant to die at thirty-two.'

'I got the impression it was only close family and friends going to the crematorium next,' I say to Meg. 'Do you agree?'

'Yes, I don't think it would be appropriate for us to go to that.'

'I felt bad enough sitting so near to the front. We ought to have arrived earlier, in hindsight, but it didn't occur to me that we'd need to.'

'Never mind. At least you got to pay your respects. Shall we head back to town in a few minutes, once the traffic has died down?'

I run a hand over my recently shaved chin. 'Um, I was considering going to the reception afterwards.'

Meg raises an eyebrow. 'Can't resist the lure of a free meal?'

'I feel like I ought to say something to Iris's parents. It's not that I really want to – it would be much easier to quietly slip off – but I don't think I'll forgive myself if I don't go. They did mention that everyone was welcome to come along.'

This isn't like me at all. It's the first time in ages that I've wanted to connect with others, particularly strangers, rather than shutting myself off as normal. But offering my condolences in person to Iris's nearest and dearest feels like the least I can do after what she did for me. Something about her and the way she died has really got under my skin. And it's more than the guilt I feel. It's like she's roused a long dormant part of me that actually cares about doing the right thing – that wants to become a better version of myself.

I tell Meg she's done enough and should go if she needs to. 'I'll be all right on my own. I can take a bus or tram back home.' I try to sound convincing as I say this, although I'm praying she'll stay with me for moral support. Plus she's had contact with the family before, so there could be an opportunity for her to introduce me, which would be better than having to present myself.

To my relief, she replies: 'No, it's fine. I'll stay.'

The do is being held at the working men's club further up the street. A lot of the other folk not attending the cremation head straight there, but we decide to take a stroll in a nearby park first and then to grab a drink – liquid courage – in a local pub.

More than an hour has passed by the time we finally enter the club. It's busy with people chatting around tables and queueing at the bar, but there's an understandably muted nature to the proceedings, rather than the usual raised voices, music or laughter you'd expect with so many people gathered in a licensed premises.

'I'll get us both a drink, shall I?'

Meg nods. 'Thanks. A tonic water for me, please, preferably with ice and lemon. There's a small table over there by the window. I'll grab it.'

As I'm waiting to order, a couple of staff emerge from the kitchen with plates of sandwiches, quiche, vol-au-vents and other buffet food, swiftly followed by a large tray of bubbling lasagne plus pie and peas.

'Goodness me,' I hear a woman's voice behind me say. 'No one's going hungry today, are they?'

Although Iris's mum and dad didn't speak at the funeral service, it was obvious who they were from the way things unfolded. I know their names – Stan and Claire – from the news reports, as well as the fact Iris was an only child. It's hard to imagine exactly what hell they must be going through, having never had children myself, but I do know what it's like to be strangled by grief. No parent should have to attend their child's funeral. It's fundamentally wrong, like nature is out of whack. Stan and Claire's grieving process is bound to be especially tough.

Would it be marginally easier if they had the comfort of another child to share the burden? Possibly. I can only surmise. Now the stark truth of the matter is they've lost a whole generation of their immediate family: gone in one fell swoop.

There's been no mention of Iris having left behind a significant other, so I assume she was single when she died. That would make sense in terms of her plans to go to Africa: probably not the kind of trip you'd embark on if you had a partner, unless they were going along too.

That's one less broken soul for me to feel guilty about – and yet also one less person to support her parents in their time of need.

What if Iris was destined to meet the love of her life in Africa? That's not hard to imagine. Trips like these are exactly the kind of situation where people who wouldn't otherwise have met spend lots of time in close quarters and fall for each other. A fellow young doctor, perhaps, from elsewhere in the world. It could have been the merging of two brilliant, selfless minds; they could have gone on to achieve wonderful things together.

'What can I get you?' the barman asks, interrupting my thought process, which I'm glad about, seeing as it was only making me feel worse. I don't know what's come over me since the accident. I barely recognise myself in some of the sentimental concerns occupying my mind. Hard-hearted and cynical have been my default settings for so long now, it feels alien to care this much, particularly about someone I barely knew. But if it wasn't for her . . .

'Could I get a pint of bitter and a tonic water?'

'Ice and a slice with the tonic?'

'Sure.'

'Aren't you going to top that up?' I ask him when he

44

places my pint in front of me with far too thick a head on it. 'Otherwise I might as well have ordered a half.'

'No problem,' he replies, frowning.

When I take the drinks over to where Meg's sitting, she looks up from her mobile, places it down on the table and smiles. 'Thank you very much. Have you spotted Iris's parents? They're sitting around the other side of the bar.'

'Yes, I noticed. I don't think now's the right time to say anything, though, as there's a constant stream of people going over to them, offering their condolences. I think I'll wait until things quieten down a bit.'

She nods.

'Who was it from the family that you spoke to at the hospital and swapped numbers with?'

'One of her cousins: Guy, he's called. I think he's the son of the aunt who spoke during the ceremony. Rita, wasn't it?'

'That's right. Where is he? Can you see him?'

Meg cranes her neck and has a good look around the club, only to then shake her head. 'I spotted him earlier, but I'm not sure where he is now.'

'What does he look like?'

'Medium height, short brown hair, designer stubble, black suit.'

'That narrows it down. Let me know when you spot him, yeah?'

A little while later she kicks me under the table. 'That's him,' she whispers, nodding in the direction of a twenty-something entering the room with a John Wayne swagger. He's brandishing a pack of cigarettes in his right hand like a weapon. Unfortunately, he's not looking in our direction, but when I see him head for the toilets, it seems like too good an opportunity to miss.

'Back in a minute,' I tell Meg. 'I need the little boys' room.'

'Didn't you go when we left the pub?'

I shrug. 'Getting old.'

When I enter the loo, the strong scent of a cheap air freshener making my nose itch, Guy is standing at the urinal with his back to me. We're alone, but now I'm here I realise this might not be the best place to make contact after all. In my experience, people don't often like being approached by strangers in the toilet. What was I thinking?

Anyway, now that I'm here, I position myself at the next urinal but one and try to go, although nothing wants to come out; I look straight ahead, hoping he doesn't notice. I can smell that he's had a fag. It's unpleasant, but nothing I'm not used to, since many of my smoking clientele tend to have one right before they come in for a haircut.

When we're both washing our hands, I say as casually as I can: 'Iris was your cousin, right? Condolences.'

As the words leave my mouth, for some reason I imagine him turning around and thumping me in the face. Luckily, that isn't what happens. Instead, he nods and says: 'Cheers, man. Appreciate that.'

I hope he might ask how I knew Iris in return, but silence ensues, so as I'm drying my hands on a paper towel, I go for it again. 'I, um, didn't know her for very long at all, but she seemed like an amazing person. I think she may have even saved my life.'

Guy looks me up and down quizzically. 'Were you one of her patients or something? Hang on: you're not some kind of weirdo stalker, are you? I know she had some problems with—'

I hold up my palms defensively. 'No, no. Sorry. I should have been clear from the start. My name is Luke Craven. I was the other person involved in the accident that killed Iris. My cousin Meg spoke to you at the hospital. She's here with me too, actually. I, um—'

He holds out his arm to offer a handshake, which I accept. 'Sorry, man, my bad. It's been a tough day so far and I'm not feeling totally with it, if I'm honest. Listen, it was good of you to come. Nice to meet you.'

'You too,' I reply. 'I'd quite like to, er, have a word with Iris's parents. Pay my respects and all that. I don't suppose you'd mind introducing me, would you?'

He hesitates for a split second, rubbing his eyes with his hands. 'Um, sure. They're pretty raw at the moment, as you can probably imagine, but yeah, okay. I'll introduce you. Give me five minutes on my own with them first, yeah?'

'Of course. Then what? Shall I come over, or—'

He smiles. 'Yeah, exactly.'

I return to sit with Meg and explain what's going on while taking a couple of large swigs from my pint to steady my nerves.

'Would you like me to come with you?' she asks when I empty the glass and tell her I'm about to go over.

'No, I don't think so. I'm probably best doing this alone.'

Meg nods, a hint of relief on her face. 'If you're sure.'

I straighten my tie and double check my flies are done up before rising to my feet. 'Wish me luck.'

A moment later I manage to catch Guy's eye as I approach the table where he's now sitting alongside Stan, Claire and a couple of others I don't recognise.

For some inexplicable reason, I find myself doing a weird kind of bow in the parents' direction as he introduces me. 'This is Luke,' he says. 'The bloke I was telling you about.'

CHAPTER 6

I have a recurring dream. I can't say how many times I've had it, but it's a lot. It can't be anything to do with the scaffolding accident, as it started ages before that. I've been dreaming it on and off for a long time – well over a year, I reckon, although I've not kept a record. As for what it means, I have no idea.

Maybe it doesn't mean anything. Does it have to?

I'd probably say no, if it had only been once or twice. But having had it so many times now, I suppose there must be some reason for it. What's my subconscious trying to communicate?

The truth is I've probably dreamed it more times than I know. You only remember the dreams you wake up in the middle of, right?

Anyway, I had it just now – and awoke while it was still unfolding. That's why it's on my mind. I'll have mostly forgotten about it by the time I've – hopefully – been back to sleep and woken up again at a more friendly hour.

It's currently 4.07 a.m. on Saturday and pitch black. I consider getting up to go to the toilet, but my bladder doesn't feel full enough to bother. So instead I dig myself deeper into the duvet and try to clear my mind in a bid to slip back to sleep.

It doesn't work. Persistent memories of the dream continue to pervade my thoughts and, after a short while, I give in and get up to go to the bathroom.

Alfred gives me a shock, appearing out of nowhere and brushing himself against the back of my bare legs as I stand at the toilet.

'Blooming heck, mate,' I say. 'Go easy with the sneaking up on me, otherwise you'll give me a heart attack. Who'll feed you then?'

He looks up at me with those big, pleading, greenish-yellow eyes of his – a pair of searchlights on the lookout for an early-hours snack – and I can't resist.

'Fine. You can have a couple of treats from the magic jar, but that's it. Then it's bedtime, okay? Not time to start annoying me, keeping me awake. Are we clear?'

He continues to stare at me, which I accept is as close to an answer as I'm likely to get. Then he accompanies me to his bowl, keeping up the leg-rubbing affection as he goes, so I almost trip over him at one point. I reach for the jar, tucked out of his way, grab a few and toss them down for him. At this point he stops sucking up to me and starts gobbling. I grab a glass of water to take back to bed and bid him goodnight.

Once I'm under the covers again, I find myself far too wide awake for my liking at this ungodly hour.

My mind returns to that damn dream. It starts in all kinds of different ways but always ends up the same: I'm living alone in a flat not unlike this one. The exact look and location of it varies on each occasion. Sometimes it's here in Manchester; sometimes London or another UK city; at other times, it's abroad or simply unspecified, as locations in dreams are wont to be.

In reality, my place is on the first floor. However, the flat where I live in this recurring dream is invariably at ground level. Another thing that's always the same is the existence of a door leading to another self-contained section: a second flat, effectively. I'm aware of it from the start in some instances; in others, I happen upon it by chance. Either way, going in there never fails to unsettle me. And what I find is always pretty much the same: a corridor leading to two fully furnished, unoccupied bedrooms decorated in neutral green and beige colours, each with a made-up double divan and a little en-suite bathroom.

Further down the corridor are a small kitchen and lounge, again neutrally furnished but unused. The latter has patio doors that lead into a luscious garden including an outdoor swimming pool. Never once have I ever dared or even considered entering the water, though. And it's not because it's in use by anyone else or neglected.

The pool and surroundings always appear empty and immaculate, yet they hold zero appeal for me. Whatever the specifics in any particular occurrence of the dream, no aspect of this secret annexe ever feels good. I want to get out of there as soon as possible; to close the adjoining door between that and my 'real' home and try to forget its existence.

That's easier said than done, of course.

After yesterday's funeral, I'm surprised I didn't dream about Iris or the accident. I have done previously, in the days leading up to it, but now I'm back to this old inscrutable chestnut.

I roll over in bed. Try to stop thinking about the dream. Instead, I cast my mind back to what happened at the funeral reception after I went over to speak to Iris's parents.

It started relatively well, despite my weird introductory bow. Claire didn't say much. She wasn't really speaking to anyone, though, so I didn't overthink the implications of that. Meanwhile, Stan shook my hand and chatted to me for a little while.

'Please accept my sincere condolences for the loss of your daughter,' I said, crouching down next to him and also trying to catch Claire's eye as I spoke, since the sentiment was intended for both of them.

'Thank you for that,' Stan replied, 'and also for making the effort to come today. We appreciate it.'

'Of course.'

'So you were with Iris when it happened: when the scaffolding fell down?'

'Yes.'

'Did you know her beforehand, or—'

'No, no. I, um . . . I was looking for somewhere to take shelter from the awful weather. The wind was bad enough, but then it started really pounding it down with rain and hail. Iris was already there before me, also trying to stay dry. Obviously neither of us had any idea that it wasn't safe to stand there. Once we realised, it was too late. Your daughter was so brave, though, even after she was injured. She was the one who called for help, possibly saving my life. Plus when the scaffolding first started coming down, she pushed me—'

Before I could finish my sentence, I was interrupted by a loud female voice asking what was going on.

I looked up from my crouching position to see Rita, the aunt who'd spoken during the funeral, standing over me and scowling. 'Who the hell are you and why are you upsetting my sister like this?' she demanded, much to my bewilderment.

My eyes turned to Claire, at which point I noticed she was sobbing into a tissue at the table. 'Um. Sorry, I didn't—'

'Get lost, will you?' Rita yelled, the large glass of white wine in her hand spilling some of its contents onto the carpeted floor.

I looked for Guy, hoping he could back me up – tell his mum that I was okay – but he was no longer anywhere to be seen. And by that time Stan was too busy consoling his wife to vouch for me. Was she really crying because of what I'd said? I couldn't imagine why, nor could I understand the reasoning behind Rita's sudden aggression towards me.

However, the last thing I wanted was to cause a scene, so rather than trying to defend myself, I apologised, rose back to a standing position and left.

'Come on, Meg,' I said, my cheeks burning as I stopped at the table on the way to the door. 'We need to go.'

She didn't argue, grabbing both of our coats and springing to her feet in one slick move.

She waited until we were outside and a little distance away from the club, walking in the direction of her car, before asking what had happened.

'Honestly, I don't know. I was having a normal chat with Iris's father, Stan, and then her aunt Rita rocked up out of nowhere, asking who I was and accusing me of upsetting Claire.'

'Claire?' Meg replies, looking confused.

'Iris's mother.'

'Oh, of course. Sorry. There have been a lot of new names to take in today. Was she upset?'

'Yes, but I'm not convinced that was because of what I said. I wasn't really looking at her by then, as she didn't seem particularly keen on talking to me. I was focusing on her husband. Clearly it was a mistake for me to try to talk to them so soon after the funeral.'

'I wouldn't beat yourself up about it,' Meg replied as we continued towards the car. 'You were only trying to do the right thing – to be a decent person. If you ask me, that Rita had already had too much to drink. I saw her throwing down a couple of shots at the bar before she came over to you. She probably got the wrong end of the stick.'

'Arguing didn't seem like a good idea. Never mind. It's done now. Let's head home.'

Back in the present, I'm still struggling to sleep when Alfred makes things worse by starting to meow loudly from wherever he is in the flat.

'Be quiet,' I say in a firm voice. 'That was the deal when I gave you a snack, remember?'

It makes no difference. He continues to meow, causing me to put a pillow over my face and thump a fist into it in a bid to vent my frustration. I eventually close the door and use ear plugs to block out the noise. It's a last resort, as it means I run the risk of sleeping through my alarm in a couple of hours. However, I'm shattered – and I desperately need some more rest before I have to get up and return to work.

If only there were ear plugs to silence inner speech. I may not be able to hear Alfred any more, but there's a monologue rattling on inside my noggin that's equally hard to ignore.

Thinking back to the funeral reception was a bad idea, because now I can't stop wondering why Rita turned on me so suddenly and with such venom. Was it because of something specific I said or did? She blamed it on me supposedly upsetting Claire, but I'm still not convinced of this.

Claire would have overheard my conversation with Stan, sure. But was that genuinely what led to her distress? She may have been upset by something or someone else entirely. Bearing in mind she'd just sent her daughter's body off to be cremated, it could also have been a natural outpouring of emotion and nothing whatsoever to do with what was happening around her.

Rita claimed not to know who I was when she came over, but that may have been a ruse to get rid of me. Her son Guy could have told her my identity. If so, perhaps

55

that was enough to make her want me out of there. It's feasible she blames me for her niece's death. If I hadn't been there with her when the scaffolding came down and she hadn't pushed me to safety like she did, things could have turned out very differently.

Such thoughts have haunted me ever since Iris's death. What even was it that she saw coming and shoved me away from? I thought there would be plenty of time to ask her afterwards, once we were both free from the wreckage, but now I'll never know for sure. I fear it was the pole that impaled her – most likely what caused her death. This of course makes me feel terrible, because it suggests that if I hadn't frozen like I did, Iris may not have been killed.

She was a better person than me in every way. It feels so wrong, so unfair. I know well enough from my own experiences how cruel life can be – how arbitrary. And yet no matter how much I try, I can't accept Iris dying instead of me as being acceptable. It isn't. I'm a miserable git who rarely does anything for anyone other than myself, while Iris appears to have been almost saint-like, or at least someone destined to achieve amazing, important things.

I need to do something to honour her memory and to justify my survival, for my own sanity if nothing else. But what that could be is beyond me right now. Especially at stupid o'clock in the morning when I ought to be fast asleep.

'Stop it,' I say out loud to myself. 'Enough is enough.'

I pull the duvet over my head, leaving only a small gap

to slowly, calmly breathe fresh air through. Next I undertake a process of relaxing my body, muscle by muscle, limb by limb, while simultaneously attempting to clear my head of all thoughts. It's a technique to beat insomnia that I read about online and have used previously with varying degrees of success.

I focus on being in a comfy, calm, safe place and try to think of nothing else but this. Other thoughts – my recurring dream, Iris's funeral, work, that pesky cat – do their utmost to assert themselves. But I'm doggedly determined to fend them off.

Each time my mind attempts to wander, I rein it in. I pull it back to that comfy, calm, safe place over and over, again and again, until eventually, at long last, I find my way back into the land of nod.

CHAPTER 7

Miraculously, I manage to get up in time for work despite my interrupted night's sleep. I'm far from fresh, though, so when I open the door to leave and spot Doreen with her back to me, watering one of the plants in the hallway, my first temptation is to close it again and wait until the coast is clear.

Glancing at my watch, I see there's no time to do that. Dammit. Why am I always running into her? Hasn't she got anything better to do than hang out in the communal areas of the building, looking for people to bother? And if she calls me Liam again this morning, I might actually lose it with her.

I decide to race past her at top speed, in the hope she barely notices me. Not that it works.

'Morning, Liam,' she chirps. 'Going anywhere interesting?'

'Work,' I reply without stopping, growling internally.

'On a Saturday?' she replies, like she's never seen me

do this before. 'You poor thing. My Bob worked his socks off Monday to Friday, I'll tell you. But he never once had to work at the weekend. That was his relaxing time. It's a different world now, I know, but not a better one. No wonder everybody's so stressed.'

I'm already at the bottom of the stairs by the time she's stopped talking. I almost walk out of the door without saying anything in response, but instead I call: 'That's life. Bye now.'

'Goodbye, Liam,' she replies. 'Have a good one.'

A couple of minutes into my walk to work, I spot a young woman in a bright pink hooded coat letting her pet poodle crap on the pavement without bagging it up, despite being right next to a bin. It makes me see red.

'Hey,' I bark at the twenty-something. 'Aren't you going to pick that up?'

She has dark, greasy hair scraped back in a high pony-tail and is sucking on one of those chunky vape devices. She looks me up and down, pouting, before puffing out a huge cloud of vapour. 'No, I don't have any bags.'

'Why not?' I ask her. 'What kind of dog owner are you? That's bloody disgusting and a health hazard.'

She shrugs, vaping some more, a bored look on her face. Then she walks on regardless, black poodle at her side.

'People like you shouldn't be allowed to have pets,' I call after her. 'You ought to be ashamed of yourself. You're a disgrace. If I see this happening again, I'll take a photo and report you to the council.'

'Whatever,' she replies, unfazed, not even looking back.

Her attitude makes me want to scream; I grit my teeth and continue on my way.

Being a Saturday, the barbershop is pretty busy. I'm not talking busy like one of those trendy establishments geared towards the cool kids: the kind where your achingly hip barber, probably wearing a waistcoat, spends as much time eyeing their own reflection in the mirror as making your hair look nice. But there's a constant stream of paying clients, which is good enough for me, and this helps the day pass quickly.

By four o'clock that afternoon, though, I'm starting to flag. My limbs feel heavy and I'm lethargic. I fear I might be coming down with something, although it could simply be my lack of sleep catching up with me.

I keep going for another couple of hours. But when I finish giving a twitchy teacher a number one buzz cut just before six o'clock and no one else is left waiting, I decide to call it a day.

As I'm cleaning up, having locked the door and changed the sign from OPEN to CLOSED, I hear someone knocking.

Not again. My mind jumps back to the last time this happened, on the night of the storm. I turn around – about to bark something arsey at whoever's there – only to have the wind knocked out of me, dumbstruck by the person I see. I blink a couple of times in case my eyes are deceiving me and I'm hallucinating.

'Hello there,' a muffled voice says through the glass of the door. 'I'm sorry to bother you while you're shutting up. I don't know if you recognise me, but . . . well, I'm here to offer you an apology.'

'Right,' I say, fumbling through my trouser pockets for the keys. 'You'd better come in.'

I certainly do recognise the visitor I let inside and offer a seat. How could I forget her after she spoke at the funeral yesterday and then shrieked at me to leave the reception soon afterwards?

I can honestly say that Iris's aunt was pretty much the last person I expected to see at the door when I turned around. And yet here she is, large as life, a visitor in my barbershop, twirling one of her red curls with her right forefinger and fidgeting in her chair. After the last time we met, it's quite a change to see her looking so uneasy. Considering how she humiliated me, I do take a little pleasure in this, I must admit. But I play nice after reminding myself who she is and that she must still be struggling to contain her grief.

'It's Rita, isn't it?' I say for want of anything better. 'Can I, er, get you a brew?'

'No, no,' she replies. 'I won't keep you. I'm probably the last person you want to spend time with after the way I treated you yesterday. That's why I'm here. I'd like to explain what happened and why I said what I did. I'm so terribly sorry. Would you hear me out?'

I'm intrigued, so of course I say yes. But gagging for a cup of tea myself, I tell her it's on the provision she changes her mind and accepts my offer of a brew. This makes her smile, immediately easing the tension in the room.

Rita's dressed in dark jeans and a grey puffer jacket, which she finally unzips while I'm topping off our mugs with milk. I'm not sure whether it's mainly down to the curly hair and brown eyes, but I can't help noticing how much she looks like her niece: even more than Iris's own mother, based on what I saw of her yesterday.

'Thank you very much,' she says when I hand her the tea. 'It's really very kind of you.'

'Hey, it's only a cuppa. It's not like I slipped in any booze.'

She grimaces. 'Just as well, I'd say. I don't think I'll be drinking for some time after yesterday. I had way too much. It was all so hard to get through.'

As Rita blinks back tears, I hand her a tissue.

Thanking me, she says: 'I'm sorry. I didn't mean to get upset like this. That's not why I came here.'

I sit down next to her. 'I understand. It must all still be very raw.'

After taking a moment to compose herself, Rita grabs my hand and looks me square in the eye. 'You seem like a nice man. Please accept my apologies for how I mistreated you yesterday in front of everyone. I'm so embarrassed, I had to come and see you. Fortunately, my son Guy, who you met, was able to put me in touch with your cousin Meg. Once I explained to her what it was about, she told me where I would be able to find you.'

'Right,' I reply, annoyed that Meg didn't give me a heads-up. Mind you, I've been so busy today, I can't even remember when I last checked my phone. Come to think of it, I stuck it on silent earlier after being bothered by one of those 'I believe you were in a car accident that wasn't your fault' nuisance callers, who I duly scolded. It's quite possible Meg has tried to contact me and not managed to get through. I resist the urge to reach into the pocket of my jeans to have a look.

'Anyhow,' Rita says. 'I'm embarrassed to admit I was already pretty well away by the time we ran into each other. That, together with my emotional state over losing my niece, was a bad combination. Essentially, I got the wrong end of the stick. I totally misread the situation and mistook you for someone else entirely.'

Hearing this comes as a surprise. 'Really? I got the impression from what you said at the time that you didn't know who I was.'

She squirms in her seat. 'I didn't, not for sure, but I had a suspicion, which turned out to be totally wrong. This is embarrassing too, although I'll try to explain. There was a patient of Iris's – Eddie – who'd been pursuing her for some time. You know, romantically. She was never interested and she did say that to him, but apparently not in a forceful enough way to get the message across. She was far too nice to tell him to get lost and leave her alone. So he kept on chasing her, sending flowers and various other gifts, hoping she'd eventually cave in and give him a go.

'He was verging on a stalker, if you ask me, always making up minor illnesses as an excuse to get an appointment with her. But again, Iris was too nice to see things that way. Even though I could tell it freaked her out from how she spoke about it, she'd then go on to argue he was lonely and harmless, albeit something of a hypochondriac.

'At the same time, she admitted being afraid to tell him about her plan to go to Africa. She knew he wouldn't react well to that, so I advised her not to mention it. What did it have to do with him, anyway? Of course, a part of me didn't want her to go, for my own selfish reasons. And yet I knew it would be a great experience for her and I was glad it would get her away from bloody Eddie. Who knew what he might have ended up doing otherwise? I thought he was downright creepy.'

'So you thought I was this weirdo?' I ask.

She shuffles her feet, briefly placing a hand on my arm as she replies: 'Yes, but please don't be offended by that. I've never met Eddie. All I know about him is that he's single, divorced, a few years older than Iris and, um, he's a little bit bald.'

'So it was mainly my age and my lack of hair, right? I am also divorced, as it goes, which makes me wonder how you could tell. Do I give off a certain sad man vibe?'

Rita's eyes stretch wide open with horror at my suggestion. 'No, no. Not at all. It was only the other two things, honestly. I had no idea that—'

'It's fine. I was pulling your leg.'

'Oh, thank goodness. I feel bad enough already, without digging myself any deeper. I really don't know why I jumped to the conclusion that you were Eddie. I suppose I'd been worried he might turn up at the funeral; then when I saw you kneeling by the table, with Claire in tears, I put two and two together and made five.

'As for my yelling at you rather than asking you nicely to leave, that was definitely down to the alcohol. Again, I can only apologise, especially now I know who you really are and what you went through with Iris. It was so lovely of you to come to the funeral. As soon as I realised my mistake, I was mortified. I did try to come after you there and then, but it was too late. You'd already gone.'

'Wow,' I say. 'At least that explains things. I did wonder exactly what it was I'd done to make you so angry. Now I understand what happened; the fact you made the effort to come and tell me this is much appreciated. You didn't have to track me down. You could have left it. So thank you. Consider your apology accepted.'

Rita breathes a sigh of relief. 'Oh good. That's a weight off my mind. It's been bothering me ever since it happened. Thanks so much for your understanding.'

I ask how she and the rest of the family are coping with Iris's death.

'So, so,' she replies, taking a sip of tea from her mug. 'As you'd expect, really. Until yesterday, everything was building up to the funeral, making all the arrangements and so on. There was so much extra stuff to think about – worrying about the press turning up against our wishes, for instance, which thankfully they didn't. Now that's over, I suppose we have to face up to the harsh reality of day-to-day life without her in it. We're only at the start of the grieving process. It's going to be tough for all of us, but especially Claire and Stan.'

Nodding, I add: 'I get the impression you were pretty close to Iris.'

Rita's eyes glisten with fresh tears. 'That's right. Living around the corner from my sister, as I always have, we see a lot of each other and our respective families. I have two sons: Guy, who you know, and Russ. Have you met him?'

I shake my head. 'No, I don't think so.'

'Okay. Well, I always quite fancied having a daughter too, although it never happened. I think that made me extra fond of Iris. She was like a surrogate daughter, if you like. I used to take her shopping when she was little – things like that – and we developed a strong bond. I think the fact I wasn't her mother actually made us closer at times. She'd confide in me about stuff she didn't tell Claire and Stan, such as what was going on with Eddie, her stalker.'

'Her parents didn't know about that?' I ask.

'Not the full details, no.'

'And did he turn up to the funeral?'

'Perhaps. Honestly, I'm not sure. If he was there, I didn't spot him and he didn't make himself known to me or any of the other family. I'm not sure exactly what he looks like, remember. Hence the fact I mistook you for him.'

I tap a forefinger on my right temple. 'Good point.'

'One of Iris's colleagues would surely know,' Rita adds. 'But I didn't fancy asking any of them at the time, especially not after making such an idiot of myself with you.'

'No one will think any the worse of you for how you reacted,' I say. 'Grief makes people emotional. Everyone understands that.'

As we continue talking, our mugs of tea growing cold, the conversation flows surprisingly easily considering our recent acquaintance. Moving on to discuss more general matters, Rita reveals she's fifty-seven years old and a semi-retired hairdresser.

'A fellow snipper,' I reply. 'If someone had told me

twenty-four hours ago that we'd be chatting like this, getting along and having things in common, I'd never have believed it. So when you say you're semi-retired, what does that mean exactly? Do you still work part-time, or—'

'I have a few regulars – mainly friends – who I cut and style from home, but that's about it. I used to run my own salon in Prestwich.' She winks as she adds: 'Unisex, so I know a little about cutting men's hair too. But a couple of years back, someone made me an offer I couldn't refuse. They bought me out and that was that.'

'This buyer of yours, they don't want a barbershop in the Northern Quarter too, do they?' I ask with a grin. 'This semi-retirement lark sounds right up my street.'

'Get away with you,' Rita replies. 'How old are you: mid-thirties? You're a young man. You've still got your best years ahead of you.'

'Thirty-nine, actually. But I'll take what you said. That sounds infinitely better than "nearly forty", which is how I tend to think of myself.'

'Hang on. You're one of those glass-half-empty types, aren't you?' she says, pulling a face and shaking her head with exaggerated disapproval.

I laugh. 'Busted. How can you tell that from one conversation?'

'I used to be married to a man like that: pessimistic Pete, I called him. We got divorced a long time ago. He used to drive me crazy with all his negative thoughts. But I loved him, more fool me, and then he ran off with someone half my age. You know how it goes.'

'More than you think,' I reply. And then, to my surprise,

I start spilling my heart out to this near stranger. Is it because I've just realised something about her reminds me of my late mother? It could be. Who knows? I definitely don't make a habit of doing this. And she really does remind me of Mum, although I can't yet put my finger on why.

CHAPTER 8

I take a phone call from Meg as I'm walking home later. One positive that's come from the scaffolding accident is that my cousin and I are back in regular contact with each other. I hadn't realised how much I missed the close relationship we once had, until she showed up at the hospital and then came to the funeral with me. We're not quite back to where we were yet, before our falling-out, but it's nice to see things improving. It definitely feels like she's on my team again.

'How are you doing?' she asks. 'Everything all right? I was getting a bit worried after you didn't reply to my texts.'

'Oh, my phone was on silent. It's been hectic at work today.'

'But you've seen them, right?'

'Yeah, I have now.'

'What does that mean? Has she been to see you already, this Rita?'

69

'Yes. And what it means is that I didn't see the messages until after she'd called by.'

My cousin groans down the line. 'Seriously, Luke? Well, don't blame me. That's your own fault for leaving your mobile on silent. Was it okay? I hope you're not mad that I told her where to find you. She seemed genuine about wanting to apologise, but after not hearing back from you, I started to question it.'

'It's fine, Meg. She's a nice woman, contrary to all evidence we saw when she bit my head off yesterday. The two of us got along well together, believe it or not. We chatted for a while over a brew and then we went for a quick drink in the pub. I left a few minutes ago; I'm walking home now.'

'What? Seriously? Wow, that's definitely not what I expected to hear. What did you talk about?'

I laugh into the phone. 'All sorts. She's a hairdresser, for a start, but it wasn't only that. We have loads in common.' I'm about to say how she reminds me of Mum, but I decide not to, because I know I won't be able to explain why and it'll end up sounding weird.

At that moment, it dawns on me where I am and the shock sets my heart racing. While chatting, I've not been paying attention to my surroundings; I've been walking on autopilot, lost in the conversation. And that's why, for the first time since the accident, I've ended up taking this route home as I often used to do.

'Can I call you back in a bit?' I say to Meg. 'I need to do something.'

'Sure.'

'Okay, bye.' I hang up and put my phone back in my pocket, take a deep breath and gingerly walk as close as I dare to the spot where, just over a fortnight ago, Iris and I were both trapped under the collapsed scaffolding.

There are flowers – dozens of bunches, old and new – marking the spot. I don't know why this surprises me. They'll be from Iris's family and friends, possibly colleagues and patients too. She was popular and well-loved, so it makes sense.

Seeing the flowers, especially the more withered ones that have been here a while, brings tears to my eyes alongside painful memories of what unfolded that evening.

I pull the beanie I'm wearing off my head and shove it into my coat pocket. It feels like the right thing to do in the circumstances: an old-fashioned mark of respect.

Weirdly, it takes me a moment to register the fact that the scaffolding is all back in place now, even though that's what the bouquets are mostly attached to. Well, I doubt it'll be the same planks and poles. Most of what came down on us is probably wrecked. But all of that's been cleared away. You wouldn't know it had even happened, apart from the flowers.

I have wondered a few times whether anyone is to blame for the scaffolding coming down like it did. Was it put up badly? Were the materials not up to scratch? Had someone tampered with it? Two police officers did come to my flat to speak to me about this a couple of days afterwards, but it was only a brief chat.

They told me the scaffolding had been put up by a respectable, well-known company, rather than a bunch of cowboys. They were suitably vague about what would happen next, saying the matter was still under investigation. But reading between the lines, the impression I got from them was that it would most likely be considered an act of God; a tragic result of the extremely high winds that day.

I will, almost certainly, be required to give evidence as a witness at the inquest into Iris's death. A post-mortem examination was carried out before the coroner released the body for the funeral. However, it sounds like the final hearing won't be taking place for a good while yet – possibly six months or more from now. There's a bit of a backlog, apparently.

As for the whole act of God thing, I'm not sure how I feel about this. It's not that I particularly want to have someone to blame for what happened. I could understand Iris's family feeling so minded but, at the end of the day, I survived the experience – as awful as it was – more or less unscathed. That's enough for me. I've no interest in the hassle of trying to sue someone. I can accept it was a freak accident, which is basically what the term *act of God* means, right?

But if you take the words literally, where does that leave me? Why would God, if you believe in his existence, deliberately take the life of someone as amazing as Iris and yet let me live?

Do I still believe in God, like I used to as a kid? Since Mum and Dad were both killed, I've told myself numerous times that I don't. So why does this term bother me so much? Why do I feel like I must make my own life mean something to redress the balance after Iris's death?

'Stop,' I say out loud, shaking my head in a bid to clear it and reset my thoughts.

I walk over to a fresh-looking bunch of flowers. They're white lilies, half of them open, half still shut, with lots of green foliage. I touch them with the tips of my fingers and imagine Iris as I saw her that evening: wide brown eyes and warm smile, encircled by the hood of her canary-yellow raincoat.

If I hadn't spotted her sheltering under the scaffolding, if I hadn't joined her there, would she still be alive now? The way I froze, causing her to push me out of the way, definitely delayed her own escape.

'I'm so sorry,' I say under my breath. 'I should have come back here sooner, Iris, but I couldn't bring myself to do it. Thank you for saving me, even though I didn't deserve it. I hope you've found peace; that you're in a better place.'

Despite my religious belief not being what it was, I haven't quite given up on the idea of an afterlife. Irrational perhaps, but it's comforting to think my parents – and now Iris – still exist somewhere, even as I continue to struggle with the idea of a higher being allowing their untimely deaths to happen in the first place.

Despite previously losing two of the people I was closest to in the world, I still can't get my head around the concept of someone dying and simply no longer existing. Forever gone. I can't grasp what a total lack of my own consciousness would be like, because for as long as I can remember it's always been there – even during sleep. I've never been anywhere without that voice in my head as a companion.

Okay, I've blacked out occasionally over the years, mainly from drinking too much on a heavy session and so on. It happened here too, of course, when falling debris hit my head. But short-term blackouts are by no means the same thing as eternal nothingness.

Having paid my respects to Iris, I put my hat back on and continue walking towards the flat. I'm starting to feel really rough. Rita's visit and the beer I had with her in the pub temporarily took my mind off whatever lurgy I'm brewing, but now there's no escaping it. My arms and legs are aching, the glands on my neck feel swollen, my head's foggy and I'm totally shattered: ready for bed or at least a hot bath.

As I step out to cross a quiet side road close to home, a male cyclist in a fluorescent orange top and matching helmet appears out of nowhere. Whooshing past, he gives me a real fright, missing me by what feels like millimetres. 'Bloody moron!' I shout after him, shaking clenched fists above my head, fury surging through my veins. 'You nearly hit me. Watch where the hell you're going, idiot.'

The cyclist continues on his way, his only response being to leisurely stretch out his right arm to give me the finger. This enrages me even further. If I wasn't so under the weather, I'd try racing after him on foot to give him what for. As it is, I have to settle for yelling a torrent of expletives in his direction.

After this, I spot a woman staring at me as she gets into a parked car further down the road. 'Yes?' I call out to her. 'What is it? Would you like a picture? Why don't you stop gawping and mind your own damn business?'

As my anger subsides, I start to regret my hot-headed behaviour, especially what I said to the onlooker. Was it actually the cyclist's fault or my own that we nearly collided? I'm still considering this as I enter my building and trudge up the stairs to my flat. It is possible I wasn't paying proper attention, considering how rough I'm feeling, but he could at least have rung a bell or something to warn me of his approach.

Anyway, Alfred's pleased to see me when I open the front door. He circles around my legs as I head through to the kitchen and I have to be careful not to trip over him.

'Chill, dude,' I say, reaching down to stroke his head and rub his cheek, before grabbing him a few treats and casting them into his bowl. 'Fill your boots.'

He's left me a present in the litter tray, which I clear up after popping some paracetamol. I'm not very hungry, but I manage to eat a bowl of tomato soup before running a bath, piping hot with lots of bubbles, which I slip into and promptly fall asleep.

The water is lukewarm at best when I wake up and most of the bubbles are long gone. Alfred is curled up in a ball on the cream bathmat.

I feel horrendous. Everything hurts, from head to toe, and I'm shivering so much my teeth are chattering. Last time I felt this way, I had the flu and it knocked me out for several days. I bet it's that again or some other horrible virus. Bloody brilliant. That's just what I need right now.

Part of me is tempted to top up the bath with some

fresh hot water, mainly so I don't have to go through the effort of moving elsewhere. But instead, I lean forward and pull the plug, lugging myself up and out, dashing for the nearest towel and wishing I'd placed it on the radiator.

No idea of the time – and not particularly interested – I dry myself en route to the bedroom, throw on a T-shirt plus a fresh pair of boxer shorts, and dive under my duvet. Still shivering, I scrunch myself into a ball and wait for some warmth to return to my aching limbs, before falling back into a deep sleep.

The next thing I know, I'm woken by a voice repeating my name.

'What? I'm trying to sleep,' I say, refusing to open my eyes. 'Leave me alone, okay? I'm not well.'

'Luke, I need to talk to you,' the voice replies. It sounds familiar, but I can't put my finger on where I know it from.

'Not now,' I say. 'It's the middle of the night.'

But the voice won't take no for an answer. She won't stop speaking, repeating my name. So eventually, I give in. I sit up in bed and pull the covers right up under my chin. Finally, I slide open my gritty, gungy eyes and peer out into the darkness, looking for the source of my irritation.

'Ah, at last,' she says, seated in the armchair I use as a dumping ground for clothes.

'Oh, it's you.'

'Expecting someone else?'

'Not really. Not at this time of night. Why are you wearing your coat?'

'It's cold.'

'True. But do you really need the hood up? I can hardly see your face.'

'Fine.' Iris reaches up with both hands and slides the rain-flecked yellow material back from around her head, freeing the bouncy brown curls of her hair. Her skin looks paler than I remember, although this could be down to the lack of lighting in the room. The only reason I can see her at all is because I've left the lamp on in the hall and my bedroom door is ajar.

Part of me knows there's something not quite right about Iris's presence here – her being dead and all – but it's only a speck of a realisation that quickly gets swept away.

'Is that better?' she asks.

'Yes, much. What are you doing here?'

'Charming.'

'Sorry, I don't mean it that way, but I get the feeling you're here for a reason.'

She raises an eyebrow. 'You might be right about that.'

CHAPTER 9

'You need to change your outlook on life,' Iris tells me, matter-of-factly, like doing so is the easiest thing in the world.

'What do you mean?' I ask, even though I have a good idea what she's talking about.

She crosses her legs and squints across the room at me. 'You're so negative. How come?'

'I dunno. I suppose, um, it's a defence mechanism. If I assume the worst, I'll never be disappointed.'

'How depressing. Surely you haven't always been that way, have you?'

'I guess not. Life grinds you down, doesn't it?'

'Only if you let it. From my perspective, it's all a matter of how you look at things. There's nearly always a silver lining hidden away in every bit of bad news. You just have to find it.'

I feel myself getting riled by this. 'That's easy to say when nothing really bad has happened to you. Try losing both of your parents in one go and then being left by your wife in the space of a year. Where's the silver lining there? Please point it out to me, because I'd love to know.'

Iris chews on her lip before replying. 'I hear what you're saying. I can only imagine how . . . awful that must have been for you, Luke. But I never claimed it was easy. Sometimes it can take a long while to find a positive perspective. It might even be something you have to create yourself, building it piece by piece from the ground up. But one thing's for sure: you'll never find it with a glass-half-empty outlook.'

'Hmm,' I reply, unconvinced. 'Where's your silver lining now, then? Sorry to be blunt, but you were killed, despite all of your positivity, popularity and good intentions. How exactly did being a glass-half-full person help you? You died and I survived. Life sucks. I was right all along, no?'

'That depends how you look at it. From your perspective, surviving against the odds, escaping with barely a scratch, isn't it the case that I was right and you were wrong? You could have been killed, but you weren't. Surely that's something to celebrate. If staring death in the face and living to see another day isn't a reason to be positive, then I'd love to know what is.'

I rub a clammy hand over my face, trying to focus my mind. 'Okay, so you've turned my argument back on me, but you've also dodged the central question: where's your silver lining?'

She smiles, her face calm and totally unfazed. 'Maybe I'm looking at it. Yes, I died too young. I never got to achieve a lot of the things I wanted to. But in my short life there's plenty that I did manage to do: I became a doctor; I helped people; I was loved by family and friends; I'll be remembered. I have no regrets.'

'What about saving me?' I ask. 'If you hadn't hung around while I froze, if you hadn't pushed me out of the way, you might have lived.'

'Why do you think I became a doctor?' Iris smiles at me in a way that instantly melts my heart. 'Saving people is my job, my calling. And guess what? I'm not quite done with you yet.

'That scaffolding wasn't the only thing you needed saving from, was it? You were dying inside when I met you. I could see it in your eyes. But you don't need to be like that any more. You have a reason to live now: to make my death worthwhile, to be my silver lining.

'Life's full of possibilities, Luke. You need to look at it the right way, that's all. Give it a try and you'll see what I mean. Start small, baby steps, and build from there. Look at how things worked out with my aunty earlier. You'd never have predicted that after what happened at the funeral, would you? So there you go.'

'But, how—'

'No more Mr Negative, right? It won't happen overnight, but get those rose-tinted sunglasses on.'

As she says this, Iris raises her right hand to eye level and clicks her fingers with a flourish, upon which the opening refrain of the ELO song 'Mr Blue Sky' starts playing.

'What the—'

'Shh!' Iris says, wedging her forefinger in front of her

lips and swaying to the music from where she's seated. 'Don't fight it. Trust me.'

Next thing, she's on her feet, arms raised above her head and shimmying across the room in time to the beat, a huge smile wrapped around her pretty face.

I can't grasp what on earth's happening. And things get even more surreal when Alfred jumps up onto the end of the bed and also starts boogieing along to the music, like something from a freaky pet food advert.

'Meow,' I hear right in my ear, deafeningly loud. 'Meow.'

My eyes open and it's broad daylight.

Iris is gone and Alfred's standing on top of my duvet-covered chest. His huge eyes burrow into mine as the song from what I now realise must have been a feverish dream continues to play – albeit with a more tinny sound – from the clock radio next to my bed. I must have forgotten to turn the alarm off in my rush to get under the covers yesterday. Soon the track fades out and an enthusiastic radio DJ announces the fact it's Sunday morning.

Alfred meows again, begging for breakfast, as usual.

'Morning, mate,' I rasp, my throat bone dry and my lips gummed up. 'Good to see you back to normal.' I wasn't sure about the groovy dancing version of Alfred I'd encountered in my trippy dream.

'What the hell was that all about?' I ask him, only for him to rub his face against my bare arm to remind me of his hunger. 'I know, I know. You're ravenous, right?'

Getting out of bed isn't as bad as I fear. I'm still not feeling great, but I'm better than yesterday, which hopefully rules out the flu and means the worst is over.

Luckily, I never open the barbershop on a Sunday. Plenty do nowadays, since lots of the shops are trading, but as a one-man band, it's not feasible to be open seven days a week. Not without running myself into the ground. No, Sunday is my one weekly day of leisure. Plus I don't usually open up until one o'clock on Mondays, giving me an extra half-day off and a second potential lie-in. As long as I remember to switch off my alarm, that is – unlike today.

Once I've fed Alfred, I make a pot of filter coffee and then give my cousin a call.

'Oh, hello,' Meg says on picking up. 'About time you called me back.'

'Sorry,' I reply. 'I did mean to get back to you last night, but I felt like crap and ended up crashing out as soon as I got home.'

'How come?' she asks, her voice laden with a sudden tone of concern. 'What's the matter? Are you okay?'

'Yeah. Well, I'm still not a hundred per cent, to be honest, but I am better than I felt last night. I really thought I was coming down with the flu then – aching limbs, feverish and all that. But now it's eased off a bit, I reckon it must be a virus or something. And before you say it, no, it's not man flu.'

Meg laughs down the line. 'Are you sure?'

'Positive.'

An hour later, she turns up at the flat unannounced, armed with painkillers, energy drinks and a family-size bar of chocolate.

'What are you doing here?' I say.

'Nice to see you too.'

'I don't mean it like that. It's good of you; I appreciate it. I wouldn't come too close, though, if I were you.'

'Fair enough.' She claims to have been passing by, although I'm fairly sure that's not true.

Later, when we're both sitting in the lounge enjoying a cup of tea, I decide to address the elephant in the room: the big argument that impaired our relationship for several months, until my accident brought us back together. We've both skirted around the issue since we've been back in frequent contact with each other, but now feels like the right time to clear the air.

'Are things good between us again, Meg?' I ask.

'Oh,' she replies, wincing. 'You want to talk about *that* now?'

'Don't you think we should? The row we had drove a wedge between us for the best part of six months. Let's be honest, we probably wouldn't be where we are now if I hadn't ended up in hospital. For what it's worth, I'm really sorry for what I said and did that day—'

'We both said things,' she says. 'I'm sorry too.'

'Yeah, but I started it, turning on you when you were just trying to be nice. And I totally overreacted, behaving like a child. Anyway, I missed having you close and I'm really glad we're getting back on track.'

'I suppose I'm also glad about that,' she adds with a wink, 'more or less.'

With hindsight, the quarrel was stupid and unnecessary. I was having dinner at Meg's place at the time; I guess we were both tired and grumpy. It started with her trying to convince me to put myself out there on the dating scene; it concluded with both of us shouting and screaming. My mind flashes back to the tail end of our dispute.

'You need to butt out, Meg, for God's sake. I'm sick of this. I'm in no rush to find love. I'm happy as I am. Why are you so desperate to get me paired up with someone? Are you tired of spending time with me? Are you looking to palm me off on someone else?'

'Maybe I am, Luke. You're not exactly much fun to be around. You're always so negative and miserable. I feel sorry for you. I was hoping a bit of love in your life might cheer you up.'

'Yeah, because that worked out so well for me last time, didn't it? Listen, I didn't realise I was such a burden to you, but don't worry, that ends today. I'm sick of your constant interfering and I definitely don't need your pity. I'm done with this, Meg, and I'm done with you.'

'Oh, really? Well I'm done with you too, Luke, and your constant wallowing in self-pity and pessimism. You don't deserve a person like me in your life. Sometimes I can see exactly why you got dumped like you did.'

'Really? Well you can go to hell! And this food is bloody disgusting.'

Happy memories. Particularly the next bit, where I flipped my full dinner plate, emptying the contents on the table, and stormed out of there. That still makes me cringe with embarrassment.

Still, I'm glad I brought the matter up. Before long, Meg

and I are hugging it out and I feel like we've turned a corner. Neither of us can believe we were too stubborn to apologise sooner, although we both admit to having wanted to do so.

'Never mind,' Meg says. 'Better late than never.'

I decide to tell her about the weird dream I had involving Iris.

'Hmm,' she says after I've recounted most of it. 'That does sound a bit odd. So initially you weren't aware it was a dream? Didn't you find it strange that a dead person was in your bedroom, chatting to you?'

I laugh. 'You'd think so, wouldn't you? I did have an inkling of something out of the ordinary, but I guess I just accepted it. You know what it's like when you're dreaming: all kinds of strange things can happen without it seeming that way. Plus I was quite feverish. The whole thing was rather trippy, and I haven't even got to the strangest part yet.'

I go on to tell her about the song starting to play, with Iris and Alfred dancing along; it makes her giggle.

'The same tune was playing on the clock radio when I woke up,' I explain. 'But don't you think that's a bizarre coincidence?'

Meg shrugs. 'It obviously worked its way into your dream via your subconscious, because it was playing in real life.'

'Oh, I realise that, but I'm talking about what you called me the other day.'

'Sorry, I'm not with you.'

'When you visited me in hospital after the accident, you

85

mentioned me being a pessimist. You told me I wasn't exactly Mr Blue Sky. It stuck in my mind.'

'Right,' she says, a puzzled look on her face. 'If you say so.'

'You don't remember? Really?'

'Um, I do recall saying something about you being a glass-half-empty person, if that's what you're talking about.'

'Yes, exactly, which was what Iris was talking to me about as well. She was urging me to change my ways to be more like her: to think and do more positive things, to make my life and her sacrifice mean something.'

Meg hesitates, her right hand kneading the cushion of the armchair where she's sitting opposite me. 'You, er . . . you know that wasn't really her, though, right? It was a dream, Luke: your mind's way of processing its own thoughts.'

'Of course. Why would you even say that, Meg? You know me. I'm not exactly the kind of guy to believe in ghosts or any of that nonsense, am I?'

Am I?

I hope the slight uncertainty doesn't show on my face.

'You've been through a lot recently,' she says in a quiet voice. 'That's all. I'm looking out for you. Checking you're doing all right, especially after that visit by Rita yesterday. I feel bad about that—'

'Why? She was fine, I told you. We got along well.'

Again, I'm tempted to mention that Rita reminded me of Mum, but I don't. Meg knows only too well how hard I was hit by the death of her and my father. Based on what she's said so far, I fear she might read something into this regarding my mental state, which she obviously thinks is fragile right now.

Instead, I try to reassure her about my interpretation of the dream. 'I'm fully aware of the fact Iris didn't really appear in my bedroom, Meg. There's really no need for you to worry about that. Yes, I have been through a tough experience, but none of my marbles have been lost along the way, okay?'

'Fine. Sorry, I didn't mean to offend you or anything, but—'

'You haven't. All I'm trying to say here, if you could give me the benefit of the doubt for a minute, is that what I dreamed ties in with what you told me.'

She knits her brow. 'How do you mean exactly?'

'You told me I'm too negative, that I always see things in a glass-half-empty way, yes?'

'Sure.'

'So what if I tried to change that, like the person who wasn't really Iris suggested in my dream? You know, the fact it wasn't actually her doesn't mean what she told me was nonsense. As you said yourself, a dream is the mind's way of processing its own thoughts. I've been feeling like something needs to change ever since Iris was killed, like—'

'You don't need to justify the fact she died and you didn't,' Meg cuts in. 'You know that, don't you? Survivor's guilt is a common response to the kind of trauma you've been through, Luke. I've looked it up on the Internet. It's considered a symptom of post-traumatic stress disorder.

87

Maybe you ought to seek professional help to get through this. I know—'

'Really, Meg? You're telling me to see a shrink?' I can't believe what I'm hearing. 'Honestly, you watch too much American TV. Who do you think I am: Tony Soprano?'

'If you like. He was reluctant to get help initially.'

'I don't need to see a therapist. Case closed. I'm fine. I barely even knew Iris.'

'That's irrelevant.'

'I managed without seeing anyone after Mum and Dad died, didn't I? And when my marriage collapsed.'

'Did you, though? It's been quite a journey – lots of ups and downs. Had you sought professional help, you might have dealt with all of that much better, much sooner. There's no shame in it, you know? It doesn't make you any less of a man.'

I let out a long, frustrated sigh, but I remind myself that I definitely don't want to fall out with my cousin again after just making up with her. 'Listen, all I want to know is what you think about me trying to be more positive. Is it a good idea or not?'

Meg rolls her eyes. 'Of course it is, but I'll believe it when I see it, Luke. How exactly do you plan to change like that? You're going to click your fingers, are you, and it'll magically happen? Real life doesn't work that way. You are who you are.'

'Now who's the glass-half-empty person?'

'Touché,' Meg replies with a weary grin.

CHAPTER 10

By Monday morning I'm feeling loads better. I didn't have any further weird dreams overnight – not that I remember, anyway – despite spending several more hours than usual asleep, having gone to bed at eight o'clock yesterday evening. I clearly needed the extra shuteye to recover from whatever illness it was that had made me feel so rough over the weekend.

I decide to walk to the supermarket for some bits and bobs and, as I'm leaving, yet again I bump into Doreen in the hallway.

'Morning, Liam,' she says, getting my name wrong as usual.

'Morning,' I reply without stopping.

'Looks nice out there today,' she says from behind me. 'Good to see the sun making an appearance, although it'll be cold too, no doubt.'

'Yep.' As I answer, I look back at her, but then I continue

forward towards the stairs, keen to get out of the building's front door as soon as possible.

Doreen doesn't say anything else immediately, which I guess means I'm off the hook. But when I reach the half-landing, where the stairway turns in the opposite direction, I see she's leaning against the metal bannister at the top, peering down at me.

'Off to work now, are you?' she asks.

Something makes me stop before I continue down the next section of stairs, which would take me out of her view. 'No, not yet. I don't open until lunchtime on Mondays. I'm popping to the supermarket.'

'Oh, I see,' Doreen replies, nodding and smiling like I've said something really interesting.

Then a voice inside my head tells me this is a great opportunity to make a start on turning over a new leaf. And before I know it, words are leaving my mouth that I've never even considered saying to any of my neighbours before. 'Is there, um, anything I could pick up for you while I'm at it?'

Doreen's eyes widen as she answers. 'Oh, right. Um, that's very kind of you to offer, love. I, er . . . let's see.'

'I'm walking,' I add. 'I don't have a car, so it'll have to be something I can carry. No crates of beer.'

This makes her laugh. 'Beer indeed. You are silly. I don't think I've had any of that stuff in the fridge since my Bob passed away. And he wasn't much of drinker. He used to get really tipsy after a couple. He was only small, you see: a good bit shorter than me. He had a big heart, though.'

I never met Doreen's husband. She's been a widow for as long as I've known her, although she seems to mention Bob nearly every time she collars me. No matter how hard I try not to get drawn into a conversation, giving monosyllabic answers to her questions and always claiming to be in a rush, she rabbits on at me regardless. Inevitably, some of what she's told me has sunk in, particularly as she often repeats herself. I know she moved here not long after Bob died, for instance, selling their old family home in Didsbury for a tidy sum. She's told me – and presumably most of our neighbours – that latter nugget of information, usually in hushed tones, more times than I care to remember.

Anyway, I'm cutting her some slack today and, in the name of change and positivity, I continue with my attempt at being jocular.

'You must enjoy a tipple once in a while, right?' I ask, winking. 'What's your poison? I'm sure I could manage to carry a bottle of something, if that's what you need.'

'Ooh, what's come over you, Liam? You're so chirpy today. And it almost sounds like you're trying to get me drunk. I do enjoy a sherry once in a while, but I don't need any, thank you.'

'Ah, I'm only pulling your leg,' I say, surprising myself with my warm tone. 'Seriously, though, is there anything you need?'

'I am a bit low on teabags, come to think of it,' she says.

'No problem. What brand do you like?'

'Yorkshire, please, if it's not too much trouble. Let me go and grab some money.'

'Good choice,' I say with a smile. 'And no rush. You can sort me out later.'

As I make my way along the street to the shop, I'm surprised to realise I'm still smiling. The thought of how long I might get held up talking to Doreen when I give her the tea makes me less happy, but I'll cross that bridge when I come to it.

'Can you spare any change?' a bearded homeless guy reading a paperback asks me as I enter the store.

'Sorry, I don't have any,' I reply out of habit, although on this occasion it's the truth.

'No problem,' he replies with a smile before looking back down at his book. 'Have a good day, pal.'

Later, as I'm leaving with two bags of shopping, I see he's still there and – remembering his chipper, no pressure attitude – I pass him a couple of pound coins I received at the till.

'Ah, thanks so much,' he says with a grin. 'I really appreciate that. You're a star. Have a brilliant day.'

'You're welcome,' I reply. 'You too.'

Giving a donation like this is most unusual for me. Homeless folk are such a regular sight in central Manchester now, it's hard sometimes not to think of them as a nuisance rather than actual human beings in need of help. I also fear they'll only spend the money on booze or drugs. That might seem unfair, but I go off what I witness, walking through the heart of the city. It's scarily common these days to see them crashed out or off their heads in public – escaping the miserable reality of their lives, I suppose.

Mind you, plenty of non-homeless people, from all social

classes, spend loads of money getting plastered in Manchester's countless pubs and clubs on a daily basis. There is an argument that the homeless have every right to do the same, if that's what they want. When passers-by give them money, it's certainly their own choice what to do with it.

Anyhow, it's not fair to tar all of the homeless with the same brush. The drunks and druggies probably only account for a small minority. This bloke I'm chatting to now is a good example. He clearly has his head screwed on the right way.

It's probably condescending of me, but I'm impressed by the fact he's reading a book. That's a much less common sight among the homeless here; it gives me the impression he has his wits about him. Plus I recognise the paperback he's reading as a book I've enjoyed myself. It's one of the early Rebus novels by Ian Rankin.

'Enjoying it?' I ask him, nodding in the direction of his reading material.

'Definitely,' he replies, tucking his long, shaggy hair behind one ear. 'Rankin's great – a cut above most crime fiction. I first read this years ago, but it's amazing how much you forget. I'm enjoying it even more this time around.'

'Yeah, I rate him too,' I reply. 'He really brings Edinburgh to life, doesn't he? My mum got me into him. She was a huge fan. Anyway, I've got to run. All the best.'

He nods. 'No problem. Thanks again.'

I'm about to leave, but a gut feeling keeps me there a little longer. 'I'm Luke, by the way,' I say. 'What's your name?'

He beams the purest smile at me. 'It's Tommy, thanks for asking. Most don't. Nice to meet you, Luke.'

'You too.'

I walk away feeling uplifted, like I've done something good, until I remember the last homeless person I spoke to: the one I saw lying in a doorway soon before the scaffolding collapse. The one I told to sling their hook without a thought for their wellbeing.

Yeah, what a nice guy I am.

I'll need to do a lot more than give a bloke a couple of quid and ask his name before I can start feeling proud of myself.

I have a few 'bread and butter' regulars at the barbershop, although not as many as I probably ought to. Is that because I don't make a fuss of them or know all about their lives by asking questions like we're friends? Maybe. But that's not my style.

As a rule, the kind of regular I tend to attract is a bloke who wants a decent cheap haircut and no small talk. I don't have any problem whatsoever with long silences, trust me. Hands down my favourite kind of cut is the type when the guy in the chair says what he wants at the start and doesn't speak again until the end. I'm happiest left to get on with my job, lost in my thoughts as a good tune plays on the radio.

There's an exception to every rule, though, isn't there? In this case, Connor is that exception. I've no idea why he's a regular at my barbershop, but he is nonetheless.

I find him waiting outside when I arrive to open up just before one o'clock.

'Luke,' he says. 'Am I glad to see you.'

'Connor, what's the problem? Haircut emergency? It doesn't look that bad to me.'

'I came for a cut on Friday and you weren't open. What happened?'

I unlock and raise the shutters. 'I had a funeral to attend.'

That explanation would be enough for most people. Not Connor.

'Did it last all day?' he asks, standing right behind me as I unlock the door and turn the lights on.

A frown is the only answer I offer to this question.

'You were closed all day. I returned several times. Why didn't you leave a note to inform customers like myself what was going on? I found the situation most frustrating.'

'I had other things on my mind, Connor. Do you know about the accident I was in recently?'

'The scaffolding?' he replies, like there's more than one accident to choose from.

'Yes. It was the funeral for the woman who died as a result of that.'

Connor, who's now helped himself to a seat in my preferred barber chair, knits his brow. He opens his mouth like he's about to say something, then shuts it again. After a long few seconds of uncharacteristic silence, he says, almost like it pains him to do so: 'I'm sorry for your loss.'

It's an odd comment, based on the fact I barely knew Iris, but it's well meant and probably as close to compassionate as anything I've ever heard Connor say.

'Please could you cut my hair now?' he asks.

'Give me a minute to get my things together.'

He taps his fingers annoyingly on the arms of the chair as he waits. 'Can you stop that?' I snap before asking if he wants 'the usual' haircut.

This isn't a question I ask many customers, but Connor has been coming in every few weeks for years now.

'Mother said it was a little too short on top last time,' he replies.

'Right.'

We wouldn't want to upset Mother now, would we?

Connor still lives with his mum in his childhood home in Sale, despite being in his early forties, fiercely intelligent, and holding down what must be a well-paid job as some kind of corporate IT boffin in the city centre. Goodness knows what he spends his money on, other than cheap regular haircuts here. I doubt it's clothes, as I only ever see him in one outfit: a plain sky-blue shirt and smart navy trousers. I'm sure he must have several versions of each, as he never smells bad, which he surely would if he was wearing the same thing every day.

When you're a barber, you can't avoid knowing what your customers smell like. Getting up close and personal is part of the job. And sometimes – trust me – it can be unpleasant. You literally have to hold your breath or breathe through your mouth. The very overweight guys can smell ripe, particularly in summer or when they've been wearing a thick coat in winter, due to how much they sweat.

Connor's lanky and doesn't have that problem. He seems

to take good care of himself: always appearing clean-shaven with a recently pressed shirt. Living with his mum might well have a lot to do with that. However, he's very precise and ordered about everything he does – almost robotic at times – so it's possible he'd be exactly the same even if he had a place of his own.

'Mother hasn't been well recently,' he tells me.

'Oh?' I reply. 'Nothing serious, I hope.'

After cutting Connor's thick, wiry, dark brown hair for so long, I almost feel like I know this woman, despite the fact I've never met her or even seen a photo of what she looks like. I don't think Connor's ever told me her name; if he has, I don't remember it. He talks about her a lot and I often switch off. If he's remotely embarrassed about still living with her at his age, he doesn't show it.

'She has the flu,' he says, which sends a shiver down my spine. I hope he's not carrying it, because I definitely don't want to catch the real thing. My flu-like symptoms over the weekend were quite enough of a taster for me, thank you very much. I make a mental note to wash my hands thoroughly after he's gone and to try to keep them away from my face in the meantime.

'Didn't she get a flu jab?' I ask as I use the bare clippers to trim the hair around his right ear. I've paid for the injection myself in past years, when there's been a lot of flu around, because I know how easy it is to pick up illnesses in my line of work. I'm starting to think I ought to have done so again.

'She doesn't like needles,' he explains. 'The GP offers her a jab every year, because of her age. I always advise her to get it, but there's no telling her. Now she'll be bedridden for who knows how long. Luckily, one of the neighbours is able to look in on her while I'm out at work. Otherwise, I don't know what we'd do.'

'Aren't you worried you'll catch it next?'

Connor throws me an odd look via the mirror, like I've said something ridiculous. 'I don't get ill,' he says. 'I don't have time for that.'

Later, as I'm showing him the back of his hair with the hand mirror, I find myself telling Connor about the homeless guy I spoke to earlier and how I was surprised to see him reading a novel.

'Hmm,' he says. 'That is unusual. It's definitely a healthier form of escapism than you normally see. I honestly don't know how the homeless manage at this time of year. Mother says it's a life choice and we shouldn't encourage them by giving money, but I disagree.

'Who would deliberately choose to live that way? I can't imagine not sleeping in a proper bed at night, not having clean clothes or being able to wash daily. When do you think this man you spoke to last had a haircut? I wouldn't feel human without any of that.'

'Good point,' I reply. 'I know what you mean.'

I'm about to undo Connor's gown, having got the nod that the back is fine, when he interjects. 'Actually, I'm not sure about the length on top, Luke. Could you take a bit more off?'

'I thought you didn't want it too short?'

'I don't, but if it's too long, it'll need cutting again in no time.'

Heaven forbid. I bite my tongue and take the scissors to his locks for another few minutes.

'Right, happy now?'

Connor turns his head from side to side in the mirror. 'Yes, that'll do. Thank you.'

I don't need to tell him how much he owes me after I've removed the gown and blasted him with the hairdryer to dislodge any remaining hairs. He's fully aware of the price, which hasn't changed for some time now and is also displayed on a list on the wall. I know not to expect a tip, because there's never been one yet, despite the countless times he's been in this chair. Just like he never looks especially pleased with the cut I've given him, which he usually refers to as 'fine' at best. I must be doing something right, mind, for him to keep coming back.

As usual, Connor hands me the exact change once he's retrieved his coat from the hanger. But before saying goodbye, he clears his throat. 'Could I make a request?'

'If you must.' I wonder what on earth is coming next.

'Should you need to close again in future, even if it's only for a few hours rather than a whole day, which would be preferable, I must say—'

'Yes?' I interject in a bid to get him to the finish line.

'Then please could you leave some kind of message on display to explain what's happening?'

'I'll think about it, Connor, okay? But relax: I don't have any other closures planned.'

I wonder if he knows I was also closed for a couple of days after the accident, while I was still recovering from the shock. I'm guessing not, since he's never mentioned it.

After he's gone, I have a few minutes to myself without any other customers. This isn't unusual for a Monday, which is why I only open for half a day.

I find myself mulling over something Connor said while I was cutting his hair. It stuck in my mind at the time and, now I've nothing else to distract me, I can't stop thinking about it.

He queried when the homeless man I spoke to before had last had a haircut. Not for a good while, from what I could tell. It was long and shaggy; possibly out of choice, but probably out of necessity. Even if he likes it that way, all hair needs cutting from time to time to stay in good condition. Otherwise, split ends become a problem.

If I was living on the streets, getting a haircut wouldn't be a priority for me either. I doubt I'd be spending any money I'd managed to gather on visiting a barber. And, if I'm brutally honest, I doubt many barbers would be happy to serve an obviously homeless person. They'd be afraid of them not being able to pay at the end, for one thing.

However, as Connor also pointed out, it's stuff like sleeping in a bed, having clean clothes and getting a haircut that makes you feel human.

There's a good reason why people visit a barber or hairdresser before a special occasion. Whatever it is – party, wedding, hot date – turning up with freshly cut hair is a confidence boost. It helps you feel like the best version of yourself.

So why can't I stop thinking about this?

Well, it's obvious, isn't it? If I really want to change

myself in honour of Iris – to try to become someone deserving of being saved by her – I need to make a real difference somehow. Trying to be a nicer person is a start, but it's not enough.

Here I have a skill I could use to do exactly that. It would barely cost me anything other than my time – and I could make some really needy people feel better about themselves in the process.

Who knows? Having a fresh haircut could even help a homeless person move forward in life, to get out of a rut. I'm probably overstating it, but feeling good about yourself can go a long way. At the very least, it could help someone walk into a public place with their head held high, not feeling like they stick out like a sore thumb quite so much.

I might need to do this.

I'll definitely have to give it some more thought, to work out the details and so on. I realise it's born of the desire to make up for past wrongs, like how badly I treated that forlorn figure crashed out on the ground near the barbershop. But before I jump in head first, giddy with good intentions, I need to be sure it's not a foolish idea.

That said, the prospect of offering free haircuts to the homeless has me feeling strangely excited.

Are those butterflies I feel in my stomach?

Wow. It's been a while.

CHAPTER 11

One of the problems with being a glass-half-empty type is how quickly negative thoughts can seep in and ruin ideas that you started off feeling excited about.

I know I'm supposed to be trying to change, but it's not easy. It was never going to be. I knew that from the start – and yet, of course, I was trying to be positive.

It's 2.14 a.m. on Tuesday. I'm lying wide awake in bed, struggling to clear my mind and get some sleep ahead of the full day back in the barbershop that awaits me in a few hours.

I could really do with a good night's sleep to ensure I'm fully over whatever it was that made me feel so rubbish over the weekend. Unfortunately, knowing that doesn't make it happen. If anything, it probably makes it less likely, because of the anxiety and ongoing thought process it generates.

How come I felt so good about the haircuts for the homeless idea earlier – and now it's all the potential downsides that are occupying my mind? Honestly, they're like tiny spiders working together to knit a giant gloomy web to snare my positive thoughts.

I'm worrying about all the little details and practicalities. For instance, would having homeless people in the barbershop put off regular customers? I'd be sure to clean and disinfect everything extra thoroughly, of course. Better safe than sorry. But I know how people think.

I'm sure some folk might fear catching head lice, although in reality a homeless person is no more likely to have them than anyone else. Those critters are happy in any hair – clean or dirty – and they're spread through hair-to-hair contact, not a person's environment. Kids are by far the worst for having head lice, in my experience, because of how they regularly and closely interact with large numbers of each other.

Then there's the fear that either no homeless folk would turn up or, conversely, I'd be inundated with too many to handle. And what if people who weren't actually homeless appeared, claiming they were; how would I know not to get taken advantage of in this way?

I have considered the possibility of going to them, rather than them coming to me, and doing the cuts in the street. However, this is Manchester – not California. It's usually chilly and wet, especially at this time of year, and I really wouldn't fancy working outside. My hands would be too cold to use the scissors properly and I'd struggle to do a good job with gloves on. Plus, without electricity, I'd be restricted to using battery-powered clippers, while I've always favoured the more bulletproof mains-powered ones.

Having these people inside the shop, sitting on the barber chair after first waiting their turn in the warmth, would all be part of what I was offering. The whole experience would hopefully be humanising, reminding them of the normality of their old life prior to living rough. I'm not convinced cutting their hair in situ, wherever they usually spend their time, would have the same impact.

I probably need to discuss what I'm considering with someone else, which I haven't done so far. I should run it by Meg in the light of day, tell her my concerns too, and see what she thinks.

That's a resolution of sorts, right? So now it's time to stop thinking about it; to clear my mind and get some much-needed sleep.

If only it was that easy.

If only my mind would stop.

Twice already I've attempted the technique of relaxing my body bit by bit and trying to clear my head of all thoughts, but tonight even that doesn't work.

Instead, I focus on breathing slowly and steadily – relaxing – while reluctantly accepting that my brain will continue doing its own thing, regardless. If I worry too much about not getting enough sleep, the very act of doing so will only work against this goal. So I try to chill out, to roll with it, as my thoughts turn to my cousin.

I'm so fortunate to have Meg in my life. I know that better than ever now. As an only child with few close friends, I could have been left feeling utterly alone after first Mum and Dad died and then my marriage fell apart. But instead, I had Meg. We were fairly close anyway, due to proximity and having got along well from a young age. But she was there for me like no one else when I was at my lowest ebb. Even in the midst of our stupid falling-out, which I'll never allow to happen again, I didn't forget that.

During times of personal crises, which I'm no stranger to, you need some kind of support network to get you through.

My first true setback in life, which felt like a fully fledged disaster at the time, came when I was eighteen years old. I was halfway through my first term at Leeds University, studying English literature, when I realised that I'd made a terrible decision and student life wasn't for me.

This was an incredibly hard thing to admit to myself, never mind my parents. But after weeks of feeling uncomfortable, out of my depth and plain unhappy, the roof finally caved in following a long, boozy night out with my then flatmates. I ended up alone in A&E, having picked a fight with a bloke twice my size after being split up from everyone else.

I'll never forget calling home from a payphone in the early hours, sobbing my heart out and pleading with Mum and Dad to come and get me, which of course they did. I slept most of the way home in the car and they didn't once ask me to explain myself. Naturally, we did have a chat the next day, upon which I broke down and admitted how deeply unhappy I was in Leeds.

'Is it the course, your flatmates or something else?' I remember Dad asking me as the three of us gathered over a brew around the kitchen table. 'Because nothing's written in stone. There are always changes that can be made.'

'It's not one thing in particular,' I replied. 'It's pretty much everything. I know you wanted this for me, but . . . maybe I'm not cut out for university.'

'Oh, love, don't you worry about what we want,' Mum said. 'Nothing's more important to either of us than you being happy. You're a bright lad. You know that as well as we do. If this isn't the right path for you, we'll find one that is – together. And I have no worries whatsoever that you'll do brilliantly, regardless. I believe in you, son. We both do. Mark my words, it'll all work out for the best, one way or another.'

They didn't let me drop out straight away, which I found frustrating. They gently persuaded me to return to uni for a bit to think over the situation. With hindsight, though, it was only right that I took a few weeks to weigh up my options rather than making a snap decision. Otherwise, I'd have probably ended up looking back after a while and wondering if I'd made a mistake.

Instead, when I did eventually drop out about a month later, I knew it was definitely the right move. And I did so with my head held high, saying a proper goodbye to my flatmates and so on, rather than skulking off with my tail between my legs.

'University just wasn't for me,' I told anyone who asked. And a lot did to start with, but soon the memory faded and the question rarely came up any more.

I'd like to say I became a barber straight afterwards, knowing that had been my destiny all along. It would be neater that way, wouldn't it? However, it took me a few years to get there, doing various other jobs along the way, from washing dishes in a hotel kitchen to tele-sales.

You could either say I fell into barbering by accident or I was led there by destiny. It all depends on how you look at it, like so much in life. What happened was I went to get a haircut while in between jobs, saw a HELP WANTED sign and, desperate for cash, offered my services on the spot.

'Do you know anything about cutting hair?' Riccardo, the owner of the barbershop, asked me in a thick Italian accent.

I told him I'd cut several of my friends' hair and never had any complaints. What I failed to mention was that this had been during my brief stint at university and it had only ever been a case of using clippers all over, rather than any actual cutting with scissors.

Riccardo was a short, barrel-chested chap in his mid-fifties, clean-shaven but with a permanent five o'clock shadow and a bushy head of grey curls. He liked to give the impression of being bad-tempered and irate, frequently raising his voice to complain about topics like the British weather and local politics, but it was an act. Anyone who really knew him – not least those like me who he employed – saw through the brash façade to the heart of gold beneath.

Riccardo taught me everything I know about cutting hair and running your own business. I worked under him for eight years, from my early days as a wet-behind-the-ears trainee to eventually becoming his right-hand man, entrusted with the extremely important task of cutting his hair.

It was only when he retired, to move back to his beloved Sicily, that he admitted seeing through my initial bravado. Chuckling into a glass of red wine at his leaving do, he said: 'I knew full well you had no experience of cutting hair when you started with me.'

'How?' I asked. 'I really thought I had you fooled. And why did you take me on?'

'You were bloody awful to begin with, Luke, but I liked your spirit and you worked for peanuts. I didn't need you to have experience. I wanted someone I could mould.'

'You could have told me,' I replied. 'I worked my arse off at the start to make out like I knew what I was doing.'

He thumped me on the back with the palm of his hand and chuckled some more. 'Exactly. Why would I do anything to stop that?'

I haven't seen Riccardo for years, although we still send each other a card and catch-up letter every Christmas. He was passionate about the art of being a barber. 'You have to treat every haircut like it's the last one you'll ever do,' he used to say. 'Never rush. Never settle for second best. Be proud of your work and your skills. You're an artist, sculpting with hair. The day you forget this is the day you should hang up your scissors.'

If I'm honest, I didn't think I'd stay longer than a few weeks when I first started working for him. But what can I say? The man inspired me. His passion rubbed off on me and, before long, I could never imagine myself doing anything else. My brief time at university felt like a distant memory. Meanwhile, Mum and Dad, bless them, were delighted to see me happy.

I bet lots of other parents would have given their child a hard time for doing what I did. Having been considered a 'gifted student' at school, I could easily have faced accusations of wasting my intelligence and throwing away opportunities. But that never happened. Not once. They supported me all the way, including when I decided to go it alone and set up my own business.

Honestly, I couldn't have wished for better parents. The problem was that this made dealing with their untimely deaths even harder.

CHAPTER 12

'Heavy night?' my cousin asks as she stands up to greet me the following lunchtime.

'Not in the way you're thinking,' I reply, removing my coat and hat before taking a seat opposite her in the café around the corner from her shop. She suggested we meet here after I texted her earlier asking for a chat. 'I had problems sleeping, that's all. My mind was racing and I couldn't switch off.'

'I'm only joking,' Meg replies with a wink. 'You don't look *that* bad. How are you feeling? Better, I hope. Or shouldn't I have given you that hug just now?'

'No, don't worry. I doubt I'm contagious any more. I'm loads better than when you called in on Sunday.'

'Good. So what's the problem? What was on your mind that kept you awake?'

'Let's get some food sorted first,' I say. 'I don't know about you, but I'm starving.'

Having scanned the menu, I order a flat white coffee and

a club sandwich, while Meg opts for sparkling water and a tuna melt panini.

As we're waiting for these, my cousin squints at me across the table. 'You've not been dreaming about her again, have you?'

I'm tempted to ask who she means, despite knowing full well it's Iris, but bearing in mind what I want to discuss with her, I bite my tongue.

'Hardly,' I reply. 'I'd have been glad of any dreams, to be honest, even that weird recurring one I've told you about with the secret annexe and swimming pool.'

'Oh, I remember you mentioning that. Do you still have it?'

'Yes, frequently. When I actually get to sleep, that is. I don't think I managed to grab more than a couple of hours last night.'

She winks at me, slipping back into our banter of old now that we've properly reconciled. 'Hence the bags under your eyes.'

'Yeah, exactly. Thanks for that.'

'What about Rita, Iris's aunt?' Meg asks.

I raise an eyebrow. 'No, I've definitely not been dreaming about her.'

Meg chuckles. 'I mean, have you heard from her again?'

I'm confused about where this is going. 'No, should I have?'

'I thought you said the two of you got along well. That you went for a drink together.'

'And? If you're trying to suggest I might be interested in her romantically, you're barking up the wrong tree.

111

She's old enough to be my mother, Meg, and not my type at all.'

'I know that,' my cousin says, 'but she used to run her own hair salon, right? And she doesn't exactly seem ready to hang up her scissors yet. She's bursting with energy.'

'What are you getting at?'

'I thought the two of you might make a good team, professionally. A woman's touch would definitely not go amiss at the barbershop; maybe she'd be able to convince you to smarten the place up.'

'Don't be ridiculous,' I reply. 'I work alone – you know that. Why would I take on anyone else? And Luke's is perfect as it is, thank you very much. No smartening required.'

Meg holds up her hands. 'Fine, whatever you say. So what did you want to talk about? I hope you don't need to borrow money, because I'm flat broke.'

'When have I ever asked you for money? The cheek of it.'

Meg giggles. 'You're so easy to wind up, Luke. Go on, what can I do for you?'

'I want your opinion on an idea I'm chewing over.'

Our drinks arrive, courtesy of a heavily tattooed woman in her mid-twenties with dreadlocks and more rings in her ears than I can count on the spot. 'Here you are,' she says, flashing a pretty smile.

'Do you ever think the Northern Quarter is becoming a caricature of itself?' I whisper across the table to Meg.

'In what way?'

'Because the alternative has become the norm, like that

waitress. I'd quite like to be served by a preppy student in brogues and chinos once in a while, but there's little chance of that here.'

My cousin shakes her head and takes a sip from her glass. 'I thought you were trying to be more positive, you old grump.'

I shrug. 'Fair point. Now you mention it, as part of my bid to improve myself and to try to do something more meaningful with my life, I've come up with a slightly hare-brained scheme, if you'll excuse the pun.'

Meg rolls her eyes. Her expression soon changes, though, as I explain my haircuts for the homeless concept.

'Wow,' she says after I've finished detailing my hopes and fears about the idea. 'That sounds incredible.'

'Seriously? You like it?'

'Absolutely. Homelessness is such a big problem. It's heartbreaking to see so many people on the streets. No one should have to be in that situation in this day and age. I know there are shelters and soup kitchens out there; I realise there are various schemes and charities doing their utmost to help. But whatever is already being done, it clearly isn't enough.'

'Yeah,' I say. 'I mean, it's not like what I'm proposing would change people's lives. It's not going to solve the problem by any stretch of the imagination. But hopefully it would make a difference to a few people and have some kind of positive impact.'

Meg nods enthusiastically. 'Absolutely. As for the concerns you mentioned, I'd definitely do it in the barber-shop rather than on the streets and I wouldn't overthink the rest. I'd try it out in a low-key way to start with and let things progress naturally. Maybe only mention it to a few people first off, sticking to word of mouth, and see what happens. If you want some moral support, I'd be happy to come along and lend a hand. Not cutting hair, obviously, because I wouldn't have a clue what I was doing, but I could chat to anyone waiting and make sure things stay organised.'

I'm a little taken aback by Meg's eager response and her offer to help. This isn't what I expected at all. I thought she'd tell me I was being stupid.

It's great she's so supportive of the proposal, particularly after my wobble in the early hours. Her words have re-invigorated my initial enthusiasm.

'That would be amazing, if it's not too much trouble,' I tell her. 'It would be good to have someone on crowd control in case it really takes off. I doubt it will, but—'

'You never know,' Meg says, finishing my sentence.

'Exactly.' I pause to drink some of my coffee before adding: 'Thanks for your support. It means a lot. I was afraid you might start talking about survivor's guilt and shrinks again.'

'I do, er, stand by what I said then,' Meg says, scratching the side of her head. 'You definitely shouldn't be doing any of this due to feelings of guilt about Iris. But that doesn't mean I'm going to try to put you off doing something so positive. A great idea is a great idea.'

'When do you think would be a good time to do it? I have a feeling I should start soon or there's a danger I'll never get around to it.'

114

'Monday's your quietest day, right?'

I nod.

'And you don't open until lunchtime.'

'That's true.'

'So how about for a couple of hours on Monday evening, after you normally close?'

'Yeah, that could work,' I say.

'I'm free next Monday evening, if that helps.'

'Okay, let's do it.'

In an attempt to rustle up some interest in my free haircuts, the next day after work I head to the supermarket instead of going straight home. I'm hoping to bump into a certain novel-reading homeless chap, since he was the one who sparked the idea in the first place.

I've even dug out another Ian Rankin paperback from my bookshelf, which I'm hoping he'll be glad to receive. It was actually Mum's – all the Rebus books I have originally belonged to her. I decided to keep them after her death, partly since she was such a big fan, but also because she got me into them as well, lending me her copies one by one. I have fond memories of chatting about them afterwards with her, often over tea and cake. For that reason, I was initially hesitant about doing this. However, having given it some thought, I doubt I'll ever get around to reading them again and I'm sure Mum would approve. She was always a sucker for supporting a good cause.

When I arrive at the store, there is someone begging outside. But to my great disappointment, it's a different bloke altogether. He's a skinny guy, who looks to be in his early to mid-twenties, wearing a black donkey jacket, army boots and a red bobble hat with a few greasy strands of hair sticking out of the bottom. Most notable, though, is a jagged scar across one of his cheeks. It doesn't look red or angry enough to be recent, but it's still very conspicuous.

Dropping a couple of pound coins into the paper cup he's holding out, I get thanked in what sounds like a light Brummie accent.

'You're welcome,' I tell him, kneeling down in front of where he's sitting, leaning against the wall, his legs enclosed in a snot-green sleeping bag with a bright orange lining. 'How are you doing today?'

'I'm all right,' he says, blowing booze-scented fumes in my direction. I lean slightly backwards to avoid this, trying to be discreet rather than causing offence.

'At least it's not raining today,' he adds. 'Listen, you don't have a fag to spare, do you? I'm gasping.'

'Sorry, I don't smoke. I wonder if you can help me, though. I'm looking for a guy I spoke to here the other day. Tommy, he was called.'

I describe him in as much detail as I can remember, including the fact he was reading a book, but the bloke shakes his head and says he doesn't know him. This is a shame, and I'm not sure I believe him, convinced I spot a shifty look flash across his face at one point, but I don't push the matter. Instead, choosing to give him the benefit of the doubt and not wanting this to be a wasted trip, I pass him my business card.

'What's this for?' he asks, turning it around in his hands,

which are dressed in black fingerless gloves. I explain, giving him all the necessary details.

'Next Monday?' he repeats as I get up to leave.

'That's it.'

'And anyone's welcome?'

'I'll give a free haircut to anyone genuinely homeless who turns up.'

He looks down at the card, which he's still holding in his left hand. 'You're Luke, are you?'

'Yes. Sorry, what's your name?'

He doesn't reply to this, responding instead: 'The big question is, Luke: are you any good?' He roars with laughter at his own words, like he's told the funniest joke ever.

'You'll have to come along to find out, won't you?'

'Maybe I will,' he says, still sniggering. 'Maybe I will.'

I consider asking his name again as I say goodbye, but since he doesn't appear to want to share it, I don't push.

I spend another half an hour or so walking around the area, keeping my eyes peeled for Tommy, who's still the person I'd really like to catch up with and invite for a haircut. I don't find him, although I do speak to a few other homeless people in the process, giving a card to each and telling them about my scheme.

A couple of them say they know Tommy to say hello to but haven't seen him today. I ask them to pass on the message about what I'm doing, if they do see him, which they say they will.

The idea of a free haircut seems to go down well with most of them, which is great. However, one – a woman with shoulder-length brown hair – says she wouldn't feel right about getting her locks cut in a men's barbershop.

'You'd be very welcome,' I say. 'Honestly, women's haircuts aren't my forte, but I'd be happy to have a go if you wanted me to.'

'Hmm,' she replies. 'Maybe. I'll have to have a think about it.'

'No problem and no pressure. The offer's there; it's totally up to you.'

Cold and tired, I head home after this, unable to shake the guilty feeling that I'll soon be warm and cosy in my own flat, unlike the folk to whom I've been chatting this evening. It must be especially tough to live on the streets in winter. I know there are shelters and other emergency accommodation options available, particularly at this time of year, but I imagine there must be limits to how many people they can take in. At least this winter has been relatively mild – definitely not as cold as previous ones I can remember. There's been almost no snow in the city so far, other than a smattering at the beginning of January. Still, it's far from toasty outside, unlike my flat, where the heating has been on for a while and, as usual, Alfred is waiting for me.

'Hello, mate,' I say as he circles around my legs, rubbing against my ankles and looking up at me with big, sad eyes. His litter is piled in a mound to one side of the tray, which means he's done a number two, so as my first job, I clean that for him.

He's always been a house cat, Alfred. I sometimes feel bad about this, particularly on nice warm summer days, but not so much at this time of the year.

I made the decision not to let him outside based on the fact I live in the city: there's way too much traffic around. Better to have a long, pampered, sheltered existence inside than a short-lived one outside that ends with him being run over. That's my view, anyway, although I know some people would disagree.

If I lived in a quiet village, it would be another story. But I don't – and it's not like Alfred knows any different. He can't miss what he's never had. Plus he has the run of the whole flat, which isn't a bad space.

I could get one of those cat leads they sell and take him for walks outside. But that would be a pretty odd thing to do, I reckon. Also, imagine if the lead broke and he ran off. He'd be terrified and, with no experience of roads and traffic, I doubt he'd survive five minutes.

I do play with him to give him exercise. He has these fake mice I buy for him, which I throw around the flat and he chases. He even does it himself sometimes, batting them along on the floor with his front paws. Plus I have a couple of sticks with string and a feather on the end, which are great for getting him jumping up and running around in circles. I used to do that a lot with him when he was younger, but he's less keen these days, now he's getting on a bit.

'What have you been up to today?' I ask as I refill his bowls with food and fresh water. 'The usual, I guess: bit of sleeping, bit of eating. It's a tough life, isn't it?'

I sometimes think it wouldn't be a bad thing to be reincarnated as a cat in a loving home. It's a nice simple existence. Carefree. Nothing much to worry about other than the time of your next meal and where the comfiest place to snooze might be.

In other news, I'm starting to feel a bit anxious about next Monday evening. It's too late to pull out now, having told various people about it, and that makes it feel more real than ever before.

I'm still vacillating between worrying that more people will turn up than I can cope with, or no one will come and I'll feel stupid. Should I spend any more time trawling the streets, touting for business, or should I leave it for now and see how things go?

It's a tough call.

I probably will go out one more time, at least, as I'd really like to find Tommy and personally invite him along. It bothers me slightly that I couldn't find him today. I hope he's all right.

CHAPTER 13

Monday evening has come around already and Meg's arrived to help out. I've had a busier than usual afternoon, which is typical of course, but at least it's kept my mind away from fretting about how this is going to go.

'What's that?' I ask my cousin, pointing to a cardboard tube she has tucked under one arm.

She grins and hands it to me. 'A present for you.'

'Really. How come? If anyone should be giving a present to someone, it's me to you, to thank you for helping me this evening.'

'Just open it, will you?'

I do as she asks and inside the tube is a rolled-up FREE HAIRCUTS FOR THE HOMELESS banner, with white lettering on a red background.

I lean over to give my cousin a hug and a kiss. 'Wow. That's amazing, Meg. You really shouldn't have, but thanks so much. It looks brilliant. How are we best to put it up in the window?'

She reaches into her coat pocket and pulls out some window suckers. 'With these. See, I've thought of everything. This way, we can put it up and take it down as often as we like. I'm assuming you'll only want it up at the times you're doing a free session, right?'

'Um, yeah, I guess so. I haven't given it any thought. I didn't even—'

'Consider the idea of a banner? No, I thought not. I did wonder about checking with you first, in case you'd already arranged something, but I took a gamble based on everything I know about you and it looks like it paid off. Shall we put it up, then?'

We spend the next few minutes doing this, after which the pair of us walk outside to see how it looks from in front of the shop. It's dark and drizzly, but the area is still fairly lively, well illuminated by street lights and the glow of the various nearby bars and restaurants.

'I'm not sure it's totally straight,' Meg says. 'What do you think?'

'It's perfect,' I reply. 'Let's leave it as it is. Thanks a million. I really hope someone turns up now or I'll feel stupid. Where did you get it from?'

'Wouldn't you like to know.' She wags one finger playfully in the air and saunters back inside the barbershop. Of course, that immediately makes me desperate to know and, after several minutes of questions, she finally caves in and tells me.

'Do you remember that girl, Ciara, who I went out with for a bit this time last year?'

'The bunny-boiler, you mean?'

'She was not a bunny-boiler. She was a bit possessive, that's all.'

'She cut up two of your favourite dresses with a pair of scissors, Meg. I'd say that was more than a bit possessive.'

'Only because she thought I was cheating on her. And I was, at the end of the day, so she was justified to an extent.'

'You've changed your tune. Last time I heard you mention her, you said she was a psycho and you never wanted to see her again. What about Ciara, anyway?'

'She's a graphic designer with excellent printing contacts and a soft spot for good causes.'

I plonk myself down on one of the barber chairs, looking in the mirror at Meg, who's standing behind me. 'You're unbelievable. You're not seeing her again, are you?'

'Um.'

'Tell me.'

'I might have agreed to go for one small drink with her next week, Luke, but that's it. I won't let things progress any further, although she was looking particularly sexy when she gave me this.'

'You'll regret it,' I say. 'Don't come crying to me when she starts attacking your wardrobe again.'

'Hey, enough of that. If it wasn't for Ciara, you wouldn't have that amazing new banner in the window.'

Before I can reply, I notice my cousin walking towards the glass and peering out.

I ask her what she's looking at, but she signals for me to be quiet and then darts out of the door without explanation. Intrigued, I get up from the chair and look outside in a bid to discover what caught her eye. I can't see Meg or anything interesting, though, so I let out a tired sigh and put on the kettle to make us a brew.

By this point, I'm seriously doubting anyone is going to turn up. Clearly my chatting to people on the street and handing out business cards wasn't enough. I'm racking my brains for better methods of promotion that will actually reach people on the street, such as contacting one of the homeless shelters or local charities, when Meg bursts back through the door with two people in tow. I immediately recognise one of them as the homeless woman I spoke to last week, who said she wouldn't feel right about getting her hair cut by a barber. She didn't tell me her name then, but I beam at her and greet her like an old friend.

'Hello there. Great to see you again. Welcome to my barbershop.'

Sounding so chipper doesn't come naturally to me, especially here; I feel like a fraud, with my painted-on smile and awkward hospitality.

Her cheeks flush and she looks down at the ground.

'This is Steph and Ralphie,' Meg chips in. 'I spotted them walking past on the other side of the street, looking over. I had a feeling they were checking out what was going on here, so I caught up with them before they disappeared and persuaded them to come on in.' She turns to look at the pair, both avoiding eye contact, and adds: 'See, I told you we don't bite. Luke might look a bit grumpy, but he's okay, I promise. We're cousins. We go back a long way. What about you two? Are you, er, together?'

Steph shakes her head vigorously at this suggestion. 'We're just friends. I told Ralphie he could do with a haircut and then I brought him here.'

'It is a bit on the, er, wild side,' I tell him, eyeing his bonce. 'No offence, but I'd be very happy to smarten it up for you, Ralphie, however you like it.'

As these words leave my mouth, I wonder if he can see through my friendly façade to the jaded soul beneath. Who on earth would call themselves Ralphie? It reminds me of Rowlf, the piano-playing dog from *The Muppet Show*, but even he didn't feel the need to add an *ie* to the end of his name.

'I d-don't have any money to pay you,' he stutters.

'I told you, it's free,' Steph snaps. 'Like it says on the sign. Don't make an idiot of yourself.'

'She's right,' I say. 'Not, um, about the last bit. No one's making an idiot of themselves here. But it is totally free of charge for you.'

'How come?' Ralphie asks. 'Is there a catch?'

I almost reply that the only catch is he has to listen to my bad jokes. But that comment is *so* not the real me, I can't bring myself to say it. Besides, I don't have any jokes to tell him – good or bad. Instead, I simply shake my head and tell him there's no catch.

'Luke's decided to give something back to our community,' Meg says, to my surprise. 'So he's offering his services for free today as a gesture of goodwill and support to people like yourselves, who might not otherwise be able to spare the money for a haircut. But don't think that means it'll be a rush job. Yes, he's my cousin, so I am a bit biased, but Luke really is an excellent barber. He's Italian-trained, isn't that right?'

She's looking at me now, awaiting an answer, which in my surprise takes me a moment to form. 'Um, yes. That's right. Thanks, Meg.' I flash her a look – eyebrows raised and lips pursed – that I hope conveys both my appreciation and a subtle signal to tone it down a bit.

'So, Ralphie,' I continue, gesturing towards my preferred barber chair. 'How about you grab a seat and tell me what you'd like done?'

He looks over at Steph, who shrugs in a get-on-with-it kind of way, and then he finally sits down.

'You'd probably be best taking off your coat,' I say, upon which he stands up again and removes his green army jacket, followed by a bodywarmer underneath, handing them both to Steph.

'Good,' I add. 'So what are we doing today?'

'I'm, er, n-not too sure,' he replies helpfully. 'Whatever you think really.'

'It's pretty long and thick at the moment. Shall I take it quite short and thin it out for you?'

He agrees, which doesn't count for much, as he'd probably say yes to whatever at this stage, so I go ahead and get on with it. I even throw in a bit of small talk, believe it or not, telling him he has a great head of hair and is unlikely to ever go bald like me.

Meanwhile, Meg makes a brew for the pair, plonks Steph down in the waiting area and puts her at ease with casual talk about the weather and so on.

Unsurprisingly, Ralphie hasn't washed or brushed his

hair for some time, so it's greasy and matted, but I soon make it look much better. I take the top more or less as short as it will go with the scissors and use the clippers on the back and sides, opting for a number four rather than anything shorter. The reason for this is simple: I don't want him to be too cold while he's out on the streets.

There is a slight smell coming off both him and Steph, I must admit, but it's not as bad as I feared. Plus I opened a couple of windows earlier in anticipation of this, so it's perfectly manageable.

Once I'm done, I get the hand mirror out to show him the back and ask what he thinks.

'Aye, that's g-great,' he says, visibly more relaxed than he was when he first came in. 'Brilliant, thanks.'

'You're welcome.'

'You look like a different man,' Meg says, standing behind the mirror and admiring my handiwork. 'Very handsome. What do you think, Steph? Maybe he's boyfriend material after all.'

Steph grimaces.

I did consider the possibility of offering people a shave as well as a haircut when I was first thinking through this idea. But since it's not something I usually offer and it's quite time-consuming, I decided not to bother. Ralphie doesn't have much beard growth anyway. He does have a few straggly bits here and there, though, which look out of place now his hair has been done, so I offer to trim them with the clippers and he accepts.

'Are you up next?' I ask Steph.

'No, no, no,' she says, shaking her head hard enough to make herself dizzy.

'Are you sure. Not even a little trim? You'd barely notice the difference in length, but I could cut off any split ends for you.'

There's no convincing her, even when Meg chips in and says I cut her hair, which isn't true, but never mind.

'Yours is short,' Steph says, 'so it's not the same.'

'No problem at all,' I tell her. 'Your hair, your choice, Steph. You know where I am, if you change your mind.'

Once Ralphie's wrapped up again, the pair say goodbye and head for the door.

'Great to see you both,' I say. 'Thanks for coming.'

'Be sure to tell everyone you know about this,' Meg adds. 'Remember, it's totally free of charge for anyone homeless; we'll be here until nine thirty tonight, so there's still plenty of time to show up.' Thrusting a wad of my business cards into Steph's hand, she adds: 'Feel free to give these out to help spread the word.'

'Where did you get those cards from?' I ask her once they've gone. 'I don't have that many, you know. We can't be handing them out willy-nilly.'

She frowns at me. 'What? You said you handed them out when you were speaking to people on the street last week.'

'I did, in limited amounts. Definitely no more than one per person.'

'Hmm. And how many people have shown up so far?'

She has a point, which grows in pertinence as the evening progresses and no one else turns up. Soon she apologises for saying it, which only makes me feel worse. She goes out into the street several times to check for people potentially loitering nearby but – like Steph and Ralphie – not daring to make the final steps into the barbershop. However, she doesn't come across any more.

By 8.55 p.m. I'm feeling really downhearted about the whole thing. At 9.15 p.m. I want to call it a day, having already used the downtime to clear up. But Meg makes me hold on until 9.25 p.m., checking outside twice more in the meantime.

'Okay,' she says finally. 'Let's close up now. It doesn't look like anyone else is coming.'

'You reckon?' Immediately regretting my snappish tone of voice, I remind myself that Meg's been nothing but supportive. 'Sorry, I don't mean it like that. I just . . . hoped more people would come. Maybe I should knock the idea on the head. What's the point if no one is interested?'

Meg holds her arms wide open. 'Come here and give me a hug. Listen, I'm really proud of you for what you've done tonight, Luke. It doesn't matter a jot that you only cut one person's hair. One is better than none; you have to start somewhere.'

As we embrace, I exhale and she ruffles what hair there is on the back of my head.

'You're not very good at this being positive business, are you, Luke? It's fantastic that you're trying, but you need to stick at it rather than falling at the first hurdle and reverting to type. You haven't got the message out there enough yet, that's all.'

'I did speak to several people,' I say. 'And I asked them to tell others. I was worried if I told too many, I might be swamped. That clearly wasn't a problem.'

'Stay positive and leave it with your cousin. I have an idea I think will help.'

I ask her several times what this idea is, but she won't tell me. All she'll say is: 'Wait and see, Luke. Wait and see.'

CHAPTER 14

There's a knock on the door of my flat soon after I get home from work the next day.

'Oh, hello, Liam,' my neighbour says when I answer. 'How are you?'

'Good evening, Doreen,' I reply, smiling to myself at the continued absurdity of not correcting her about my name. 'I'm fine. How are you?'

'Good, thanks. I have a present for you.'

'Really? That's, um, very nice of you. It's not my birthday, though.'

'Oh, it's not a birthday present. And don't get too excited, it's only . . . well, I spotted it in a charity sale this afternoon and thought of you, that's all.'

I'm intrigued. 'Would you like to come inside?' I ask without thinking, surprising myself.

'No, no,' she replies, remaining on the doorstep, holding one arm behind her back. 'My tea is on the stove, so it's only a flying visit. Thanks, though.'

131

Swinging her arm forward, she hands me a boxed DVD. It's *Edward Scissorhands*, the Tim Burton movie from the early nineties. I remember seeing it once when I was younger.

'Wow,' I say. 'Superb.'

'It was the scissor thing I thought might appeal,' she explains. 'You being a barber and all. You haven't seen it already, have you?'

'No, no, I don't think so,' I lie, also not mentioning the fact my decrepit DVD player, which I really ought to throw out, hasn't worked in a while. 'Thank you very much, Doreen. That's really kind of you.'

'My Bob used to love watching films,' she adds. 'I prefer normal TV myself. What about you?'

'Oh, I definitely enjoy a good movie. I'll look forward to watching this. You really shouldn't have, though. I don't want you spending your money on me.'

'It's nothing. They were basically giving it away. The thing is, you've fetched me a couple of items from the shops over the past week or so and I wanted to let you know that I really appreciate it.'

'Well, I appreciate this too, Doreen,' I say, genuinely touched. 'But don't you be spending anything else on me, okay? I mean it. Next time, you treat yourself instead.'

Iris visits me in my sleep again that night. I'm having the latest version of my recurring dream when she makes a surprise appearance.

This time the imaginary flat where I'm living is in Corfu, where I've been on holiday a couple of times in real life.

There's a huge picture window in the lounge, overlooking a deserted sandy beach and beautiful azure sea.

Having been drawn to enter the hidden extra section of the flat, I've found the usual corridor leading to two unoccupied bedrooms, a small kitchen and lounge, and patio doors looking on to the luscious garden.

And it's while peering through the glass of these doors that I see Iris, standing next to the pool.

The outside area and everything inside the secret annexe look exactly as I expect, based on all the previous versions I've had of this dream. But I don't ever recall encountering someone else here before. Until now, I've always been alone in this strange, movable place.

I slide open the patio doors and call out to Iris, who's looking into the distance. She turns and smiles, beckoning me over.

Based on her surroundings, I'd expect her to be in a swimming costume or perhaps a summer dress. Instead, she looks the same as when I first met her: wrapped up in that canary-yellow raincoat, which seems odd in such warm, sunny weather. At least she doesn't have the hood up.

'Hello,' I say. 'This is a surprise.'

She nods and smiles, a soothing serenity about her. 'Hello, Luke. It's nice here.'

I look around at the emerald-green, neatly mown grass; the thick, tall laurel hedges that enclose the garden; the imposing palm tree in the centre of the lawn and a colourful variety of shrubs, plants and flowers that I won't even attempt to name.

Then, of course, there's the immaculate pool next to her: oval-shaped with submerged steps at one end.

'The water's lovely and warm,' Iris says.

'Right,' I reply, wondering again why the pool has never held any appeal for me; why I'm never happy to discover anything in this garden or the hidden annexe that leads here. They always feel like dirty secrets. After pacing through, I usually end up returning to the main flat and closing the door to this other section, wishing it didn't exist. I've no idea why, though. The whole thing is a mystery.

'Aren't you hot, wearing that big coat?' I ask Iris.

'This is a dream, Luke,' she replies. 'Your dream, for that matter. Ask yourself why I'm dressed this way. It's not like we're really in Corfu, is it? This garden is the same wherever the main flat happens to be, right?'

Hmm. She's correct on all counts. I suppose the reason she's wearing that yellow raincoat again is because it's the only thing I ever saw her wear in person.

'Can't you take the coat off?' I ask her.

'Well, I could if you desperately wanted me to, but why?'

I realise I'm slipping into thinking that this really is Iris, rather than a creation of my subconscious mind, which is dangerous territory.

She's not real.

She's a figment of my imagination.

She squints at me like she can tell what I'm thinking, which she probably can, because she's also me. Wow, this is getting confusing. I'm probably better not overthinking such things.

'It's fine,' I say. 'Leave the coat on, if you prefer. It really doesn't matter, does it?'

'Exactly,' she replies. 'And I do think this colour suits me. I love how bright it is. You could say it promotes positive thinking.'

'You'll be glad to know I've been working on that and everything we discussed last time.'

She nods. 'That is good news.'

Do I need to tell her everything or does she already know? I've no idea how this works. There must be a reason why I'm seeing her here, but what that might be is anyone's guess.

I should probably avoid overanalysing the ins and outs of this. Last time Iris appeared to me, I just accepted it and the conversation proved useful. Maybe I can take something from chatting to her again, if I give myself half a chance.

'I came up with this idea to help the homeless by offering them free haircuts,' I say. 'The problem is that only one person turned up. Well, two technically, but only one of them wanted a haircut. It's made me feel quite demoralised. If I can't even give away my help, then—'

'That's not a very positive way of looking at things, is it?'

I frown. 'Give me a break, Iris. I'm trying here, but how exactly can it be a good thing that barely anyone turned up?'

'It's better than no one turning up, isn't it?'

'Hmm.'

'Don't be so hard on yourself. You should be proud of

135

the fact you did it at all. Why not consider it a trial run? Think back to when you first started your own business. How did that go initially? I bet it took a while before you started turning a profit.'

She's quite right. That was a scary time for me, going it alone without Riccardo, who wasn't even nearby to offer advice. He was still reachable in Sicily by phone, but I didn't like to bother him, nor to look like I was struggling. I wanted him to be proud of me and to enjoy his well-earned retirement; not to waste time worrying that I couldn't hack it on my own. And knowing Riccardo, that's probably what he would have done, given half a chance. He was always such a supportive, caring boss. I couldn't have wished for a better mentor.

A key difference between then and now was the support structure I once had – namely my parents and my wife – which I've had to learn to manage without. I have Meg now, thankfully, who's amazing, but that'll never be quite the same.

I often wonder what I'd be like today if things had turned out differently: if Mum and Dad were around and I was still with Helen. That's the name of my ex-wife, by the way. I've deliberately avoided mentioning it until now. I don't like wasting my time and energy thinking about her after she let me down so spectacularly. However, it's pertinent while considering how much all of that bad stuff scarred me.

Would I have ended up so guarded and cautious? As I discussed with Iris last time, glass-half-empty thinking is all about having low expectations in a bid not to end up dispirited, like I feel now. It's a kind of pain-avoidance strategy. I'm pretty sure I haven't always thought that way. Why would you try to avoid pain if you'd never felt it in the first place?

'You look pensive,' Iris says. 'Why not tell me what's on your mind rather than stewing alone? I might even be able to help. Here, come and sit with me.'

She plonks herself down on the edge of the pool, removes her black leather shoes and socks, rolls up her dark trouser legs and dips her feet in the water. 'Mmm, this is nice, Luke. Go on, be a devil, come and join me.'

I hesitate for an instant and then I do it. Why the hell not? I'm already in shorts and sandals. In no time at all, my legs are dangling over the side, my feet and ankles soaking in the lovely warm water alongside hers.

'So?' Iris asks. 'Penny for your thoughts?'

'I was thinking about why I struggle to be positive; how it's probably down to past experiences. We are a result of what we've been through, right?'

'Our experiences certainly shape us,' Iris replies, first staring into the distance and then turning to face me. 'But we also get to choose how we respond to them. It's normal to want to close off or harden your heart after having it shattered into a million pieces. But while doing so might protect it from being broken that way again, it also stops it from being able to love and—'

'Hang on,' I say. 'How did we get on to love? I thought we were talking about being positive.'

Iris places her hand on mine and smiles at me with a sudden crashing wave of such incredible kindness and warmth, it catches me unawares, punching a hole through my defences. I feel a brick-size lump in my throat; I can barely swallow, never mind say anything else. I turn away from her intense gaze as I feel tears forming in my eyes, blinking repeatedly, fighting them back.

'W-what . . . is that?' I ask, still reeling.

'Love,' she replies. 'Powerful, isn't it? Sorry to shock you like that, but I wanted to emphasise the point I'm about to make. Love's a big word, you see. It encompasses a lot of things. Much more than being in love with another person or loving a family member, although of course these are important aspects. What do you think of as positivity, Luke?'

'I suppose it's, um, looking at things optimistically. It's seeing the good ahead of the bad in a given situation. It's—'

'Love?'

'How do you mean exactly?'

'Being positive is opening your heart to the world without being afraid of potentially negative outcomes. It's choosing hope rather than fear. It's opting to live in the now, rather than the problems of the past or the fears of the future. It's accepting life for what it is – with all its ups and downs – and embracing it with enthusiasm, come what may. Choosing love means, quite simply, rejecting all that horrible negative stuff like hate, fear, desperation, bitterness and anxiety.'

'That's easier said than done,' I reply.

'True. When you choose to love above all else, your heart is unshielded. It's open to being hurt. And yet love

138

is a great healer: better even than time. If you truly surrender yourself to love, it will always win in the end.

'Closing yourself off to it might appear to be the safer option, but it's like if someone in the UK shut themselves alone in an underground bunker during the Cold War, fearing a nuclear attack. They might have survived like that for a long time – years perhaps with the right supplies – and yet that doesn't mean they made the right decision, because the nukes never came. Choosing love is the key to finding true happiness, Luke, trust me.'

'But how do you know that, Iris? Where's the evidence?'

'Oh, it's there all right,' she replies with a tone of absolute certainty. 'You just have to open your eyes.'

'Sorry?'

'I said open your eyes.'

I wake up in my bed at the flat – my real flat, rather than the one transported to Corfu in my dream. I'm covered head to toe in a sheen of sweat. My hair's soaking wet; my duvet, bottom sheet and pillow are drenched too.

'Yuck!' I throw the covers up and away from me and jump out of bed.

It's still dark. I look over at my clock radio and see it's only 4.17 a.m. Brilliant.

I walk through to the bathroom and towel myself down. Then I pick an old T-shirt out of the washing basket and put it on before heading through to the kitchen and pouring a glass of water.

I don't hear Alfred, but I feel him as he sneaks up on me and rubs his warm fur against my bare ankles.

139

'Hello, mate,' I say, leaning down to pick him up and give him a cuddle. 'Sorry if I stink. I've been sweating.'

He rubs his cheek against my shoulder and starts to purr. 'You're a good boy, aren't you?' I tell him. 'But I know you too well. You want a snack, right?'

He meows like he knows what I've said and wriggles free, so I drop him gently onto the floor, where he races greedily to his bowl.

Once I've scattered some treats in there, I head back to my bed, which is still soaking. The pungent odour of my own sweat is far from appealing. I pull the duvet right back to air, throw on my dressing gown and go through to the lounge, opting for the couch instead, where I hope I'll be able to catch a few more winks before I have to get up for work.

I lie there briefly before accepting it's not going to happen, sitting up and switching on the TV. I tune into a news channel for a few minutes, but there's not much happening that I care enough about to continue watching. So I proceed to flick between stations, settling on nothing.

After a while I find myself watching an episode of *The New Avengers* – which isn't new at all and nothing to do with the recent Marvel movies. It dawns on me that I'm viewing it in mini mode, with most of the screen taken up by the TV guide, so I rectify this.

Seeing a young Joanna Lumley literally kicking butt alongside Patrick Macnee and Gareth Hunt entertains me for a few minutes. But eventually I find it all a bit too dated, so I flick over to Netflix instead and proceed to settle on nothing there either. There's too much damn choice nowadays.

Alfred runs into the room and jumps onto the arm of the sofa. He perches there, staring at me.

'You're not getting any more snacks,' I say without looking at him. 'I literally just gave you some.'

He starts rubbing his head against my arm and then my chest, his eyes looking longingly up into mine.

'Stop being greedy,' I say, still doing my best to ignore him. When he inevitably moves on to his favourite party trick of reaching forward with one paw and poking me on the cheek, I shake my head at him and scowl.

'If I gave you a treat every time you begged me for one, you'd be the fattest cat in Manchester, Alfred. Chill out. You're doing my head in.'

When he pokes me again a moment later, I get to my feet to make a cup of tea, which he interprets as me caving in. He darts off the chair and makes a beeline for his bowl.

'You're wasting your time,' I say. 'Go and do something else.'

But then I feel mean, so I do actually cave in. 'Fine. You can have two more treats, but after that no more, okay?'

He must think I'm a right sucker.

CHAPTER 15

I receive an odd phone call from my cousin on the Thursday following our disappointing homeless haircuts session.

'Hi, Meg,' I say, answering my mobile. 'How are you doing?'

'Excellent, thanks. You?'

'Fine.'

'Are you at work?' she asks.

'It's mid-afternoon on a Thursday. Where else would I be?'

'I'll take that as a yes, which is perfect.'

I'm suddenly suspicious. 'What do you mean by that?'

'Oh, nothing. You might get a visitor later today, that's all. Her name's Nora. Be nice.'

'Hang on, what? Who's Nora?'

'Trust me. Talk to her; give her what she needs. You can thank me later.'

'What is this, Meg? What's going on? Tell me you're not trying to set me up with a potential girlfriend again.'

'After our legendary row? Seriously? No, Nora's visit has nothing to do with dating, Luke, I promise. It's a professional matter, but I'm saying no more than that. Sorry, I have someone on the other line. Got to go.'

With that she hangs up and I let out a long sigh. What's her game?

Nora eventually shows up just after five o'clock when the barbershop is empty and I'm sitting down with a coffee and today's paper. I guess it's Nora, anyway, since it's a relatively unusual occurrence for a woman to come here alone. Most of the time they're accompanying a husband, partner or child. Occasionally women do turn up wanting their own hair cut, which is totally fine with me, but that tends to be when they have a short style. However, this person has long, wavy blonde hair that's been profession-ally dyed recently enough that she's barely showing any roots.

She looks to be a professional in her early thirties: tall, slim and pretty, dressed in smart grey trousers and a cream blouse, under a black, knee-length leather jacket. Over her shoulder is a leather satchel that I suspect contains a laptop or tablet.

What on earth does she want with me? I have absolutely no idea, thanks to Meg being so cryptic. I decide on the spot to play a game of my own and pretend I haven't heard anything about her visit. She looks capable enough, so I'm sure she'll be able to handle it.

'Hello, can I help you?' I say. 'I'm guessing you're not here for a short back and sides, although . . . do you know what? I wouldn't rule that out if I were you. A drastic

143

change can be really liberating. I think you could have the bone structure to carry it off.'

'Hmm, interesting you say that,' she says in a husky voice with a gentle Mancunian accent. 'I was planning to go a step further and ask you to shave it all off for me – totally smooth, like a boiled egg. I woke up this morning feeling daring. You only live once, right? What the hell. I reckon I could make it work.' She flashes me a toothy grin. 'Meg warned me you could be a bit of a handful. Did she tell you I was going to call in?'

I shrug, deadpan, egged on by this. 'Sorry, you've lost me. Meg? I'm racking my brains, but no . . . I'm pretty sure I don't know anyone by that name. Are you definitely in the right place?'

She stares at me in silence for a long moment, her green eyes narrowing to slits as she scrutinises my face, and I fight not to crack a smile.

'Not bad,' she says eventually. 'But you'll have to do better than that.'

I hold my hands up in mock surrender. 'Okay, you got me. It's Nora, right? Meg did ring up to say you were coming. She didn't say who you were or what it was about, though, and that's the truth, I swear.'

She holds her arm out, offering me a handshake, which I accept. 'Nora Mills,' she says.

'Luke Craven,' I reply. 'Pleased to meet you.'

'You too.'

'How is it that you know my cousin, then?'

'We've socialised together a few times. Friends of friends, you know.'

I don't ever remember Meg mentioning a Nora previously, so I'm guessing they don't know each other that well. I wonder if this means they actually had a thing at some point and hooked up or whatever. Meg's always had a far more exciting love and social life than I have, so I wouldn't be especially surprised.

'Come on, then,' I say. 'I'm dying to know what it is she's told you and why you're here. Are you going to put me out of my misery or what?'

Nora has a glint in her eye as she replies. 'Hmm. That sounds a bit easy, considering how you gave me the run-around. What do you think I'm here about? Do you reckon you can guess what I do for a living?'

This should be annoying, but there's a certain charm about her, so I decide to play along.

'Fine,' I say. 'I'm guessing a professional role: solicitor perhaps; maybe something in finance.'

'Wow,' she says. 'Do I really look that dull?'

I walked straight into that, I suppose, but I thought they were both fairly safe, inoffensive options. 'How about marketing, then? Any closer?'

'A little,' she says, 'but no. You're still not right.'

'Graphic designer?'

She shakes her head.

'Entrepreneur?'

'Nope.'

I'm getting nowhere here, so I decide to say something silly rather than running the risk of offending her. 'Street magician?'

She smiles this time, at least. 'No.'

'Okay, I think I've nailed it. Trapeze artist?'

'Yes, finally,' she says. 'I thought you'd never get there. So the reason I've come to see you is that one of the clowns at the circus where I work is sick and we desperately need a replacement. What do you think? The money's not great, but all clothes and makeup are included.'

She's quick-witted, this one. I'll give her that.

Laughing, I offer Nora a seat and a cup of tea. 'Anyway,' I say as the kettle boils. 'You'd better tell me what you're really here for or we'll be at this for hours.'

'Your cousin told me about your idea to offer free haircuts for the homeless,' she says, clasping her hands together and leaning forward. 'It sounds like a wonderful plan, but Meg said you could do with some publicity to get the ball rolling. That's where I come in.'

How did I not see this coming? It makes perfect sense, now I think about it. Why else would Meg send someone I've never met before to come and see me? I really can be dense sometimes.

'Right,' I say, pouring water over the teabags and reaching for the milk.

'Oh, none of that for me, thanks,' she says.

'Sorry?'

'The milk. I don't have any. I take my tea black and not too strong, thanks.'

'Oh, of course. Shall I take the bag out now?'

'Please.'

'Does it taste nice that way?' I ask, handing her the mug.

'I think so. It's a matter of opinion, though, isn't it?'

'So, tell me,' I say, sitting down next to her in the waiting area after first changing the sign on the door to CLOSED to avoid any potential disruptions. 'It's great that you're able to help, but in what way exactly? What is it you do professionally when you're not, um, hanging from a trapeze?'

She shuffles in her chair and clears her throat. 'I'm a freelance journalist.'

This really wasn't what I was expecting to hear – and it throws me. 'I see.'

'Listen,' she continues. 'Meg explained about the recent accident you were involved in. I heard about it at the time; how that poor young doctor was killed. Such an awful tragedy. Anyhow, I believe a few journalists approached you then, but you didn't want to speak to them. I totally respect that. And I must assure you that I'm not into muckraking or sensationalism.

'I know that's how we often get portrayed in TV shows and so on; certain pockets of the industry possibly are closer to that stereotype than I'd like. But I only write things I believe in and know to be true. I can promise you that. I don't send my work to the kinds of editors who might over-tweak it to make what they consider a better story. I know the right people to deal with. I've been in this business for a while now.'

She goes on to reel off a long list of publications she's written for, including various national newspapers and glossy magazines. She also challenges me to look her up online and have a read of some articles she's written. I'm about to say I'll need to have to think first when, to my surprise, she beats me to it.

'Don't worry, I'm not looking to interview you today. I want you to go away and think it over, because I've no interest in doing a piece unless you're totally comfortable.'

These words are music to my ears. They actually go a long way towards allaying my fears.

My previous experience of journalists isn't only related to the scaffolding accident; Mum and Dad's death attracted media attention too. And back then one particularly pushy tabloid reporter left a bad taste in my mouth. He badgered me to speak, despite my obvious grief; when I did eventually say a few words, chiefly to get rid of him, my comments got taken out of context and reported in a way I found to be insensitive and misleading.

Knowing Nora isn't like that, or at least she doesn't appear to be, is very reassuring. So too is the fact she knows Meg and we've had a bit of a laugh together. I'm also in a better head space now than on previous occasions when I've had to deal with the press. Consequently, I don't tell her to do one, like I have to previous journalists, and instead agree to think about it.

I query what she has in mind and how getting coverage is likely to help promote my scheme.

She says she'd ideally like to interview me here with a photographer present to take some 'nice pictures'. I don't necessarily have to mention Iris or the scaffolding accident, she adds, although it would give the story more depth and emotional appeal to readers, particularly if that experience played any part in my decision to do this.

I ask: 'If what you write doesn't get read by homeless people, how's that going to boost the numbers I have coming into the barbershop?'

She says that she thinks the story would go down well with both the *Manchester Evening News* and *Big Issue North*, which should really help spread the word on the streets. She's also hopeful that with the right angle, it could get picked up nationally too.

'Getting it in those titles could help,' I say, careful not to sound like I'm definitely onboard with the idea yet. 'I wouldn't be bothered about it going national, if I'm honest. But I guess that would be better for you, in terms of payment, right?'

She chuckles. 'We all have costs to cover and bills to pay. There wasn't much money in journalism when I first joined the industry. Nowadays, with so many people consuming news for free on their smartphones, budgets are tighter than ever. National newspapers and magazines help keep us freelancers in business, because they have the biggest pockets.'

I'm impressed by the honesty of this response and Nora's apparent unflappability, whatever I've thrown at her so far.

I take her business card and give her one of mine when she stands up to leave, telling her I'll need to give the matter some serious consideration. If I'm honest, though, I've pretty much made my mind up already.

I'll need to grill Meg for some more details about Nora first. But to my surprise, this particular journalist might well have managed to convince me to put my historic concerns about the press to one side and do an interview.

Nora is clearly good at what she does, so I'm hopeful she would write a decent piece. There's also the argument that being a positive person is all about saying yes to things and opening yourself up to new opportunities.

The old me would have said no straight away. He'll no doubt pop into my mind later on with all kinds of compelling points to support that position. But if I really want to move forward, I need to ignore him and trust my gut, which is definitely telling me to do this.

CHAPTER 16

It's weird seeing yourself in the paper. I remember being featured once as a child. We'd gone away down south on an Easter break when I was seven or eight. I can't remember exactly where – and it's not like I have anyone to check with – but I'm fairly sure it was in Devon. It was definitely near the sea: I remember walking along some sprawling sandy beaches. I desperately wanted to go in the water, but I wasn't allowed because it was way too cold.

Anyway, one morning, the three of us were walking along the main street in whatever town we were visiting that day and we got stopped by a young reporter. I remember him being covered in spots, proper acne, and for some bizarre reason, finding that a desirable look. Dad wound me up for years about that. Apparently, I whispered something to him along the lines of: 'What does that man have on his face? It looks really cool.' This never failed to make both him and Mum roar with laughter whenever it got brought up afterwards.

The reporter was looking for a child around my age to pose for a photo as part of an April Fools' Day prank. He said he'd picked me because I had a cheeky look about me, although with hindsight I was probably the first kid of the right age to walk past.

'What would he have to do?' Dad asked, to which Spotty explained that I'd need to pose for some pictures with a huge ice cream – and then I'd get to eat as much of it as I could manage.

That was all it took to get me interested. At that age, ice cream was probably my favourite food in the whole world. So we trundled along to a café around the corner and there, as promised, they made this ridiculously large cone with about twenty scoops of various flavours, held together with a long metal spike.

I had my photo taken holding it, tongue out ready to lick, and then they put all the ice cream into a huge bowl and I ate as much as I could until I started to feel sick.

A couple of days later, on 1 April, we picked up a copy of the paper – and there I was on the front page.

'You're a celebrity now,' Mum told me. 'How does it feel?'

'Not just any celebrity either,' Dad added with a wink. 'Luke's a front-page star, my love, and don't you forget it.'

They must have bought about twenty copies of the paper to give to family and friends, and a cutout of the article remained on our kitchen noticeboard for years, gradually yellowing with age.

I remember being a bit taken aback initially, but as the

day went on, I started to quite like the idea of being famous. Dad kept nudging me while we were out and about, claiming people were looking and pointing at me. He even got me to practise my signature in case someone wanted my autograph – and sure enough, when we were out for dinner that night, the waiter came over to ask me for it, saying he was honoured to have someone so important as a guest in his restaurant.

I realised years later that Dad had set the whole thing up, even though he never admitted to doing so. It was a typical Dad-style stunt. He was always great fun like that: a friend as much as a father to me, particularly when I was little. Don't get me wrong, Mum was brilliant too. She always had a big smile on her face and a wonderful ability to see the silver lining in even the gloomiest of situations. They were both always on hand as playmates, so I never especially minded being an only child. I think Dad often stands out in my memory because he had such a great sense of humour. He was forever making me and Mum laugh.

They were both such warm, happy people. I wish I'd ended up more like them.

As for the news story that landed me that front page, it was a purely fictional affair – as April Fools' Day articles are wont to be. The line was that I'd supposedly walked into the café on my own, ordered the biggest ice cream they'd ever heard of, eaten it and then confessed to having no money. I'm sure it didn't take the paper's readers too long to twig it was a joke.

All the same, it was a great tale to tell my friends when

I got home. I took the newspaper into school and my teacher even read it out to the class. Being as gullible as I was at that age, my pals were gobsmacked to hear about the autograph incident. I think for a while they genuinely believed I'd become famous over the holidays.

Now I find myself on the front page again as an adult – and this time it's in Friday's *Manchester Evening News*, which does actually feel like quite a big deal to me. Nora's article isn't on the front, but one of the pictures of me is there with a taster headline, guiding people to read all about it on page seven, where there's a prominent page lead.

I agreed for her to come and interview me on Monday morning, four days after she'd first called in, when the barbershop would usually have been closed. This meant no customers getting in the way of our chat – although, of course, a couple did try their luck despite the CLOSED sign and I did my best not to bite their heads off. It also meant more natural light for the pictures, which the photographer that Nora brought along with her – a fellow freelance called Rudy – was keen on.

Nora had initially suggested turning up to the next free cuts session. But in light of the poor turnout last time, I told her I was keen to hold that after publication, so the article would hopefully promote it. She agreed and, sure enough, there's a decent plug for next Monday's planned session in the piece. As I look at this, it both excites and terrifies me all at once. My major concern now is whether I'll be able to keep up with demand.

Relax, I tell myself, sitting alone in the barbershop just

before midday, waiting for my next customer. Stop thinking like a glass-half-empty person. This is amazing free publicity. And yet, even as this thought occurs to me, that old negative voice in my head is chattering away in the background, saying I look ridiculous in the photos: my cheeks too flushed and my teeth not white enough.

It is a really good article, I must admit. It's more or less exactly what we discussed it would be, focusing primarily on the free haircuts, while still acknowledging the impact of the scaffolding incident and the role it played in leading me to this place. Nora had convinced me that a brief mention of this would give the story greater depth and increased human interest appeal. So I told her an edited version of the truth, skipping the part about trying to turn myself from pessimist to optimist, and focusing on how Iris's death had inspired me to do something meaningful.

I'm accurately quoted in the article as saying: '*I decided to put my barbering skills to good use somehow. This is about me trying to help the needy in my own small way, paying tribute to Iris and her plans to be a volunteer doctor in Africa, which she tragically died before realising.*

'*I only got to know her very briefly, but she was clearly a wonderful woman with such a drive to help others. I had to do something in her honour.*'

My mobile rings and I see it's my cousin. She rang earlier, having already got hold of the paper, sparking me to pop over the road to the nearest newsagent to grab myself a copy.

'Well?' she asks as soon as I pick up. 'Have you got one?'

'Yep.'

'So, what do you think?'

'I'm pleased.'

'You don't sound it. You're on the blooming front page, Luke. How often in their life can someone say that?'

I don't have the heart to tell her it's my second time, assuming she doesn't remember the April Fools' Day article all those years earlier. She no doubt heard the story as a girl, but since she wasn't there when it happened, I'm not surprised it's slipped her mind.

'I'm really pleased with the article, Meg. Thanks for helping to arrange it.'

'That's better.' She chuckles down the line. 'You still don't sound that happy about it, though. What's up? Are you embarrassed by the attention?'

'No, not really. It'll be someone else's turn in the limelight tomorrow. If anything, my main concern now is that we'll be swamped next Monday and I'll struggle to cope. Are you still able to help?'

'Definitely. I only wish I could be more useful to you and actually get involved with the cutting. I mean, I could have a go if you like, with the clippers or whatever, but—'

'I'm sure we'll manage and it won't come to that,' I say, silently horrified at the idea of Meg making a hash of some poor guy's first haircut in ages.

Changing the subject, I ask about the drink she went for with Ciara, her psycho ex-girlfriend, in return for her help arranging the window banner for the barbershop. The meet-up was scheduled for last night.

'Don't ask,' she replies.

156

'Come on, Meg. You have to give me a bit more than that.'

'Well, things started off all right, but before I was halfway through my G&T, she made a couple of comments that really sounded like she'd been stalking me on social media.'

'What kind of comments?'

'Oh, I really don't want to go into it, Luke. Let's say she knew a bit too much about what I've been up to over the past few months. It rang alarm bells; I made my excuses and left.'

'No chance of any further fancy banners, then?' I ask as a gentle wind-up.

'Definitely not. And don't say I told you so.'

'As if I would,' I reply with my tongue firmly in my cheek.

CHAPTER 17

The following Monday evening comes along in a flash, as does a second article, in the latest edition of *Big Issue North*.

My picture's not on the front page on this occasion, but the piece they run on the inside is longer and more feature-like, using different photos. I've fallen on my feet getting Nora's help, I realise, since this article is as accurate as the first and provides a really good plug for my free haircuts. Plus there's the fact that homeless folk are the ones who sell this magazine, meaning the information is highly likely to disseminate to the right people one way or another.

It was Nora herself who rang to tell me about this second article being published. At the time, she asked if I'd mind her coming along tonight to see how things turned out. I said that would be fine as long as it was only her and not the photographer, explaining I didn't want to discourage any folk unsure about whether or not to come inside, like the pair we encountered last time.

'The sight of someone snapping shots with a big professional camera might be enough to put some people off,' I said.

'Okay, fine. But you won't mind me taking a few subtle shots with my phone, right? I'll check with them first, of course.'

'No, that shouldn't be a problem,' I told her, not wishing to sound contrary after she'd come good on all of her promises so far.

She and Meg arrive a couple of minutes apart. They chat with each other while I get things ready, trying to hide how anxious I feel. As much as I tell myself to focus on the positives, it's hard when I'm so nervous and don't want to reveal this fact to Nora in particular.

'Luke,' Meg says, drawing my attention to the door, where I see a rangy, scruffy-looking bloke with a mop of curly ginger hair. We race each other to greet him and, five minutes later, Michael is wrapped in a gown in my barber chair, shoulders covered in hair cuttings, chatting away about how he ended up on the streets.

He talks about it so matter-of-factly, his descent from having 'the odd flutter on the gee-gees' to being made redundant and developing a full-blown gambling addiction that lost him his home and family. It's shocking, as is the fact he's only twenty-eight but looks a decade older.

You can tell from the way Michael speaks – the language he uses – that he's a chap with a decent education. His life could have turned out a whole lot better had he made a few different decisions along the way. I find myself wishing I could offer him something more substantial than

159

a haircut. And then the smile on his face when I finish, show him the back using the hand mirror and ask if he'd like me to style it with some gel – that gives me such a great feeling. To my surprise, I even fear I might cry for an instant – happy tears – as he shakes my hand and thanks me for making him feel human again.

'I'll tell you what,' he says. 'I haven't sat in a barbershop like this for goodness knows how long. I haven't had a proper haircut in forever. And it feels great. It's like stepping back into my old life for a few minutes; resampling normality. You're a star, Luke the barber, and this is very much appreciated.'

'You're very welcome, Michael,' I say, trying to ignore the lump in my throat. 'It's been a pleasure.'

And then I'm on to the next guy, who walked in two minutes earlier, as three more men arrive. I'll have to work quickly to stay on top of things.

Meg catches my eye in the mirror and winks at me. I nod and smile back before cracking on.

By the time I've finished a couple more cuts, there's quite a queue forming. All the seats in the waiting area are full and there are already two more people standing. This level of busy is nothing I haven't dealt with by myself before. However, I've never previously offered free cuts supported by two prominent press plugs. So how am I supposed to know which way things will go from here? This could be my peak time or merely a warm-up.

Don't panic, I tell myself. Get on with it, one cut at a time, like you always do.

At least people are turning up this evening. Plus Meg's

doing a great job of keeping everyone happy while they wait. There are already too many people present for her to be offering out brews, but she's greeting folk when they enter and constantly keeping some chit-chat on the go. This is helped by the fact that a lot of the clients already know each other. I'm pleasantly surprised to see Nora lending a hand too, in between asking people for comments after I've cut their hair. It's all very informal – not pushy in the slightest.

About forty minutes into the session, though, the mood starts to change. It's really hectic now – uncomfortably so. I'm going full throttle, keeping the cuts as quick and straightforward as possible, and yet people are cottoning on to the fact that I'll struggle to get around everyone. I can hear the mutterings, but I try not to be fazed, pushing on.

Harder to ignore is a row about who's next, thankfully settled by Meg and Nora. Then a few minutes later, while Nora is outside taking photos, two blokes standing in line behind me start to jostle, arguing with each other about a can of lager one claims the other stole from him earlier.

'Come on, guys,' Meg says. 'Calm it down, please.'

Putting on my most authoritative voice, as loud and deep as I can manage, I add: 'Any scrapping and you'll be out of here, gents, no second chances.'

As I turn to them to say this, I recognise one of the jostling pair. It's the skinny guy with the jagged scar across his cheek, who I met when I was first trying to spread the word on the streets last month. The bloke who wouldn't tell me his name. He turns to me with a sneer. 'You're going to kick me out, are you, Luke? You and whose army?'

His words remind me I'm not exactly well equipped to deal with any kind of trouble at one of these sessions. I look over at Meg and our eyes meet, clearly both thinking the same thing.

'Don't be a dickhead, Moxie,' a familiar-sounding voice from further down the queue pipes up. 'There are plenty of us here that'll help him turf you out if you can't behave yourself. This guy is trying to do something good. Calm down and let him get on with it. Otherwise, get lost.'

Several others voice their agreement with the speaker, who turns out to be Tommy: the book-reading bloke from outside the supermarket, who inadvertently inspired this whole idea. He nods at me and I smile back to show my appreciation. Meanwhile, Moxie – who clearly does know Tommy, despite what he told me when I was trying to track him down previously – backs down and does as he's told, calmness thankfully resuming.

Shortly after this, Nora shuffles her way past the queue to get back inside. To my confusion, she has an angry-looking Rita – Iris's aunt – in tow.

'Rita,' I say. 'What are you—'

'Can we have a word, please?'

'Now's not a great time,' I say. 'As you can see, I'm pretty swamped.'

Arms firmly crossed over her chest, Rita shoots daggers at me. 'We can do this here, in front of everyone, or outside. Your choice. Either way, we're doing it now.'

This doesn't sound good. I ask Meg to hold the fort

for a minute before I follow Rita outside to the sound of various sighs and groans from those waiting in line. 'Don't worry, I'll be back in a minute,' I say in a loud voice, hoping it's the truth.

Out on the pavement, Rita stomps a short distance away from the barbershop before turning to face me and immediately letting rip. 'Who the hell do you think you are?' she asks in a tone reminiscent of the way she spoke to me after her niece's funeral.

'Sorry?' I reply. 'What's going on? Am I missing something? I thought we were on good terms now.'

'How dare you use Iris's name to push your business in the press!'

'Is that what this is about?' I say. 'Because that's not what I'm trying to do at all. I only—'

'What right have you got to talk publicly about my niece? You barely knew her. I couldn't believe my eyes when I saw it; nor could her mum and dad. To think I came to apologise to you after what I said at the funeral reception. I was obviously right to send you packing then. Using her legacy for your own personal gain. How could you? Honestly, I'm fuming.'

'I see that, Rita, but can I have a chance to explain? This is nothing to do with me trying to plug my barbershop in the media. I'm offering my services totally free of charge. I'm genuinely trying to give something back to the community.'

Rita vents some more of her fury before finally allowing me to try to clarify the situation.

I recount how my first attempt at offering free cuts for

the homeless fell flat without publicity, in contrast to tonight's big turnout. Apologising for not running the press coverage by her and the rest of Iris's family – which I now acknowledge as a stupid oversight – I plead with her to believe me that the whole idea truly was inspired by the wonderful nature of her niece.

'I can't tell you how many times I've relived that night in my mind,' I say, 'wondering if there's anything I could have done differently that might have saved her. If I could go back in time and change things so she survived and I died, I'd do so in a heartbeat. It eats me up why I'm still here and she's gone, when she had so much more to offer the world than I do. And how am I dealing with that? By trying to be a better person – someone more like Iris. That's what tonight is all about, I promise you. Nothing more.'

She takes some convincing, but eventually Rita starts to soften. Just as I seem to be getting somewhere with her, a fraught Meg bursts out of the barbershop. 'Oh, there you are,' she calls to me. 'Are you coming back? Things are getting a bit chaotic in here.'

'Um, yeah, I'll be with you in a sec,' I say.

Turning to Rita again, I add: 'I really need to get back. Is that all right?'

'Okay,' she says. 'Maybe I got this wrong. Maybe. Although you definitely should have run it by us first.'

'I know that now.'

'Good.'

A few minutes later, once I'm back in the shop, doing my best to calm everyone down and catch up, Rita walks back through the door with a glamorous, petite blonde woman at her side.

I fear she's about to cause another scene, but instead she announces: 'This is my good friend Sharon. She gave me a lift here tonight after my car broke down. She also happens to be an excellent hairdresser, who used to work with me and, luckily, keeps her cutting equipment in the boot. Luke, I noticed you had two empty chairs and lots of customers, so I thought perhaps you might appreciate some help.'

'Seriously?' I reply, gobsmacked. 'That would be amazing.'

The waiting homeless folk clearly agree, as they let out a cheer.

The two new additions get right down to it and make a huge difference. Although they come from a primarily women's hairdressing background, it's clear they've both cut plenty of men's hair too; they do a cracking job.

Sharon, who's in her late thirties, is pretty quiet while she works. She chats a little here and there, but her primary focus seems to be on getting the job done.

Rita, on the other hand, is a revelation. A total chatterbox throughout, her original anger is nowhere in sight as her vibrant personality and infectious laugh lift the whole mood of the barbershop. It might not be my usual style of running things, but I can't deny it works a treat – and she gets plenty of cutting done too. There's no sign of any more trouble or unrest among those in the queue. She's so bubbly and optimistic. On reflection, I think that's what it is about her that reminds me of my mother, because she was the same way. Plus Rita seems extremely efficient and, as I just discovered for the second time, she can be fiercely protective of her family and has no qualms about speaking her mind. These were also qualities Mum had.

Aside from that initial outburst, you wouldn't have a clue of the pain Rita's been going through since her niece died. It reminds me how far I still have to go if I truly want to become a positive person.

Was Iris like her aunt when she was at work? Probably not to quite the same degree, bearing in mind she was a doctor rather than a hairdresser. And yet I bet she always had a huge smile for whoever walked into her surgery and a lovely way of putting her patients at ease.

I wonder if she's looking down on us now from wherever she is, a big smile on her lips and eyes twinkling. I'd like to think so. I really hope she'd be delighted to see this happening in her honour.

I make sure Tommy ends up in my chair and the first thing I do is thank him for his earlier intervention.

'Oh, you're welcome, pal,' he says. 'I think I recognise you, by the way. Have we met before?'

I assumed he'd come tonight because he remembered chatting to me, but apparently not. Mind you, he must have spoken to loads of people since we met. Why would I have stood out?

'Yes,' I say. 'A little while back. You were reading Ian Rankin.'

'Okay,' he replies, narrowing his eyes like he's trying but can't quite remember.

'Funnily enough, I dug out another Rebus novel that I wanted to pass on to you, but you seemed to move spots.'

'Really? That was kind of you. Yeah, I went for a wander, but I'm back now, like the proverbial bad penny.'

'Hang on,' I say, remembering I left the paperback in a drawer here at the shop. I dig it out and hand it to him. 'Here you go. Hope you've not read it.'

'Brilliant,' he replies, grinning. 'No, I've not read it. Not for years, anyway. That's amazing. Thanks so much.' He pauses before adding, in a more solemn tone: 'I can't believe you thought of me like that. I . . . really appreciate the gesture. People don't often do such things for you when you're on the streets. Most passers-by barely notice you're there, never mind see you as a fellow human being. It's, um, really kind of you, really thoughtful.'

'No problem. There are more if you want them. Let me know. I'm afraid I don't have any of the most recent ones, though, as it was my mum who collected them and she passed away before they came out. I should buy the new ones myself, I suppose, but I struggle to find time to read these days. Too many other distractions.'

What I don't say is that it wouldn't feel right not being able to chat to Mum after finishing one of these books, like I always used to. Those mother-and-son talks, chewing over the highlights and so on, were always half the fun.

'Sorry about your mother,' Tommy says, which I acknowledge with an appreciative nod. 'Are you sure it's okay for me to have this, if it was hers? Would you like it back after I've finished?'

'Of course it's all right,' I say. 'Books are meant to be

read – not to gather dust on a shelf. And no, there's no need to return it. Maybe you can find someone else to pass it on to instead. Mum would be happy to know it was being enjoyed.'

I look his long, shaggy hair up and down. 'So what are we doing today? Would you like me to take off a little bit or a lot?'

'It's been a long time since I visited a barber,' he replies.

'I guessed as much.'

'No, but really a long time.' He clears his throat. 'To put it into context, my last haircut was a number four with the clippers on top and a two on the back and sides.'

I look at the length of his hair now, which is well past his shoulders, and give a low whistle of surprise. 'Seriously? That's, um . . . wow. And no scissors to it at all in the meantime?'

He shakes his head and strokes his bushy beard with his right hand. 'This thing's been growing for a while too, although I have trimmed it once or twice when it was getting annoying.'

He eyes himself in the mirror. 'I look like a proper hippy, don't I? Oh, let's cut it all off.'

I raise an eyebrow. 'Are you sure? You might find it cold outside without all that hair to insulate you.'

'Stuff it. I've got a woolly hat I can wear if necessary. Give me a four and a two, for old times' sake – and maybe a quick beard trim too, if that's possible.'

'Really? That's pretty short, especially compared to now.'

'No, I'm definite. Let's go for it.'

So I do – and the man who leaves the barbershop after

I've finished is almost unrecognisable from the one who walked in. Waving goodbye, I joke: 'How will I know you next time I see you, Tommy?'

He holds up the paperback and grins. 'I'll be the one reading this. Thanks for everything, Luke. You have a great night.'

CHAPTER 18

We finish about an hour later than planned, once we've finally got through everyone.

The amount of hair swept up is truly impressive – way more than a normal day's worth. That's not a huge surprise, though, considering how long it's been since most of these guys last had a proper cut. Plus there were three of us cutting for much of this evening, whereas normally there's only me.

To her credit, Nora's still here and she's even been getting her hands dirty, helping with the clean-up operation.

'Pleased?' she asks me, leaning on the broom she's been using on the floor.

'Definitely,' I say, 'and totally knackered. I can't believe how much your articles helped get the word out there on the street. Do you think it'll be this busy at every session we do from now on?'

'Only time will tell,' Nora says. 'I suspect it will ease off to a more comfortable level once the initial buzz dies down. It was pretty manic this evening, wasn't it?'

I mime staggering backwards in exhaustion. 'Whatever do you mean?'

As happy as I am about how today has turned out, especially compared to the previous occasion, I do hope Nora's right. Going forward, I can't expect to rely on the good will of others, particularly Rita and Sharon, to be able to cope. What I'd really like is to be able to get things to a level where I can manage alone, like I do with paying customers during the day.

'Are you still planning to do this fortnightly?' Nora asks.

'Yeah, I think so, for now. In the long term, we'll have to see how it pans out. Thanks for helping tonight, by the way. I didn't expect that.'

'You're welcome. I've enjoyed myself. Plus I've got a fair bit of extra material from chatting to people today and taking photos, so hopefully I'll have something good to tout elsewhere. I'll let you know how I get on.'

Lowering her voice, she asks: 'Everything all right between you and Rita? She looked pretty angry earlier.'

'Yeah, yeah. Bit of a misunderstanding, that's all.' I say no more for fear of rocking the boat. So far Rita's been fine with Nora – and I'd like to keep it that way.

'Quite a character, isn't she?' Nora adds. 'It's great that she got involved.'

'I know. And I'd never have managed without her and Sharon. They really saved my bacon.'

I pull Rita for a chat later, after Nora has gone. 'I can't thank you and Sharon enough for tonight,' I say, 'especially considering your initial feelings. I couldn't believe my eyes when you came back to help. I now see where Iris got some of her charitable nature from.'

She shakes her red curls out of her face. 'It's not what I expected to happen either, but it looks like I misjudged you again, Luke. Sorry for biting your head off. I've been so up and down since Iris died. I saw red after reading the article in the paper – that picture of you on the front page and Iris being tied into it all. I mistook it as a publicity stunt. I wanted to stop you before it even began, but thanks to my car breaking down, I didn't arrive until it was well underway. I'm glad, with hindsight; if I hadn't seen everyone waiting in line, I'm not sure I'd have understood.'

'It was wrong of me not to talk to you first,' I reply. 'I can only apologise again for that.'

'Let's put it behind us, Luke. Do you know what? As shattered as I am now, I've really enjoyed myself. It felt great to be able to put my skills to good use. Despite everything I said earlier, I think Iris would be as pleased as punch to know that she inspired you to do this. They were such nice blokes. My heart goes out to them. Anyone could end up homeless. All it takes sometimes, by the sound of things, is a bit of rotten luck or some bad decisions.'

When they leave, I reiterate my huge thanks to her and Sharon for their help. Surprising me yet again, Rita says she'll happily get involved next time and will smooth things over with the rest of Iris's family regarding the press coverage. However, a shattered-looking Sharon stays quiet, looking like she bit off more than she could chew tonight.

I offer to take them both out for a drink to show my appreciation, but they decline, saying they have to get home to bed.

Meg, on the other hand, does agree to come for one with me so, after locking up, we head to a bar a few doors along. It's lively, but we manage to find a small corner table to grab a seat and rest our weary limbs.

My cousin takes a long sip of the G&T I bought for her. 'Mmm, that's nice. I feel like I've earned it tonight. Went well, didn't it? Thank goodness for the two extra cutters. It would have been chaos if they hadn't shown up when they did. Great job turning things around with Rita.'

I shrug. 'Thanks.'

'What about Nora?' she asks, swirling her drink around in the glass.

'What about her?'

'Nice, isn't she?'

'Yeah, definitely. Nowhere near as many people would have turned up without her writing those two articles. Hats off: it was a great idea of yours to involve her, Meg. I'll admit to being a bit sceptical originally, but you were right on this one.'

She nods thoughtfully before adding: 'She's single at the moment.'

'Okay . . . any particular reason for telling me that?'

I'm grinning, assuming this means Meg's about to announce her intention to pursue Nora romantically.

Instead, she replies: 'Don't take this the wrong way. I'm not pushing anything here – just saying it as I see it – but I'm pretty sure she likes you.'

This totally throws me. 'Hang on, what? I thought you were into her. Isn't she—'

'Oh, seriously? You thought . . .' Meg roars with laughter. 'No, no. You've got the wrong end of the stick there. Nora doesn't bat for my team.'

'Really? I assumed—'

She rolls her eyes. 'You should know better than to assume, Luke. I'm disappointed in you. I don't only socialise with—'

'Sorry,' I cut in. 'Listen, I'm shattered. I really didn't mean it that way.'

She calmly places a cold hand on mine, which is resting on the table. 'It's fine, Luke. I'm not offended. I'm messing with you.'

'Messing how?'

She shakes her head. 'You really are tired, aren't you? I'm messing with you about being offended – not about Nora. I genuinely think she has a soft spot for you.'

'Based on what?'

She winks. 'Women's intuition. And before you ask: no, I definitely didn't plan this when I introduced the pair of you. It didn't even occur to me until I saw you together.'

'I don't see it at all.'

'Well, you wouldn't, would you? Listen, I definitely don't want to spark another row with you, Luke. But know this, you're quite a catch: tall and handsome, in good shape, with those piercing eyes that run in our family. Plus you're a successful business owner with no personal ties – and you're not half as grumpy as you used to be, which is a huge bonus.'

Now it's my turn to roll my eyes.

Later that night, nursing a beer at home in front of the TV news, my mind wanders into the past. I find myself thinking about Helen, my ex-wife. She's not a topic I often dwell on nowadays, but after what Meg said about Nora and the lack of romance in my life, it's no surprise I've ended up here. It's an obvious mental journey, since Helen leaving me was what brought me to my current situation.

She broke me at a time when I was already in bits, grinding down what was left of me into specks of dust. And there's been zero romance since. It's not something I've wanted to open myself up to again, knowing the terrible pain it can lead to. So, other than a few meaningless, functional one-night stands, I've steered clear.

If Helen ever truly loved me, I don't understand how she could have left me when she did, when the death of my parents was still so raw. She claimed she'd already waited longer to break the news than she wanted to, because of that. But where's the comfort in knowing she was longing for another man while I was sinking in a pit of grief? Was she thinking of him every time she consoled me? I can only assume the affection she gave me then was born out of guilt.

There was no hint of any such tenderness when, a fortnight before Christmas that fateful year, she picked her moment to break the bombshell news.

'Grub's up,' I called, entering the kitchen with the fish and chips I'd picked up from the chippy around the corner on my way home from work. I placed the white plastic bag on the table and, after quickly digging out placemats, cutlery, plates and ketchup, I removed the hot, paper-wrapped contents. 'Are you coming or what?' I called. 'It's getting cold.'

When Helen finally appeared, a minute or so later, I remember she looked pale. 'Everything all right?' I asked. 'You're not coming down with something, are you? You look a bit peaky.'

'I'm fine,' she replied, monotone.

'How was your day?'

'Fine. Yours?'

'Not too bad,' I replied, blissfully unaware that this was about to change.

I must have been about halfway through my meal when, noticing that Helen had barely touched hers, I asked again if she was okay.

'I need to talk to you,' she said, voice wavering.

I ought to have guessed that something bad was about to happen, but I was oblivious. Naively, up until that moment, I hadn't considered my marriage a matter I had to worry about.

'Go for it,' I said, in between mouthfuls of my takeaway.

She took a slow, deep breath before speaking. And then came the words that hit me like poisoned arrows puncturing my chest. 'I've met someone else.'

'What?' I replied after almost choking on a chunk of battered cod. 'Is this some kind of joke?'

I'm not sure why I said that. It was a kneejerk response, I suppose. Why on earth would she have made a joke about something so serious?

'No,' she said. 'I've been trying to tell you about this for a while, Luke, but there's never been a right time. After what you've been through, losing your parents, I didn't want to—'

'Have you slept with him?'

She looked down at the floor as she nodded that she had, permanently shattering a piece of my soul. 'I, um, it's not . . .' She sighed. 'I think I'm in love with him.'

A voice started screaming inside my head. I pushed away my unfinished plate of food, knowing on the spot that I'd never again enjoy fish and chips. I closed my eyes for a few seconds to try to calm myself down. It didn't work, but my self-defence systems – employed so frequently since my parents' deaths – were already in play, closing down any outward signs of my inner turmoil.

'So you're saying you don't love me any more?' I asked, my voice taking on a dispassionate, android-like quality as I feigned indifference.

'I do love you, Luke,' she said, a solitary tear rolling down her left cheek. 'That's why I waited as long as I could, so I could help you through your grief. But – this is really hard to say – I'm not *in love* with you any more.'

'I see.'

With an audible gulp, she added: 'I'm sorry, but I'm leaving you. My bags are packed. I'm moving out tonight.'

And with that, my marriage was over, before I even

knew it was in trouble, and I was hurtling down a deep, dark chute towards despair.

Looking back, right to the start, it's hard not to believe Helen once loved me as much as I loved her. I remember the way she used to look at me in the early days, like I was all she ever wanted or needed. She sobbed happy tears on our wedding day. I honestly thought we'd grow old together. Clearly, I was wrong. I hadn't factored in the possibility of her finding someone else – someone better than me. She didn't say that last bit specifically, but it didn't take a genius to work out she was thinking it. Otherwise why would she have chosen him over me?

An hour or so after breaking the news, she was gone. First to a local friend's place for a couple of nights, and then to him – her new man, my surprise nemesis – leaving me to have the worst festive period ever. While she presumably enjoyed turkey and all the trimmings at his place, I spent it drinking myself into oblivion, sobbing, and smashing up the expensive crystal glasses I'd bought her as a Christmas present.

Meg was away on a long trip to visit her parents in New Zealand at the time, which was incredibly tough, because I could have really done with her support. I felt utterly bereft, so worthless, miserable and alone at that point, it was a struggle to keep on going. In my darkest moments, which were thankfully fleeting, some truly scary thoughts went through my mind.

Two things kept me going: Alfred and the memory of my parents. The latter was important, because although the pain of losing Mum and Dad was still red raw, I knew what they'd want more than anything would be for me to pull through this. They'd wish for me to move forward and make the most of my life, like they no longer could, having had their own lives so cruelly ripped from them ahead of time.

As for Alfred, well, he was there for me, day and night. I hugged him more than ever before and kept him close, talking to him incessantly, as if he could understand my problems. As I negotiated those dark moments of the soul, I also reminded myself of my responsibility to look after him. He'd always been more my cat – my boy – than Helen's. That was presumably why she hadn't even suggested taking him with her, thank goodness. Honestly, if she'd tried, after everything else, I think I'd have totally lost it with her.

By the time Helen made contact to let me know she was pregnant with the new guy's baby, a few months after she'd run into his arms, I'd encased my heart in an icy coat of armour. I still felt the force of the blow, though, especially when she admitted it was planned.

She'd always said she hadn't wanted kids when we were together. It turned out she just hadn't wanted them with me.

They have two little ones now: a boy called Euan and a girl called Gwen.

How perfect.

I've heard people say the signs are always there when your partner is having an affair, but honestly, I was clueless. I still can't spot them looking back. Mind you, my mind was elsewhere for months prior to Helen leaving me. I can't remember how I spent vast swathes of that time after Mum and Dad's funeral.

I was walking around in a daze, on autopilot, while my brain battled desperately to come to terms with how both of my parents could really be gone.

Forever.

So what about this Prince Charming who swept Helen off her feet?

He's no one special, apart from to her. His name's Adrian and he's a university lecturer in Edinburgh, where they both now live. Physics is his subject, apparently. I've only met him very briefly a couple of times. He seems incredibly dull to me, but I was never going to like the bloke who stole my wife.

They went to secondary school together, going out for a year or so towards the end of their time there. They fell out of touch and then the magic of bloody social media brought them back together.

Helen had been chatting with him online for a few months – and then they secretly met up while he was attending a work conference in Manchester. I imagine several further clandestine meetings took place before she made the decision to leave me for him, although I never asked for further details. I couldn't see the point: knowing the ins and outs of the deception would have only added to my misery.

For the same reason, I never asked her to clarify how and why she thought she'd fallen out of love with me. Perhaps I should have. Everything had seemed fine to me when evidently it wasn't. It might have been useful information in a self-knowledge sense. But then again, I'm not convinced the act of falling in or out of love with another person is the kind of thing one can easily explain.

Did I fight to keep her? No, not really. I didn't have the strength. Plus I knew Helen, or at least I thought I did, and in my experience she wasn't someone to change her mind once made up. Ironically, of course, that's exactly what she did do with regards to our marriage, but let's not split hairs.

When she asked for a divorce so she could marry him, I wasn't surprised. By that point I was glad of an option to cut her out of my life once and for all, so I didn't stand in the way, and once that was done, so were we. I haven't heard a peep from Helen in ages and I can't see that changing now.

It's good that she's far away in Scotland. I wouldn't want her to be nearby, as there would always be a danger of bumping into her with him or the kids – and that would only serve to reopen the wound. It's pretty much healed now, I reckon, although I do still have my maudlin moments from time to time, especially when late nights and alcohol are involved. There will always be a scar.

I think the part of me that fell in love with Helen as a hopeful, happy young man is gone forever. I truly believed she was my soulmate. Now I doubt such a thing even exists.

And yet, saying all that, if I'm totally honest and I put myself back in the head of the person I was at the start of our journey, we really were a good fit: best friends with an intense romantic and sexual attraction. At that point, we felt perfect for each other. The problem is that over a period of time, people change. And if they don't change in the same way or at the same pace, how can their connection stay the same?

As much as I resent the Helen who abandoned me when I needed her most, the same doesn't apply when I think back to our joyous early years together. Those memories remain untainted. They still make me smile.

Maybe there is hope for me to find love again one day, then. That's the positive way of looking at things, which is how I'm supposed to be thinking these days.

Not that I'm in a rush to find love. Hence why I've never got involved in online dating and so on.

I suspect Meg planting the seed that Nora might be interested in me is purely wishful thinking on my cousin's part. I mean, why would a pretty professional like Nora be interested in a balding barber? We're from different worlds. What would we have to talk about? And apart from her being out of my league looks-wise, I'm not even sure she's my type. No, it's nonsense. I don't even know why I'm wasting my time thinking about it.

'Meow.' Alfred brings me back into the moment by bounding into the room and on to my knee.

'Oh, hello. Where've you been?'

He stares at me before starting to knead my trousers with his front paws. His claws would hurt if I was wearing jogging pants or something similarly thin; fortunately I'm in jeans so don't feel it.

I press my fingers into the fur on the top of his stripy head and give him a massage in return, which gets him purring like a lawn mower.

'We don't need a woman to make our life complete, do we, mate?' I say.

He responds by circling around on my lap and then flopping down into a curled-up ball.

'I'll take that as a no.'

CHAPTER 19

'Evening, Doreen. How are you today?'

'All the better for seeing you, Liam. Are you sure you don't mind doing this for me?'

'Of course not. I wouldn't be here if I did, would I?'

'Well, it's very kind of you.'

Last time we spoke, my neighbour asked me if I knew a reliable plumber. When I asked why, she said she needed someone to redo the silicone seal around her bath, which is something I've done myself loads of times. So rather than letting her fork out for such a simple job, I told her I'd do it.

It'll only take me half an hour and, since I've got to know Doreen better of late, I've started to feel quite protective and fond of her. Weird, I know, considering how long we've been neighbours and the fact she still can't get my name right, but I'm not overanalysing it.

'What's that amazing smell?' I ask. 'Have you been baking?'

She winks. 'There's no getting anything past you, is there? It's a chocolate cake. It was my Bob's favourite. He always used to say it was the best chocolate cake in the world. I thought you might enjoy a slice or two and a nice cup of tea while you're busy.'

'Now we're talking. By the way, that film you gave me, I watched it the other night and thought it was brilliant. Thanks again for that.'

I haven't really watched it. I can't, thanks to my broken DVD player, but I figure a white lie is appropriate here, which Doreen's beaming smile confirms. 'I'm so glad you liked it,' she says.

I head to the bathroom and get to work removing the old strip of silicone from around her bath. It is in a poor state, more black than white and already coming away in places, so it doesn't take me long to tear away with the help of a sharp knife and screwdriver.

I give the area a good clean down before patting it dry with some kitchen towel. Next, trusty sealant gun in hand, I squeeze out a thin, bright white bead all the way along between the bath and the tiles, before standing back to admire my handiwork. Hmm, not bad for the first pass. I fill a couple of obvious gaps and then lay the gun aside, dipping my forefinger in the small glass pot I prepared earlier. It's filled with a fifty/fifty mix of washing-up liquid and water – a top tip passed down to me by my dad – which allows me to work the bead into a neat, consistent strip with one or two gentle smoothing motions.

A couple of minutes later, I'm done. Easy as that. It's a

185

job I've always found strangely relaxing and enjoyable; with the right technique, a professional-looking result is pretty easy to achieve.

It's up to Doreen's standards, anyway. At my request, she comes in to inspect what I've done and squeals with joy at what she sees.

'Wow. That looks so much better, Liam. And you've only been busy for a few minutes. It had been annoying me for ages like it was. I preferred to shower rather than bathe because it looked so mouldy and unhygienic. Now I can enjoy a good soak again.'

'Well, not right away,' I say. 'You need to leave it to dry for a while yet – twenty-four hours if possible; definitely at least twelve. After that, it's all yours.'

She leans over and plants a kiss on my cheek. 'I appreciate this so much. You're an absolute champ. Now come and have that tea and cake I've made for you, and you can let me know how much I owe you.'

'Oh, don't be silly. You don't owe me anything, Doreen. I had the silicone already and it's hardly taken me any time. The worst part of the job is usually removing the old seal, but that came away easily on this occasion. It's my pleasure to help. Besides, you already baked a cake for me. If it tastes half as good as it smells, I'll be more than happy with that.'

On my way out of the bathroom, I catch a glimpse of a smiling face I barely recognise as my own. 'Who are you?' I mouth silently at my reflection.

The cake is in fact every bit as delicious as I hoped. 'Goodness me,' I tell her, sitting on the floral beige fabric sofa in her lounge, which is a mirror-version of my own. 'Bob wasn't wrong when he told you how good this was. It could in fact be the best chocolate cake in the world. I can't remember ever having a better one.'

We chat for a while about various bits and bobs. Eventually, Doreen mentions having spotted the article in the *Evening News* about me and my haircuts for the homeless. She digs out her copy from under a pile of other papers and magazines on a shelf under the coffee table and shows it to me, like I might not have seen it already.

'It's very good of you to do that,' she says, 'but don't they, um . . . Aren't they a little bit, er, you know . . . whiffy? It's not like they get to wash very often, is it?'

Her question makes me smile. I love how direct and honest people can become when they get older. It's refreshing in a society where so many folks' true feelings are often hidden away behind politeness or social awkwardness.

'You must be annoyed, though,' she adds before I've had a chance to answer.

'Sorry, I don't understand,' I say. 'Annoyed about what?'

'Them getting your name wrong throughout the article,' she replies. 'They keep referring to you as Luke instead of Liam. I was thinking of phoning the paper to let them know.'

I can't help smiling at this point. 'Oh, Doreen,' I say, taking her delicate little hand in mine. 'I hate to break it to you this way, but my name *is* Luke. I'm not sure where you got Liam from. You used it so often, I got to the point where I didn't know how to tell you any more.'

She gasps, holding her other hand up to her mouth. 'No! Really? How embarrassing.' Her cheeks flush and then she starts to chuckle. 'Dear me. What must you think of me, Luke? Oh, that sounds strange. You don't look like a Luke to me after all this time. I'm going to have to keep saying it: Luke, Luke, Luke. So where did I get Liam from?'

I shrug. 'Don't worry about it, honestly. I always found it funny.'

She cuts another fat slice of chocolate cake and plonks it on my plate before I can resist. 'It's the least I can do,' she says. 'More tea?'

'You're spoiling me, Doreen, but go on then. I'll need something to wash down all this delicious cake, won't I?' I wink. 'It's as well I'm not watching my figure at the moment.'

As I'm eating some more cake, she nearly makes me choke on it with a particularly blunt serving of directness. 'I was wrong about more than your name, wasn't I? I used to think you were an arrogant misery guts who considered yourself better than the rest of us. But now I can see that's not true at all. You're a teddy bear beneath that brash exterior. I don't know what changed to bring out your softer, kinder side, but it's a huge improvement.'

Cackling, she adds: 'Your face! It's true, though. So maybe it's fitting that I got your name wrong until now. I prefer Luke over Liam one hundred per cent.'

At work the next day, my usually chatty regular Connor shows up, although I can tell something is wrong as soon he enters the barbershop.

He gives me a weak nod and, without saying anything, takes a seat to wait his turn behind a couple of other guys who arrived before him.

Puzzled, as he tends to greet me by name and usually has something to say for himself straight off the bat, I turn away from the wispy blond hair of the heavy smoker currently in the hot seat, and address him directly. 'Morning, Connor. How are you today?'

'It's afternoon now,' he says in barely more than a whisper. 'Five past twelve.'

This is a typical Connor comment, but it's delivered with none of the regular uptight energy and focus. Typically, he reminds me of a coiled spring, but today he's behaving more like a toy robot whose batteries are about to die.

He's unshaven for the first time in memory and, when he undoes his coat, I'm surprised to see that his usual sky-blue shirt is covered in creases rather than neatly pressed.

'Everything all right?' I ask him.

He shuffles in his seat before replying. 'I just need a haircut.'

I don't press him any further for the time being. I assume, based on the countless occasions he's been in previously, that he'll start talking soon enough.

'What are we doing today, Connor?' I ask when his turn in the chair comes around, fixing the gown in place over him.

'Whatever you think's best,' he replies with zero enthusiasm.

'Not too short on top, like last time?'

'Fine.'

Wow. Monosyllabic answers like this aren't what I've come to expect from Connor at all. Something most certainly is going on. I think back to our last conversation and recall him mentioning that his mother was ill. I hope she's not taken a turn for the worse.

I start work in silence, hoping he might say something unprompted. But when that doesn't happen, I come out with it. 'How's your mum getting on, Connor? I remember you said she had the flu last time you were in.'

He looks straight ahead into the mirror, face reddening and eyes steely. 'I don't want to talk about that.'

'Okay,' I reply. 'No problem. Sorry, I didn't mean to intrude.'

Is he keeping quiet because of the other man who walked in after him, currently glued to his smartphone? Possibly, but that's never stopped Connor from chatting before. I doubt that guy's even listening. Whatever he's looking at on his mobile appears to have his undivided attention.

Could Connor's mum have been taken into hospital? Flu can be nasty, especially for the elderly and those with underlying health issues. I've no idea of her age – I don't even know her name – but based on various things he's told me, I've always got the impression she's older rather than younger and probably had him late. As for his father, I've no idea. He's never mentioned him to me, so I assume he's not on the scene, for whatever reason.

Who have I become? In days gone by I'd have relished the peace and quiet, instead of the usual chitter-chatter, while cutting Connor's hair. Now I'm behaving like his counsellor. I can't help myself.

I try to coax him out of his shell another way, by talking about something else. 'Last time you were in, do you remember we spoke about a homeless man I'd seen reading a book?'

Connor nods but still doesn't look at me, not even via our reflections in the mirror.

'Something you said to me that day struck a chord. You asked when I thought this man would have last had a haircut. You said you wouldn't feel human without being able to get one. Does that ring a bell?'

'Of course,' he replies. 'I have an excellent memory. It's very unusual for me to forget things.' This sounds more like the Connor I know, although his words are still lacking their usual conviction, delivered in an uncharacteristic mumble.

'Well, it inspired me, that comment of yours, particularly the bit about not feeling human. It gave me the idea to start running free haircut sessions for the homeless – to help them to feel more human; to give them a reminder of normality and their old lives before living on the streets. I held the second session earlier this week, on Monday, and it proved really popular.'

Connor nods a few times as I talk about this, going on to explain about the articles in the *Evening News* and *Big Issue North*, although he doesn't say much.

'So, anyway,' I conclude. 'Thanks for giving me the idea.'

'You're welcome,' he says in a quiet voice. I notice his

191

eyes silently scanning the long counter that runs along the bottom of the mirror in front of us, upon which rest the various tools of my trade. 'I assume you thoroughly clean everything afterwards.'

'Absolutely,' I reply. 'You've nothing whatsoever to worry about there, Connor. Trust me.'

'Good.'

To my dismay, he falls silent again after this, rather than moving on to talk about his mother. I'm out of ideas and, before I know it, I'm showing him the back of his hair with the hand mirror. 'How's that looking?'

'Fine, thank you.'

'What about the top? Short enough or a little more off?'

I ready the scissors, expecting him to say something's not quite right, but he simply nods and repeats that it's fine.

As he's paying, I ask him again in a low voice if everything is all right. 'You don't seem yourself, Connor. What's going on?'

He closes his eyes for a long moment and exhales through his mouth. Then he looks me in the eye and says, with a quiver of emotion in his voice: 'Mother died. There were complications with the flu. She developed severe pneumonia. So now you know. Please don't ask me about this again, Luke.' He pauses to take another breath. 'I find it very difficult to discuss.'

'Oh, Connor. I'm so sorry. I had no idea. You must be—'

'I have to go now. Thank you for the haircut. Goodbye.'

Before I have a chance to say anything else, he turns and heads for the door.

'You know where I am if you need anything,' I call after him. 'Anything at all.'

He doesn't respond. I'm tempted to run after him and say something else. Tell him I know what he's going through, having lost both parents myself.

I stay put, though, since that's clearly not what he wants right now.

Poor, poor Connor.

He has my utmost sympathy.

From what I gather, his mother was his world, outside of work. I hope there are other family members and friends out there to support him; to help him through this.

I wish he could have confided more in me and properly opened up about it. But why would he? He might have been coming here for a long time, but I'm only his barber. Plus, for years I've let him talk at me without ever showing any real interest in his life, too wrapped up in my own issues and problems. Too busy being angry at the world.

I'd like to contact him at home or work to follow up this conversation. But the cold hard facts are that, despite having cut his hair for ages, I don't know his home address or the name of the company he works for. I only know vague details. Come to think of it, I'm not even sure of his surname. I have a feeling it's something Irish-sounding; I'm sure he said that's where his mum came from originally. But anything more than that would be guesswork.

The guy next in line for a cut is growing impatient.

He's put his phone down and is looking at me expectantly, so I gesture for him to step into my chair and I get on with my job.

I feel truly awful for Connor, though, and that stays with me for the rest of the day.

CHAPTER 20

'Okay, I'm sitting down. What is it? Please tell me. Are my mum and dad all right?'

'I, er . . .' The faceless, heavily accented voice paused, like he was searching for the right words. I'd already forgotten his name, although he'd said it down the phone-line a moment ago. My mind, consumed by panic and fear, didn't have space for such things. 'I am afraid it is very bad news, Mr Craven.'

My heart was in my mouth as he stopped again.

Just say it, I wanted to scream. But I could no longer move, never mind speak. I was rigid with terror.

'Your parents . . .' He repeated their names for some reason, as if I might suddenly shout that he'd got the wrong person and they weren't my mother and father after all. If only.

And then, finally, he said it – the awful, unimaginable truth – and my coffee cup tumbled, exploded on the floor, as my world teetered on its axis.

'No! That can't be true. I don't accept it. You must be mistaken. Can you check? They can't both be—'

'I am so very sorry, Mr Craven, but there is no doubt.'

'Is there someone else I can speak to? I don't even know who you are. How do I know this isn't some kind of—'

'I can pass you to my superior, should you wish,' he enunciated slowly, calmly. 'However, she will only tell you the same thing. Are you alone? Is there a person you can call?'

I wasn't listening to him any more. My mind was reeling, desperately trying to comprehend the impossible nightmare that had somehow smashed through into real life.

'How? How the hell? How could this have happened? Please!'

Mum and Dad were keen skiers. The three of us went on a couple of skiing holidays when I was in my teens. As the youngster of the family, I was probably the one people might have expected to develop a passion for winter sports. But it went the other way: I wasn't especially keen, whereas my parents got hooked.

As their passion for the slopes grew, they started going on annual skiing holidays, visiting numerous popular resorts in France, Italy, Austria and Switzerland. They often tried to tempt me along, despite knowing it wasn't my bag, arguing that I might view things differently as an adult than I did as a teenager and, if not, I could just enjoy the après-ski.

On the last occasion they went, Dad was on the cusp of turning sixty. The pair of them had really tried to convince Helen and me to join them in their beloved Alps as a one-off to mark the special occasion. However, neither of us had been keen, so we'd politely declined.

It's a decision I've regretted ever since, because neither of them returned alive from that trip. They were both killed in an avalanche while skiing off-piste – and to this day, I've never stopped questioning whether the same thing would have happened if we'd joined them.

According to investigators, they'd set off on the morning of the accident with a Danish couple they'd met at the resort. Not one of the four survived. I'll never know for sure, but I suspect it was this other couple who'd convinced Mum and Dad to venture on that particular outing. Would they have still met these holiday friends if Helen and I had been there too? And even if they had, would they have joined them on such a treacherous, unprepared route? I like to think I would have talked them out of it, advising them to stick to an official resort slope for their own safety. I also doubt they'd have ventured too far from base, knowing we'd left our comfort zone to join them on the holiday. It's far more likely they'd have invested their time in making sure we were having fun, coaching us and so on. That's the kind of people my parents were. They always put others – especially me – before themselves.

Okay, I'll admit to thinking and occasionally saying otherwise while on the roller coaster of emotions I experienced in the aftermath of their deaths. Anger featured quite heavily at the start. I felt waves of intense fury at them for taking their lives into their own hands like they did, putting their own thrill-seeking ahead of their responsibilities as parents.

I later accepted that, by thinking in such a way, I was the one being selfish – not them. I was a fully grown man by that point, with a wife and a life of my own. They were perfectly within their rights to do whatever they wanted with their time on holiday.

Would they have taken a similar risk when I was still a child, reliant on their care? I doubt that very much. They were amazing parents, always putting me first as I grew up. And they never judged me for the many mistakes I made on their watch, like that night they picked me up from A&E in Leeds; or when I was brought home by a policeman at the age of ten for climbing into a nearby building site for the thrill of it.

Realistically, I doubt they had any idea of the danger they were putting themselves in when they set off that day. They would probably have judged it a slight calculated risk at most, especially in light of how experienced they were at skiing.

In the absence of survivors, no one will ever know exactly what happened out there when they lost their lives. However, if the avalanche was in any way caused by human error – stupidity or recklessness, for instance – I'd bet my bottom dollar it was nothing whatsoever to do with either Mum or Dad.

I'm thinking about all of this as I make myself a homemade cheeseburger, salad and chips for my tea. Not the healthiest option, I know, but it'll be damn tasty, that's for sure.

It's hearing about the death of Connor's mother earlier today that's sparked these memories. I can't stop thinking about it, wondering how he's coping and wishing I could have offered more in the way of support.

Losing Mum and Dad is hands down the worst thing that's ever happened to me. Being dumped by my wife less than a year later was bloody heartbreaking too, especially on top of my grief. But the nauseating, suffocating pain of losing both parents at once, without warning . . . words don't even come close.

Maybe my grief was intensified by the fact I was an only child with no siblings to share the burden. I'd also remained in regular contact with my parents as an adult, relying on them both as mentors and my closest confidants outside my marriage.

It was Mum and Dad I desperately wanted to turn to when Helen left me, since up until their deaths, they were the ones who'd always been in my corner when things went wrong in my life.

The suddenness with which they were gone, with no chance to say goodbye, was one of the hardest aspects of the situation. I spent so long afterwards regretting that I hadn't offered to see them off at the airport, for example, or even popped around to their house on the night before they left. That way we could at least have had a few more precious moments together.

I spent ages overanalysing the last conversation we'd had – over the phone – wishing I'd used that opportunity to tell them how much I loved them and to be safe. Instead, I'd mainly wittered on about an insignificant issue I'd been having at the time with the boiler at home playing up.

The legal, logistical and financial issues of them dying abroad didn't make things any easier. Nor did the press attention I mentioned previously. But nothing compared to the agony of actually losing them – of knowing I'd never get the chance to talk to or see either of them ever again.

They were relatively young too and fighting fit: Dad a couple of weeks shy of turning sixty and Mum only fifty-four. I felt like they still had years left. I hadn't even started to consider a time when they wouldn't be around any longer.

My grief was all-consuming. My heart literally ached in my chest and, for a long time, I found I could barely think of anything other than how much I missed them. Nothing else seemed to matter. Hence, I guess, why I didn't notice the foundations of my marriage crumbling beneath me.

The irony is that soon before Helen told me she didn't love me any more and wanted to leave me, I'd been considering talking to her about the possibility of having a child together. It was something we'd agreed neither of us wanted prior to getting married. But having lost both parents, I felt a gradual shift in my viewpoint. My family, which had been small anyway, had been decimated by this one tragedy – and I slowly realised I wanted to do something about that before it was too late.

Unfortunately, Helen was already busy plotting her future elsewhere. My family was destined to shrink again; I just didn't know it yet.

I've come to terms with all of that now. I'm okay with not rebuilding myself a new family. I think I am, anyway. I don't have much choice, do I?

After Helen had gone, I consoled myself with the fact that at least I'd never have to feel the pain of losing anyone so close to me again.

Imagine if things had been different; if Helen hadn't left and we'd had a child or even children together. What if they'd fallen seriously ill or got into an accident and died? How could I have coped with that kind of torment again? Surely it would have ripped me apart and finished me off for good.

As I carry my food over to the couch on a tray, I picture the Iris from my dreams frowning at this last thought and shaking her head in disapproval.

'That's no way for a positive person to think now, is it?' I imagine her saying to me. 'Life is meaningless if you hide from its many possibilities because you're afraid of getting hurt.'

CHAPTER 21

Nora calls at the barbershop unannounced that Friday. She taps on the window as I'm sweeping up after closing time. It's been really busy today – most of the week, come to think of it – and I'm longing to get a cold beer down my throat.

'Hello,' I say, letting her inside. 'This is, um, unexpected. How's it going?'

'Good, thanks.' She smiles. 'I have some news for you and, as I was in the neighbourhood, I thought I may as well deliver it in person.'

'That sounds intriguing. Grab a seat. I need to finish cleaning up, if you don't mind, but I can talk while I go.'

She tells me how she pitched my story to *The Sunday Times Magazine* and, although she wasn't sure whether it would be their kind of thing or not, they turned out to be really keen on it. 'They want to run it the Sunday after next,' she says.

'That's brilliant,' I reply, making a mental note to give Rita and family a heads-up this time.

'It is, but there's one small hitch.'

'What's that?'

'They're not entirely happy with the photos I have so far.'

'Why not? What's wrong with them?'

She purses her lips. 'The nationals can be quite, er, specific about what they want when it comes to these things. Basically, they'd like some pictures of you actually cutting the hair of a homeless person.'

'You got some shots like that on your phone, didn't you?'

'I'm a writer. Photography isn't my forte, Luke, and phone pictures are never likely to be as good as photos taken with a professional camera. Plus I think they'd like some images that haven't been used anywhere else.' She shrugs, explaining they liked the shots Rudy, the photographer who came here previously, had taken. But as those had been of me alone in the barbershop, they'd requested that he take some more.

'So what were you thinking?' I ask. 'Because the next session isn't until a week on Monday, which will be too late.'

'Exactly. I, um, was hoping we might be able to set something up beforehand. Tomorrow, maybe?' She flashes me a doe-eyed look. 'Do you think one of the guys who came to the session earlier this week might be up for popping back to get involved? What about the man you gave that paperback to? It seemed like you already knew each other.'

'Tommy? I wouldn't say we're close or anything. That was literally the second time we met, but yeah, we'd had a chat previously. We'd spoken about the book he was reading at the time, which was why I'd dug out that other one for him. He might be up for getting involved, I suppose, if I can track him down. Leave it with me.'

'Perfect. Could I give you a call tomorrow morning?'

'Fine.'

When Nora first showed up, I was tempted to ask her if she fancied joining me for that cold drink I've been looking forward to all afternoon.

A naive part of me must have swallowed Meg's nonsense about her liking me and, in a state of delusion, let myself believe that was why she'd dropped by. Now I know the real reason for her visit, all I can think about is whether I'll be able to find Tommy and persuade him to help. Hopefully he'll remember me this time – assuming I can locate him.

As I'm letting Nora back out, I ask: 'What if Tommy's up for it but doesn't want to be identified?'

She screws up her face, looking pensive, before replying: 'I don't think that would be a major problem. I'm sure Rudy would be able to take the photo so you can only see the back of his head or something. Yeah?'

I nod.

'Okay, speak tomorrow. Have a great night.'

It's tempting to say my night would have been better if she'd not showed up, sending me on a potential wild goose chase. I don't, of course. I feel like I owe her for getting me the publicity I needed and helping out here the other day. It would have been nice if she'd offered to give me a hand to find Tommy, mind; then again, I could have asked for her help and I chose not to.

Once I'm done locking up, I head for the supermarket where I first met Tommy. I'm not too hopeful of finding him, based on previous experience, and – sure enough – he's not there. No one is camped outside the store today, which surprises me, although when I walk along the road a little further and turn a corner, I almost trip over a woman in a grimy pink bodywarmer. She's sitting on a pile of cardboard boxes with a tartan blanket over her lap and a dog at her side.

'Could you spare any change?' she asks in a hoarse, smoker's voice, clearing her throat before flashing me a brief weary smile.

'Um, sure.' I root through my pockets and dig out a few coins, which I hand to her. 'You look like you could do with a hot drink,' I say.

'Thanks, love.'

I turn to her dog, a black and white Staffie, who looks up at me with sad, kind eyes and then opens his mouth so his long pink tongue flops out and he appears to be smiling.

This leads me to reach into my pocket again and hand over a couple more pounds, adding: 'Treat this one to something nice too, yeah? He looks like a great companion.'

The woman thanks me again and reaches over to tickle her pet under the chin. 'Did you hear that, Milo? This nice man thinks you deserve a treat. I reckon he's right.' Looking back at me, she adds: 'Milo's my watchdog. He's always got my back. He knows straight away if someone's to be trusted or not, and he likes you, right enough.'

I smile. 'That's nice to hear. I'm looking for a guy called Tommy, by the way. I don't suppose you know him, do you?' I describe him as best I can, both before and after his recent haircut, making sure to mention the fact he likes to read.

'Yes, I know Tommy,' she says. 'You're the one who's been cutting folks' hair, are you?'

'That's right,' I say, offering her a handshake, which she accepts. 'I'm Luke, and you are?'

'Maggie.'

I tell her she's most welcome to come along to the next free cutting session, giving her the details, and she advises me to try near the bus station, where she thinks I might find Tommy.

'Don't bank on him being too chatty,' she adds, miming someone smoking. I don't understand this comment; rather than querying it, though, I nod and thank her for helping me.

When I eventually find Tommy, after circling around the bus station a couple of times, I understand what Maggie meant. The reason I didn't spot him straight away was because I was expecting to find him sitting on the ground reading near a shop or a cashpoint, perhaps. The last thing I anticipated was for him to be standing frozen in the middle of an alleyway like a zombified statue.

I've seen people in this state before, so I know straight away what's going on. He must have taken spice: the former legal high that's caused a lot of problems across the city centre, not least among the homeless.

I've read numerous articles about it in the papers and online. Also known as 'fake weed' or 'synthetic marijuana', it's usually smoked in rolling paper, like cannabis, but is far more potent and dangerous. Essentially, it's a cheap mix of nasty, lab-made chemicals sprayed on to herbs to give the appearance of being natural when it's actually anything but.

It's common to see those who've taken it crashed out on benches or pavements, dead to the world, or – even scarier, like now – rooted to the spot while still standing, in a zombie-like catatonic state.

I've never tried speaking to anyone I've encountered in that condition before, and I'm sad to say there have been plenty. I've always shuffled past, bemused – one of the herd – assuming someone else will deal with them. How can I do that now, though? I know this guy, unlike the various others I've seen. Days ago, I was cutting his hair and chatting to him; giving him one of my old paperbacks.

Previously, although I feel bad admitting it, I suppose I tended to think of the people who took spice as being either desperate or foolish. And yet I wouldn't consider Tommy either of those things, based on my limited experience of him. You could argue that no one would live on the streets in the first place unless they were desperate. But equally Tommy has never come across as desperate to me. Until this moment, I thought he carried himself with an impressive level of self-respect.

But there's no dignity in what I see in front of me now. It's horrific. Every bone in my body is urging me to turn and run, but still I can't bring myself to leave. I have to do something. I have to try to help him.

'Tommy,' I say, gingerly walking up close. 'Are you all right? Do you remember me? It's Luke. I cut your hair the other day.'

I'm standing right in front of him, but I get no response other than a guttural groan, which may or may not be anything to do with my presence. His eyes are unfocused and glazed over. It's freaky as hell. My pulse is racing.

I click my fingers right in front of his face several times, but it makes no difference. He's away with the fairies. It's like his mind's gone somewhere else and his body's been left behind. What's so disconcerting, though, is the way he's still standing up, staggering and twitching. Part of me fears he could suddenly turn violent and attack me, although that's probably down to watching too many zombie movies.

Standing back a couple of metres, I pull my phone out of my pocket, ready to call 999, when – to my surprise and considerable relief – an ambulance pulls up at the end of the alley.

'Was it you that called us?' a young male paramedic asks me after stepping out of the vehicle and walking over in his yellow hi-vis jacket, radio attached to the breast.

'No, I've just got here,' I say. 'I was about to phone for help, but someone obviously beat me to it. He's in a right mess. I can't get him to respond.'

'He'll have taken spice,' the paramedic says. 'He'll be like that until the drug wears off. Do you know him?'

I'm not quite sure what goes through my head at this point, but rather than telling the truth, I lie. 'No, I was, um, passing by and saw him like this.'

'Okay, well, don't worry about it. You can leave him to us. We'll check him over.'

'Is he going to be all right?' I ask.

The paramedic frowns. 'It's nasty stuff, but he's in safe hands now. It's nothing we haven't dealt with lots of times before.'

Back at the flat later that night, Alfred curled up on my knee in front of the TV, I'm beating myself up about the way I disowned Tommy. What was I thinking? Why didn't I tell the paramedic his name and admit that I knew him?

I'm really not sure why I reacted in such a strange way. I guess I panicked, thinking I might get drawn into that whole mess. They might have wanted to leave him in my care, for instance, once he came to. And what would I have done then: brought him back here? No way. Not after seeing him in that horrendous state. Not knowing he's into taking spice. I'm not stupid. Welcoming a destitute druggie into my home would be like inviting them to steal my stuff.

I may have cut Tommy's hair, had a chat with him and given him a book; that doesn't make him my responsibility. And yet I still can't help feeling bad about disowning him. I wonder if he'll have any recollection of that. Unlikely, considering the condition he was in. He didn't seem remotely conscious, but who knows? I haven't got a clue what it's like to be on spice – and I never want to find out.

Regardless of whether Tommy remembers or not, I'm ashamed of my actions. Iris would never have walked away like I did. Not a chance.

CHAPTER 22

Nora phones me the next morning, as promised. I'm at the barbershop when I take the call and I have to be brief, as several people are already waiting in line. Earlier in the week, I put the recent rise in customers down to coincidence, but now I'm starting to believe it's because of the press attention. Several people have even mentioned the free cuts for the homeless, mainly to say that they approve.

'Bad news, I'm afraid,' I tell Nora.

'You didn't manage to find that guy?'

'No luck.'

'Is there anyone else you can think of who might get involved?' she asks.

'Sorry, there's not. I'm swamped here today too, so I doubt I'll have time to look. I wish I could be more helpful, but—'

'No, no,' Nora replies. 'Don't worry. I'll see if I can rustle someone up instead. Rudy's not free today, anyway,

211

as it turns out, but he could do tomorrow at a push. Would that work for you?'

I'm tempted to say no, on the grounds it's my one day off. However, I don't have the heart to let her down, particularly after my disappointing behaviour yesterday, which I feel I need to make up for.

'I don't usually open up on Sundays, but as long as it's not going to take too much time, I'm sure we can work something out.'

Nora hesitates, like she's considering suggesting to leave it until next week, but then she says: 'Thanks so much. That would be great, if you don't mind. No, it won't take long at all. I'll make sure we keep it as brief as possible.'

She calls me again early that evening to say she's got someone lined up to help, so I agree to meet her and the others at the barbershop at midday tomorrow.

They're already waiting for me when I arrive.

'Sorry, am I late?' I say, looking at my watch to see it's only a couple of minutes past twelve.

'No, no. Not really,' Nora says. 'We were early, to be honest. This is Ivan, by the way. Ivan, Luke.'

I shake hands with the man she brought along with her – someone I don't recall meeting before – who's wearing a *Big Issue* hi-vis vest and ID card.

Nora must have got in touch with him via her contacts at the weekly magazine. Clever thinking on her part.

'And you remember Rudy, right?' she adds, gesturing towards the photographer.

'Of course.' I smile and shake his hand too.

The three of them have been for breakfast at a nearby café, I hear. I'm guessing this was part of the deal she made to get Ivan along – Rudy too, perhaps.

Ivan's also in need of a haircut, which I soon find myself agreeing to throw in while Rudy snaps various pictures of us both.

'I heard about you doing this,' Ivan says to me, as I'm busy giving him the skin fade he's requested, despite my concerns that he might find it nippy out on the streets. 'I thought about coming along on Monday, but something came up. How did it go?'

'Really well, thanks.'

'It's a nice idea. I'll spread the word.'

'Cheers.'

Once I'm done with the haircut, Rudy asks if we can do a couple of shots outside too, saying he'd like to try incorporating some of the Northern Quarter street art as a nice backdrop.

'Really?' I say. 'But I don't do any cutting outside.'

'That doesn't matter,' Nora chips in. 'No one's saying you do. It would just be for effect. It's a good idea: a way to convey that you're helping people who live on the streets. It brings the two things together in a nice visual way.'

It does kind of make sense when she puts it like that, so I agree. We get a few funny looks from passers-by but not as many as you might expect. This is the Northern Quarter, after all.

We're finally done by 1.10 p.m., which isn't bad. Rudy has to rush off and Ivan – who's clearly chuffed with his new haircut, as he keeps looking at himself in the mirror – is keen to get to his patch to sell some magazines. Nora and I are left alone and, before I have time to overthink it, I ask her if she fancies grabbing a quick coffee together.

She looks at me with raised eyebrows. 'Oh, right. I thought you were pushed for time.'

'This didn't take as long as I expected, to be honest. But no pressure. I won't be offended if you have to get off somewhere else.'

'Um, yeah, okay. Sure. Why not? Where did you have in mind?'

Awkwardly, my brain freezes and I can't immediately think of anywhere, despite the fact I work and spend so much time around here.

'I, er, don't mind,' I say, feeling stupid. 'Is there a place nearby that you particularly like?'

She throws me a blank look. 'Not really.'

Finally, my brain kicks into gear. 'I'll tell you what, I know a little place around the corner that has brownies to die for. I mean, they have other cakes too, obviously, which are probably also really nice. And drinks: coffee, tea and so on.' Realising I'm rambling, I rein myself in before she starts to think I'm a total idiot. 'Sound good?'

Nora chuckles. 'Perfect. You had me at the brownies, to be honest.'

I grin. 'Excellent.'

As we're walking to the café, I panic it might be closed, seeing as it's Sunday. Most places we pass are open, though, so I keep my fingers crossed and luck turns out to be on my side.

214

'Here we are,' I say, like there was never any doubt. There's even a spare table in the window, which I grab, and I pass Nora a menu.

Without conferring, we both order a flat white and a brownie from the waiter, who's freckly with long ginger hair, a matching bushy beard and large black-rimmed specs.

'Jinx,' we both say at the same time before erupting into a fit of giggles.

'No brownies today, I'm afraid,' the waiter says in a deep, deadpan voice.

'What?' Nora says in mock outrage. 'This is a disaster. I only agreed to come here to sample one of the legendary brownies.'

Beardy is no fun at all and doesn't even acknowledge this comment. He simply asks: 'Anything I can get you instead?'

'What would you recommend? You look like a man knowledgeable about his sweet treats.' Nora winks at me when he's not looking in her direction.

'That's really a matter of personal preference,' Beardy replies. 'Everything we have is detailed on the menu. Shall I give you a few more minutes?'

'No, I'll tell you what,' I say to him. 'Surprise us.'

'Sorry?' He peers down his nose at me like I've said the most ridiculous thing in the world.

I smile in a slightly exaggerated manner, careful not to push it too far. 'You pick something for us that you think we might like, bearing in mind the fact we both love brownies.'

'Chocolate cake?' he asks with a sigh.

Nora rolls her eyes. 'You've ruined the surprise now. I'm sure that'll be fine, though. Luke?'

'Fine.'

Beardy walks off without saying another word.

'He's a bundle of laughs,' Nora says. 'I thought we'd best not push him too far. Otherwise he might spit in our food.'

'I know. He wasn't here last time I came. I wouldn't have suggested it if he was. Not exactly service with a smile, is it?'

We have a good chat. The conversation flows easily and we cover various subjects, from how I got into being a barber after quitting uni to a bad date Nora went on the other day, which ended soon after the man she met asked her if she was open to water sports in the bedroom.

I clench my teeth. 'Really? That's when you, um—'

'Urinate on each other,' she says, grimacing as she finishes the sentence for me, saving my blushes. 'He seemed relatively normal when I was chatting to him beforehand, but – honestly – it's a minefield. I had to text a friend to call me and pretend there was a family emergency so I could get out of there.'

'You met him through a dating website, app, whatever?'

She nods, squinting at me across the table and smirking. 'Are you judging me right now?'

I hold up my hands. 'No, no. Not at all. That's how most people meet these days, right? It's just never been my thing. Call me old-fashioned—'

'You are quite old-fashioned, come to think of it. What age are you again?'

'Charming,' I reply. 'Thirty-nine.'

'Ooh, nearly forty. It's all downhill from there.'

'Thanks for that. How old are you, then?'

'Guess,' she replies, to my dismay.

Erring on the side of caution, aiming to flatter rather than offend, I say twenty-seven.

'Yeah, right,' she replies, grinning. 'Try thirty-three. When's the big day, anyway?'

'Not until October. I've plenty of time left in my thirties.'

'If you say so,' she says with a wink. 'Old man.'

'Wow.' I shake my head, narrowing my eyes, and pretend to be offended. 'That's a low blow, playing the age card. Next you'll be calling me a slaphead.'

Nora snorts with laughter at my comment, holding her hand to her mouth after doing so and turning pink. This sets me off and when Beardy walks past, frowning, we both end up having a full-on giggling fit.

We've almost recovered when Nora nudges me and points out of the window. 'Hey, isn't that the bloke you were trying to track down for the photo? The book guy. Sorry, I can't remember his name. Terry, was it?'

'Tommy,' I say, spotting who she's pointing at, strolling by on the other side of the street, a sleeping bag under one arm and a rucksack over his shoulder. 'Yes, you're right. That's him.'

I hesitate for a second, unsure what to do. Is it best to leave him be or to go after him? My mind says to do the former, especially since Nora's here with me, but my gut has other ideas.

I look Nora in the eye with sudden sincerity. 'I could

do with having a quick word with him. Would you mind if I—'

'Not at all. Go for it.'

'I'll be back in a minute, I promise.'

'That's fine. I'm not going anywhere.'

I dash out of the café and up the street in the direction Tommy was walking. I can't see him straight away, due to all the other pedestrians milling around, but after a moment I spot him and make chase.

When I've nearly caught up with him, I stop running and try to slow my breathing so it's less obvious how keen I am to chat. What do I want to say, actually? I've no idea now the moment is upon me. All I know is that I feel bad about what happened on Friday and I want to make sure he's okay.

'Tommy!' I call out when I'm about two metres behind him, with no one in between.

He turns around, stares at me blankly and then, slowly, a look of recognition lights up his face. 'Barber dude, right? How's it going?'

We both stop walking and, to get out of other people's way, stand towards the inside of the pavement, under the canopy of a children's clothing store. This works out well because it's started spitting with rain.

'I'm fine, thanks, Tommy,' I say before reminding him that my name is Luke.

'That's it. Like the geezer from *Star Wars*. Nice one.'

Tommy looks dog-tired. There are a couple of scratches on his cheek, but otherwise he appears more or less back to normal, compared to the last time we met.

'How are you doing?' I ask.

He shrugs. 'Can't complain. Still liking my haircut, although you were right about it being a bit cold.'

'I thought you said you had a hat.'

'Yeah, I do,' he replies. 'Somewhere.'

'How's the book?' I ask, half-expecting him to say he's lost it.

Instead, for the first time in the conversation, a spark briefly returns to his eyes. 'It was brilliant. I raced through it in no time. I couldn't find anyone to pass it on to who'd actually bother to read it, so I swapped it for a different one at a book exchange. Not a Rankin, though. There weren't any. Hope that's okay.'

'Of course,' I reply. 'Would you like another?'

'Definitely.'

'No problem. Leave it with me.'

I'm tempted not to say anything about Friday, particularly as Tommy doesn't appear to have any memory of the incident – or at least of seeing me there – but my bloody gut won't let me. He looks more or less fine now, but . . . I can't simply forget what I saw. And I feel like I have to do something to make up for my shameful behaviour.

'Hey, I'm guessing you don't remember this, but I ran into you on Friday. You weren't really with it. I got the impression you must have, um, taken something. Does that ring a bell?'

Tommy's eyes widen upon hearing this and he looks from side to side, no longer meeting my eye. 'Sorry, what?' he says eventually. 'I don't know what you're talking about.

Are you sure you've got the right person? Maybe it was one of the other guys who—'

'No, it was definitely you, Tommy,' I say. 'You were properly out of it. I was a bit concerned, to say the least. It seemed to me like you might have taken some of that, um—'

'Listen, I have to get going,' Tommy says, interrupting me before I can finish. 'It's good to catch up and all that, but I need to see a man about a dog, so to speak.'

'Are you in trouble?' I ask him. 'Is there anything I can do to help?'

'I live on the streets, mate. Every day is trouble. I do what I can to get through it, yeah? And no offence, but how I manage that is my business. If you really want to help, a bit of change is always useful.'

'I'd rather buy you a sandwich, Tommy. Are you hungry?'

He shakes his head. 'Not right now.'

'Sorry, I don't have any change,' I say, not willing to fund his next drug binge. 'I only have a card with me. But seriously, I'll happily buy you a coffee or whatever, if it's not food you want.'

'Maybe next time. Gotta go.'

He pats me on the shoulder and, before I can stop him, darts off.

Feeling dazed by our encounter, I stand there alone on the pavement for a minute, gathering my thoughts. And then my mind turns to Nora. Dammit. How long have I been gone? I need to get my arse back to that café sharpish.

CHAPTER 23

I've got to know a few more of my neighbours, thanks to Doreen. She's pally with several of the block's older residents and, since we've become friends, she's been introducing me to them in her own unique, direct way.

So, for instance, I was picking up a couple of bits from the supermarket for Doreen the other day, which I seem to do quite frequently now, and her friend Pauline was there on my return. I vaguely recognised her, but I'd never spoken to her or known her name until that point.

Doreen introduced me by saying: 'Pauline, this is Luke, the one I was telling you about.'

'That sounds ominous,' I replied, shaking Pauline's limp hand.

'Well, exactly,' Doreen said. 'You were pretty ominous until recently. I'd written you off as a grumpy, selfish sod until I finally got to know you and realised how nice you are.'

I nodded. 'Right. I, um, don't quite know what to say about that.'

'Oh, sit down and join us for a cuppa, Luke,' Doreen said. 'I was showing Pauline your handiwork in the bathroom earlier. She was very impressed, weren't you, love?'

Pauline nodded and, before I knew it, I was agreeing to replace the sealant around her kitchen sink.

Today, on my Monday morning off, I got roped into helping their friend Sylvia – another older, single resident of our block of flats – rearrange the furniture in her lounge.

It's not just me and loads of pensioners living here, by the way. There are plenty of younger folk too, but they tend to be out a lot: at work or partying. As a man on the cusp of turning forty, I guess I fall somewhere in between the two camps.

The funny thing is, I quite enjoy helping Doreen and her friends. The jobs I've done for them are only little tasks, which don't take me long, anyway. And they're always so appreciative, often plying me with tea and cake in return or even, in Sylvia's case, handing me a four-pack of lager. To be clear, it was supermarket own-brand beer that went out of date twelve months ago – but it's the thought that counts, right? And I was only there for half an hour or so, anyway, lifting the lighter stuff and sliding the settee, etc., a few metres across the room.

I also managed to 'fix' Sylvia's iPad for her, which she said was broken, although all it needed was a quick reboot. I reckon she thinks I'm some kind of computer whizz now, which definitely isn't true.

If Mum and Dad were still alive, I'd probably be doing

things like this for them all the time. I often hear people my age moaning about how their parents treat them like an IT helpdesk. It makes me want to scream how lucky they are to still have them around. I wish I had phone calls like that. Still, at least I've found a way to be of help to others now rather than simply dwelling on the past, seething and moping.

That's one of the most surprising, rewarding things I've found so far about being positive; about saying yes instead of no and opening myself up to new people and possibilities: it makes me feel good.

It's the same in the barbershop too. I've started listening more to what customers tell me. I've asked some questions back, if that's what they seem to want, and I've offered the odd piece of advice. I may even have smiled and laughed a few times.

'So how long have you been into collecting comics?' I found myself quizzing one guy last week after he mentioned his hobby. 'And do you own any really rare issues?'

An hour later, I was advising a Glaswegian on a business trip about where he might buy his wife a nice gift. 'What kind of thing are you looking for?'

'Jewellery always goes down well,' he replied. 'But she tends to prefer the more unique, artisan kind of stuff.'

'I know just the place,' I said. 'And as it happens, it's run by my very talented cousin, Meg. If you mention my name, she'll take good care of you.'

'Fantastic. Thanks, Luke. I wish my regular barber back home was half as helpful as you.'

'I do my best,' I said, feeling pleased with myself.

On another day, a customer actually enquired if I'd won the lottery.

'Um, no, sadly not,' I replied. 'If so, I'd be drinking cocktails on a sunny beach right now, not working. Why do you ask? Is it because of my snazzy outfit?'

The man – a big chap in his mid-forties – looked me up and down in my old jeans and T-shirt, then threw his head back in the barber chair and gave a booming laugh. 'You must be getting laid, then, mate. Something's definitely changed for the better. You're like a different person from the last couple of times I was in here. You barely said two words to me then, frowning like it was going out of fashion. And on the last occasion, I remember you ripping the poor postman a new one because some parcel he delivered was soaking wet from the rain outside.'

The scary thing is I don't even recall that particular incident. I've bitten off too many people's heads over too long a period to remember them all.

The old crotchety me does still come out from time to time, especially first thing in the morning before I've had a couple of coffees, but I am really trying to stay upbeat.

I don't know whether it's down to that or the fact the barbershop has been busy of late, but I've been finding my working days have been flying by when they often used to drag. I've certainly got no regrets so far about the life changes Iris has inspired in me.

I'm still beating myself up about the way I dealt with Tommy when he was on spice, though. Disowning him was cowardly and selfish. Yes, he was in good hands when I walked away – professionals trained to deal with that kind of thing – and, based on what he told me in the street yesterday, he doesn't even remember me finding him in that state.

And yet if I'd stayed, maybe I could have made a difference. If I'd been there when he'd come to his senses, perhaps he'd have opened up to me about his issues. Who knows? It's all pointless speculation, because I don't have a time machine at my disposal, so I can't change the past. If I could, I would. Anyway, at least I've got another Rebus book for him, as promised, which I'll keep at the barbershop until I next see him.

I get a phone call from Nora as I'm walking to work at around 12.30 p.m.

'Good morning,' I say. 'How are you today?'

'Great, thanks. It was good to, um, see you yesterday. I enjoyed our coffee, despite the lack of brownies and the grumpy waiter.'

I laugh. 'Me too. Sorry again for leaving you alone with him while I chased after Tommy.'

'You're forgiven.'

I'm about to suggest we should do it again sometime, but I hesitate and then the moment's gone.

'So,' Nora continues. 'I wanted to let you know that Rudy's new photos have turned out really well. I sent them over to my contact in London—'

'Ooh, that makes you sound like a spy,' I interject. 'You're not, are you?'

'If I was, I wouldn't tell you, would I?'

'True. Sorry, you were saying?'

'Yes, before you so rudely interrupted me, I was about

225

to tell you how much they love the pictures too. They're definitely going to run the piece next Sunday.'

'Great,' I say. 'That's good timing, as the next free haircuts session is the following day. You're welcome to come along again if you need anything more.'

Nora falls silent before replying to this and, in that pause, I immediately regret what I said.

'Oh, um, right,' she responds eventually. 'Yes. I, er, think I've got everything I need for now, to be honest, Luke. I'm not sure whether we'll be able to get the story anywhere else, although you never know. Someone might see this one and want to follow it up. All the same, I think I'm good. Hope it goes well.'

'Cheers, no problem,' I say as casually as I can. 'Thanks for the update. Fantastic news. I'll see you around, yeah?'

'Sure.'

'Okay. Bye, Nora.'

'Bye, Luke.'

I frown at my phone before shoving it back into the pocket of my jeans. Wow, that ended awkwardly. Analysing the conversation, I wonder if my spy comment was misjudged. Surely she realised it was a joke, but was her 'rudely interrupted' remark semi-serious? And why on earth did I ask her if she wanted to come along again next week? Idiot. She probably thought I was angling for her to help out. As if she hasn't already done enough for me.

Just as well I didn't ask her out on a date. That would only have made things even more embarrassing. Bloody Meg. I wish she'd never put the idea of Nora liking me

226

in my head. It's clearly nonsense. Yes, we might seem to get along well, but that's what journalists do, right? They're specialists at getting on the level of their interviewee in order to get the best out of them. Based on that phone call, I wouldn't be surprised if I never see or hear from Nora again. Oh well. *C'est la vie.*

As I approach the barbershop, I notice someone waiting in front of the door.

They're keen, whoever they are.

Drawing closer, I recognise the forlorn figure, hands in his coat pockets and eyes firmly focused on the pavement, as Connor.

'Hello there,' I say once I'm within earshot. This causes him to look up, alarmed, but he relaxes again when he sees my face.

'Oh, it's you, Luke.'

'I'm glad to see you, mate. I was worried about you after last time.'

Connor's only reply to this is to shuffle awkwardly on the spot as I open up.

He follows me inside and takes a seat in the waiting area. I'm wondering what he's here for, as it's only been a few days since I last cut his hair, but I don't question it, not wanting to scare him off.

'Right, I'm ready for you,' I say a short while later, gesturing towards the barber chair.

He looks better than last time. He's had a shave for a start and his shirt, while not perhaps as perfectly ironed as usual, is passably smart.

'Oh, okay. Great.' He walks over and sits down; I cover

him with a gown, like his returning so soon is the most normal thing in the world.

'What are we doing today?'

Connor fidgets in the chair as he tells me, with a catch in his voice: 'You're probably wondering why I'm back again already. It's Mother's funeral tomorrow morning, you see, and I, er, want to look my best.'

'Of course. So you want me to tidy it up?'

He nods without saying anything, but his face twitches here and there like he's struggling to keep a neutral expression.

Treading delicately, I wait until he settles down again before adding: 'I know you find it hard to talk about, so don't feel like you have to say anything in response, but I must tell you that you're in my thoughts and I hope you get through the funeral all right tomorrow.

'I know how hard it is to lose a parent, having lost both of mine. If you ever need someone to talk to, I'm here for you. I'll give you my mobile number before you leave. You can call me any time.

'I won't say any more now, because I don't want to make you uncomfortable, but I had to say something. I hope you understand.'

Connor's fighting back the tears as he utters a strained 'Thanks, Luke', meeting my eye for the briefest of moments and then looking away again.

A short while later, another customer arrives to wait his turn, making me glad I said what I did while the two of us were alone.

True to my word, I don't say any more about Connor's

loss or the funeral. To put him at ease, I even make a bit of the kind of small talk I traditionally avoid, about the weather and so on.

At the end of the cut, I give him my number as promised and refuse his money. He looks confused at this, so to clarify, I say: 'It's on me. No debate.' With a wink, I add: 'But don't get used to it. It's a one-time only reward for my most loyal customer. All the best for tomorrow, yeah?'

'Thank you,' he whispers.

'Of course, and make sure you use that number, if you need it.'

'Okay.'

I think about Connor a lot for the rest of that day and the next. I'm glad he called in. Was it really because he wanted another haircut? Possibly, knowing how fastidious he can be. However, part of me wonders if he simply fancied seeing a familiar face and doing something normal, which I would totally understand. Normality is something you miss when you go through the grieving process. Well, that was my experience, at least.

Maybe it was a chat he wanted, despite the fact he didn't end up saying much.

Whatever the reason, I hope I've helped him, even if only a tiny bit. I certainly feel better about the situation than I did after his last visit.

Poor Connor. I wouldn't wish what he's going through on my worst enemy.

CHAPTER 24

'Thanks so much for your help, Rita. You're an absolute star.'

'I enjoyed myself,' she replies, giving me a hug goodbye. 'Sorry I couldn't tempt Sharon along again. She was a bit overwhelmed by it all last time. At least my car didn't let me down today.'

'No, I totally understand about Sharon. I think it was perfect with the two of us, anyway: just the right amount of busy. See you later.'

'Bye, love.'

I lock the door behind her and set to finishing off the cleaning up, which is almost done.

So that's the third free haircuts for the homeless session completed. It came around in no time and, despite the fact I had a bit of a private meltdown about it yesterday, everything went well in the end. The reason for my panic was that I feared I might have to go it alone and wouldn't be able to cope. I knew Meg wasn't able to make it due to work commitments, and Rita didn't confirm that she was coming until this morning.

Anyway, it was all right on the night. Definitely not as hectic as the time before – thank goodness – but plenty busy enough to keep Rita and me on our toes. I'd have struggled by myself, put it that way.

The article went in *The Sunday Times Magazine*, as promised. Thankfully, Rita said she and the rest of the family were happy with the content and appreciated me telling them about it in advance. It was a good spread, using several of Rudy's photos, so I feared it could lead to another mad rush that I wouldn't be able to handle alone. Realistically, though, homeless folk probably aren't the biggest readers of Sunday supplements; I doubt it made much of a difference to the numbers we saw this evening.

I was fine once I knew Rita was coming. She was brilliant, like last time: her bubbly yet no-nonsense personality every bit as useful as her cutting skills. Having her by my side really helped me to relax and take things in my stride.

Rita's presence also proved useful when Steph and Ralphie, the only two homeless people who came along to the first free cutting session, turned up again this evening. As I gave Ralphie another short back and sides, Rita managed to convince Steph that, unlike me, she was up to the task of giving her shoulder-length brown hair a cut.

'Come on with you,' she said. 'I don't blame you for not letting Luke near it – he's a barber, not a women's hairdresser – but I used to run my own unisex salon. I've got plenty of experience with hair like yours, honestly. You've nothing to worry about. I don't even have to take much off, if you don't want me to. How about a little trim to tidy it up?'

'Okay,' Steph replied. And after a few minutes in the chair, it was wonderful to see her unwind and start to open up.

Until then, I'd considered Steph a tough nut to crack, but in Rita's hands, she lowered her defences, chatting about the harsh reality of her life.

'It's not easy living like this,' she said. 'You're always watching your back and feeling edgy, wondering when the next bad thing's going to happen, but I just get on with it. My life has been hard for as long as I can remember. My mum was a junkie and I never knew my dad. Mum died when I was a teenager, but I'd spent most of my childhood in care by then, so I was used to being alone. I've always felt homeless, if you know what I mean.'

Later, when Rita had finished working her magic on Steph's hair, she asked: 'What do you think, love? Ideally, I'd have liked to wash and condition it for you too, but I'm afraid we're not kitted out for that.'

Watching Steph turn her head left and right in the mirror and then crack a satisfied smile was priceless.

'It's really nice,' she said after a long pause, sounding a little choked up. 'Thanks a million.'

'You're very welcome,' Rita replied with a catch in her voice.

'Amazing!' I mouthed at her, a swell of emotion also catching me unawares as a sudden sense of us touching people's lives – making a difference – washed over me.

*   *   *

232

Back in the present, cleaning done, I'm about to switch the lights off and head out when there's a knock at the door. That's the only part of the shopfront where I haven't yet lowered the shutters. The sound makes me jump and when I turn around, half-expecting to see Rita again, maybe because she's forgotten something or having more car trouble, I'm surprised to see someone else.

I recognise the skinny young man peering through the glass straight away. He's wearing the same black donkey jacket and red bobble hat I've seen him in before. But, as usual, the jagged scar across his cheek is what really stands out. It's the homeless guy I first bumped into while looking for Tommy, who then caused a scene at the last free session, a fortnight ago, challenging me when I threatened to kick him out for fighting; only backing down when Tommy intervened.

What did Tommy call him? Moxie, was it? Yes, I'm pretty sure that's right.

I have a bad feeling as soon as I spot him, but this eases when he smiles pleasantly and waves at me. 'All right, dude?' he shouts in his friendly-sounding, light Brummie accent, so I can hear him through the locked door. 'How are you doing?'

'I'm fine, thank you. I'm afraid we're closed now, though. There'll be another free session in a fortnight.'

'Sorry?' he says, cupping a hand around one ear and holding it to the glass.

I repeat my words, only for him to point to his ears and shake his head.

Is he taking the piss? I wouldn't put it past him, based

on how he behaved on the last occasion he was here, although I don't get that impression this time. Perhaps he's hard of hearing. It's a reasonable possibility, which could even go some way to explain his previous behaviour. Not being able to hear things properly is bound to be frustrating and a potential cause of misunderstandings.

I take pity on him and open the door, realising my mistake almost instantly as he wedges his foot, encased in a chunky black army boot, into the gap. His eyes harden to a look of stone-cold determination.

'Let me in,' he demands.

'Get lost!' I shout, trying to shove the door closed, but failing.

Then he pulls a knife out of the inside pocket of his coat and starts waving it near my hands. I jerk them away in shock, my heart thumping with sudden fear; my vision blurring.

Next thing I know, he's inside. He has me pinned up against the wall, left hand vice-like on my throat, so I can hardly breathe; right hand brandishing the blade.

'If you don't want to die tonight, you need to do exactly what I tell you,' he says. 'Got that?'

I nod, terrified, my insides churning like my bowels are about to open.

'Say it then, prick,' he snarls, tiny flecks of his spit firing on to my cheek. 'Tell me you understand.'

His face is only a few centimetres away from mine. I can smell the hot, foul stench of booze and cigarettes on his breath.

'I understand.'

I manage to squeeze this response out of my compressed throat, although it emerges as little more than a whisper. I feel sick, dizzy; like I'm about to pass out.

How have I let this happen to me?

'Move away from the door,' he barks, removing his hand from my throat and backing off while keeping the weapon and his eyes firmly directed at me. Now I've had a chance to view it properly, I can see it's a branded paring knife – the kind used for cutting and peeling fruit and veg – with a sharp, solid-looking blade that's probably three or four inches long. It looks like something swiped from a kitchen.

I do as he says, moving into the body of the shop and thus out of view of anyone walking past on the street, which is clearly his intention.

Dammit. Being spotted by a passer-by was my best hope of getting help. I'm totally screwed now – my fate entirely in the hands of this unhinged, violent man.

But what else can I do other than what he demands?

Surely, that's my safest play now, isn't it?

God, I can't even think straight.

My limbs are shaking.

I wish I could be brave or calm, but I'm neither.

Utterly petrified is what I am.

I fear for my life now like never before.

'What do you—'

'Shut it,' he says. 'You speak when you're spoken to.'

'Right.'

'I said shut it.' He brings the knife closer, waving the tip dangerously close to my eyes, making me flinch.

He sneers at me. 'Not so high and mighty now, are you?

Think you're so much better than me, don't you? Well, you're not. Like a free bloody haircut is going to sort my life out. It's an insult, that's what it is.'

I can't believe what I'm hearing. Why did he come here last time if he finds it so offensive? Why did he take a free haircut? I can't understand his extreme anger towards me. Is it because of my threat to kick him out that time? He definitely didn't like it. I still remember the defiant, aggressive look he threw at me before Tommy got involved. Is this some kind of warped revenge for him having felt humiliated in front of the other homeless guys? Bloody hell.

I get the feeling he's on some kind of drug: likely a stimulant – speed, coke, crack maybe – because the pupils of his eyes look huge and he keeps sniffing and chewing. I've noticed a few involuntary muscle twitches too, particularly on his face. He's almost definitely wired.

Is this a good or a bad thing? God knows. Perhaps it'll start to wear off and he'll calm down a bit. On the other hand, if he's off his face on whatever, he could be capable of anything.

He could be prepared to do anything to get another fix.

'Right,' he says, slapping me around the face with his empty hand and then pushing me down into one of the seats in the waiting area. 'Where's all the money? I want it right now. No bullshit.'

This is what I feared he was going to ask for. I take a deep breath before answering, knowing he's not going to like what he hears. 'There are a few pounds of petty cash in the till, which I can get out for you no problem, but that's it. It's only a small float for giving people change. I don't keep any real cash on the premises.'

'Bollocks!' he shouts, standing over me, the knife firmly gripped in his hand, edging ever closer to my skin. 'You're a liar. You have loads of customers. You must make a fortune. Why would you be offering free haircuts if you weren't rolling in it?'

If only. Has he seen how little I charge? I'm tempted to draw his attention to the price list on the wall, but anything that might upset him seems like a dumb move. It could even be fatal. So I reiterate that I'm telling the truth, pointing out there's even a sticker in the window saying as much.

'It all gets banked before closing,' I say. 'And lots of people pay by card.'

'Why do you have the shutters, then?'

'You need to around here. Everyone does. It's mainly to stop the windows getting smashed.'

'I don't believe you. Open the till. Now. I want to see for myself.'

Slowly, afraid of making any sudden moves that might trigger him to do something stupid, I stand up, walk over to the till and open it, before moving to one side and letting him look.

'Prick!' he shouts, grabbing a handful of change and flinging it against the wall. Then he turns back to me, teeth bared. 'It must be somewhere else. Tell me where or I swear I'll kill you.'

I hold my quivering hands up. 'Please, there's nothing else here. Like I said, it's all in the bank.'

237

'Aargh!' he screams, his empty hand balled into a fist that he shakes in fury, stomping his feet on the ground like a stroppy teenager and still waving around that scary damn blade.

Subtly, I shuffle as far away from him as I can, putting a precious bit of distance between us. But he's in my face again an instant later and my back is against the wall.

His eyes scan mine, like they're looking for clues, and then they narrow, suggesting he's thought of something. 'Pockets,' he snaps. 'Empty them now.'

I do as he says, pulling out my phone and wallet. I wonder for a second where my keys have gone, but then I realise they're still in the door from when I made the mistake of opening it and starting this nightmare.

He snatches my phone immediately, looks it over and then, sneering, shoves it inside his manky jacket. Next he opens my wallet, pockets the two twenty-pound notes in there and examines the bank cards.

'Take them,' I say. 'They're yours.'

'Oh, I'll do whatever I want,' he replies with a menacing snigger. 'I don't need your permission for that, Mr Hairdresser. There's only one person in charge today and guess what: it's not you.'

'Listen, it's Moxie, isn't it? I just meant—'

'I don't care what you meant. And don't you dare say that name. Shut your mouth or I'll carve it wide open.'

I nod and look down at the floor, attempting to steady my frantic breathing. Trying to hold myself together and not totally lose it, despite my entire mind and body being gripped by panic.

'Hmm, three cards,' he says, turning his attention back to my wallet. 'All your money's in the bank, you say. Well, why don't we pay a little visit to the cashpoint and see if we can't get our hands on some of it?'

Initially, my heart sinks on hearing these words, as it means this ordeal is going to continue, whereas I hoped he might take my stuff and leave. However, on the bright side, we'll be going out into the street with other people who could spot something untoward and raise the alarm. Plus there'll be lots of space to potentially break free from him and make a run for it.

There's a cash machine around the corner and that's where he wants us to go. He instructs me to lock up the barbershop first to avoid suspicion, but he's right at my side the whole time, whispering that if I do anything stupid, it'll be the last thing I do.

Once that's done, he jostles me along the street, one arm clamped around my shoulders, the other inside his open jacket, still holding the blade but keeping it out of sight.

I hope he might accidentally stab himself while doing this, but he keeps reminding me that I'll be the one impaled by it if I make even the slightest wrong move.

'Try to escape or call out for help and that's it for you: game over,' he rasps into my ear. 'And don't think I wouldn't do it, because you'd be wrong. There's nothing I'd enjoy more than to gut you like a pig.'

I believe him. It petrifies me.

Although we pass various people on the street, I say nothing. I don't have the guts.

I walk with him, his horrible arm feeling like a rod of steel across my back. My mind is racing, my eyes scanning all around, looking for a way out, but nothing presents itself.

'Listen to me, prick,' he says in a low voice, so no one else can hear. 'When we get to the cash machine, this is how it works: you calmly put in each of your cards, one by one, and withdraw the maximum amount you can. No funny business with forgetting the PIN or trying to raise the alarm somehow, because I'll be right next to you with this knife in my hand. Got it?'

'Yes.'

He squeezes my shoulders hard enough to hurt. 'Good.'

What do I do? The money is the last of my worries. But if I get it out for him, what then? Will he stab me anyway once he's got what he wants? I know who he is, meaning I could report him to the police.

Am I going to die here?

How on earth am I having to ask myself that question again?

Five minutes ago, I was trapped under the fallen scaffolding, wondering exactly the same thing. What if I never actually escaped from that situation and everything since has been a figment of my imagination?

Maybe I'm still lying there on the ground, unconscious.

Maybe I'm already dead.

No, please don't let that be the case. That would mean I haven't changed; that I'm still the nasty, negative person no one would miss – someone my parents would have been ashamed to call their son. That would mean Meg and I never made up after our falling-out; no haircuts for the homeless; no being a good neighbour to Doreen and her pals; no meeting Rita or Nora.

I'm ashamed of that old version of myself, trapped under the collapsed scaffolding: unpleasant, unhappy and friendless. I'd rather die now, knowing I've at least tried to become a better man, than back when I was still him.

God, what am I doing?

What am I thinking?

The fear's making me delusional.

Of course this is real. I desperately wish it wasn't – but if I'm going to find a way to survive, I need to focus, not get lost in flights of fantasy.

I have to do something – and soon. That's risky, of course. But surely doing nothing is worse than trying to help myself. Isn't it?

What would Iris have done in a situation like this? I don't know why that's relevant, but it's the thought that pops into my head. I know the answer straight away: she'd have tried to reason with Moxie; to wake *him* up to the reality of his actions.

The right words elude me. My lips are quivering and won't form the necessary shapes. I fear saying something that will put his back up and cause a kneejerk reaction. That could get me killed.

My skin is covered in sweat and I'm so on edge it feels almost like I'm on drugs myself. I guess I am, in a way: there must be huge amounts of adrenaline pumping through my body right now. The fight-or-flight response.

That's what they call it, right? I'm not currently doing either; if I do, which one is it going to be?

We're almost at the cashpoint now. I can see it up ahead on the left. We'll be there in less than a minute, I reckon. I'm still considering how to handle things when we reach it, part of me praying it's out of order to buy me some time, when Moxie stands on a discarded water bottle on the pavement, stumbles and momentarily loosens his grip on me.

Time slows down as my brain grasps what's happening and makes a series of desperate, split-second decisions about how to respond.

This is arguably the best opening I'm going to get to escape.

It's now or never.

So I go for it.

As I feel his arm slacken and his body twist away from me, I fire my elbow back into him with all the force I can muster. It doesn't land in his stomach, which I hoped it would in order to wind him, but it does make contact – possibly hitting his ribcage – and I feel him fall further back from me at the same time as he yelps in pain.

It's enough.

I sprint ahead as quickly as I can, pulling away from him. But when I look back after what must be a few seconds, I see he's coming after me: red bobble hat discarded on the pavement behind him and knife now on full display, glinting in the headlights of a passing car.

He's gaining fast.

'You're a dead man!' he shouts, apparently no longer bothered about hiding his intentions from other people. Shit.

There's no one in view on this side of the road, but a couple of pedestrians on the opposite pavement have stopped walking and are gaping in our direction. We're also attracting plenty of rubberneckers in passing vehicles, and yet no one is actually stopping or doing anything to help me.

Can I blame them? Would I intervene if I saw someone being chased by a knifeman?

'Somebody help me!' I cry out. 'Call the police.'

The echoing sound of his heavy boots pounding the pavement behind me fills me with dread and despair. He's so damn close now I can even hear the rapid pace of his breathing. I want to go faster – to push myself harder – but this is all I've got.

I already know it's not going to be enough.

If only I'd winded him like I wanted to. That might have made the difference.

As soon as I feel the kick of his boot in the back of my knees, I know it's all over. Time crawls again as my legs crumple and, instinctively, I throw my arms forward in a bid to soften the impact of hitting the pavement on the rest of my body. Then bang: pain everywhere as I hit the ground running, in the most literal sense, only to be pounced on a second later and thumped on the chin by Moxie.

'You're going to regret that,' he pants, punching me again, on my cheek this time, as I bite my tongue and my mouth fills with the metallic taste of blood.

Why is no one helping me?

We're in a public place, but not a soul is stepping in.

Out of nowhere, a sense of fury swells in my belly and surges through my chest. Fired up by the injustice of what's happening here and a desperate sense that if I don't fight back now, it could be curtains for me, I let out a guttural yell and headbutt my attacker in the nose. He cries out in pain, cursing and staggering backwards, holding his free hand up to his freshly injured snout.

Where did that come from?

I didn't think I had such an aggressive move in me.

It's done the trick, though. He's no longer on top of me and . . . oh crap.

He still has the knife.

He's coming back at me now, pure fury burning in the heart of his saucer-like eyes.

And he's holding the knife like he's about to . . .

'No, no, please! Not that. I'm sorry. Please don't. You can have—'

CHAPTER 25

'How are you, Luke?'

I turn my head to the left and admire Iris's beautiful brown eyes, brimming with warmth and kindness. Is that why her parents named her so?

Possibly. And yet it could be after the plant, or the Greek goddess of the rainbow and messenger of the gods; maybe they simply liked the sound of the name.

'Good, thanks,' I tell her, looking down for a moment at our bare ankles and feet, soaking in the warm water as we sit next to each other on the side of the swimming pool, sun beating down.

She replies with a smile.

'Why do you ask?' I say after a brief pause.

'Why do you think?'

'Hmm. Something feels a bit off to me. Or am I imagining it?'

Iris, wrapped in her customary yellow raincoat, shrugs. Not very helpful.

'Can I ask you a strange question?' I say.

'Of course.'

'How did I get here? I don't remember.'

I've been to this place before, plenty of times. That's how recurring dreams work. But in the past, I've always had to find my way to the garden via the flat's unused secret annexe and its unsettling rooms: furnished but empty of life. I can't think of a previous instance when I've simply appeared by the pool in such a way.

On this occasion, I was here all of a sudden, with nothing particular preceding that in my mind.

Definitely not how this usually unfolds.

I blink and we're no longer by the pool but sitting on the beige furniture in the small lounge of the annexe. Iris is on the sofa and I'm on a facing armchair. I look down and see my feet and ankles are no longer bare. They're encased in a chunky pair of black army boots, topped by faded jeans and a red polo shirt. Iris's trouser legs are no longer rolled up either and she's wearing black leather shoes.

'What the hell's going on?' I ask her. 'We were outside by the pool a second ago, weren't we?'

'Try not to worry,' she says.

But I do, not least because the weather has changed too. The sun we were basking in just now is nowhere to be seen through the patio doors. Instead, it looks dull and gloomy outside.

The vagueness of Iris's response reminds me that she never answered my earlier question about how I got here. When I put it to her again, she asks: 'You can't remember?'

'No, genuinely. It's like I appeared out of nowhere.'

'That's interesting,' she replies, resting her chin on her hand and looking pensive. 'What's the last thing you recall before being here?'

'Good question,' I say. 'I'm racking my brains for the answer, Iris, but I'm not getting anywhere. My memories seem to be, um, muddled. I can't sort them into any kind of logical order. What's wrong with me?'

I stare outside into the garden, looking for some kind of inspiration, I suppose. But when I look back at Iris, I get a nasty shock. She's gone, and in her place – still dressed in Iris's clothes – is my mother's frozen corpse, icicles hanging from her nose and ears; hair coated in snow; eyes open and rolled back like she's trying to view her own forehead.

I gasp. Cry out in shock. Squeeze my eyes shut to block out the awful, ghastly image and cover my face with my hands.

Then Iris's voice asks me what's wrong. Gingerly, I peek through the tiniest gap between my fingers, relieved to see her face back where it belongs.

'What's the matter?' she asks me. 'You look like you saw a—'

'Please, don't finish that sentence,' I beg. 'I don't even know what that means any more. I don't know who or what you are; I'm utterly confused about what I'm doing here and where here even is. Nothing makes sense. And I'm not even going to try to explain what I saw, because it scared the bejesus out of me.'

Iris scratches her head and twists her mouth to one side. 'I'm not sure what to suggest.'

An idea comes to me, so, telling Iris I'll be back in a minute, I get up and walk into the bland corridor of this weird little flat within a flat. Passing by and ignoring the usual two unoccupied bedrooms, I head towards the door at the end. I figure it should lead to the main flat, where this dream traditionally begins; hopefully, I might find some answers waiting for me there.

I walk up to the door, which can vary in appearance from dream to dream. On this occasion, it's solid wood without any glazing, painted in white gloss. I reach out and grab the silver handle, turning it decisively, heart pounding at the thought of what I might find on the other side, only for nothing to happen.

Locked. Dammit.

I look around to see if there's a key anywhere nearby, but I can't spot one.

For some reason, I then knock on the door. I'm not sure who I'm expecting to answer, since the person usually on the other side is me.

I'm about to return to the lounge, planning to ask Iris if she knows where to find the key, when I'm startled by a knocking sound from the other side of the door.

'Hello? Is someone there?'

There's a pause for a long moment and then comes a reply.

'Hello? Is someone there?'

The voice speaking to me from the other side is my own, as if what I said was recorded and played back to me.

What? Just when I thought this experience couldn't get any stranger.

I kneel down and put my eye to the keyhole, only to jump away from the door at what I see on the other side: another eye, the same light blue colour as my own, watching me.

'Who is that?' I ask.

'Who is that?' comes the reply shortly afterwards.

'Is there a key on your side?'

The only response I get, which I'm expecting now, is my question fired back at me.

Frustrated, I storm off down the corridor to where I came from; to my confusion and dismay, the lounge and kitchen are empty. Peering out through the patio doors, there's no sign of Iris in the garden either. Brilliant.

I call her name at the top of my lungs. 'Iris, where are you? I need your help.'

Apparently, she's no longer here to offer it, so I start rooting around in the kitchen drawers and cupboards, hoping to find what I'm looking for. They're mainly empty, apart from some white crockery, a few pieces of cutlery and two pans, but eventually I come across a set of six keys of various shapes and sizes on one ring.

This has to be it.

I grab the keys and head straight back to the locked door. After pausing for a moment, fearing another spine-chilling apparition of Mum or Dad might await me on the other side, I throw caution to the wind and shove the first of the keys into the lock. It slides in but doesn't turn at all. Not the right one, apparently. The second key I try doesn't even fit.

Third time lucky?

Well, it goes in and turns, if that counts. Lucky, I'm not

so sure about, considering all that's happened so far in this eerie dream.

I take a deep breath and turn the door handle, at which point things go from weird to off-the-scale freakish.

I'm looking a mirror-version of myself in the eye. And instead of the main flat I was expecting to see on the other side of the door, I'm facing an inverse replica of the corridor I've just walked up.

My doppelgänger is dressed exactly as I am: red polo shirt, faded jeans, black army boots. The only visual difference between us, as far as I can see, is that he has a jagged scar across one cheek. This reminds me of someone else, although I can't put my finger on who.

'What the hell's going on?' I ask. 'Who are you?'

Copying my words and tone of voice exactly, he repeats them back at me. Then a huge, creepy grin erupts across his face, which he holds for a long moment while eyeballing me, before throwing his head back and starting to laugh, shoulders jumping up and down, in a maniacal frenzy.

'Where's the main flat?' I demand, only for him to say the same thing in reply, but this time in a high-pitched, whiny voice, obviously intended to wind me up. Once he's said it, he returns to laughing.

I try to pull the door shut again, to close him off from me, but it won't budge even the slightest bit; when I look down, I see he has one of his boots jammed against it.

'Get lost!' I say, unsurprised when the words get fired back at me in the same grating tone as before.

Unexpectedly, he reaches forward and shoves me. I'm forced back a couple of steps and want to do the same to him in retaliation, when I notice blood on my hands. They're covered in the stuff; it's dripping off them on to the floor, although I can't tell where it's coming from, as I don't feel any pain and there are no visible wounds on myself.

Is it mine, his, or someone else's blood?

'Who are you?' I ask, almost screaming. 'What have you done?'

I'm so busy watching my hands that I don't see how he responds. However, when for the first time he doesn't repeat what I've said, I look up at him, only to find someone else staring back at me, their face screwed up, oozing hatred.

'You're a dead man,' the skinny young guy growls. I know him. What's his name? He's wearing a black donkey jacket and red bobble hat. He has the same scar on his cheek as my doppelgänger did. But that's the last of my concerns when I see the bloodied knife in his hands. Shit.

I spin on my heel and tear down the corridor as fast as I can. 'Iris!' I cry out. 'There's a guy with a knife. Wherever you are, get the hell out of here.'

To my horror, she appears from the doorway I'm racing towards, shoots me a look of panic and lets out one hell of a blood-curdling scream.

'Run for your life, Iris!' I shout.

Then there's a sharp pain in the back of my legs and I'm sprawling forward, heading for the floor. I squeeze my eyes shut and tense all of my muscles, readying myself for the impact.

My eyes snap open and I gasp for air.

I'm back in the real world. I know this immediately,

although it takes me a little while to get my bearings, to remember where I am and why, and what really happened.

It's dark everywhere, which doesn't help. But once my eyes acclimatise and my breathing steadies, the panic in my chest starts to ease, allowing rational thoughts to return. I recognise my surroundings: suspended ceiling tiles, cubicle curtains, beds on wheels, LED lights, and mysterious medical equipment hanging from the walls.

I'm on the six-patient hospital ward where I was admitted after having my injuries from the knife attack treated. I check the time on the old phone Meg brought me as a temporary replacement for the one that bastard stole. It's 11.43 p.m., so still Tuesday night for another quarter of an hour or so. Hard to believe it was only yesterday that Moxie tried to kill me. It feels like it happened much longer ago.

I hold my bandaged hands and forearms up in front of me and move them slightly to see how much they hurt. Quite a lot, as it turns out, causing me to grimace and groan, triggering yet more pain in my bruised, grazed face and where I bit my tongue. My body aches and throbs all over, particularly when I shift around in bed, although a lot of that is bruising and muscle strain. I could press my button to call a nurse over and ask for some more pain-killers, but I don't want to at the moment. I suspect the various meds they've given me already may have contrib-uted to my bewildering, trippy dream, which I'd rather not experience again. Plus part of me doesn't mind feeling the pain, because it serves as a reminder that I'm still here – roughly in one piece – alive rather than dead.

There were several times during my horrendous ordeal when I actually thought I was a goner. The terror and helplessness I felt while in Moxie's drug-fuelled, deranged hands was so much worse than my last near-death experience under the collapsed scaffolding. I've never encountered fear like he put me through – and I never want to again.

How many times over the past day have I been told how lucky I am to have escaped with the injuries I have? A lot, that's for sure, by various members of the amazing medical team who've helped me: from the paramedics who tended to me on the street, to the doctors and nurses who checked me over and tended to my wounds. I think some of the police who've spoken to me have said so too.

I'm not sure I feel as lucky as I ought to: it's hard with all this pain. However, considering I was attacked by a man on the edge, who was armed with a blade he wasn't afraid to use, I am lucky. My wounds might be sore at the moment, but they're defensive, as in I suffered them while fending off potentially far worse injuries. We're talking incisions and lacerations, rather than puncture wounds, which is very much a good thing . . . As good as any knife wounds are ever going to be, anyway.

Put simply, Moxie didn't manage to stab me, but I'm not going to be cutting anyone's hair for a while. Again, the doctors say I've been extremely lucky. No bones are broken and there doesn't appear to be any tendon or nerve damage. It looks like I'll make a full and relatively speedy recovery – at least in terms of my physical injuries.

Mentally, who knows? Counselling has been mentioned, since post-traumatic stress could be an issue. Despite pooh-poohing Meg when she suggested this after I survived the scaffolding collapse, now I'm coming around to the idea. Objectively, trying to manage such things by myself in the past – mainly due to pride, shame and stubbornness – hasn't worked out too well for me.

Every time I close my eyes, I see Moxie's face, knotted with anger and hatred as he tried to finish me off. I don't understand how someone I knew so little could harbour such resentment for me. Ironically, this would never have happened if I hadn't tried to do something nice for him and other homeless folk.

It's hard not to question my attempts to change – to become a better person – considering where that journey has landed me. Optimism and good intentions returned me to hospital, in a worse state than last time. And if I hadn't been so lucky, they could easily have killed me. Maybe I was better off as I used to be: looking after number one and viewing things with a wary eye.

At least Moxie's not around any more to do further harm to me or anyone else. I can still picture the wide-eyed look of disbelief on my cousin's face when she visited earlier today and I filled her in on the gory details. Meg was in tears when she first clapped eyes on me, my hands and arms all bandaged up, plus the various cuts and bruises on my face.

'Oh my God,' she said, gasping and holding her hand up to cover her open mouth. 'You look dreadful.'

'Thanks. That's good to know. It's not as bad as it appears, honestly. I'll be fine once everything's healed.'

'Sorry, Luke. I feel awful. If only I'd been there to help.

Now you're back in hospital and I can't stop thinking it's my fault. You should never have been left alone.'

'I wasn't alone until right at the end of the night. Rita was with me for the whole session. This was afterwards. It could have happened on any day. I'm usually alone at work, remember? You've really nothing to feel bad about.'

'I do, though. How could I not when I see you like this? Are you in a lot of pain, you poor thing? Is it okay if I give you a hug?'

I spread my arms wide. 'Of course it is, Meg, as long as you're gentle with me.'

It did hurt a bit, although I didn't let on. I was too glad of the warm, calming sensation of being embraced by someone I love and trust. Comforted by my family.

She wanted to know every little detail of what had happened to me; I told her, even though it pained me to do so. I'd already been through the story several times with the police, but that didn't make it any easier to relive.

When I got to the part where I'd broken free and then Moxie had caught up with me and sent me sprawling on to the pavement, I noticed Meg's hands gripping the metal bar on the side of my bed, her knuckles white with exertion.

'And?' she asked, her eyes stretched like CDs, hanging on my every word. 'How did you escape? How did he end up—'

'Well, I didn't,' I continued. 'Not straight away. He launched himself at me, raging, and I really thought he was going to kill me. In that moment, believing it could be my last, I found some kind of inner strength: a sort of survival instinct, I guess. I fought him with everything I had. I headbutted him in the nose, but even that wasn't enough.

'He was like a man possessed, on top of me, screaming and shouting, trying to use the knife on me. And then we were rolling around on the pavement and I was kicking and punching and biting and scratching. Doing everything I could to save myself. The only thing going through my head was that I couldn't let him kill me. It seemed to go on forever. And then, out of nowhere, I was surrounded by flashing lights and sirens, and he was gone.'

'How do you mean, gone?' Meg asked, her features screwed up in concentration.

'He pulled away from me, got to his feet and ran. One minute he was there; the next he wasn't. I lay on the ground, dazed, believing at first that I'd somehow managed to avoid being hurt at all. Then, as paramedics rushed to help me, I realised there was blood everywhere, particularly on my hands and arms. I think I might have passed out a few times. It's all a bit of a blur, to be honest.

'The only part I remember distinctly is what happened next: the screech of a vehicle braking suddenly, followed by the loud thump of it hitting something. There was a pause before this awful screaming sound started. It was so high-pitched and deafening, like the kind of shriek you'd hear in an old slasher movie, and it seemed to go on and on. It was a woman, I think. I can only assume she witnessed what happened, although maybe she was the one driving. I really don't know. I'm glad I didn't see it. I'd have taken no pleasure from that, despite what that man put me through.'

Meg shook her head, slowly running her hands down her face. 'I'm struggling to take all of this in,' she said. 'What you're telling me is jaw-dropping, even though I had a rough idea already. It's the sort of thing that happens in cop shows on TV, not real life. And I can't get my head around why this bloke – Moxie or whatever his real name is – had it in for you. I remember him from when he came to get his hair cut and got into that argument. I tried to calm him down. He didn't seem very nice, but . . . I had no idea.'

I explained that, based on what the police had been able to tell me so far, he was a troubled man dealing with significant mental health issues, who was already known to them. His real name was Jonathan Moxford.

'And the sound you heard, that was him being hit by—'

'A bus, yeah, on the busy main road that runs across where he attacked me. He raced out in front of it, they say. Whether that was by accident, because he was so desperate to get away, or on purpose, who can say? It killed him, though. That's for sure.'

'Good riddance,' Meg said, steely-eyed.

Part of me wanted to agree with her, but I couldn't quite bring myself to do so. 'Well, as I say, it seems that he had psychological issues, so—'

'It sounds to me like he was pure evil. Honestly, after what he put you through, the world must be a better place without him.'

CHAPTER 26

They wake you up early in the morning in hospital – before seven o'clock. You might be lying in a bed all day, but that doesn't mean you get to sleep in. Mornings are all about sudden bright lights and an array of different people visiting patients' bedsides with medication, brews, breakfast, bed pans, washing bowls and fresh sheets.

This might only be my second morning on the ward, but I already feel like part of the furniture, experienced, institutionalised. I recognise a few of the faces now. Today I'll even get the food I ordered yesterday rather than what the bloke who occupied this bed before me fancied before he got discharged or moved on. Not that I feel particularly hungry. Near-death experiences tend to take your appetite away for a while. I should know; I'm an old hand.

I've been here a little longer than three of the other ward occupants, all of whom arrived over the last twenty-four hours. Not that I've spoken much to anyone else here, other than the staff. I'm not in the mood for socialising.

That said, the elderly chap in the bed next to me – Neville, who was here when I arrived and has two broken legs after falling down the stairs – has collared me a couple of times and spoken at me for a bit. He keeps telling me how he's worried about his dog, who's currently being looked after by his sister, because his sister isn't very reliable, apparently. He hasn't given me enough of a chance to speak to tell him about Alfred, who Meg is looking after for me again.

I've taken to wearing headphones, which Meg kindly brought in for me, in an attempt to avoid such interactions. I get that Neville's lonely and frustrated by his injuries, but I don't feel charitable at the moment and I don't have the energy to deal with him. I'm utterly drained, mentally and physically.

Around mid-morning, a smiley woman in her early twenties approaches me to ask if I need any help washing or shaving. I want to say no, out of pride more than anything else, but it is tricky with all these bandages on. We reach a compromise, whereby she comes into the washroom with me, rather than giving me a bed bath, and I do as much as I can while she assists, retaining my dignity and modesty. I skip the shaving part, figuring that a bit of facial hair is the least of my worries.

I don't know why I'm bothered about getting help from this woman; she must have seen it all before. I guess I need to feel independent, particularly as I'm hoping I'll get discharged in the next day or so.

I do feel better as a result of the wash, although once I'm done, alone again with my thoughts as I wait for the doctors to make their rounds, a black cloud descends. I could listen to the radio or watch something – TV or a movie – on the bedside screen provided, which Meg insisted on paying to activate for me yesterday. I don't want to, though. I have zero interest in engaging in anything. I feel rubbish in every way I can think of. I want to feel sorry for myself and wallow.

It's at times like this that I really miss Mum and Dad. I know I'm a fully grown man and all, but I wish more than anything that they were here now to offer their help and advice. They were always amazingly supportive when life threw obstacles into my path, knowing exactly what to say and do to help get me back on my feet. Were they still around today, I'm certain one or both of them would be camped out at my bedside. They'd be asking the doctors a million questions; doing whatever they could to make me as comfortable and happy as possible, from bringing me grapes and magazines to insisting that I shave and, if necessary, helping me to do so.

I can picture Mum now, walking in and frowning at my stubble. 'You look so scruffy,' she'd say. 'No one will take you seriously in life if you don't take care of yourself.'

What advice would she offer to help me recover from nearly being killed by Moxie? Always upbeat and bubbly, she'd definitely encourage me to look on the bright side; to focus on the fact I escaped without major injury and my attacker was no longer on the loose. 'Come on, love,' I imagine her telling me. 'You need to pick yourself up and dust yourself down. Life's too short to dwell on the negatives.'

Dad would find a way to make me smile with a joke, no doubt, while being crystal clear that he had my back, come what may.

It's making me teary, thinking about my parents like this. I even find myself missing my ex-wife, Helen, who was once a great source of comfort when I was feeling low – until she betrayed me.

At least I have Meg . . . and Alfred. I should focus on that, rather than the negatives, and take my mum's imagined advice. I could be in the situation of having no one, like plenty of other people. I could even have no flat or job, like the homeless people I've been trying to help. Thinking about them inevitably leads me back to Moxie, refuelling my anger and upsetting me all over again.

This is going to be hard to move on from.

I seriously doubt I'll be able to run another free hair-cutting session for them now. Why would I want to put myself at risk like that again? And it's not just me, is it? I also have to think about the safety of the people who've helped me, like Meg, Rita and even Nora. I wouldn't forgive myself if any harm came to them.

After lunch, some of the other men on my ward have visitors. Neville's is clearly his 'unreliable' sister, based on what I hear of their noisy conversation, which seems to be almost entirely about how often she feeds, waters and walks his dog. I'm already wearing my headphones, mainly for show, but I decide to actually listen to something for a bit in the hope of tuning them out, opting for my regular workplace choice of Radio 2.

Meg warned me yesterday that she wouldn't be able to

261

visit again until this evening, so I'm not expecting any company of my own. There is a chance of me getting another visit from the police at some point today, but I'm hoping they've got all they need for now. It's not like they have a criminal to track down, is it? Moxie's death will have lightened their workload considerably, I imagine, once all the necessary paperwork is out of the way. How considerate of him.

The Lightning Seeds' 'Pure' starts playing and I turn it up. I remember my dad loved this song and used to listen to it all the time when I was a boy. I close my eyes and think back to happier days, losing myself and my troubles for a precious few minutes in the hazy euphoria of the track. I picture him and Mum in the front seats of our old white Ford Escort on a red-hot summer's day, windows down and elbows jutting out. He's turned it up full blast, singing along; belting out the lines about love, first to Mum and then to me. Meanwhile, she and I are both grinning like crescent moons and nodding in time to the music.

As the tune ends and a radio jingle starts, I slide off my headphones and let out a wistful sigh, knowing whatever record they play next will never match up to this one for me. I keep my eyes shut for a moment longer, holding on to that precious image of the fabulous family I once had. Then I open them and nearly jump out of my skin.

'Bloody hell!' I yelp reflexively as I find myself staring straight into the face of Rita, who's standing at the end of my bed looking puzzled.

She jerks back in surprise at my exclamation and then

we both burst into laughter at the sheer ridiculousness of the situation.

'Sorry,' she says. 'I didn't mean to scare you. I saw you were listening to something when I arrived and, well, I wasn't sure what to do. I thought about tapping you on the leg or something, but I didn't want to alarm you. So much for that.'

Next she apologises for laughing, after the nightmare I've been through, but I tell her not to be silly.

'It's nice to have a bit of comic relief,' I say. 'I was feeling blooming miserable until a few minutes ago, when a song I like came on the radio and briefly cheered me up. Laughing was even better, as it turns out. It's so kind of you to come and see me. I didn't expect that at all. How did you—'

'It was all over the news. I don't know if you saw or heard it, but—'

'Meg said something to that effect yesterday, but I've decided to steer clear. It was the same after the scaffolding accident. You know that better than anyone. I'm not sure what to make of it all. I guess I'm still in shock.'

Rita slowly shakes her head. 'I'm sure you are. I spoke to Meg last night to get the details of where to find you here, and she told me everything that had happened. It sounded horrendous. I can't imagine how awful it must have been for you. And to think I only left a few minutes earlier. I feel terrible about that.'

'You shouldn't,' I reply. 'I'm glad you didn't get dragged into it.'

She stares into the distance. 'I keep thinking that if I'd

still been there with you, we might have been able to do something between us to nip it in the bud at the barber-shop. To stop it from escalating like it did.'

'I survived, Rita. You might not have been so lucky, had you been there. He was seriously deranged. On drugs too, I think. There was absolutely no reasoning with him. It was always going to end badly, one way or another.'

'But look what he did to you, Luke: your hands and arms, especially. Meg said the doctors are optimistic, but – please don't take this the wrong way – you look awful right now. How are you going to run your business in the state he's left you in?'

I shrug. 'I'll cross that bridge when I come to it. I don't know if you realise, but he – the guy who did this – was one of the homeless guys we cut the hair of the first time you got involved: a bloke with a nasty scar across one cheek. He kicked up a fuss before you and Sharon arrived. I think it might have been you who cut his hair. I know I didn't do it.'

'No, it wasn't me.' She drums her fingers on the side of the bed. 'It was Sharon. She, um, saw his photo on the TV when they were reporting on it. She called me straight afterwards to see if you were okay, which was a bit of a shock, because it was the first I'd heard about it. Anyway, turns out he was a nasty piece of work back then too. He was whispering all kinds of horrible stuff to her, apparently, when no one else was in earshot. Things he wanted to do to her and so on. I'm sure you can use your imagination.'

I'm stunned by this. 'What? Seriously? Why didn't she

say anything? I can't believe neither of us noticed. I feel awful.'

'That's what I said, Luke. She told me she didn't want to make a fuss, particularly as it was only words. She felt sorry for him. Now I understand why she didn't want to help out again.'

'Yeah, totally. Oh, I wish she'd told me at the time. No one should ever have to put up with that kind of thing. God, that's so awful. She was there to help me. I should have been watching out for her.'

'You can't feel any worse than I do, Luke, for the same reason. I was probably too busy laughing and joking with the others to notice.'

'How's she doing now?' I ask.

'She says she's fine. If anything, she feels bad for not speaking up, as she thinks that might have stopped what happened to you.'

'I doubt that very much. If he came at me like this after I threatened to kick him out for arguing, imagine what he might have done if I'd barred him for talking to Sharon that way. She has nothing to feel bad about. Nothing at all.'

I'm still wrapping my mind around this latest shock revelation, even though we've moved on to discussing other things, when, to my complete surprise, another visitor I wasn't expecting walks into the ward and up to my bed.

'Hello, Luke. I'm so sorry for what you've been through. I want to ask how you are, but it seems like a stupid question. I hope you don't mind me visiting. I was so upset when I heard, I had to see you.'

CHAPTER 27

I can't believe Nora is here in the hospital. All of a sudden, I feel self-conscious about how I look, in a way I didn't when Rita showed up. Thank goodness I had a wash earlier and changed out of the hospital gown into my own clothes, even if they are just a T-shirt and jogging bottoms.

She leans over the bed to greet me with a kiss, which is nice of her. Then, as she turns to say hello to Rita, who of course she's met before, part of me starts to worry that maybe she's only here because she wants to report on my story: my account of what happened with Moxie.

As if she can read my mind, she says: 'To be clear, I'm not here on a professional basis. I'm here as a friend. Anything you say about what happened is strictly between us and off the record.'

Looking at Rita, she adds: 'Hard news isn't my kind of thing. I've always hated the pushy, door-knocking stuff. I had to do my share when I started out on local newspapers, but I was glad to leave it behind. I've always been much more comfortable as a feature writer, like I am now.'

Rita, who no doubt met her share of news hounds after Iris's death, nods her acceptance. Despite her initial fury at me over the haircuts for the homeless press coverage, she never seems to have had an issue with Nora's involvement, presumably because what she wrote was so accurate and only showed Iris in a good light.

'Pull up a chair,' I say, gesturing towards a small stack near the door, wishing I was in a position to be more gentlemanly.

'Actually,' Rita says, 'take mine and I'll get another in a minute. I could murder a brew. I saw a vending machine down the hall earlier; I think I'll pay a visit. Can I get anything for anyone else?'

'No, thanks,' Nora and I say in unison.

'I had one before you got here,' I add, smiling.

'And I have some water in my bag,' Nora says.

Rita is already on her feet. 'Back soon.'

She flashes me a discreet wink as she says this, which confirms what I already thought: she's deliberately giving me some time alone with Nora. I want to tell her it's really not necessary, since things aren't like that between us, but there's no easy way to do that, so I simply smile back at her.

Once we're alone and Nora is sitting at my bedside, she asks me the kind of questions I'm getting used to answering now, about the severity of my injuries and how it all unfolded. She too feels bad about not being there at the barbershop that evening, particularly since I'd asked her if she wanted to come along. However, I reassure her that the attack was something none of us could have predicted or should beat ourselves up about.

'There was only one person to blame for what happened,' I say, 'and he's dead now.'

'You're so brave, talking about it like you do. I'd be in pieces if I was the one in your shoes.' After saying this, Nora unexpectedly places a hand on my leg; to my considerable embarrassment, especially after being called brave, this makes me jump.

'Sorry,' she says, holding her hands up and grimacing. 'I didn't mean to. You must be—'

'It's fine,' I reply. 'I'm still a bit on edge, I think. It'll probably take me a while to, um, you know.'

Changing the subject, I ask her if she's been up to anything much recently.

'Not really,' she replies. 'Apart from going on the date from hell the other evening.' She pauses, her face turning pink, as she appears to struggle to find the right words. Once she does, it's obvious why. 'I, um, feel awful saying this, but that was what I was doing when, er, you went through what you did. It was a blind date a friend of mine had set up a few weeks ago, so I felt like I had to go along. Anyway, I wish I hadn't. It was a total disaster from start to finish. Sorry, Luke, I'm sure this is the last thing you want to hear about right now.'

'On the contrary. I'm only too happy to be distracted with other more normal things. This sounds perfect – do tell.'

I accept that encouraging Nora to share this story with me is effectively friend-zoning myself once and for all, but I'm pretty sure that's already how she sees me. Plus I could do with a good laugh.

'Fine,' she says, smiling and shaking her head. 'If you're sure you can stomach it.'

'Come on,' I reply. 'It can't be worse than the water sports bloke you told me about last time. Can it?'

Keeping a straight face while looking up into the air, she jiggles her head from side to side, like she's seriously weighing up my question.

'Oh dear,' I say. 'That does sound ominous. So, come on, take me through what happened.'

'Well, he looked okay – tall, dark and relatively handsome – so my initial impression wasn't bad. But then he opened his mouth and had this absurd Mr Bean voice. Honestly, I thought he was putting it on as a joke to start with, but I soon realised that was actually how he talked.'

'Nice.'

'Not really. Anyway, the next thing he did, about five minutes into the date, was ask me how many sexual partners I'd had, before announcing that he'd lost count once he'd passed the one hundred mark.'

'Wow, what a gentleman. I hope you didn't give him an answer.'

'Too right I didn't. I'd have been out of there already if it was a date I'd arranged myself, but I felt obliged to stick it out because of my friend's involvement. I figured there must have been some reason she'd thought we would be a good match. There wasn't, though. He was disgusting.

He talked with his mouth full, his fingernails were dirty and he kept making lewd comments about how we should sneak off to the toilets together to get properly acquainted. He even suggested using the disabled loos because there would be more room.'

'Oops,' I say, chortling. 'He sounds like the date from hell. How long did you put up with him?'

'I had a starter and main. But after watching him chew his way through a large steak with his gob almost permanently open, boasting about how loaded and successful he was, that was all I could manage. I feigned having a bad headache, which he delightfully offered to "shag away". When he eventually grasped that I really was about to leave, he said he was going to stay on for pudding and coffee, regardless; he called me "mardy" before asking the waitress what time she knocked off and if she wanted to go clubbing with him.'

I roll my eyes. 'Lucky her.'

'Oh, she wasn't having any of it. She laughed it off and flashed her wedding ring. I didn't hang around to see what happened next, but he probably continued to proposition her, thinking she was playing hard to get. He loved himself so much, I don't think he could understand why anyone else wouldn't feel the same.'

'What was your friend's explanation for putting you through that? Was she angry at you or something?'

'Good question. I spoke to her about it afterwards, obviously, and she said she'd never seen him behave that way, putting it down to nerves on his part. Turns out he was more of her husband's friend than hers and she'd only met him briefly a couple of times. Anyway, that's me done with blind dates. Never again.'

Rita returns empty-handed, pulling up another chair. 'Didn't you manage to find a brew?' I ask her. 'You were gone for ages.'

'I, er, drank it out there,' she says. 'I wasn't sure if I'd be allowed to bring it back in here.'

I don't query this, knowing full well the real reason for her delay, although it was totally unnecessary.

She ends up staying longer than Nora, who has to head off to interview someone for a feature, so before long it's just the two of us again.

'Lovely lass that one,' she says. 'What's the, er, situation between the two of you?'

I'm surprised at the directness of Rita's question. 'Um, we only met fairly recently. She was already a friend of Meg's and, um, she was good enough to agree to write the articles about the homeless stuff. That's it really.'

'Hmm,' Rita says in response. 'If you say so.'

'What does that mean?'

She tries to keep a straight face, but the hint of a smile slips through. 'Nothing. Nice of her to call by and see you in hospital. She obviously thinks highly of you. Cares enough to make the effort. Anyway, that's none of my business. There is, er, something else I wanted to speak to you about, though.'

'Sure,' I say, glad of a change in subject. 'What's that, then?'

She pauses before continuing, biting her upper lip and giving me the distinct impression that she's choosing her words carefully. 'I've been thinking, Luke. You're not going to be able to cut hair for a while with those injuries of yours. Saying you'll cross that bridge when you come to it is all well and good, but you're already there as far as I can see.

'The barbershop has been closed since Monday night. You're not going to be opening up any time soon – and that's not good for business – so I've got a suggestion I'd like you to consider.'

'Okay. What kind of suggestion?'

'I'm getting to that. Bear with me.' She takes a deep breath. 'How about I run the business for you until you're ready to take over again?'

CHAPTER 28

Rita has been gone for a couple of hours now, but she's barely left my thoughts. Her proposal took me completely by surprise; I'm still not sure what to make of it.

Is she serious?

Has she thought it through?

The answer to both of these questions would seem to be yes, from what she told me before she left.

Is she up to the job?

Absolutely, based on what I've observed from working alongside her. She has all the necessary haircutting skills and a far better manner with the clients than I do. She even used to run her own salon, so the practical side of things – opening and closing, dealing with the money, keeping the place clean and tidy, etc. – shouldn't be a problem either.

So why am I hesitant to take her up on the offer?

Why aren't I snapping her hand off?

I'm not exactly sure. That's why it's been on my mind so much ever since she suggested it.

I suppose part of me is concerned about her reasons for making the offer. Is it because she feels bad about what happened to me and wants to make up for what she perceives to be partly her fault?

If so, I have major issues with that, since it isn't her fault in the slightest. And a misplaced sense of guilt shouldn't be the cause of her doing something she wouldn't otherwise want to do.

My other worry, and it's a big one, is about her safety. After what happened to me in the barbershop, how could I in good conscience allow anyone else – Iris's aunt no less – to work alone there? Imagine if something similarly horrific befell her while she was helping me out. I'd never forgive myself.

Rita didn't give me a proper chance to discuss these concerns with her after making the suggestion.

'Don't say anything for now,' she said, already standing up to go. 'I wanted to mention it and then give you some time to consider. I know it's a big decision, so have a good think about it. Take as long as you need. You know where I am. Once you're ready, I'll happily address any questions you might have. And if the answer's no, for whatever reason, that's fine too. I won't be offended.

'I'll leave it with you. But know this, Luke: I'm making the offer in all seriousness and having thought it through at length, so please give it proper consideration. I'm sure we could reach terms that would be financially amicable for both of us. Plus it would give you an easy path to gradually return to work rather than having to do it in one go.'

That last point in particular definitely got me thinking. If she was to run things in my absence, it would certainly allow me to ease my way back into the job, doing the odd cut alongside her to start with, for instance, and progressing from there. But that doesn't address my concerns, which is why I'm still scratching my head about what to do. I'm glad Meg's coming to visit me again later today, as I'll be interested to get her take on things. Hopefully she'll be able to help me decide.

I'm feeling a bit sorry for myself by the time Meg's due to arrive that evening. It's frustrating trying to do things when your hands are sore and bandaged up. I also had another visit from the police late this afternoon, which meant going over various details of what happened with Moxie for the umpteenth time, wearing me out and leaving me miserable.

I was expecting my cousin at seven o'clock, so when it gets to quarter past, I'm all for believing she's not coming at all.

Something must have come up; nice of her to let me know.

No sooner have I thought this than I start to worry that she might have been involved in an accident on the way here.

I check the old mobile Meg's lent me to see if I've received any messages, but I haven't. Is that a good or a bad thing?

I consider calling or messaging her myself, but now the idea of her having an accident is in my head, I can't shift it. I even worry that if she's still on her way, I could be the one to cause her to crash by making contact and distracting her.

What's wrong with me?

Why am I thinking like this?

I tell myself to stop being so pessimistic; to remember my quest to become a glass-half-full person and to honour Iris's memory. However, the argument sounds half-hearted and hollow to my ears.

It's not pessimism but realism, another part of me asserts in return; optimism is akin to delusion in a world where shit can and usually does happen.

It's hard to disagree with this contention in light of everything bad that has occurred in my life so far.

And it's not like I haven't tried optimism. I've given it a good go; the results speak for themselves.

Where has my attempt at changing myself got me? What have I gained?

At that moment, I hear a voice in the corridor that I recognise.

It sounds like . . . no, I must be mistaken.

Only I'm not.

It really is my neighbour Doreen, I realise, as she strolls into the ward ahead of Meg and, to my further surprise, my other neighbour Sylvia, whose iPad I fixed and furniture I rearranged.

'There you are,' Doreen says. 'I've been worried sick about you. We all have, haven't we, Sylvia? Pauline wanted to come too, but she has a terrible cold and we didn't want her to pass it on to you in your fragile state.'

'This is a surprise,' I say, flashing my cousin a quizzical look. Her brow furrows in return, causing me to add: 'How lovely of you all to come and see me.'

Doreen looks from me to her friend. 'It was the least we could do, wasn't it, Sylvia?'

'Oh, yes,' Sylvia adds. 'We were terribly shocked to hear what happened to you. What's the world coming to?'

'Exactly,' Doreen says. 'I bumped into your lovely cousin when she was feeding your cat earlier. I told her how much we wanted to visit you in hospital and she was good enough to pick us up and bring us along with her. How are you, my love? Are you in a terrible amount of pain?'

'I didn't know you had a female fan club,' Meg whispers into my ear with a little giggle as she greets me after the other two. 'You're a dark horse.'

One of the nurses pops over to say I'm only supposed to have two visitors at once – not something that's ever been a problem before – so Meg takes herself off for a coffee, agreeing to come back and swap with one of the other two in a few minutes.

It's sweet how they fuss over me, Doreen and Sylvia, asking if they can pour me a glass of water or do anything else to help, concern etched in the wrinkles on their foreheads. I'm touched that they've come to visit me at all, particularly considering how I've only got to know them recently. I didn't expect it.

Luckily, they don't ask for a blow-by-blow account of

what happened. Their main questions concern my current and future wellbeing; they're especially interested in knowing how long I'll be staying in hospital for.

'Not too long, I wouldn't think,' is my response. 'I should be home in a day or two.'

Doreen gives me an intense look. 'Well, don't you worry one jot about struggling to do certain things on your own, Luke, because you're not – on your own, that is. Anything you need, we'll be there to help you, like you've helped us. And that includes Pauline. She was really sorry not to be able to join us here today.'

Part of me wants to tell them I'll be fine and won't need any help. But that's probably not true. They also look so earnest and kind in their desire to assist me, I couldn't bring myself to reject them like that.

'Thank you,' I say instead. 'That means a great deal.'

'If you ever needed me to,' Doreen adds, 'I'd be only too happy to feed the cat for you as well. I already told Meg this, although she said it's no trouble for her.'

'The same goes for me,' Sylvia adds. 'I love animals.'

I nod and smile at them both. 'You're too kind.' I do appreciate the offer, although I'm secretly glad Meg said what she did; I'm not sure I'm ready to start handing out keys to my flat willy-nilly just yet.

One step at a time.

When Meg returns, the other two go off to grab a brew and stretch their legs.

'I didn't do the wrong thing bringing them along with me, did I?' Meg asks once they're out of earshot.

'No, no. Not at all. It's nice to have so many visitors.

'I'm a bit taken aback, to be honest, especially after Rita and Nora coming this afternoon too.'

'Mum and Dad also send their love and best wishes from Auckland, by the way.'

'Really?' I say. 'That's nice of them.'

'Yeah, we had a video chat last night. They were so shocked and worried. They actually made me promise to keep a close eye on you to make sure nothing else bad happens.'

Soon I steer the conversation towards Rita's proposal. Now that I have a few moments alone with my cousin, I'm keen to get her advice about what to do.

Meg's instant reaction, once I bring her up to speed, is resoundingly positive. 'Wow,' she says. 'That's amazing. How generous of her. It sounds like the perfect solution to me. What did you say?'

'She, um, told me to give it some thought. She didn't want an answer straight away.'

The hint of a frown forms as Meg scrutinises my face. 'Yeah, okay, but surely you're going to say yes, right? Why on earth wouldn't you? Remember, a while ago, when I suggested the idea of her working with you? And that was before she started helping out with the homeless haircuts. Maybe you should try listening to me once in a while.'

I voice my two main concerns, the first of which Meg brushes aside. 'It's not for you to question her motives, Luke. She wants to help you. That's what matters. She probably does feel bad about what happened, like I do. It's only normal when you consider she was the last person to see you before he turned up. I really don't see why that's a problem. If she's running the barbershop, you'll have plenty of opportunity to put her straight. And it's not like she'll be doing it for free, anyway. She'll keep the business ticking over and make some cash for herself in the process. It's a win-win situation.'

'What about her safety, then?' I ask. 'That's a genuine concern for me after what happened. Moxie might be gone, but that doesn't mean someone else won't turn up and do something similar. I've seen first-hand that even the people you think have their heads screwed on tight can have issues with drugs and so on.'

'What does that mean?' Meg asks.

I explain about my encounter with Tommy after he'd taken spice. 'It was gut-wrenching,' I say. 'He was like a totally different person. In fact, scratch that, he wasn't like a person at all. He was like a zombie. And if taking drugs can do that to him, well . . . Moxie was clearly on something too. It really scares me, Meg. I invited these guys into my barbershop. Who knows what might happen next?'

My cousin looks at me with pity in her eyes. 'Oh, Luke. I totally understand where you're coming from and why you say that, but you can't live that way. No matter what you've been through – and I know you've been through way more than most – you mustn't allow fear to rule your life. You've been opening and closing that barbershop alone for years. How many other businesses in the area do the same every day?'

Citing her own jewellery store as an example, she adds: 'I manage alone a lot of the time. Ellen's only there with me a couple of days a week. And don't forget we're talking

280

about Rita here. She's not exactly wet behind the ears. She's a strong woman who ran her own salon in the past. She's more than capable of doing this. I literally can't think of anyone better to help you out.'

I want to argue with her, to say that my concerns are based on common sense rather than fear, but I can't. Her words have shifted something in my mind. She's right: I am afraid. That's where trying to be an optimist has landed me. Positivity doesn't allow you to prepare yourself for the worst-case scenario like negativity does, and now I'm itching to return to the security of contingency planning, of believing in Sod's Law and actively preparing for it.

And yet when I was permanently pessimistic, I was miserable. I was lonely as well, although too stubborn to realise it. I might have been more ready for dealing with bad news, but at what cost? I never really got to enjoy the good.

Who visited me in hospital after the scaffolding accident? Meg and no one else.

Look at the difference this time around.

Yes, I might have been less prepared for dealing with Moxie's attack, but I've also got a far better support structure to help me get over it.

And I'm still alive, aren't I?

I take a few deep breaths before responding to Meg. 'I hear you,' I say eventually. 'And I think you're probably right. But after what happened to me, I'm still struggling with the idea of Rita being there alone, particularly at closing time. I'm coming around to the idea, but I'll need some kind of security blanket in place before I can truly get behind it.'

CHAPTER 29

Two days later, I'm released from hospital and head home. My wounds are healing well, I'm told. They still hurt, don't get me wrong. But the bandaging is already less than it was, making it easier to do things by myself. I can feel a slow improvement day by day.

I was given the option of regular visits to the nurse at my local GP surgery to have the dressing changed, or for someone to be shown how to do it for me in between check-ups. Luckily, Meg agreed to the latter, which should make things easier.

It's 8.06 p.m. and she's just left after helping me to get settled and promising to call in again first thing tomorrow.

'In the meantime, give me a call if you need anything at all,' she said as I saw her out.

Handing me a small piece of paper, Meg added: 'And here's a list of the phone numbers of your female fan club, in case you need someone on the spot. Doreen wasn't sure if you had all of their details; she assured me that she,

Sylvia and Pauline would be at your beck and call, should you need them. I wouldn't be at all surprised if they call in to check on you tomorrow, regardless, so best not lounge around in your pyjamas. Otherwise, they might need medical help themselves to slow their pulses.'

I shook my head at this. 'You're hilarious, Meg.'

She shrugged, keeping a straight face. 'What, hot stuff? It's not my fault you're so popular with the pensioners.'

I'm now sitting on the sofa in the lounge. The news is on, but I'm not really watching it. I'm too busy stroking Alfred, who's barely left my side since I returned and is currently on my knee, staring at me and purring. I'm also going through the small pile of letters that arrived in my absence and Meg has left for me to open. Most of it is the usual boring stuff – bank statements, bills and so on – but then I come across a handwritten envelope that instantly sets my pulse racing.

Even without the telltale Edinburgh postmark, I'd recognise that swirly style of writing anywhere. How could I not after living for years with the person it belongs to? There's definitely no mistaking it. Long before I build up the courage to tear it open, I'm certain it's a letter from my ex-wife.

So why am I staring at the envelope rather than reading the contents?

I haven't heard a peep from Helen – the woman who nearly destroyed me when she cast me aside – in ages. What's changed? Why now?

Do I even want to know what she has to say?

Is this about me being attacked? The date stamped on

the envelope is from the day after the incident took place, so that's a possibility.

I won't ever know for sure unless I look inside, will I?

Why can't I bring myself to do so, then?

What am I afraid of?

'What do you reckon, Alfred?' I say to the cat, since no one else is around to ask. 'Should I open it or not?'

He continues to stare at me, so I thank him for his insight and put the letter to one side for a bit.

It feels strange to be home, particularly because I'm by myself now, rather than surrounded by other people like I was at the hospital. There is a small part of me that's anxious about this, which is probably natural in the circumstances, but I push that feeling to one side rather than engage with it.

I've no idea whether or not this is a good way to deal with my hang-ups, as no appointment with a counsellor, therapist or whatever has materialised so far. I'd probably self-medicate with a beer if there were any cans or bottles in the fridge, but unfortunately there aren't. So I settle for a cup of tea instead. Alfred follows me to the kitchen to watch me make it, jumping straight back on my knee once I sit down again.

'Wow, you are pleased to see me,' I tell him, stroking the soft fur on his little head. 'You haven't even pestered me for food yet. Has Aunty Meg been overfeeding you?'

As much as I try to ignore it, the unopened letter won't leave my mind. It may as well be lit up in bright neon. My eyes keep landing on the small rectangle of paper, scrutinising the familiar script detailing my name and address; wondering if it holds any clues as to Helen's mood when she gripped the black ballpoint pen to write it. If it does, they're lost on me.

The only sure-fire way to find out what Helen wants is to read the damn letter.

Right then.

I grab the envelope and rip it open in one movement to make sure there's no opportunity to change my mind. I pull out the contents: three sheets of plain A4 paper, each covered with the same handwriting. I take a deep breath and start reading.

Dear Luke,

How are you? I hope you're well. You've been in my thoughts a lot recently. I've been meaning to contact you for a while. I've almost phoned you on countless occasions but always ended up chickening out at the last minute.

I'd love to chat to you, but I'm afraid the feeling won't be mutual. Hence my decision to contact you by letter. I could have messaged you or sent an email instead, which would probably have made more sense in this day and age, but that didn't feel right somehow.

A handwritten letter felt more appropriate – more personal.

I can't remember the last time I sent a letter like this to anyone. I think that's probably the point. I want it to stand out and for you to see how much this matters to me.

So what's going on? That must be what you're

wondering. Why is Helen contacting me out of the blue like this?

You probably hoped never to hear from me again after everything I put you through. I'm right, aren't I? It's fine. I totally understand. To be honest, I wouldn't blame you for hating me with a passion, the way I abandoned you while you were still grieving for your parents.

I hated doing it even then, especially right before Christmas, but I couldn't help myself. I'm sorry to say this, but I was head-over-heels in love with another man, and I desperately wanted to be with him. I'd stayed with you for as long as I possibly could, because of your grief, but the time had arrived, difficult as it was, to come clean and stop lying to you. It felt like the lesser of two evils by that point.

I don't expect you to understand, but I honestly thought I was doing the right thing by everyone in telling you.

You must be wondering why on earth I'm spilling my guts to you now about all of this. There's a reason, which I'll come to in a minute. But first I want to apologise to you for never properly clarifying this before.

I don't remember us ever really talking it through. I told you about Adrian; you were angry, understandably, and needed time alone to process it. Then I was gone. The only real conversations we had after that were about practical matters to do with the separation and then the divorce, which I can only thank you for *making as painless as you did when you could have dragged your heels. That was far better than I deserved.*

Anyway, recent developments in my life have given me a new perspective on what happened, making me realise that you were the one who deserved better. For a start, I should have given you a clearer explanation. I also should have told you straight away, rather than dragging it out because I feared you wouldn't be able to handle it. I genuinely thought I was being kinder that way, but now I know the truth is always better than a lie, no matter the circumstances.

It wasn't you, Luke, it was me. I'm very aware of what a cliché that is, but it also happens to be true. You didn't do anything wrong. That's not why I left – and I don't think I made that clear enough.

Yes, you were consumed by grief throughout the end of our time together. Of course you were. But that wasn't the reason I fell out of love with you. It happened before that, gradually, over a long period. It wasn't an overnight thing. It wasn't even caused by me reconnecting with Adrian. I'd never have done that in the first place if something hadn't already been missing.

We grew apart, that's all. Me in particular. The love I felt for you at the start and when we got married was genuine. It truly was, Luke. But that faded – and one day it dawned on me I was unhappy. I felt like there was a gaping hole in my life and, for some reason, I couldn't talk to you about it. I should have. I see that now. Maybe we could even have worked things out if I had . . . maybe.

But that's not what happened, is it? We both know what I did instead and where that left us.

One thing that's always bothered me is what your take must be on my change of heart in terms of having children. We both agreed that we didn't want them, and then look what happened when I got together with Adrian: I fell pregnant in no time.

I remember calling you up to tell you the news as if it was yesterday. I felt like I had to, but the conversation didn't go as planned. I'd intended to assure you then that it wasn't any reflection on you; to admit it was an accident. I was all ready to confess that my first reaction to the positive test had been one of horror, only for Adrian to talk me round, convincing me to keep the baby. I wanted to tell you, knowing that you'd understand better than anyone how terrified I was feeling about the idea of being someone's parent.

But I couldn't do it. My pride kicked in, together with a sense of not wanting to betray Adrian. So I found myself lying to you – saying the pregnancy was planned, when that couldn't have been further from the truth.

I'm so sorry for doing that, Luke. I really hope it didn't make you feel like I'd always secretly wanted children – just not with you – because that wasn't the case at all. You'd make a wonderful father, if that was something you wanted. I know you would.

Personally, I don't regret becoming a mum. I fell in love the moment my eyes landed on Euan's little face; all my fears and doubts about parenthood soon ebbed away, to the point where our second child, Gwen, really was planned. I adore them both and can't imagine life without them now.

As for Adrian, karma's a bitch, isn't it? I don't need to imagine life without him because that's been my reality for several months now.

Yep, you've guessed it, he left me for another woman. Well, more of a girl really: Jess, a twenty-something former postgrad student of his from the university, who he's currently shacked up with and thinks is his soulmate. The only time I see him now is when it's his turn to take the kids.

I won't bore you with the rest of it. Not your problem. And I'll forgive you if you're thinking I got my just deserts, because you're probably right.

I certainly don't expect your sympathy. That's not what this letter is for. It's about me being able to see things from your perspective, having gone through a similar experience myself, and wanting to make amends; to set the record straight.

As I wrote at the start of this letter, I've been meaning to contact you for a while. The thing that finally sparked me to do so was when my mum mentioned seeing an article about you in her Sunday newspaper supplement, which she made a copy of and emailed to me.

I was so proud of you when I read about what

you've been doing for the homeless in Manchester. It sounds like you've found your place in life and that things are going brilliantly for you and the business. I'm really glad, honestly. You deserve it.

That said, how awful what took place with you and that poor young doctor who died in the scaffolding accident. I'm shocked not to have heard anything about this previously, especially considering how close we once were. It feels dreadful to think what you must have gone through. Still, it's amazing that you've turned what happened around and built something so positive out of such a tragedy.

Lastly, I pray you can find it in your heart to accept my apologies for everything I did to you. I hope you have a wonderful life and that one day we can perhaps meet up as old friends and reflect on the good times we had together.

Love and best wishes,
Helen X

CHAPTER 30

Wow, that letter. Not what I was expecting at all. Although, honestly, I'm not sure what I was expecting. It's not like I had any idea Helen was going to write to me until she did.

I'm confusing myself now, but that's how I feel – utterly bewildered – and I've read it through several times, one immediately after the other.

I'm tempted to go straight in for another read, but taking some time to reflect on the letter's contents seems like a better idea, all in all.

It feels downright weird to have heard from my ex-wife after all this time – and in such detail. I've not had this kind of insight into her mind in forever. It's a lot to take in, particularly considering what she's written; how honest she's been at last.

The detail that strikes me most, apart from the shocking revelation about Adrian having left her, is her confession about that first pregnancy. So it wasn't planned after all.

And it wasn't some inherent fault in me that stopped her from wanting children when we were together.

That's huge, because I think it's something that's weighed heavily on my mind, consciously and subconsciously, ever since we had that telephone chat about her being pregnant. Prior to the call, I didn't think there was anything more Helen could do to hurt me than she already had; it surprised me how injured I felt afterwards.

I analysed the breakdown of our relationship against the backdrop of that single conversation and deduced that it was probably all my fault.

My conclusions: I wasn't good enough for her; I wasn't the kind of person with whom anyone would want to have a family; I was fundamentally flawed and unlovable.

Had Mum and Dad still been around, I'd have discussed it with them and they'd have no doubt helped me to see things from a more reasonable, detached perspective. But they weren't. They were gone. I should probably have talked about it with Meg or someone else instead, but I didn't, for whatever reason. Foolishly, I convinced myself I could handle it alone and accepted my skewed interpretation of events as fact. I used that as the foundation for a new hardened, bitter version of myself, created with the prime purpose of protecting me from ever getting hurt by anyone in the same way again.

Helen really did a number on me, didn't she?

And yet I don't feel even the slightest bit happy about what's happened to her. I don't think for one minute that she got her just deserts. Mainly I feel sorry that Adrian let her down so spectacularly when she gambled everything on him being the right guy for her. I know exactly how that feels, although it's probably even worse for Helen than it was for me when you factor in the children too.

Poor things, having to grow up in a broken family. That's bound to affect them in one way or another for the rest of their lives. They'll probably end up believing it was partly their fault; that their father didn't love them enough to stay, perhaps. Or maybe they'll even end up blaming their mum, thinking she drove him away. Not fair, of course, but that's the kind of polarising fallout you get from breakups.

No, rather than being glad about this, I genuinely hope Helen and Adrian manage to work things out. It is still possible, I guess, although the odds don't sound particularly high at the moment. Hopefully he'll wake up one morning, realise what a huge mistake he's made and head home with his tail between his legs. Whether she would take him back at that stage is another matter. But like she wrote in the letter, none of that is my problem.

When Helen first left me, I used to consider what I'd do if she came running back, full of apologies. My predicted response varied from one day to another, depending on my mood. Sometimes I was convinced I'd tell her to sling her hook and never to darken my door again. On other occasions, I imagined making her beg and then, perhaps, after a long period of penance, giving her another chance.

That all changed after she had kids. It ended once and for all for me at that point, not least because of my perception that she considered wife-stealing Adrian more suitable, capable or whatever to father children with her than me.

Now, even though she's blown that theory out of the water, my feelings about this – about the possibility of us ever being a romantic couple again – haven't changed. That door remains permanently closed. And yet after the way she poured her heart out to me in this letter, I wouldn't mind speaking to her. I think I could be ready at last to forgive her and be her friend. I'd also like to thank her for finally providing this explanation and, in doing so, giving me the closure I didn't know I needed until I got it.

It does surprise me that I'm not at least a bit angry with her. Particularly for lying to me about that first pregnancy, bearing in mind how much it's affected me.

But do you know what? Life's too short. I've twice looked death in the face in less than two months – and yet, somehow, I'm still here.

It puts things into perspective.

Why be angry at Helen now for something she did so long ago, which she clearly regrets and told me about of her own free will? Especially considering the pain she's already going through, thanks to that idiot Adrian. Why choose hate when I can rise above it and choose love instead?

Wow, I sound like Iris now, or at least the version of her I've got to know in my dreams.

I look down at my bandaged arms and hands, still holding the letter. Weirdly, I've not noticed my injuries once since I started reading and considering Helen's words.

How strange to think she doesn't even know about them or any of what happened with Moxie. But still she chose to send her letter at this particular time. I have an eerie sense that she may even have been writing it while the incident with Moxie was unfolding.

She thinks my life is going well, which couldn't be further from the truth. How far apart we've grown from the time when we used to share everything with each other.

I'm woken up the next morning, having allowed myself to sleep in, by the sound of someone knocking on my front door. It's 10.03 a.m. on Saturday. Since whoever's there is already inside the building, I assume it must be one of my neighbours: Doreen, most likely.

Feeing groggy and sore, I'm tempted to ignore the noise until it stops, so I can catch some more Zs. But then I picture Doreen panicking and calling Meg or even the emergency services, worried that something might have happened to me. Keen to dodge such hassle, I throw on my dressing gown, narrowly avoiding tripping over Alfred, who's curled in a ball in front of my bedroom door, and go to see who's knocking.

'Luke Craven?' a young man's voice snaps at me the moment I swing open the door.

'What? Who are you?'

I'm looking at a short, wiry chap with pockmarked skin. He has dark, slicked-back hair and a smattering of stubble on his chiselled jaw and upper lip. He can't be much older than early twenties and I'm sure I've never clapped eyes on him before. Dressed in smart trousers and a thick grey coat, he grins at me with the brash bravado of a car salesman, before flashing a press pass.

'I'm Billy,' he says. 'From Billy Broome Media. I'm here to make your day.'

Seriously? I really don't need this right now.

'I'm not interested,' I reply. 'I don't know where you got my details from, but I'd appreciate it if you could leave me alone.'

'Please could you hear me out for a minute?' he says, eyes wide and arms apart with his palms facing up. This makes him look a bit needy and pathetic.

I sigh. 'Fine, you've literally got sixty seconds, but that's it. And I'm not inviting you in.'

'No problem,' he says. 'So I'm a journalist. I run my own press agency and I work with all the big media names. I know for a fact that some of them would pay good money to publish your story after the terrible ordeal you went through the other night. I'm here to facilitate that in one go: no need to deal with anyone other than me. How does that sound? You deserve some cash after what you went through, right?'

'Still not interested,' I say. 'Thanks but no thanks. Have a nice day.'

'Listen,' he continues. 'I'll be completely honest with you. If you don't talk to me, there will be a sea of other people hounding you. And if you don't talk to them, things will probably get made up. Not by me – I don't work that way – but there are some people in this business without my moral fibre, if you know what I mean.'

'I'll take my chances,' I tell him.

'Okay, I'm sorry to say this, but there are rumours circulating about you selling drugs out of your barbershop. I'm sure they're not true. I don't believe them for a minute. But don't you want the opportunity to respond to them and set the record straight?'

I can't believe what I'm hearing. What the hell is this guy on about?

I'm so shocked and disgusted that I try to shut the door without saying another word, only to find he's placed his foot in the way. It's a tan brogue this time, rather than the black army boot Moxie wore, but it's more than enough to cause a flashback to the other night and the start of my nightmare ordeal.

I see red and, next thing I know, I'm shouting and screaming uncontrollably at this bloke, bellowing all kinds of insults at him at full volume. His expression turns to one of horrified bewilderment. Some of my neighbours emerge out of the doors of their flats to see what's going on, and he turns on his heel to scarper.

'Go on, get lost, scumbag!' I call after him. 'And don't come back or I'll report you for harassment.'

My blood still boiling, I'm about to go back inside to calm down when Doreen appears before me, her face knotted with concern. 'Is everything okay, Luke?' she asks. 'Who on earth was that? What's going on? Should we call the police?'

'Doreen,' I say, taking a deep breath to steady my voice before continuing. 'Sorry about the noise. He was, um, a journalist. Not the nice kind either. He must have tricked his way inside the building and then he wouldn't leave.

He stuck his foot in my door and it reminded me of . . . I guess I, er, panicked.'

Doreen's brilliant. She takes me back inside and, after explaining the situation to the rest of the neighbours, she tours the building to check Billy has really gone and then makes me a cup of tea to calm my nerves.

Later, once I'm alone again, I start to worry about what Billy said to me and what he might do in retaliation for the way I got rid of him. There's only one person I can think of who might be able to help, so I call her mobile, which unfortunately goes straight to voicemail.

'Nora,' I say, leaving a message. 'Sorry to bother you. It's Luke. Is there any chance you could give me a call whenever you get this?'

CHAPTER 31

'You really didn't need to come and see me,' I tell Nora, handing her a glass of water. 'But it's very nice of you and I do appreciate it.'

It feels strange for her to be here in my flat, since she's never visited before. Once I knew she was coming, I found myself tidying up, shifting various bits of junk from the living room to my bedroom. I also made sure to get out of my dressing gown and into some presentable clothes. I'm not a patch on her, though. She looks effortlessly fantastic in black jeans and a white jumper, ruby-red lipstick, hair up in an immaculate bun.

I offered her a tea or coffee when she first arrived. Did she opt for water instead to make it easy for me? She may well have been worried how I'd manage, with my injuries, although they're improving all the time: my hands in particular. I'd be lying if I said it didn't hurt to do certain everyday tasks, but I'm getting there.

'How are you doing now?' she asks. 'I bet it's nice to be home.'

'Definitely. I'm feeling better every day. Well, I was until that idiot Billy Broome called by this morning. Do you know him?'

She wrinkles her nose. 'A little bit. We've run into each other a couple of times on jobs, although we mainly work in different fields. He's all about the tabloids and news stories, really, unlike me. He always seems very, er, full of himself.'

'You can say that again.'

'He started out at one of the regional press agencies a couple of years back and soon became chief reporter there. Next thing, he set up on his own. I've heard it said that he doesn't always do things by the book. What exactly did he tell you? What questions did he ask?'

I recount in detail what happened; Nora raises an eyebrow several times during my account but waits until I've finished before commenting.

'I see,' she says. 'I feel like I ought to apologise on behalf of my profession. It's people like him that give us a bad name.'

'How did he even find out where I live?' I ask. 'And why's he bothering me on a Saturday morning, the day after I get home from hospital?'

'It's surprisingly easy to find out people's addresses, I'm afraid. The Internet's like a backdoor key into everyone's private lives, if you know where to look. With regards to him calling here today, I wouldn't read too much into that. He's probably been trying to get hold of you for a few days. His aim will have been to speak to you first; to beat anyone else to it.'

'It's the drug-dealing allegation he mentioned that's really bothering me,' I say. 'I've no idea where that came from, but obviously it's total rubbish. Have you heard any rumours along those lines?'

'Absolutely not.' Sitting across from me in the lounge, she reaches for her glass and takes a sip from her water. 'It sounds to me like something he made up to try to scare you into talking to him. Typical strong-arm, bullyboy tactics. I'll check it out for you, to be sure. But don't worry: I'll be extra careful not to inadvertently spread any misinformation myself.'

'Thanks,' I say. 'That would be great. I worry he might get vindictive after the way I saw him off. I wouldn't usually have reacted like that, but him blocking the door with his foot . . . I lost it.'

'No, I totally understand. Leave Billy Broome to me. He might think he's well connected, but he's not been around half as long as I have. A couple of chats with the right people and I could get him into some trouble, business-wise. Let me fire a shot across the bows and I bet you'll never hear from him again.'

'Really? Could you? That would be amazing, if you're sure it's not too much trouble. You've done such a lot for me recently, Nora. How can I ever thank you?'

She smiles, looks down at the floor and seems like she's about to say something. Then Alfred appears out of nowhere and springs on to her knee, causing her to jump up and let out a little squeal. This in turn scares the cat, whose tail fluffs out like a racoon's before he tears off again towards my bedroom.

Nora holds both hands to her mouth and slowly starts to laugh. 'Wow. That scared the life out of me.'

Chuckling, I say: 'Nora, meet Alfred, my flatmate of sorts. That was his way of saying hello. You should feel honoured. It's rare for him to be that friendly when he first meets someone. He obviously liked the look of you, until you scared him off. Don't you like cats?'

'I do, actually. I don't have one now, as most of the places I've rented over the years haven't allowed pets, but I did when I was a girl. Prudence, she was called: a beautiful black cat with one white paw—'

'Like in the book *Gobbolino the Witch's Cat*,' I say.

'Exactly,' she replies, her eyes lighting up. 'Gobbolino was my nickname for Prudence, although she did have a small white patch on her chest too, so she wasn't exactly the same. Did you also read that story at primary school? I loved it.'

'I did – and I was a big fan too.'

'I adored Prudence. We spent so much time together. She slept on the end of my bed most nights when I was growing up. She also used to watch me doing my homework for hours on end. Then she got run over during my first term away at university. I was heartbroken. I sobbed for days.'

'I can imagine. I don't know what I'd do without my little lad.'

Nora twists around to face the direction of my bedroom. 'Sorry, Alfred,' she calls. 'You scared me, that's all. I'd love

302

to meet you again later if you'll give me another shot. You're very welcome on my knee.'

Turning back to me, lips contorted into an exaggerated sad face, she adds: 'He probably won't give me another chance now, will he? I reckon I've blown it.'

I grin. 'Don't worry. I'll have a word with him later and tell him how good you've been to me. If anyone can talk him round, I can. We go back a long way.'

'Purrfect. Alfred's a great name for a cat, by the way.'

'Thanks. I like it when pets are called non-typical animal names. If I ever have another male cat, I reckon I'll call him something like Alan or Kevin.'

Nora claps her hands together. 'Yes! Kevin the cat. Love it.'

'Anyway, you were about to say something when Alfred rudely interrupted. About how I might thank you for helping me.'

I regret saying this as soon as it's come out, because Nora's cheeks flush and she looks awkward as hell. 'Um—'

I flash my gritted teeth. 'Sorry, you don't have to answer that. It's just . . . I thought maybe. No, never mind. Can I get you another water?'

'No, thank you,' Nora replies. She looks down at the floor for a long moment, her hair hanging in front of her face. Then she slowly starts to chuckle. 'I feel like a schoolgirl,' she says. 'I'm so used to doing this kind of thing online – through apps and so on, or via well-meaning, if misguided, friends – I'm struggling with what to say in real life, person to person. I almost chickened out then, after Alfred interrupted me, but I'll regret it if I don't say something. I know I will. So here goes nothing.'

She smiles, her white teeth glistening.

Pauses.

And in that gap, time appears to draw to a halt.

My mind and my heart race each other with anticipation.

I think I might know what she's about to say, but I daren't believe it until I actually hear the words.

The silence is killing me, but I force myself not to break it, while doing my utmost to hold her gaze.

An old-fashioned part of me wonders if I ought to be the one to say these words, if they are indeed what I think they might be, but I can't bring myself to interrupt her and risk ruining the moment again.

I gulp and, as my Adam's apple jerks forward, time kicks back into gear.

'I like you, Luke,' she says. 'I felt like we had an instant connection the moment we met. I think we're on the same wavelength. We make each other laugh, which is always a good start, and when I heard what happened to you the other night, I really felt it – like a punch in the gut. That was when I realised how much I cared about you, even though we've not known each other long at all. And I'd like to get to know you better, if that's something you're interested in. At your own speed, of course. I'd never rush anything after, um, all you've been through. So, to get to the point, you asked earlier how you could ever thank me for helping you.'

I nod, smiling. 'I did indeed.'

She attempts a nonchalant shrug but ends up holding

her hand in front of her flushed face, giggling. 'I told you I didn't know how to do this in person.'

'Nonsense,' I reply. 'I think you're doing a great job. But please tell me what it is I can do. I'm dying to know now. And in case it helps, I am definitely interested too. How could I not be?'

'Well, that is nice to know.' She fans her face with both hands. 'Do I look as red as I feel? I reckon you could probably fry an egg on my cheek.'

'I think you look absolutely gorgeous,' I tell her without having to consider it or feeling awkward. The words slip out, although I've never said such a thing to her before. It's as if there used to be an invisible barrier between us – and now it's gone, thanks to Nora's honesty. I can literally feel a shift in the dynamic between us now that we both know where we stand. The air in the room is so charged, I can almost hear it crackling.

She meets my gaze and holds it. 'Maybe you should do something about that, then.'

'Maybe I should.'

We're still staring intensely at each other, on the brink of who knows what, when there's a loud knock on the door, followed by the sound of a familiar voice. 'Hello, Luke, are you there? Don't worry, it's not that nasty man again. It's me, Doreen. I've got some cake to lift your spirits.'

CHAPTER 32

I'm up early this Monday morning, because Meg's got a surprise for me.

She was visiting yesterday afternoon and, before leaving, she instructed me to be ready with an overnight bag by 10.30 a.m. today.

'How come?' I asked her. 'What's going on?'

'You and I are going on a little trip,' she replied. 'It's nothing for you to worry about. Quite the opposite. Just a gift from me to my favourite cousin to help with your recuperation.'

'Where are we going? What about Alfred?'

'Not far and it's only for one night, so the cat should be fine with a big bowl of food and water. Plus Doreen or one of the others can check on him, if needs be. Leave all that to me. Be ready in time with a change of clothes and anything else you need for a night away. Okay?'

'I guess so. Can you really not tell me any more? Surprises make me nervous.'

Meg placed a hand on my shoulder and looked me in the eye. 'Do you trust me?'

'You know I do, Meg. More than anyone else.'

'So trust me, then.'

I look at the clock: 10.21 a.m. Nearly time.

I'm as ready as I'll ever be.

I had yet another freaky dream last night. Well, it was this morning, really; my alarm went off in the middle of it.

I don't recall much, apart from the bit right before I woke up, which still sends shivers down my spine when I think about it. I was in the middle of a particularly large double bed. Lying to my left was a zombie-like version of Iris: a decaying corpse, essentially, which was moving and groaning but did not appear to contain her consciousness. To my right was a similar version of Moxie, although his body was more crushed and mangled than rotten, like you'd imagine it might look after being hit by a moving bus. And he was able to talk, despite his jaw being partly detached from the rest of his head, and one of his eyes having popped out of its socket.

'How does it feel?' I remember him asking me in a gruff voice.

'How does what feel?' I replied.

'Killing the two of us,' he said before erupting into a creepy belly laugh. 'You're almost a serial killer. Maybe we should start calling you the Sweeney Todd of Manchester.'

'I haven't killed anyone. It's not my fault that you died.'

'Are you sure about that?' he said. 'Would either of us be dead now if we hadn't run into you when we did?'

'Seriously? You're the one who came after me with a bloody knife. I wasn't driving the bus that killed you.'

'Whatever helps you deal with it, Luke. You and I both know the truth, though, don't we? Iris does too, but I think her tongue must have rotted away. Shame.'

'That's not Iris,' I told him defiantly. 'She was cremated.'

'Hmm,' he replied. 'I think I'd rather take my chances underground and be buried.'

At that point, I realised we were no longer in a bed but a giant coffin. Suddenly the lid was being shut and I was in the dark, with Moxie's nasty comments in my right ear and Iris's groans in my left.

Moxie cackled. 'Buried alive! Perfect. Ain't karma a bitch?'

And then, thank goodness, I was saved by the bell, aka my clock radio, which I'd set to buzz for once to ensure I got up in time to be ready for Meg's surprise.

There is a part of me that does feel guilty about Iris and even Moxie dying like they did, I must admit. It's only normal to feel like that, I suppose, considering how they were both killed while I survived. Another thing I probably need to discuss with my therapist, whenever I actually get an appointment with one.

Before I have time to dwell on this for too long, the buzzer sounds.

'It's me,' Meg's voice says. 'I'm downstairs with the car. Do you need a hand carrying your stuff?'

'No, I only have a small rucksack. I'll be fine. See you in a minute.'

'Bye, Alfred,' I say, giving him a stroke before I leave.

'You're in charge until I get back, yeah? If Doreen calls in to check on you, be nice.'

He glances at me and then his eyelids slide shut.

'So, come on, where are we going, then?' I ask Meg once I'm in the Mini and she's driving us through the city, our destination still a mystery to me.

She smirks. 'You'll find out soon enough.'

'Really? You're going to make me wait until we get there?'

'Yep.'

'Brilliant.'

'How are you doing today?' she asks. 'Much pain?'

'I'm okay, thanks. My hands are always a bit stiff and sore when I first use them after sleeping, but yeah, they're coming along.'

'Good. Heard any more from Helen?'

'Since her letter, you mean? No. I'm not expecting to either, unless I decide to contact her.'

'Hmm.'

Meg's been funny about this ever since I showed her what my ex-wife wrote. I thought that, like me, she'd be impressed; instead, she's warned me to be wary.

'I'll never trust that woman again,' she says, taking one hand off the steering wheel to wag her forefinger at me. 'Neither should you.'

'I hear you, but I think you're wrong. I've no reason not to take Helen at face value this time.'

Rolling her eyes, Meg moves on to other matters rather than picking a fight. 'Any more unwanted press attention since I saw you yesterday?'

'No, thankfully not. Hopefully Nora's chat with the charming Mr Billy Broome has done the trick. That's not to say I won't be bothered by anyone else, but at least I'll be prepared, if so. Plus, it's not like I haven't been through this kind of thing before. It happened after Mum and Dad were killed and, to a lesser extent, when I survived the scaffolding accident. To be honest, it's usually a case of saying no and they go away. Billy Broome, with his fictional rumours of drug-dealing, was something of an extreme example.'

Meg looks across at me from the driver's seat with a glint in her eye. 'It was good of Nora to help you.'

'Definitely.'

I haven't yet told Meg about the discussion Nora and I had on Saturday when we admitted to liking each other. I probably will do soon, but while she's not telling me where we're going, I'm in no great rush to share this. It is possible that Nora has already mentioned it to her, but I don't think so. I'm pretty sure my cousin would have said something if that was the case. Besides, it's not like she and Nora are that close. They occasionally socialise together; they're not BFFs.

I'm sure Meg will be delighted to hear the news, although things haven't progressed much further than words so far. Doreen turning up when she did saw to that. Nora made her excuses a few minutes after my neighbour's arrival and, while there was a lingering hug goodbye at the door, it didn't feel like the right time to go in for a kiss.

That said, we have been messaging each other a lot

since then; I've also asked her out for dinner on Friday, and she's accepted, so that bodes well.

I have the feeling Meg's about to ask me if there's anything going on between us, but instead she turns the conversation to Rita and her offer to run the barbershop in my absence.

'Made any decision about that yet?' she asks. 'You ought to because, in the meantime, your business is closed.'

'I know that, Meg. I'm working on it.'

'Working on what? What does that even mean, Luke? One way or another, you need to give her an answer – and you need to do so soon. I honestly can't see why you wouldn't take her up on the offer. It's the perfect solution.'

The truth is I am coming around to the idea. I was thinking that maybe I could turn up just before closing time every day and lock up with her. That way she's not on her own and I'm not worrying about it. In my current state, I'm not sure how much help I'd be if anyone did try anything, but at least there would be two of us to face it. Plus I'd still be actively involved in the business, which should make it easier to return to cutting once I'm ready.

So why haven't I told any of this to Rita yet? In truth, it's more about me than her at this stage. I haven't even been back to the barbershop since Moxie forced his way in, held me against my will and robbed me. Since he threatened to kill me with the knife that eventually caused all these injuries to my hands and arms.

The police have been to gather evidence. I lent them the keys, but I didn't join them there, because I was still recovering in hospital at the time. Now the idea of returning to the scene of my real-life nightmare fills me with dread. I know it's something I'll have to face soon, but I'm putting it off as long as I can.

'I'll speak to her later this week, Meg. I promise. And, between you and me, I probably will take her up on it. Please could we drop the subject for now, though? I need a break.'

She replies with a nod and a 'No problem', moving on to easier topics like traffic and the weather.

'It's a lovely sunny day today,' she says. 'More like April than late March, even if the temperature still needs to climb a bit before it truly feels like spring has sprung. It's perfect for where we're heading.'

'I'll have to take your word for it,' I say, 'since I'm clueless about where that might be. Are we nearly there yet?'

'Not too far now.'

CHAPTER 33

We head south out of Manchester and, before long, city and suburbs give way to the open fields and windy lanes of rural Cheshire.

'I've got it,' I say, tongue-in-cheek, as the car takes us deeper into the countryside. 'We're off to a petting zoo. Do I get to ride on a donkey?'

'How did you guess?' Meg replies with a grin.

Eventually, urban familiarity well and truly left behind, we arrive at our actual destination: a swanky four-star hotel in sprawling, immaculate grounds. According to the sign at the entrance, it boasts a golf course, gym, tennis and squash courts, pool and spa facilities.

'Surprise!' Meg says as she negotiates the private road that weaves its way through the estate and up to the main building: a grand Georgian-style structure in red brick with white stonework.

'Wow,' I reply. 'This looks very fancy. So we're staying here, are we?'

'That's right. I thought it would do you good to escape the city for a day or so and enjoy some country air. There are several leisurely walks to be had around the grounds here, apparently. According to reviews I've read online, it's a wonderful place to get away from it all and unwind.'

As Meg drives the Mini into the block-paved car park, to the side of the imposing main building, I see there's a large, more modern extension at the rear and, behind that, a luxurious spa annexe. Floor-to-ceiling tinted glass envelops the large indoor pool and whatever other goodies are on offer, which I imagine include a jacuzzi, sauna, etc., plus treatment rooms. Not that I'll be able to make use of any of these things with my injuries still so fresh.

We saunter into the hotel through the pillared main entrance. A porter offers to help us with our bags but, since we're both travelling light, we politely decline.

Meg instructs me to have a seat while she takes care of checking us in. Ten minutes later, we're settling into our recently refurbished adjoining bedrooms, which each include a wetroom-style en-suite and all the mod cons.

'This is amazing,' I call to my cousin. 'Have you seen the size of the showerhead? It's like a dinnerplate.'

Later, after we've ordered a spot of lunch in one of the hotel bars, I tell her: 'I can't let you pay for all of this. It must be costing you a fortune.'

Sitting across from me, she shakes her head. 'You don't have a choice. It's my gift to you and I want you to enjoy it without thinking about any of that. I got a good deal, don't worry.'

With a sudden catch in her throat, she adds: 'I nearly

lost you – again – the other day, Luke. Let me spoil you a bit, yeah?'

'Fine, but lunch and dinner are on me, no arguments.'

She reluctantly agrees.

'I'm lucky to have you, Meg,' I add, struggling with my own feelings now. 'I love you. I'm so glad we got past our stupid falling-out.'

'Me too. Let's never do that again.'

'Agreed.'

This sets her off crying as I also find myself blinking back the tears.

Gently, I place my damaged right hand on hers, which is resting on the table, and leave it there as we stare at each other in silence, both fighting to contain our emotions in this public place. I'm stuck in a strange no man's land between wanting to sob my heart out and to laugh at myself for being so soppy.

By the time the waiter comes along with our food, we've both just about managed to pull ourselves together.

'So what did you have in mind for this afternoon?' I ask. 'I'd love to jump in the swimming pool or whatever, but I don't think that's on the cards for me while I'm still bandaged up.'

'I thought we could go for a nice leisurely stroll through the grounds while the weather is so lovely. And then I have one more surprise for you.'

I try to get her to tell me more about this surprise as we're walking, but it's soon obvious I'm wasting my breath, so I give up and focus on enjoying the moment, which isn't hard considering the gorgeous surroundings. I wear my usual beanie hat initially, but the weather is so nice, my head starts to get hot, so I whip it off.

'This is lovely,' I say as we reach a large fish pond and stop for a breather. 'And I don't just mean the scenery. I'm talking about the whole visit here. I don't know what gave you the idea, but it's perfect. I feel so chilled, like we're on holiday.'

'We are,' Meg says with a smile.

'That's true, I guess. What I meant, though, was that it feels like we're hundreds of miles away from home, even though we're not. Everything is different here. The hotel is fantastic, the air is so fresh and, I don't know, it's all wonderful. Thank you so much for doing this.'

I pull her into a hug, feeling myself getting emotional again and hoping she doesn't notice. I shouldn't be embarrassed about this, but for some reason I am. Who knows why? Maybe that's another thing I should query when I eventually get this counselling.

After a little more walking, blissfully enjoying the sun's caress on my light-deprived face, Meg looks at her watch: a dainty but striking silver piece that's one of her own creations. She announces it's almost time for what she has planned next.

To my confusion, she leads us towards the glass spa annexe we spotted earlier.

'Time for us to put our feet up for a bit after all that walking,' she says. 'When I booked this trip, I realised you wouldn't be able to use the pool and so on. I'm not going to do so without you, because that would be mean. But I didn't want us to miss out on the spa experience altogether.'

'So?' I ask as we approach the entrance.

'We're both booked in for a pedicure.'

I give my cousin a double take. 'What, seriously?'

'You're going to love it.'

The funny thing is that, although I've never even considered having a pedicure before in my life, it turns out to be quite pleasant. My feet are ticklish, so that's a bit awkward at the start. It's hard not to be on edge with a stranger's hands delving in between my toes. But once I relax into the experience, aided by the reassuring presence of old-hand Meg being treated alongside me, my tension eases. For the most part, I avoid squealing and giggling like a child.

It's a varied mix of sensations, from the soothing, tingling feeling of the initial herbal footbath, to the stinging discomfort of my soles being scrubbed with a pumice stone. There are also moments of actual pain – thankfully brief – when my cuticles are snipped. However, by the time we get to the foot mask and then the final massage, I feel like I've earned my pedicure stripes and it's all rather enjoyable.

I walk away genuinely light-footed and relaxed, thanking Meg once again for such a thoughtful surprise.

Later, having chilled in our rooms for a couple of hours, we enjoy some pre-dinner cocktails in the bar next to the restaurant where we're booked in to eat.

After a glass of prosecco each with our starters and a bottle of red between us with our mains – a lovely medium rare ribeye steak, in my case – we're both a bit tipsy when our desserts arrive, which we agree to share. I've gone for

317

the peanut butter cheesecake, which is to die for, and Meg has a comparably delicious crème brûlée.

One minute we're debating which is the tastier of the two and the next, seemingly out of nowhere, my cousin's asking about my psychological wellbeing.

'Sorry, Meg, where did this come from?'

She shrugs. 'I'm worried about you, that's all. You've been through so much lately; I feel like you don't talk about it enough. I've read several newspaper articles about how men can be reluctant to seek support for their mental health. There's still a stigma attached to it, for some stupid reason. Did you know that suicide rates are around three times higher among men than women in the UK?'

'Whoa!' I say, taken aback by the sudden directness of her words. Lowering my voice so I'm not overheard by anyone else, I add: 'I have no intention of trying to kill myself, Meg. After everything I've recently survived, why on earth would I want to do that?'

'I don't know,' she replies. 'I'm not saying you necessarily would, but don't kid yourself that you're equipped to deal with all the stuff that's happened to you. I know I wouldn't be, if I was in your shoes. I'd be a mess. And the fact you're not, or at least you don't seem to be, concerns me. I fear you're bottling things up rather than dealing with them – and that's not good.'

I sit back in my seat and let out a long sigh. 'Fine. What would you like to talk about? Let's go. I mean, personally I was enjoying escaping my troubles for a couple of days. I thought that's what this trip was for, but apparently I got it wrong.'

The moment I see the hurt look in my cousin's eyes, I regret my kneejerk reaction to what she said, which, let's face it, was only her demonstrating how much she cares about me. I'm an idiot; I've had too much to drink.

I reach for her hand, glad to find she doesn't pull it away. 'Sorry, Meg. Please ignore the thoughtless crap that just came out of my mouth. I don't mean it, honestly. I feel pissed.'

Taking a deep breath before answering, she says with a slight slur to her voice: 'I wasn't trying to suggest we talk about it in detail now, Luke. I totally get that you're not in the mood. I'm a little tipsy too, so maybe my choice of words gave you the wrong impression. If so, I'm sorry.

'What I was trying to tell you was that I'm here for you, twenty-four seven, if and when you ever need to talk. Also, I've said it before and I'll say it again, I really think you'd benefit hugely from speaking to a professional.'

I drain the dregs from my wine glass. 'I think you're probably right, Meg, but I'm still waiting for counselling to materialise after they mentioned it to me at the hospital.'

Meg nods her head, biting on her bottom lip. 'Fair enough, but you don't have to wait for them to organise it. Who knows how long that will take? You could also contact someone yourself.'

'Like who?'

She scratches the back of her head. 'There's, um, a woman I could give you a phone number for who's helped me through a few issues here and there. She's very nice and not particularly expensive. If she can't help you herself, I'm sure she'd have a colleague she could refer you to.'

'Really?' I reply. 'I didn't know you—'

'Everyone needs help sometimes, Luke.'

'Wait. What were you saying about men not sharing their issues? And yet you've not shared this, whatever it is, with me.'

'Not with you, no, but with someone. And that's what counts, Luke. You don't have to talk to me either. It's entirely up to you who you choose to speak to. And please don't be offended that I didn't talk to you. It's absolutely nothing personal. I have my own way of dealing with things, that's all.'

I nod, but I can't help feeling offended – and guilty. I've always thought of Meg as being someone independent, confident and secure in her own skin.

How many times have I spoken to her about my problems without ever realising she has issues of her own?

How self-centred and insular does that make me?

I know her sexuality must have made life tricky for her at times, particularly growing up when there wasn't the same level of social acceptance as nowadays. But having come out as lesbian in her late teens, she's always seemed so comfortable with the situation; I've never thought of it as being a concern.

Who says it's even anything to do with that? It could be totally unrelated.

I'm in the dark here.

As if she can read my mind, Meg says: 'It's depression, okay? I don't have it all the time – it comes and goes. I'm not embarrassed about it. Mental illness is like any other sickness; it's part of who I am and, when it flares up, I deal with it, mainly via counselling and mindfulness. Yoga too, in theory, although I'm not very good at finding time for that. I'm not a fan of taking medication if it can be avoided.'

I shake my head in disbelief. 'How am I only hearing about this now?'

'I've never deliberately hidden it from you. I guess you've just never noticed – and that's fine with me. Depression has been part of my life, on and off, since my college days. I was living with it long before we became close, like we are again now, thankfully, after our blip. You needed me to be there for you after your parents died and Helen left, and so I was. If anything, helping you has put my own problems into context, particularly after what you've been through recently. Life's dealt you some really bad hands, Luke.'

'I feel awful now,' I say, pausing as the waiter comes to ask if we'd like any coffee, which we both would. 'You've been way more supportive of me than I ever have of you. I owe you big style, especially after this trip away.'

'You don't owe me anything, Luke. We're family and I love you. I'd do it all again in a flash. But if you do want to do something for me, get the professional help you need. Make the phone call.'

'Roger that.' Still perplexed by Meg's revelation, I add: 'Do you mind if I ask what kind of thing makes you depressed? I don't mean that in a funny way. I'm trying to understand what you've told me. I've always thought of you as a happy-go-lucky person. That's the way you come across to me, so I'm feeling pretty foolish.'

My cousin shakes her head. 'Please don't. I'm glad you think of me that way. That is how I feel a lot of the time, only there are lows too. I can't explain what triggers them. That's not really how it works.'

'Well, if you're ever feeling depressed in future and you do fancy talking to someone other than your counsellor, you know where I am, Meg. I mean that. I want to be there for you too. It's about time, I reckon.'

CHAPTER 34

By the time Friday comes around, Meg's lovely hotel treat feels like it happened ages ago rather than earlier in the week.

I wasted yesterday, spending most of my time pacing up and down the flat, worrying about today. Now it's here, I wish I'd allowed myself to rest – to live in the moment rather than panicky projections of the future. Then I might not feel as wiped out as I do.

My anxiety is threefold because, in a fit of planning stupidity, I've booked myself a triple whammy of things to keep me busy today, none of which I feel comfortable about doing.

Kicking things off is the first appointment with my counsellor at 11.30 a.m., which mainly bothers me because I have no idea what to expect. I rang the phone number Meg gave me and her counsellor referred me to a man called Charles Stewart, who she assured me was 'very good'. Next, having finally accepted Rita's offer to run the barbershop, where I've still not returned since *that* night, I'm due to meet her there after lunch to go over everything and get her set up. And last but not least, it's my first date with Nora this evening, by which point I fear being so frazzled I'll either bore her to death over dinner or say something stupid enough to blow my chances.

What could possibly go wrong?

I arrive to see my counsellor five minutes early. Neither he nor the location are quite what I was envisaging. I suppose my expectation of such things is coloured by all the New York-set movies I've watched, where it's a given that there'll be luxurious furnishings, huge windows, a view of Central Park, and a scholarly shrink in an expensive suit.

Instead, I get an unassuming ground-floor office space near Piccadilly railway station with small opaque windows, carpet tiles and traffic noise. Charles, as he asks to be called, is a scruffy chap in his early fifties with a few days' beard growth and unkempt, wavy, salt-and-pepper hair. He's wearing black jeans, tan slip-on shoes and a plaid shirt.

He doesn't have a secretary. He is very welcoming, though, greeting me with a warm smile and a firm handshake. He offers tea or coffee before sitting me down in the 'waiting area' – three brown plastic chairs next to the door of his inner office – and disappearing for a few minutes.

He returns with two steaming cups of what he's already warned me is instant coffee.

Next thing, we're sitting opposite each other on comfyish grey chairs that wouldn't look out of place in a school staffroom, and I'm giving him the synopsis of my life so far.

I do most of the talking for the hour I spend with him, while he asks open questions, scribbles notes on to an A4 pad and nods a lot.

His ears prick up when I tell him about my quest to become a more optimistic person.

'How's that working out?' he asks.

'It's taken a bit of a knock, to be honest, thanks to recent events. But it was going pretty well beforehand. Life's definitely more lively and varied when you open yourself up to things and people. But on the flipside, in doing so, you tend to make yourself more exposed and vulnerable.'

When Charles tells me that our time is nearly up, I think he's joking. It feels like I've only been there for a few minutes, even though we've covered a lot of ground and I've told him so much. I suppose what surprises me is that he doesn't end our session with a diagnosis or a remedial action plan, as you might expect after seeing your GP, for instance. He simply requests that I keep a diary of how I'm feeling between now and our next session, with an emphasis on any particular highs and lows I experience during that period and any external factors that might have sparked them. He says he'll also email me a list of books I might be interested to read, some specifically about post-traumatic stress and others about relaxation and mindfulness.

'That's it?' I ask.

'For now,' he replies. 'How have you found your first session?'

'Um, good, yeah,' I say, for want of anything better.

He nods and smiles. 'It's great you were able to open up as much as you did. Not everyone can do that straight away; it's a big help.'

'Good,' I say, wondering if it's normal to feel bewildered at this stage. I probably should ask him, but he seems so happy with the way things have gone, I decide not to.

As I'm walking back towards the barbershop afterwards, I unexpectedly feel a strange sense of elation, like a weight has been lifted from my shoulders.

Is this normal after a session?

I pull out my mobile – which is actually still the temporary replacement Meg sorted for me while I was in hospital – to put this question to the Internet.

But before I get a chance, Meg's photo pops up on my screen to indicate she's calling. Right on cue, it's almost as if my cousin has telepathically sensed my query.

'How did it go?' she asks. 'You did turn up, right?'

'Of course I turned up. Why would you ask that, Meg?'

'Oh, I'm only pulling your leg. What did you think of your counsellor? Did you get on well with him?'

'He seemed nice, yeah. He definitely put me at ease.'

'And?'

I'm not sure what she's fishing for here – what she's hoping I'll say – so I answer her question with one of my own: the very same I was about to look up online when she called.

'Oh yeah,' she says. 'It's totally normal to feel buzzing afterwards. I always find my sessions really cathartic. It's like by saying things out loud to someone independent, you offload your psychological baggage and leave feeling liberated. A word of warning, though: it won't last forever. Sooner or later, that buzz will wear off and you might even feel worse for a bit before you pick up again. That's how it works for me, anyway. I don't think there's a long-term quick fix for mental health issues. You have to chip away at them, piece by piece, day by day.'

When I ask her about my initial sense of bewilderment when the session ended, she pushes me for more of an explanation.

'Um, I don't know really. I suppose I expected more, or at least something different. All I did was talk him through the highs and lows of my life. He didn't say a great deal. He definitely seemed pleased with how it went, but there wasn't much offered by way of advice.'

'I wouldn't worry about that,' Meg says. 'It's early days. A counsellor's first job is to understand you and your issues. Then they help you to do the same. From there you can start moving forward.'

'How many times do you think I'll need to see him?'

'He should advise you on that, but don't be afraid to voice any concerns you might have. He'll be happy to answer your questions, I guarantee it.'

I've been walking while chatting to Meg and, by the time I hang up, I'm back in the familiar territory of the Northern Quarter, only a short walk away from the barbershop. Realising this, a feeling of panic grips my whole body. I picture Moxie's snarling face as he shoves his way in through the door and overpowers me. The flashback stops me in my tracks and, suddenly feeling dizzy and out of breath, I grab hold of a nearby lamppost to steady myself.

'It's going to be all right,' I say under my breath.

I knew it would be hard returning to the scene of the crime for the first time. That's why I'm heading there alone now, so I can get my head around it before Rita arrives. But I wasn't expecting it to be this hard. Why on earth didn't I bring it up with Charles, so I could ask him to give me some coping mechanisms?

Oh well. Too late for that now. I'll have to face it head-on.

Spotting an empty bench a little further along the street, I take a couple of slow, deep breaths and then make a dash for it. Once there, I lean forward with my elbows resting on my knees and focus on calming myself down.

Moxie's dead.

He's gone for good.

There's nothing to fear.

I play these words on repeat in an internal monologue designed to help me pull myself together.

It's all kinds of wrong that I'm afraid to step foot in my own business: the place where I've comfortably worked alone for years without issue. All because of one incident. Okay, it was rather a big deal. But in all my time there, nothing on this scale has ever happened before. I've had odd instances of vandalism and a couple of attempted burglaries at night. What city centre business hasn't? People have run off without paying and swiped odds and ends when my back's been turned. But there's never been anything remotely like this until now, so logic would suggest it's very unlikely to happen again, especially considering Moxie's fate.

Right?

It's not about logic, though, is it?

It's about emotion.

It's about how Moxie's attack made me feel.

Weak.

Helpless.

Vulnerable.

Small.

I look down at my bandaged wounds: healing, but still there to remind me of what happened. And to stop me from returning to my job, at least for the time being.

That's another thing. What if they don't heal as expected? What if my hands continue to ache as they do now when I use them? What then? If I can't use my hands properly, how can I continue to do the one thing I know I'm good at?

I have to stop thinking in such negative terms, or I'm never going to be able to leave this bench.

I close my eyes and imagine Iris sitting down next to me in her usual yellow raincoat. She has a tiny MP3 player in her hand and, with a calming smile, she slots a pair of earbuds into the jack plug and hands me one while placing the other into her own ear.

'Smile,' she whispers before pressing play on the device.

She starts nodding her head in time to the beat as 'Mr Blue Sky' kicks in and we listen to the song together, heads leaning towards each other. I surrender to the buoyant vibe of the music and tell myself everything is going to be all right.

A hand on my shoulder jolts me back to reality. I snap open my eyes and, for an instant, I'm convinced Iris really is there. Her brown eyes are looking at me; her brunette curls. 'What? How's this—'

'Luke? Are you all right, love?' another person's voice says.

And it dawns on me that it's not Iris I'm looking at, but her aunt.

'Rita,' I say, shaking my head to clear the cobwebs. 'I almost didn't recognise you. I thought . . . Your hair. You've—'

'Dyed it,' she replies. 'Yes, I fancied a change. What do you think?'

'Very nice,' I say. 'That colour suits you well. It, um, actually reminds me of Iris's hair.'

'Yes, I suppose it is similar.' A wistful look crosses her face. 'I wonder if that's why I did it? Subconsciously, I mean. I miss her so much, it's quite possible. She was such a sweetheart. The tiniest little things remind me of her every day. I mean, I saw a girl eating a KitKat yesterday – and even that made me think of her, because it was her favourite chocolate bar. I always used to get her a KitKat egg for Easter. I've done so for as long as I can remember. She won't be needing one this year, though, will she?'

I shake my head and look down at the pavement, my eyes falling on a hardened piece of pink bubble gum in a shape that reminds me of a tear.

It's sad to hear Rita talk this way. I ask after Iris's parents and she tells me they're not coping well at all. Her mum has barely left the house since the funeral, apparently. Poor woman. Poor family. And here's me wallowing in my own misery – my own fears and anxieties – rather than appreciating every fresh breath of air I'm able to take, thanks to Iris.

In the time I've got to know Rita, I haven't considered nearly enough the awful grief she must still be going through in the aftermath of Iris's death. She's so vivacious on the surface – no doubt part of the way she deals with her pain – that it's easy to forget the truth.

How did I become so self-absorbed without realising it? It's like when I found out about Meg's depression for the first time the other day.

I've been battling my pessimism ever since Iris's death, but perhaps the root of my problems lies deeper than that. Maybe the whole glass-half-empty thing is merely a symptom of me being an egotist.

And there I go once again, making this about myself. I should be focusing on Rita, who, in spite of her grief, is about to do an amazing thing for me, which I've barely appreciated until this very moment.

'Are you all right?' she asks me again.

'Yes, fine.'

'Because you looked—'

'No, really. I'm okay. What are you doing here, anyway?

331

I thought we weren't meeting at the barbershop until two thirty.'

'Sorry, I arrived early. I was feeling keen and thought you might already be around; when you weren't, I decided to go for a stroll, maybe buy a sandwich. It was a total surprise when I spotted you sitting here.'

'Don't be sorry. It's great to see you. We can head there now if you like. Or how about I treat you to lunch first? I've not eaten yet either and I know a nice little café around the corner from here.'

She flashes me a toothy smile. 'Now that sounds like a great plan.'

CHAPTER 35

Having been through everything I can think of regarding the day-to-day running of the barbershop, I pour myself and Rita a brew and ask her if she has any other questions.

'No, I don't think so. Not at the moment. You've been very thorough.'

'Sorry, I've not been mansplaining, have I?'

She giggles. 'No, no. You're behaving like someone who's run their own business for years and is now handing the keys over to someone else. Don't worry, I've run my own business too, remember. I totally understand. It's a bit like entrusting a new babysitter with looking after your little kids for the first time.'

'I'll have to take your word for it on that analogy,' I say, grinning and taking a seat next to her in the waiting area. 'I really appreciate you doing this, Rita. I haven't said that enough. We've not known each other for long, but it doesn't feel that way, probably because of what we've both been through lately. You have my full trust and support. I wouldn't have agreed to this otherwise.'

Rita nods. 'That's nice to hear, Luke. I'll look after the place like it's my own, I promise, without forgetting that it's not. And I know exactly what you mean about us knowing each other far better than we should on paper. We had a couple of rocky starts, didn't we? But I think there's a real bond between us now, like we're meant to be friends and will be for a long time. It might sound mushy, but . . . maybe this was Iris's last gift to us.'

There are tears in her eyes as she says this, voice wavering. It sets me off too, so I give her a hug.

It was a huge help to have her at my side when I first walked back through the door. I'd already confessed over lunch how nervous I was about it; Rita made me feel better, saying it was totally understandable.

And in the end, probably because I wasn't alone with my memories, it wasn't as bad as I'd feared. Apart from having to pick up the change from the till that Moxie had thrown at the wall, there was no real sign of what had happened the last time I was here. It was plain old Luke's Barbershop – home from home.

It also helped that a couple of traders from shops nearby bobbed their heads in to see if I was okay and to voice their support. That was particularly nice, considering I've never made much of an effort to be neighbourly in my time here. The way Rita was laughing and joking with them after a couple of minutes suggested that may well change on her watch, which can only be a good thing, I reckon.

'Don't feel like you need to open for exactly the same days and hours as I usually do, by the way,' I tell Rita once we've both calmed down to a less emotional state. 'That's entirely up to you while you're at the helm. Just give me a heads-up, so I can make sure I'm here for closing time.'

'Great,' she says. 'Will do. That's good to know.'

She hasn't specifically said so, but I'm pretty sure she thinks me coming by at the end of each day is unnecessary. At the same time, I hope she appreciates why I need to do that, for my own peace of mind as much as for her safety. I have at least explained that it's not about me checking up on her. And she says – probably for my benefit more than hers – if there's ever a day I can't do, she could always ask one of her sons to drop in, as they both work nearby.

We're about to close up when there's a knock on the door, which I've kept locked, since we're not open for business today. The sound makes me jump and gives me a momentary flashback to Moxie knocking and then peering through the glass, pretending to be a nice guy. I turn around, ready to shout that we're closed, only to see Connor's familiar face staring back at me.

I say his name under my breath and Rita throws me a quizzical frown. 'Who's Connor?'

'A regular,' I whisper. 'He's a good bloke, but a bit eccentric. He just lost his mother.'

'Really? Poor thing. Are you going to speak to him then or what?'

I nod, stand up and walk over to the door. After

hesitating for the briefest of moments, I fumble with the key in the lock and then let him in. 'Hello, Connor. How are you doing? I haven't seen you since the funeral. How, er, how was it?'

In reply he mutters something I can't make out, eyes wandering everywhere apart from at me.

'They're always hard, funerals,' I say. 'My friend Rita over there lost her niece recently.'

He glances in her direction for a second and scratches the side of his nose. 'I see.'

'If you're after a haircut today, I'm afraid we're not open.'

'You've been closed for several days now, Luke, with nothing on display to explain why to your customers. You said you didn't have any other closures planned after the last time this happened. I've been confused and concerned. I tried calling you several times on the number you gave me, but it didn't work.'

I look over at Rita, who's pulling a bemused face, then turn back to Connor.

'I guess you haven't heard, but there was a bit of an incident. It was in the news. A man forced his way in here to rob me. He took my phone, which is why you couldn't get hold of me. He also attacked me with a knife.' I hold up my bandaged limbs. 'As you can see, I'm going to be out of action for a bit. But there is good news: from Monday, Rita will be running things in my place.'

Connor looks ahead blankly and doesn't say anything for what feels like an age. I'm about to break the silence when he finally replies. 'No, I hadn't heard anything about that, Luke. I haven't been following the news lately. I'm sorry for your, um . . . Are you okay?'

'I've been better, to be honest, but I'm getting there.'

'Right.'

'So, as I say, if you'd like a haircut, Rita will be able to help you out from Monday afternoon.'

'But you cut my hair, Luke. You always do it. No one else knows how I like it. Couldn't you do one quick haircut?'

'No, I'm sorry, Connor. I'm not up to that yet. That's why Rita is covering for me. She's very nice and excellent at cutting hair. I wouldn't team up with her otherwise. Come over and say hello.'

Connor looks terrified at this prospect. 'Oh. I, er, need to get going, actually.'

'I don't bite, love,' Rita says, taking the initiative and walking over to introduce herself. 'Connor, is it?'

'Yes,' he says, shoving his hands firmly into his pockets and shuffling his feet.

'Very nice to meet you. I'm Rita. I used to run a unisex salon of my own and, to be honest, I miss it. I've also been struggling a bit since my niece, Iris, died. We were very close, you see, and I need something to take my mind off how much I miss her. I don't know about you, but I cope better when I'm busy than when I'm twiddling my thumbs at home.'

Connor grunts something monosyllabic and incomprehensible in reply. His cheeks are flushed and he seems particularly twitchy, but if Rita's noticed, she doesn't let on.

'Hey, I've got an idea for you. How about I cut your

337

hair now? We're not open yet, as Luke said, but I'm prepared to make an exception for a handsome regular customer like you. Luke could even watch over me and make sure I do it right. How does that sound?'

I'm totally blown away by how well Rita is handling this situation and I assume Connor will take her up on her generous offer.

But that's not what happens.

Instead, he starts vigorously rubbing his forehead with the fingers of one hand and stutters: 'I, I, d-don't th-think that's a g-good idea. Sorry.'

He turns to leave, grabbing the door handle.

'Wait, mate,' I say. 'It's fine. There's no need to race off. You don't have to get a haircut now if you don't want to. Why don't you stay for a brew?'

'I have to get b-back to work.'

'Right. Well, don't be a stranger. I'll have my old phone number back up and running again soon. I've been meaning to sort it, but with one thing and another, I haven't got around to doing so yet. I do have a temporary number I can give you, if you like. Hang on, I'll grab it for—'

'That's okay,' he says, a fresh look of alarm on his face at the prospect of me leaving him alone with Rita. 'I really have to g-go.'

And with that he leaves.

'Sorry,' Rita says.

'What for? You were amazing with him. So much so, I thought he'd go for what you suggested. He blooming well should have.'

'He didn't, though.'

338

'Please don't take it personally. He's, er, unconventional at the best of times. And he was very close to his mum, who died suddenly. He still lived with her and he's obviously struggling. That's why I gave him my number last time he was in, which was just before the funeral. I don't usually hand it out to customers. In fact, I'm struggling to think of a time I've ever done so before. But I don't think he has a lot of friends or people to look out for him, so—'

'It's all right. I get it,' Rita says. 'There's a heart of gold hidden away somewhere deep inside that chest of yours, isn't there?'

Her comment throws me. 'I, um, don't know about that. He's been coming here a long time, that's all.'

'Whatever you say, Luke.' She pinches my cheek like my mum used to do. 'I wish my boys were half as thoughtful as you are.'

I head to the supermarket on the way home, having declined the kind offer of a lift from Rita, telling her a walk in the fresh air will do me good. It's pretty warm today, albeit a bit drizzly. Now we're near the end of March, I'm hoping we'll start to get some more consistent spring-like weather.

I'm feeling a lot more relaxed than earlier, now Rita and the barbershop are sorted. I've still got my date with Nora ahead of me, but knowing how she feels is a big help. Hopefully I'll be able to enjoy that rather than get too worked up about it.

However, on approaching the supermarket entrance, my

new-found calm goes out of the window when I spot Tommy sitting on the pavement outside, chatting to a departing female shopper.

Heart racing, I consider trying to slip past him without being noticed. But the woman moves on at just the wrong moment, having handed over some change, and he spots me.

'Luke! Bloody hell, are you all right, mate? I heard what happened with Moxie – that frigging psycho. I called by the barbershop a couple of times to see if you were there, but it was closed.'

'Hello, Tommy,' I say, employing slow, deep breaths. 'I'm on the mend, thanks.'

He eyes my bandages and, standing up to chat to me, pulls a pained face. 'It's true that he took a knife to you, then?'

'Yes.'

He shakes his head and frowns. 'I'm really sorry to hear that, Luke. I knew he was trouble – I've had a few run-ins with him myself – but I didn't think he was capable of that. And after you've done so much for us. I bet you wish you'd never got involved.'

'I think he was on some kind of drugs,' I say. 'He was after money, probably to get another fix.'

Tommy nods but falls silent at this.

'I understand why people take stuff when they're on the streets,' I continue, pulse rising as I say what I feel I must. 'It's a temporary way out, I guess, a means of escaping reality. But it's not a real answer to any of your problems, is it? Ultimately, it's only going to make things worse.'

340

Tommy looks into the distance, still not responding. I think he knows I'm not talking about Moxie any more, so I take the opportunity to hammer the message home.

'You're an intelligent guy,' I say. 'You know what I'm talking about. I've no idea how you ended up where you are, but I bet you could use that brain of yours to get yourself into a better place if you really wanted to. Okay, lecture over. But think about it, yeah, before it's too late?'

He meets my gaze for the briefest of moments and nods once.

'Good.'

I continue into the store, adding to my small shopping list a pre-packed sandwich and a bottle of water. I hand these to Tommy on my way out instead of cash I fear he'd waste on spice.

'Cheers, Luke,' he says. 'All the best with your recovery.'

'You too. I didn't forget about digging you out another Rebus book, by the way. There's one waiting for you in the barbershop whenever you're ready. Just pop by.'

'Really? After everything that's happened? Wow. I don't know what to say, other than thank you.'

'No problem. I may not be there, as I'm taking some time off, but I'll make sure Rita knows where it is. She'll be running the place in my absence.'

I'd like to tell him that the free haircuts for the homeless sessions will be continuing at some point soon but, honestly, I don't know if that will happen. It's all still too raw at the moment to make a final decision.

CHAPTER 36

I get home at around 4.15 p.m. and decide to put my feet up for an hour ahead of my date with Nora.

We're going to a new cicchetti place that recently opened not far from Albert Square. The style of food is a Venetian take on tapas. I've heard excellent things about this particular restaurant, which is very authentic, apparently. As the location is a fair slog across the city centre from here, Nora has kindly offered to pick me up in her car. It's not remotely on her way, as she lives in Chorlton, but she was insistent.

'I can always walk or get a cab,' I told her. 'Wouldn't it be easier for you to take the tram?'

'No, no,' she said. 'I prefer to drive and it's no trouble, honestly.'

I'm really looking forward to spending some quality time with Nora. And I won't be letting her open her purse at all while we're out. I want to treat her, although, knowing how independent she is, I'll probably have to insist. It's the least I can do after how much she's helped me. On top of everything else, she did an amazing job of getting rid of that Billy Broome idiot and his sham drug-dealing rumours. Luckily, as she predicted, it turned out he'd simply made the whole thing up to try to force me to talk. I haven't heard a peep from him since; Nora seems certain he won't cause me any more bother.

I'm expecting her at about 6.30 p.m., half an hour before our table is booked, so plenty of time to spare.

After showing initial affection when I returned from hospital, Alfred has grown a bit standoffish with me, like he knows I'm not a hundred per cent and doesn't like it. However, this afternoon he's back to his usual friendly self. The moment I sit down on the sofa, he claims my lap and falls asleep.

One minute I'm stroking him, feeling a little heavy-eyed myself, and the next I'm woken by a loud buzzing sound.

Dazed and blinking away the sleep, it takes me a moment to get my bearings. Then I look at the time on the wall clock and nearly jump out of my skin. Crap! It's already 6.20 p.m. That must be Nora, running ahead of time.

I lift Alfred off my knee and race to the intercom by the front door.

'Hello?' I say. 'Sorry, I—'

'Luke?'

Hang on. That's not Nora's voice. It sounds like . . . no, it can't be. Can it?

'Yes, this is Luke. Who's that?'

'It's Helen. I'm sorry to turn up unannounced, but I was in Manchester and – well – I just heard what happened to you. I had to visit and see if you were all right. Could I come up?'

My God. How could her timing be any worse? And what's she doing in town? She didn't say anything about that in her letter. I hesitate, unsure what to do, only to realise I have to let her in, especially after everything she wrote to me and having not seen her for so long.

So I tell her it's fine and press the button to let her inside the building.

About thirty seconds later, as I'm waiting by the door to greet her, the buzzer goes again. 'Isn't it working?' I say into the intercom, assuming she's having problems.

But it's Nora's voice this time on the other end of the line. 'Luke?' she says. 'Sorry, isn't what working?'

'Oh, Nora, it's you. Hello.'

'Were you expecting someone else?'

'Um, it's complicated.'

'Oh, right. Are you ready to go?'

'No, I'm not. I'm having a bit of a—'

I'm interrupted by a knock on the front door, which must now be Helen. This is a disaster. 'Could you come up, so I can explain?' I ask Nora, wincing as the words leave my mouth, and she says she will.

A couple of minutes after that, having hastily tried to explain the situation to Helen before Nora caught up with her, I'm sitting in the lounge with the two of them, wondering what on earth to do next.

I've made brief introductions, so everyone knows who's who, but now an uncomfortable silence has fallen on the room.

'Well, this is awkward,' I say to both of them before focusing my attention on Nora, who's not yet even had the rushed, garbled explanation I gave to Helen. 'I sat down on the sofa for a moment a couple of hours ago and, apparently, I fell fast asleep. The first I knew of it was when the buzzer went a few minutes ago. I thought it was you, Nora, but it turned out to be Helen. She arrived right before you, although it was a complete surprise. We haven't seen each other in a long time.'

'I should have called first,' Helen says.

She looks good: a little older than I remember and tired around the eyes, but otherwise much like when we were together. In fact, seeing her and Nora alongside each other for the first time, it strikes me – to my discomfort – that they look a little alike. They have similar long, wavy blonde hair, for a start. They're also both attractive, tall and slim.

Nora is a few years younger than Helen, who'll be thirty-eight now. And at least they're wearing totally different outfits. But spotting the resemblance between them is only adding to my embarrassment. Their eyes are a different colour, I note to my satisfaction: Helen's are hazel, while Nora's are green. That's something at least.

'Is there any chance you could perhaps call back tomorrow?' I ask Helen. 'Nora and I do have a table booked.'

Not that I'm dressed as intended. I've missed my chance to get changed. But I could probably get away with staying in these smart jeans and shirt – worn, unknowingly, for my scruffy counsellor's benefit – as long as I use some deodorant, splash a little aftershave and brush my teeth.

'I would, of course,' Helen says. 'But I'm booked on a train back up to Edinburgh first thing tomorrow morning. I can go, though. I should. It's my own fault for barging in without any warning. I had to see that you were okay, Luke. I only heard about the knife attack this afternoon and I was so shocked.'

I'm racking my brains for a way out of this mess that will keep everyone happy. If Helen's only around tonight, I don't see how I can let her go without a catch-up. And yet how can I turn Nora away when we're supposed to be heading out on our first date? She could be my future, but I'm loath to disregard my past.

How on earth have we ended up here?

Thankfully, Nora speaks up with a potential solution. 'Why don't I make this easy and step aside to give you two some space? I can ring and cancel our dinner reservation, Luke. We can always do it another time.'

'Are you sure?' I reply, immediately regretting not putting up more resistance, based on the look of disappointment that flashes across her face.

'Yes, of course,' she says, by which point her guard is back up and her true feelings hidden. 'It's the most sensible solution.'

'I feel awful now.' Helen sighs dramatically. 'I really didn't mean for this to—'

'It's fine, honestly,' Nora replies with a wooden smile. 'You don't need to feel bad.'

Did she place an emphasis on the *you* – as in my ex-wife doesn't need to feel awful, but I do – or did I imagine it?

A part of me wants to resist her suggestion now, but it

is the only obvious way I can see to break this unexpected deadlock.

Next thing she's on her feet. 'It was nice to meet you,' she tells Helen, who also stands up to say goodbye. Nora moves to shake her hand, by which point my ex-wife is already leaning in to kiss her, resulting in some awkward shuffling around and yet more red faces.

'Lovely, um, to meet you too, Nora,' a flustered Helen replies eventually. 'So sorry for spoiling your plans.'

I walk Nora to the door and, in a quiet voice intended only for the two of us, I tell her: 'I'm so sorry about this. I feel terrible. I won't try to make an excuse for falling asleep like I did, but I genuinely had no idea that Helen was going to turn up. I don't see her for years and then she appears out of nowhere, now of all times. I'll make this up to you, I promise.'

She gives me the briefest of pecks on my cheek. 'It's fine, Luke. Seriously.'

'It's not,' I whisper. 'I promise I'll make it up to you.'

Then she's gone and I'm alone with my ex-wife for the first time in forever.

'So I got your letter,' I say. 'Sorry to hear about you and Adrian. If it's any consolation, I don't think you got your just deserts, as you put it. You have my sympathy. It's a horrible feeling to be cheated on, and I wouldn't wish it on anyone.'

'Not even me?' she asks from her seat in the lounge, where I also sit back down so we're facing but not on top of each other. 'The person who cheated on you.'

I rub the coarse stubble on my chin, exhaling. 'I might

347

have felt like that at one point, Helen, but not any more. It was a long time ago. A lot has happened since then. I reckon life's too short to hold grudges, particularly against someone who was once such an important part of my life. How are you coping? It can't be easy with the children.'

She talks about this briefly and, when I ask, explains that she came back for a job interview this morning, after which she met up with an old colleague for lunch, who told her about me, having seen it in the news.

'Hang on,' I say. 'So you're thinking of moving back to Manchester?'

She shrugs. 'There's no harm in exploring my options, is there?'

'No, I suppose not. Are the children both with their dad at the moment?'

'Yes, him and his young floozy.' She frowns, shaking her head. 'Sorry, force of habit. Adrian thinks I'm on a social trip. I couldn't bring myself to tell him about the interview, although I don't think it went very well, anyway.'

She speaks a little more about this but soon wants to bring the conversation back to me and my injuries – all that I've been through.

I start talking, recounting everything, from the scaffolding accident at the end of January, which Helen read about in the article forwarded by her mum, right up to handing Rita the keys to the barbershop this afternoon. By the time I've finished, a good while later, Helen's eyes are bulging, her mouth agape.

'My goodness, Luke. What a couple of months. You have my sympathy, for what it's worth. And there was me

348

thinking I'd had a tough time lately. It certainly puts things into perspective, doesn't it?'

'It does,' I say. 'It really does.'

As I was telling my story, Helen cut in with various questions: the usual stuff, which I'm used to answering by now. The only subject I particularly avoided mentioning was that of the weird dreams I've had involving Iris. I'm not comfortable sharing these with her. Out of context, I fear they could make me sound unhinged.

After putting two frozen pizzas in the oven, since we're both getting peckish, I say I appreciated her recent letter and its contents. However, I stop short of admitting how much it means to me to know the truth about her not getting pregnant on purpose that first time and that she thinks I'd make a good father. It's a pride thing. I don't want her to know quite how much she broke me when she left.

There's a weird moment when Alfred walks into the lounge and she squeals with delight, calling him over to her. He gives her a suspicious stare from a few metres away. A childish part of me secretly hopes he'll snub her, despite us once caring for him together. But then, with a happy, bird-like chirrup, he bounds up to her and springs on to her knee, letting her stroke and rub him like she's never been away.

'Oh, Alfred, you funny thing,' she says as he soon settles into a comfy sleeping position on her lap. 'I've missed your furry hugs. You look so old and wise now.'

'Did you ever get another cat?' I ask her.

'No, not so far. Adrian is allergic to most pets, although

now he's gone, perhaps it's time. The kids would love a cat.'

'Don't get any ideas about kidnapping this one,' I say, smiling but half serious, just in case.

'No, no,' she says. 'I wouldn't even joke about that. He was always more your cat than mine. He might be sucking up to me now, not having seen me for ages, but in the old days he never used to choose my knee to sit on over yours. You were number one, without a doubt.'

I don't disagree with her.

Helen is staying at a hotel near the train station and, not long after we've eaten, she says she could do with heading back there and orders a taxi.

As we're saying goodbye, we hug and it's a nice way to end things: the most amicable it's ever been between us since she left, reinforcing the sense of closure I already felt from reading her letter.

'Thanks for calling by,' I say. 'You didn't have to, but I appreciate that you did.'

'You're welcome, Luke. It was the least I could do. I'm only sorry my timing was so off. Nora seemed lovely. I hope I haven't messed things up for you there.'

'Not to worry. It's early days. If it's meant to be, one hiccup shouldn't ruin it.' I laugh. 'Although it was a pretty big hiccup, all things considered, and half of that was down to me dozing off. Never mind. It was good to see you after all this time, whatever the circumstances.'

'You too. Take care. I don't want to hear about any more near-death experiences.'

'I'll do my best. Good luck with the job interview. Do

let me know if it works out and you end up coming back to Manchester.'

She shakes her head. 'Thanks, but I'm pretty sure that's not going to happen. Even if the interview had gone well, I think this trip was more about me getting away for a couple of days to get things into perspective; to remind myself that I'm my own woman and I have options. It might be nice for me to get away from Adrian, but I don't honestly think I could do that to Euan and Gwen in the long term. He's their parent as much as I am. If I moved them here, I'd effectively be severing their relationship with him, which they might grow up to resent me for. And Edinburgh is their home. Mine too, to some extent.'

She wrinkles her nose before adding, with a wicked glint in her eye: 'I probably will tell Adrian about the interview when I get back. It won't do him any harm to know what I could do if I chose to be vindictive.'

I bet she won't be afraid to drop in the fact she met her ex-husband either, as that's bound to wind him up. He might yet come running back to her, full of regret. Would she forgive him and offer him another chance to make their marriage work for the sake of the family? That's not my place to ask and, luckily, not my concern. I wish her all the best with it, regardless.

As soon as she's gone, my thoughts turn to Nora. I'm gutted our date didn't work out and I'd like to get something else on the calendar as soon as possible, if she's still interested.

I call her mobile. It rings twice and then goes to

voicemail midway through a third ring, which is sooner than usual, suggesting she rejected my call.

It's hard to know the best way to respond to this. I almost hang up so that I can either call again later or send a thoughtfully constructed text message instead. But fearing that not leaving a voice message might give the wrong impression, I make a split-second decision to stay on the line and speak.

'Hi, Nora,' I say after the beep. 'It's Luke. I'm probably the last person you want to hear from at the moment, but I feel so bad. I want to apologise once more about this evening and, if you're still up for it, to invite you out again as soon as you're free. No need to call me back. I'll, um, try you again tomorrow. Sorry. Anyway, have a good night. Toodle-oo.'

I end the call and then hang my head in shame. *Toodle-oo?* What was I thinking, using such an archaic expression? When do I ever normally say goodbye like that? What an idiot.

And why the hell would she have a good night after I ruined it for her by bailing on our date? Another perfectly stupid thing to say.

Brilliant.

Just brilliant.

CHAPTER 37

It's getting on for a month later when I brave an April shower to arrive at the barbershop just before closing.

Rita, who's already in the process of cleaning up, has her back to me as I enter. 'Hello, hello,' I say. 'Only me. Have you had a good afternoon?'

'Hi, boss.' She turns around and smiles, winking to acknowledge the fact I've told her umpteen times not to call me that. It's her little joke. 'Not bad, thanks. Pretty busy for a Monday. Rainy out today, isn't it?'

'Yep,' I say, drying myself off and then hanging up my coat and umbrella. 'But it's warm too, don't you think? I was sweating on the way here. Anyway, happy anniversary.'

She throws me a blank look. 'Sorry?'

'You've been running the place for three weeks now. And doing a fine job of it, I must say. How about I treat you to a drink to celebrate?'

'Go on, then,' she says. 'I'm in the car, but a small wine wouldn't go amiss. I have a couple of things I'd like to discuss with you, anyway.'

'That sounds ominous.'

'Oh, don't be such a drama queen, Luke. What have you been up to today, anyhow? Anything interesting?'

'Oh, this and that. Nothing to write home about.'

I've actually come from my latest counselling session with Charles but, since I haven't told Rita I'm seeing him, I don't mention it. Just because we get along well and she's currently running my business, I don't have to share everything with her.

That's not to say I'm uncomfortable or ashamed about being in counselling. I would tell Rita if there was a particular reason to do so, but there hasn't been so far.

I'm getting used to seeing Charles now and the process is definitely proving helpful. We talked a lot today about the effect on me of my parents' sudden deaths, in conjunction with my subsequent split from Helen and her recent reappearance.

He's asked me to draw up a list at home of the ten things I miss most about each of them, including my ex-wife. He feels it will help me to better understand my current needs, as well as the way I've responded to my own two brushes with death.

Charles still doesn't offer me much in the way of answers, though. I've come to accept that his role is more about guiding me towards working things out for myself, which I think I'm starting to do. Self-knowledge and acceptance are key to finding happiness, he claims.

'So, should I simply accept myself as being a pessimist, rather than trying to change?' I put to him earlier.

'No, not at all,' he replied. 'Optimistic thoughts are great. Mind over matter and all that. It's far healthier and better for your spiritual wellbeing to be positive than negative. But it would be a big ask for anyone to go from one extreme to the other overnight. Understanding why you've traditionally been a pessimistic thinker is important. You can also test out the pros and cons of each approach in real life.'

'How would that work?' I asked.

'Okay, you live in a flat, right?'

'Yes.'

'Well, let's say for the sake of it that you live in a house. Imagine one morning you get up and discover a small leak coming from the ceiling of an upstairs bedroom, so you call out a roofer to look at it. Optimistic Luke would tell himself it was probably a minor issue. Pessimistic Luke, on the other hand, would fear the whole roof might need replacing. How do you think each different version would cope while waiting for the roofer to turn up?'

I thought for a moment before replying: 'I reckon the optimist would be fine, forgetting about it and doing other things. The pessimist would be riddled with worry. He'd probably struggle to think of anything else.'

Charles nodded. 'Exactly. And if the optimist turned out to be right?'

'The pessimist would have wasted a lot of time being anxious.'

'And vice versa? Would the pessimist be any better off

355

if his worst fears were realised and the whole roof needed replacing?'

'Not really, other than being able to say that he was right to worry. They'd both be in exactly the same situation.'

'But at least the optimist wouldn't have wasted any time worrying about it beforehand.'

'True,' I replied. 'And because he was right, the pessimist would probably be all woe is me, like he was bearing the weight of the world on his shoulders. Plus the validation of his concerns would almost certainly fuel future fears.'

'What about the optimist?'

'He'd probably take it on the chin and focus on getting the roof fixed, thankful he found the problem before worse leaks or damage occurred.'

Charles gave me a thumbs-up. 'Perfect. So the next time you have to choose between positive and negative thinking about something in your real life, try analysing that in the same way.'

Back in the present, Rita and I have just entered a small but busy pub around the corner from the barbershop. After waiting to get served for several minutes, I order a pint of bitter and a small white wine at the bar before carrying the drinks over to a cosy table in the corner, which Rita grabbed when it came free.

'Thank you,' she says. 'Sorry, I should have offered to help you carry them.'

'Don't be silly,' I reply. 'I'm perfectly capable.'

'It's good to see the bandages have gone from your hands now, Luke. How are they?'

'Still healing,' I say, flashing her the scabs, 'but a lot better.'

A few deeper wounds on my arms are still bandaged up but also improving.

'You'll be back in no time,' she says, to which my only response is a smile in her direction. In truth, I still don't feel remotely ready to return to cutting hair or working alone, but I don't want to sound negative.

'How are you finding it, three weeks in?' I ask. 'No regrets, I hope.'

After taking a sip from her wine and nodding approvingly, she says: 'Not at all. I'm loving it.'

'Good. So what are the couple of things you want to discuss with me?'

'Well, for a start, your friend Connor came by today.'

I grimace. 'He didn't cause a fuss, did he?'

'No. He didn't actually step foot in the barbershop, although he looked badly in need of a trim. But he was outside for quite a while, pacing up and down the pavement and peering in through the window from time to time.'

'Really? That's a bit weird.'

I wish it didn't, but Connor's behaviour makes me think of Moxie. Connor couldn't end up doing something stupid, could he? Surely he's not going to go off the deep end about me not being available to cut his hair. Yes, his manner can be a bit odd, and he's obviously been hard hit by the death of his mum. But no, I can't believe that about him. I've been cutting his hair for years. Despite everything I've experienced lately, I'm convinced he's not

357

got anything bad like that in him. Rita doesn't know him like I do, though. She could be intimidated.

'Did it bother you?' I ask.

'Not especially, no.'

'You're sure?'

'Yes, but I thought you might want to know about it, with him being a regular. Plus I remember you gave him your mobile number and it was out of service when he tried to call you. Has he used it at all since?'

'No – and it's been back up and running for more than a fortnight now.'

'Maybe you should try calling him,' she suggests.

'I would, but I don't have his number. I only gave him mine. I'll tell you what, Rita, if you notice him hanging around again, you phone me and I'll come and speak to him. He's a good guy at heart, honestly.'

She seems happy enough with that, even though it still troubles me a little. I hope she's telling the truth about not being bothered by his actions today. I'd feel awful if she was worried about it. It's important to me that she feels safe there.

The next thing she brings up is an idea to introduce a few new services at the barbershop. My heart sinks when I first hear this. But recalling the discussion Charles and I had earlier about positive and negative thinking, I listen to what she has to say with an open mind and try to focus on harnessing her enthusiasm rather than suppressing it with my own obstinacy.

'I'm not talking about huge changes,' she says, 'but little tweaks.'

'I'm listening.' I fight the urge to say something cynical.

'So I couldn't be bothered with hot towel shaves,' she adds, to my relief. 'They're too time-consuming and messy. But – hear me out – I do think nose and ear waxing could work, as well as eyebrow threading. These things don't take long, but I reckon they'd be popular with the younger men in particular. They could rake in a few easy extra pounds too.'

'Eyebrow threading? You know how to do that?'

'Absolutely. I've done it all before and the costs involved are minimal. I'd be happy to demonstrate on you. I could even teach you how to do it, if you like, once you're back at work. Meanwhile, it could be on a trial basis. What would be the harm? Nothing ventured, nothing gained.'

'Okay,' I say quickly, before I have a chance to change my mind. 'Why not? Let's give it a try.'

She flashes me a big toothy grin. 'Great. You won't regret it.'

'We'll see. I don't mind a few changes, as long as we don't go down the route of some of those poncey barber-shops with their silly prices, exposed brickwork, craft beer and guys in waistcoats. I want to cry when I pass those places.'

'Noted.' Rita giggles. 'I'll leave the waistcoat at home. What's happening regarding the free cuts for the homeless, by the way? A *Big Issue* seller – Ivan, I think he said he was called – bobbed in today to ask. I said I wasn't sure.'

I shrug. 'I don't honestly know, Rita. After the living hell of the whole knife incident, I'm not sure I've got it in me to do it again. I can barely think about cutting anyone's hair at the moment. I did really enjoy giving something back to the community, but—'

'Don't worry,' Rita says. 'I totally get what you're saying. If anyone else asks, I'll tell them we've postponed things for the time being because of the attack. No one's going to argue with that.'

'I'm not totally ruling it out,' I add. 'But no promises.'

As we leave the pub, pushing our way past two prune-skinned old smokers blocking the entrance, she asks: 'How are things going with that lovely Nora?'

Rita already knows about me having to cancel our first date; since then, try as I might, I haven't been able to tie Nora down. We've messaged each other and spoken several times on the phone. But on every occasion that I've suggested we meet up, Nora's claimed to be busy, usually with work.

She was staying with her sister in Bristol over Easter. Now she's miraculously found a window in her hectic schedule to jet off on a last-minute holiday to Gran Canaria for a fortnight. It gets better: she's going with her old schoolfriend Jeff, whose marriage has apparently recently broken up. They're due to leave later this week.

I don't tell Rita any of this. I can't face it. Instead I say, as casually as I can: 'Oh, we've not had much of a chance to see each other lately, so nothing to report, I'm afraid.'

'That's a shame.'

I dream of Iris again that night for the first time in a while. She's in the barbershop this time – a version of it, at least. But there's now exposed brickwork on all the walls and a large glass-fronted fridge full of fancy beers next to the till.

'Nice waistcoat,' she says to me from where she's sitting in my preferred barber chair, still wearing her yellow raincoat, of course. Looking around, she adds: 'I like what you've done with the place.'

'You're joking, right? I would definitely never do any of this. It's pretty much my worst nightmare.'

I rip off the brown waistcoat, not having noticed it until she commented. Unfortunately, when I look down again, another sits in its place. 'Great. Someone's having a laugh at my expense.'

'You have to move with the times,' she says.

'Hmm. Not like this.'

It's nice to see Iris looking like herself again. I'm still haunted by the image of her lying next to me as a decaying corpse in that earlier dream with Moxie and the giant coffin. Luckily, she seems pretty normal this time.

'How do you feel about returning to work?' she asks.

'You sound like my counsellor.'

She leans right back in the chair with her lovely curls dangling down over the headrest. 'Well, I am a trained medical professional. Not much call for my services any more, though, so I'll take what I can get.'

'You really know how to make a guy feel wanted. Okay, I'll be honest with you, I'm nervous about it. Apart from the fact I'm afraid that someone else could walk in off the street with a knife at any moment, I'm also anxious about my ability to cut after my injuries. My wounds are healing well, but my hands are still stiff and sore. What if they never fully recover?'

'You know what they say about getting back on a horse as soon as you can after falling off.'

'Hmm.'

'How about you give me a trim now, as a bit of a warm-up?'

'How does that work? This is a dream and, well, women's haircuts aren't my forte.'

'Stop making excuses, Luke.' She leans forward, grabs a nearby gown and starts wrapping it around herself.

'Fine.' I pick up a pair of scissors and get to it.

Iris flashes me a smile that reminds me of her aunt. 'A couple of centimetres off will be perfect, thanks.'

After I've been cutting her hair for a while, she clicks her fingers and 'Mr Blue Sky' starts playing from somewhere.

'This again?' I say.

'What? It's such an awesome song,' she replies. 'And I thought you might need a reminder of where you're supposed to be heading. I have a feeling now might be the last time we see each other like this.'

That last part makes me put down my scissors. 'Why do you say that?'

'You didn't think these were normal dreams, did you?'

'Um, I don't know. I haven't really thought about it too hard. What are you saying?'

'Don't stop cutting unless you're done. You've only got until the end of the song.'

'What? Seriously?' I say. 'But I've got a million questions. I hope this is the long version with the extended ending.'

Iris laughs. 'We've probably got time for one question. If you're quick. But keep cutting.'

I let out an exasperated sigh before picking the scissors back up and continuing. I want to ask her something – so many things – but now I know I'm up against the clock, my mind has gone blank. I focus on the cutting, quickly but carefully finishing the job, and then I stand back to admire my handiwork.

'Right, there you go,' I say. 'What do you think?'

She turns her head from side to side in the mirror, fanning out the bottom of her curls with her hands before eventually giving me a thumbs-up, reminding me of Charles earlier. 'Very good. I think you've still got it, Luke. And your question?'

Suddenly, loads flood to mind. Is this really Iris? If so, how is she here with me and where has she come from? Is she happy? Why has she appeared previously in my recurring dream about the flat within the flat, but not this time? Will I ever have that dream again and what did it mean? There are so many more things I could ask her.

However, in the end, forced to make a snap decision, the question I put to Iris is a simple but pertinent one: 'Do you have any regrets?'

She nods, sucking her teeth. 'Interesting. I'm guessing that's partly because you still think it's your fault I died, because I pushed you out of the way. Don't. I'd do it again in a flash. And in direct answer to your question: no, I have no regrets whatsoever. I led my short life to the full and I loved it. Could it have been longer? Of course, but it wasn't meant to be. What would be the point in having regrets? They'd only make me miserable. Nothing would change. Positivity – blue-sky thinking, if you like – was at the heart of everything I did then and it remains so now. And with that, I bid you farewell, my friend. Choose love. Be happy.'

She pulls me towards her and kisses my cheek as the song ends and so does my dream.

CHAPTER 38

I receive a phone call from Rita as I'm walking through Piccadilly Gardens on a warm, sunny Wednesday at the end of April.

'Hello there,' I say. 'Everything all right?'

'He's here again.'

'Connor?'

'Yep. I saw him a moment ago, walking past for the first time.'

'Right. I'm only a few minutes away. I'll be there as soon as I can.'

It's just over a week since I told Rita to call me when Connor next appeared.

I spot him passing the barbershop and stopping for a moment to look through the window as I approach from further down the road. I'm tempted to shout something to get his attention but decide against it, not wanting to scare him off. His hair is the longest I've ever seen it. Being wiry and thick, it's grown up and outwards, reminding me of the stereotypical image of a science boffin. He's unshaven too, I see as I get closer, with quite some beard growth evident. Oh dear. Things clearly aren't going well.

'Hello, Connor,' I say once I'm within a few yards of him. He's still standing in front of the window and jumps when I speak, like he's been caught out doing something wrong.

Turning to look at me, his eyes are wild for a moment and then they soften. 'Luke,' he says. 'You're back.'

'Um, yeah, I'm not exactly back, back,' I tell him. 'I'm just calling in to see how Rita's getting on.'

Eyes falling on my hands, he adds: 'But the bandages have gone.'

'Yes, I know, Connor. But I've not returned to work yet. I—'

'Please, Luke,' he says. The desperation written all over his face startles me. Makes me re-evaluate my position. Do I understand why it's so important to Connor that I'm the one to cut his hair? Absolutely not. But I know what it's like to feel despair; to be wretched; to be riddled with grief, to the point where up feels like down and down feels like up.

As much as I don't want to cut his hair right now – as afraid as it makes me feel – I think back to the head-scratching dream I had last week in which I cut Iris's hair. I know it was only a dream. Well, I think it was, although Iris's words were confusing and, so far, I've not dreamed of her again, as she predicted. Anyway, the point is that I cut her hair in the dream without issue. And, as Charles

366

said to me in our latest counselling session, sometimes optimism means taking a leap of faith.

Before I can change my mind and start doubting the decision I've already made in my head, I tell Connor: 'Fine. Come inside and I'll cut your hair.'

His face lights up like a lamppost at dusk. 'Really? You'll do it for me?'

'Yes,' I say, 'on one condition.'

'Name it.'

'You stop with the weird walking up and down outside the barbershop. I'm worried you'll freak out Rita, especially after what happened to me with the knife guy.'

'I'd never hurt anyone,' he replies, looking hurt himself at the suggestion. 'I've been waiting for you to come back, that's all.'

I pat him gently on the shoulder. 'I know that, Connor. But she's only met you once, remember. She barely knows you. Next time you want me and I'm not around, call. My phone number's back up and running now. Anyway, come on in and let's make you look human again.'

I sit Connor down in the chair next to the one Rita's using and explain what's going on. If she's surprised or perturbed by this in any way, she doesn't let on. In fact, if anything, she seems pleased.

'Good to see you both,' she says.

'Sorry if I freaked you out, Rita,' Connor says to my surprise. 'It won't happen again.'

My hands shake with nerves when I first pick up the clippers to start the haircut, but I manage to steady them and my breathing; I blank my mind and get on with it.

Connor doesn't say much, but Rita helps, making jokes and small talk to take my mind off the bigger picture.

It goes all right, muscle memory kicking in and taking care of much of the process. Still, it's a relief when I reach the point of getting the hand mirror to show Connor the back. 'How's that for you?' I ask.

He turns his head left and right in the mirror. 'Yes, that'll do nicely. Thank you.'

Wow, he's happy first time. Thank goodness.

I did consider offering to trim his facial hair too but decided not to overcomplicate things.

Instead, with a wink, I say: 'Unless you're growing a beard, you might want to have a shave when you get home to complement your new smart look on top.'

Luckily, he takes it in good humour.

Later, after Connor has gone, promising to call me if I'm not around next time he needs a trim or even just to chat, Rita and I get five minutes alone during a quiet moment between customers.

'How did that feel?' she asks.

'Better than expected.'

'It was good of you to do that for him – and for me.'

I raise an eyebrow.

'You think I didn't know that you were worried about me feeling safe?' she says. 'After all these years of hair-dressing, I can read people pretty well. I also know you didn't feel ready to start cutting yet, but you did a great job of hiding that. And it was a good cut, of course, but I'd expect nothing less. I hope it's helpful with your recovery.'

She goes on to chat about how several people have taken her up on the new services she's trialling, following our conversation in the pub last week. And when she gives me a breakdown of the figures she's predicting they'll rake in, I'm seriously impressed.

'You're making me wonder whether I ought to leave you to it and not come back at all,' I say, grinning.

'Who says it has to be one thing or another?' she replies. 'I'm really enjoying it here. It's confirmed what I already suspected: I'm way too young to be semi-retired. I have too much left to give. If you wanted me to, I'd be happy to carry on alongside you, for a while at least. That way, you could also ease yourself back in as gradually as you like, starting part-time and working up from there. If that's what you want, of course. You're the boss.'

Her response blindsides me, but my instant gut reaction is that it's a great suggestion. I hadn't really considered that she might want to stay here beyond this period of covering for me, but now she says it, I can't think of anyone I'd rather work alongside. Plus, if I'm totally honest, one of the key reasons I've resisted cutting, until Connor forced my hand today, is the fear of eventually having to work alone again here. This suggestion would negate that problem. My one concern is whether we could consistently generate enough business to support two salaries. Mind you, the numbers have been good of late and Rita's new services might help as well.

I say most of this to her, skipping over the bit about me being afraid to work alone, and next thing I know, she's pulling me into a hug and getting emotional.

'It's so strange how Iris brought us together, isn't it?' she says, her voice catching. 'We'd probably never have met otherwise, but I really feel like we have the makings of a great team. I also have a few more suggestions that might help boost takings. Nothing crazy . . . I know poncey isn't your style, and it's not mine either. But a lick of paint and a few new fixtures and fittings wouldn't go amiss. That, um, sign outside could really do with replacing.'

She hesitates before continuing: 'It's totally up to you, obviously, but, er, maybe a change of name might even be worth considering as a way to attract new business.'

I automatically bristle up at this but, rather than getting shirty, I make myself listen to what she has to say.

'Change can be good,' I imagine Charles telling me. 'Don't reject it before you give it a chance.'

'Anything you have in mind?' I ask Rita.

'There is, but I'm afraid to tell you in case you hate it.'

I laugh. 'What makes you say that?'

'It's very different from Luke's Barbershop – but it's actually, sort of, inspired by Iris.'

My ears prick up at this. 'Right, you've got me interested now. Come on. Spit it out.'

'Well, there's this song she loved. It's a classic from the seventies; she'd play it all the time. She said it always put her in a good mood. Helped her stay positive after a tough day at work, that kind of thing. We even talked about playing it at the funeral, but it wasn't right for that. I, er—'

'Are you going to tell me what it is, Rita, or do I have to guess?'

'Okay, but don't say no straight away. Promise you'll at least give it some thought.'

'Fine.'

'So the song's "Mr Blue Sky". Do you know it? It's quite famous. Anyway, I was thinking something along the lines of Blue Sky Barbers? Oh no, what does that look mean? Why are you laughing? You hate it, don't you?'

'No, not at all,' I say, shaking my head and grinning so hard my face hurts. 'It's perfect. I can't even begin to explain why, but . . . I love it.'

CHAPTER 39

Until recently, I didn't think people wrote letters to each other any more. I assumed it was all emails and phone messages nowadays. In fact, it turns out that letters are like buses: you don't see one for ages and then two come along in succession.

The second handwritten letter sent to me this year arrived at the barbershop today, only a few weeks after the previous one from Helen. Rita handed it to me earlier, following our remarkable, illuminating conversation about the future. It was part of a small pile of post delivered this morning.

I didn't even notice it until I got home, assuming the pile contained only the usual collection of bills and junk mail. Honestly, I was still too dazed by Rita's surprise suggestion of that new name for the business to think of much else. It's an amazing idea, which couldn't be more apt. However, the mind-bending implications of the real Iris having loved that particular song continue to make my head hurt to this moment.

Have I actually been talking to her in my dreams all this time?

I know that's what Iris suggested when I was cutting her hair. But that happened in a dream too.

Believing in an afterlife is one thing – but seriously, how could her appearing to me like this be true?

There must be some other logical explanation. Maybe Iris mentioned that tune during the brief time we were together before she died. Or perhaps I overheard one of her friends or relatives say that she liked it at the funeral and it slipped into my subconscious.

I guess I'll never know for sure, just like I'll never know the meaning of that original recurring dream. That said, with hindsight, I now suspect the latter has always had a lot to do with Helen: the way she left me at my lowest point and made me feel like I wasn't worthy of being a husband or father. Perhaps the second flat represented a part of me I'd closed off as a result. Who can say? If I ever have it again, I might bring it up in a session with Charles. Somehow, though, I suspect I won't be troubled by that dream any more.

Answers are neat, but life doesn't always provide them. I can live with that. It's the positive way. Religious people do it all the time. Where would they be without hope and faith, neither of which is tangible? Mum and Dad took great comfort in these things. I've grown so far away from the church they brought me up in, I can't see myself ever going back to that now. And yet, undeniably, some kind of core faith remains ingrained in me, deep in my soul. A part of me wants to believe that Iris did find a way to come back to help me, as incredible as that might sound.

Either way, whether it was really her or a subconscious part of myself, the Iris I met in my dreams did help me. She gave me a leg-up to get where I am now, despite all the obstacles thrown in my path. She inspired me to be a better person, to open myself up. And that in turn helped me to form a new support structure I didn't have when I first met her under the scaffolding.

Now, as my wounds heal, both physical and mental, I have a growing sense that things are going to be all right. You could even call it optimism.

Anyhow, this letter. Standing in the kitchen of my flat, I turn it over in my hands before opening it. I don't recognise the small handwriting on the envelope and I'm surprised to see a York postmark this time.

Who could be writing to me from there? Only one way to find out.

I run a finger under the seal and pull out the single sheet of lined paper inside. It looks to have been torn out of an A4 notebook and smells faintly of cigarette smoke.

Dear Luke,

I wanted to let you know that I've left Manchester to sort myself out. It's because of you. The stuff you told me the last time we spoke, outside the supermarket, hit home. You said I should use my brain to get myself to a better place. I knew what you meant. Off the streets and away from the spice before one of them finished me off.

So I did something about it. I went to York. That's where I am now. Why here? It's where my little sister lives. She's actually in her late twenties, but I'll always think of her that way. She's the one person I knew would help me if I asked, but previously I was too proud to do that, worried I might mess up her life in the process.

About an hour after you and I spoke that last time, I called her up from a payphone. She was so happy to hear from me, she drove over here that night to pick me up and took me home with her.

I have a job interview tomorrow with a guy she knows. He's supposed to be a good bloke, who's given people second chances before. It's nothing fancy – just serving tables in a café – but if I get it, it'll be a fresh start.

I want to thank you for helping me to get here, Luke. I know I fobbed you off the first time you tried to speak to me about the spice, pretending not to know what you were talking about. But seeing you again after what bloody Moxie did to you, it was the wake-up call I needed.

I thought I had things under control, only doing spice every now and again, but I was kidding myself. Hopefully I can stay off and away from that shit for good now.

I really think I have a decent chance of getting my life back on track here. My sister's got loads of books to read, which is an added bonus, although I think I need to get her into Ian Rankin, as she doesn't have any of the Rebus novels so far.

Thanks again for the much-needed haircut and, of course, the book you so thoughtfully gave me. That meant a great deal, especially knowing it used to belong to your mother. You really made me feel human – seen rather than ignored – that day at your barbershop. I'll never forget it. And to think you were prepared to give me another novel, despite knowing about the spice. So kind. Sorry I never got a chance to come for it.

I'm also massively sorry about what happened to you because of Moxie. He was a bad apple, but most of the folk on the streets aren't like that, as I hope you've seen for yourself. They're regular people who've hit hard times, that's all.

I hope you're still recovering well and get back to work soon. Look after yourself, pal, and I'll try to do the same.

All the best,
Tommy

Tears are rolling down my cheeks by the time I finish reading Tommy's letter. I'm so touched that he's written to me – and incredibly happy that my words had this effect on him. His future looks so much brighter now, in such a small space of time; it's fantastic. I only wish he'd included his address so I could write back.

A tiny part of me feels I don't deserve his appreciation, because of the time I abandoned him when he was off his head on spice. But I must stop being negative, as that's not who I am any more. I left him in safe hands and, as he put it himself, I helped him to address his drug problem and get off the streets.

As Charles likes to tell me in our sessions, we must celebrate our wins unconditionally, however big or small. And this is a big one. Who knows? I might even have helped to save a guy's life.

CHAPTER 40

The grand reopening of my barbershop – to be known from now on as Blue Sky Barbers – takes place on a lovely balmy Friday evening at the end of May.

Everything has happened so quickly. It's amazing what you can get done when you put your mind to it, particularly when you have an amazing motivator and organiser like Rita at your side. She has some great connections when it comes to booking reliable tradespeople and the like. I never could have done it in such a short space of time without her.

We closed for a week to get the place redecorated and smartened up, also adding a refreshed services menu and so on, plus of course the new shopfront sign, which Meg designed for us and looks amazing. It's a sky-blue background with the words embossed so they look like they're crafted out of clouds. I couldn't be happier with how it's turned out.

At Rita's suggestion, we've continued the white and blue

theme inside too. It's so bright and airy now, it feels like a whole new place.

Before we closed, I was already back working most afternoons for a couple of hours alongside Rita. And that's been going really well too. My injuries continue to heal as the doctors hoped. Apart from a bit of stiffness and a few aches and pains here and there, I'm taking it all in my stride.

Plus Rita and I get along brilliantly. We laugh all the time and she's so vibrant, it makes for such a happy place to be. I hardly ever think about what happened here with Moxie now.

Rita's good for business too. We've already racked up loads more regulars than I ever used to get on my own and, as she predicted, the waxing and threading she's introduced are proving popular.

We've not started offering the free haircuts for the homeless again yet, although I'm warming to the idea. Maybe we'll reintroduce it once a month or so.

The thing I'm most excited about at the moment is the apprenticeship scheme we're going to introduce in conjunction with a local college. An old friend of Rita's teaches hairdressing there. We've been in talks with her about collaborating to offer someone – ideally a person in need of a second chance – the opportunity to learn the trade while working alongside the two of us.

We still need to iron out the exact details of how it will all work, but I'm determined to make it happen. The idea emerged after I told Rita about Tommy's letter and how great it was that he was getting another shot at life. She

pointed out the spare third barber chair here and it esca-
lated from there. In theory, we could offer the position to
a former homeless person looking for a fresh start, like
Tommy, or maybe a school dropout trying to sort themselves out. As long as they're dependable, hard-working
and ready to develop a passion for barbering, I'm up for
giving pretty much anyone a go.

Rita and I both arrive early for the reopening do, as
agreed, so we can get everything ready before people arrive.
The haircutting doesn't start until tomorrow, when I'll be
doing my first full-time shift since coming back. This
evening is all about drinks and nibbles in the revamped
barbershop, with family, friends and regulars invited to
join us. I'll have to be careful not to drink too much, or
tomorrow will be tough.

'How are you feeling about tonight?' Rita, who's
wearing a gorgeous coral dress, asks me.

'Excited,' I reply without hesitation.

'It's going to be marvellous,' she adds with the usual
twinkle in her eye.

And it is.

So many people turn up, they're spilling out on to the
pavement. There's Meg, of course, who's already gleefully
reminded me of her early suggestion that Rita and I would
make a good team. Plus there are Rita's two sons, Guy
and Russ, and her old colleague Sharon who helped out
with the homeless cuts. Iris's parents, Stan and Claire, both
make an appearance, which is wonderful, albeit a bit
emotional. Connor pops in, only staying for a quick glass
of bubbly but, thankfully, looking much more like his old

380

self. Then there are my neighbours and newfound friends Doreen, Pauline and Sylvia, who drink like fish and get rather merry and loud, much to my amusement.

Thanks to Rita befriending them, several of our business neighbours come along too.

But the biggest surprise for me is when, towards the end of the evening, Nora shows up. She's in a striking canary-yellow dress that immediately makes me think of Iris.

I sent Nora an invite, of course, but she replied that she didn't think she'd be able to make it. I first spot her chatting to Rita outside on the pavement, alongside Rudy, her photographer friend. He starts taking some photos to send to the *Evening News*. Unfortunately, I get caught up in that, bustled around by him and Rita, before I get a chance to catch up with Nora.

I've haven't seen or spoken to her since she got back from her holiday with that old friend of hers, Jeff. I assume any chance of something happening between us now has gone out of the window. Still, I'd like to have a chat with her, to apologise once again for what happened with Helen, if nothing more.

I approach her a little later when the crowd has thinned out and she's talking in a quiet corner with Meg. 'Hello stranger,' I say. 'I'm so glad you could make it after all. How are you? I love the dress. That colour really suits you.'

She smiles. 'Thanks. You look well. Great to see you've made such a good recovery. The place looks wonderful, by the way, and Meg and I were just agreeing what a fantastic new name it is.'

'I can't take credit for that: it was Rita's idea. But I couldn't agree more. I'm excited to see what the future holds.'

Meg gives me a discreet wink before making an excuse to disappear and leaving the two of us alone.

'So how was the, um, holiday?' I ask.

'Well, the weather was kind, but Jeff was miserable. I spent most of the time passing him tissues and listening to him lament the death of his marriage.'

'So you two were at school together?'

'That's right.' She giggles. 'We actually went out with each other for a while.'

Brilliant. This gets better and better. How long until this Jeff idiot falls into her arms? If he hasn't already, which he probably has, let's be honest. That's what happens on holidays. Especially after a breakup.

'It's a shame the way we left things,' I add, although I'm not sure there's any point now. Not with jammy Jeff on the scene. 'I was keen to make it up to you. I've already told you how bad I feel about the whole thing. But I got the impression you'd had enough.'

'Is that why you stopped calling?' she asks, circling the top of her glass with her finger.

'Well, you were on holiday and then . . .'

'Then what?'

'I assumed maybe you and Jeff . . . You know.'

She bursts out laughing. 'Me and Jeff? Seriously?'

'Yeah, why not? He's your ex and his marriage has ended. I thought sun, sand—'

'Jeff's gay. His marriage failed because his husband,

Alvin, cheated on him with their piano tuner. He's devastated. Getting together with anyone else, least of all a woman, was the last thing on his mind.'

'But you said he was your boyfriend at school.'

'Lots of gay guys go out with girls before they come out, you know.'

I hold my palms over my reddening face for a moment. 'Well, don't I feel like an idiot. Although in my defence, you weren't exactly receptive to my advances after the Helen incident. You were always busy.'

She shrugs. 'Fair enough. I was pretty busy, but I may have exaggerated my diary engagements a little. I was pissed off with you. I know your ex was only around until the morning, but we had plans. I felt like you shouldn't have let me leave. That disappointed me. It also made me wonder if there was still something between the two of you.'

'Really?' I say. 'No way. There's absolutely, categorically no chance of us ever rekindling what we once had. Not after how she left me. Our marriage is ancient history. We needed to talk things out, that's all.'

Nora bites her bottom lip as she looks me square in the eye. 'I spoke to Jeff about you while we were away, when I could get a word in edgeways. He said he liked the sound of you. That I ought to give you another chance. But then you didn't call. Your invite to this was the only time I heard from you.'

'You said you probably couldn't come.'

'I had a work thing, but I managed to wriggle out of it.'

'I'm glad you did.' I place my hand on the top of her

arm, which feels cool to the touch. 'Are you cold? The temperature has dropped away a little. Would you like me to get my jacket? It's hanging up over—'

Before I can finish, her warm, soft mouth is pressed up against mine, her body close and her arms wrapped around my waist. It's as wonderful as it is unexpected.

I lose myself in a long moment of pure passion, adrenaline and euphoria.

And it feels fantastic. Like the last piece of the puzzle has slotted into place and I'm staring at the big picture – finally revealed to me in all its glory.

I can't stop smiling.

Everything is going to be okay.

I know this for sure now. At long last.

How?

Because I'm Mr Blue Sky.

ACKNOWLEDGEMENTS

So this is how it feels to release a fifth novel. I'd love to be able to hop back in time and boost the spirits of my unpublished younger self by telling all.

I believed in what I was doing when I started out on my writing journey, of course. I'd never have sent my work out to anyone otherwise. But the inevitable early rejections gnawed away at my confidence and it wasn't always easy to be optimistic. Without the unwavering support of my close family and friends – particularly Claudia and Kirsten, Mum, Dad, and Lindsay – I'm not sure I'd have been able to keep dusting myself off and persevering, undeterred.

Thank goodness I did. First I found my amazing literary agent, Pat Lomax, who's been at my side every step of the way since, offering sage advice and positivity, ably backed up by the BLM team. Then I found my publisher, Avon, where I've always been made to feel very welcome. I've been lucky enough to have Molly Walker-Sharp as my editor this time, who's been an absolute pleasure to work with and brilliant throughout.

Huge thanks to all of the above, plus everyone else who's supported me in creating this and my four previous books.

Finally, I must thank my readers for buying, borrowing, and, most of all, reading my stories. Without you, I wouldn't be able to keep doing this dream job of mine. Helping to spread the word by telling others about my novels and leaving positive online reviews is so incredibly helpful too. It's all very much appreciated.

How do you leave the person
you love the most?

Is there ever a right time to let go?

time
to say
goodbye

S. D. ROBERTSON

A heart-rending story about
a father's love for his daughter.

Is holding on harder than letting go?

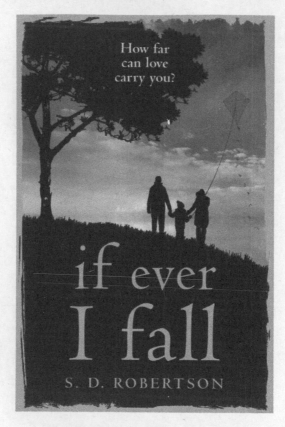

How far
can love
carry you?

if ever
I fall

S. D. ROBERTSON

A beautiful story of love,
grief and redemption.

Best friends since the day they met . . .

True friendship can last a lifetime . . .

'A heartbreaking tale' *Sun*

stand
by
me

S.D. Robertson

They'll always have each other,
won't they?

Hannah's life is pretty close to perfect.
But someone to close to her is hiding
a secret that will turn
everything upside down.

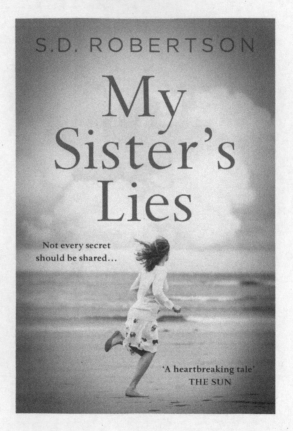

An emotional story that delves into the true
meaning of family, sisterhood and secrets.